BLAZING GUNS

*Though she'd grown up in Australia's wild frontier,
emerald-eyed Penelope had never lacked material
comforts. As a Cranston, she'd been spoiled and
pampered; as a blossoming beauty, she was the belle of
every dance up and down the Hawkesbury. Then Aaron
Aylesbury returned from England, and Penelope's blood
rushed with hot desire under his smouldering gaze. He was
an explorer, a man not of her class. But that couldn't stop
Penelope from yearning to feel his lips bruising hers, her
flesh yielding to his, the flames of his passion searing her
with forbidden ecstasy beneath the blazing Australian sun..*

STARLIT PLEASURE

*All his life Aaron had known that one day he'd discover
the exotic secrets of the outback and explore the lush,
virgin land that lay beyond the distant ridge of sapphire
mountains. No woman could keep him—certainly not the
spoiled daughter of his father's enemy. He'd take his
pleasure, then leave her at dawn. But once he'd trapped
Penelope in his arms and felt her hungry response to his
demanding, lingering kisses, he knew that he needed more.
He wanted to feel her come alive beneath the stroke of his
hands and hear her cries of rapture shatter the Australian
night. He wanted nothing less than her complete*

Wild Surrender

01841

ISBN 0-8217-1841-X

0 71268 00395 9

FORBIDDEN FLAMES

He was there.

He had removed his hat and coat and tie, and his shirt was open at the neck. He was leaning against a tree where the horse was tethered, watching her.

Penelope rode slowly to the cottage, not taking her eyes from him. She dismounted and tethered the brindle. Aaron had not moved; neither had his expression changed.

She went to him then, and it was as if time had not passed since she was in his arms. Desperately he held her, pressing her to him. With each beat of his heart against her breast she grew weaker with want, with need.

With a low moan, he pulled her inside the cottage door and kicked the door shut, crushing her against him so close to his thudding heart she could not breathe. Then his lips were on hers—bruising, searching, demanding. She dug her fingers into the hard muscles of his back and wanted to climb inside him, to melt there, to be him.

Grasping him, pulling him to her as she arched her body against him, she felt herself drowning in forbidden passion. He was the one man she had always loved, the only man who could truly make her a woman. . . .

Wild Surrender

Gina Delaney

ZEBRA BOOKS
KENSINGTON PUBLISHING CORP.

ZEBRA BOOKS

are published by

Kensington Publishing Corp.
475 Park Avenue South
New York, NY 10016

First printing: June 1986

Printed in the United States of America

To Jan Edsall and Carolyn LaFlower

Part I

1822

Chapter I

Penelope ran up the stairway to her own room, gritting her teeth against replying to her mother's complaints. She had learned a long time ago that there were only three ways to deal with her frustrations and resentments: She must either paint, play her harp, or go back to the east pasture where the sheep were. But since her mother objected to her interest in watching the sheep and the lambing, and the harp was in the ballroom next to the living room where her mother sat with her personal maid planning the day's menu, Penelope decided she must paint.

The easel was set as always by the north window. Hers was the northeast room. People in the colony called such rooms "bedrooms," though her mother still referred to them as "bedchambers," which was the old-fashioned word for them, brought over from England. Penelope hated England, though she wouldn't dare say so, except to special friends. She had never been there, but she hated it because her parents worked so hard to make Cranhurst like the estate in England, and they compared everything else in the colony to things in England. It was like

comparing melons to hay. It was ridiculous to try. For this was New South Wales. Governor Macquarie called the continent where the colony of New South Wales was located Australia.

There was another reason Penelope hated England. It had taken Aaron away.

Penelope sat down on the clerk's stool and took her sable brush from the old tankard sitting on the flat-topped traveling trunk under the window. Old Greta always kept water in another tankard for her, and in this water she now swished her brush.

The first thing one must do when making a water coloring is to make a wash. That was the first thing the art tutor had told her when she was just ten years old and had begun to show an interest in painting. Since then she had developed her own technique of water coloring, producing exquisite and detailed paintings of the countryside, and of the towns, Windsor, Parramatta, and Sydney. She had a complete portfolio of bush flowers, too, but her paintings of the Blue Mountains and of the paddocks and runs with their cattle and sheep and the pastures with grazing cattle and horses were her favorites. She must have had a hundred of those paintings.

Now she made her little puddle of water about the size of a shilling and twirled her brush in the blue tub of color, staining the puddle of water with blue. Next came just a hint of yellow, for New South Wales's skies were never absolutely blue this late in the spring.

With the color mixture just right, Penelope filled her brush with it and stroked the wash from left to right, again and again. While she was making her wash of sky colors, she became aware of the spot of light dancing on the wall across the room and she turned and blinked at the light—only a spot that

10

quivered on the wall above her bed. It brought back memories of Aaron, but over the past four years every spot of light, even those dappling the ground beneath the gum trees, reminded her of Aaron. Smiling a little, she turned back to her painting, wiped her brush, and swished it around in the tankard of water to cleanse it.

The spot of light flashed on her face, startling her, then danced across the white plaster ceiling. Now she was watching it, her lips parting as the light quivered, went out, flashed again, moved across the ceiling and down the wall. Her mouth was wide open now, her green eyes widening. Then, suddenly, she turned toward the window so abruptly her knees knocked over the easel, which crashed to the floor, but she was unaware of it as she leaned on the window sill and peered out.

On the ridge. On *that* ridge, on *their* ridge the light flashed, flashed again, and Penelope's breath caught in her throat. Open-mouthed, she watched as the light flashed from the ridge a mile away onto her face.

It wasn't possible. It was too early. Or was it?

Her breath caught in her throat again and she felt as if all the blood in her body had rushed to her face, to her head. She turned away and ran toward the door of her room, remembered she had just come from the paddock, and dashed to her mirror. Ringlets of dark brown, almost-black hair framed her face, her cheeks were pink from too much sun, and oh, her dress was soiled at the hem. She ran to her armoire and flung its door open, but her mind was so much awhirl that she was blind and could not understand what she saw.

And what difference did it make? She must run. Now. Hurry. But carefully.

Reminding herself that he was an Aylesbury and

11

that Cranstons hated Aylesburys and vice versa—depending on which Cranston and which Aylesbury—Penelope composed her face and checked her haste, but despite her efforts to control her excitement, her feet flew down the stairs into the small hallway.

"Where are you off to now?" called her mother from the drawing room, which was actually a living room, but Elaina Cranston still persisted in calling it a drawing room like they did over in England. "Not out in that paddock again, Penelope."

"Riding!" Penelope flung back over her shoulder.

"You will be in time for tea?" came the plaintive voice of her mother.

"Yes, Mum."

"You mustn't go far, the country's full of bushrangers—"

Impatient but attempting to control it, Penelope said, "I'll be careful, Mum."

And then she was out in the yard making every effort to keep her feet from running. She was breathless because it might not be true, might not be he, after all.

The groom grinned and bobbed his grizzly head and touched his beaver hat when she ran into the stable, "M-M-Miss Penelope," he greeted her.

"Cricket, please saddle Bayleaf," she said. And while the little servant who cared for the horses did as he was bidden, Penelope stood at the stable door gazing toward the ridge. One could see only an occasional flash of light from here, but she knew the light would be dancing on the ceiling or walls of her bedroom and prayed that Greta wouldn't see it. Abigail, the housemaid, wouldn't tell, but Greta would, because she was her mother's personal maid.

Once Cricket, an emancipated convict whom her

father had employed before and after his pardon, brought Bayleaf to her, she was on the horse in a flash and kicked his sides, tearing out of the yard.

She did not see Cricket's smile, his small eyes going to the ridge, then back to the girl racing west so that no one would guess the direction of her destination. Young Aylesbury was back then, Cricket thought nodding, and he was glad. And he would never let anyone know about the two young people who used to meet on the ridge. Nay. Never. For he wished them well. In spite of everything that was against it.

Penelope raced west, although the ridge was north. But it wouldn't do to let anyone at Cranhurst see her riding north. When she was on the track out of sight of the house she took the path up the ridge through the wattle and gum trees. Blind with excitement, hope, and the dread of disappointment she rode, urging the horse along the well-worn path, a path she used often and one her father used when he thought no one noticed.

She barely noticed that the young forest, just eight years old, was alive with birds. Australian birds were not numerous, but they were exotic and colorful. Jade and scarlet parrots, blue and yellow lorikeets, white and pink galah and white cockatoos with yellow crests played hide-and-seek in the branches of the gum trees, which her father and the other men called eucalypti. Penelope did not care that the brilliant, frothy blooms of the wattle bush, which had been bright yellow just a month ago, were fading and now surrounded with the scarlet and purple blooms of the pea vine. She urged the horse on, and without caution burst out of the forest on the crest of the ridge.

Her stomach seemed to have come up in her mouth and she swallowed as she reined the mare and looked

13

about. There was nothing here but the sounds of quiet. Penelope looked around her. The grasses waved in the breezes and butterflies flitted like her anxious hopes in search of blooms on which to light. The sun burned down like a midsummer sun, and only the cool of the breezes from the west proved that summer was not yet here.

He was not here, either. Aching with disappointment, Penelope dismounted, and shading her eyes with her hand, looked north from the ridge.

The ridge was a natural upheaval in the land running between the Aylesburys' and the Cranstons' properties for about two miles, a natural division separating the two holdings, a rocky, but not necessarily untillable, narrow hill. It was just that the two families liked having the ridge there between them with no crops on it. Penelope's father had let the gum trees and wattle grow up on his side of the ridge, while the Aylesburys had left theirs barren, except for the grass.

From here she could see down to the Crawfords' and the Aylesburys' properties for miles. In the distance, not too far away, was the Hawkesbury River, seen from here as a snake of green vegetation— the gum trees that followed the river. This side of the river was the Crawfords' holdings: black, tilled fields, plowed, raked, harrowed, and other fields green with new rye and yellow with ripened wheat. Stubble fields, too, then an orchard of peaches, and gardens with melons and vegetables. Then there were the paddocks for the horses and a few milk cows. More to the east, she could see Tad Crawford's horse farm, with its white paddock fences. Then farther east would be Ben Crawford's dairy farm, but you couldn't see it from here.

She could see the convict workers in the fields

below. Settlers hired convicts from the superintendent in Parramatta and Sydney to work on their farms because they were cheap labor. She could see someone leading a horse to the house below. The house was a tall, rambling reddisk-pink brick, the extravagance of which seemed to infuriate both her father and mother for reasons of their own.

But Penelope did not see *him*.

Tears sprang to her eyes. Madam Aylesbury, Parramatta's distinguished dressmaker, had said *summer*. She had told Penelope that her nephews, Aaron and Mark, would return home this summer from England, and this wasn't summer. This was spring. Penelope wanted to cry with disappointment. Apparently some object had caught the sunlight and flashed it into her window as Aaron used to do with his mirror to signal her. She had been fooled, and here she stood about to cry. Oh, wretched waiting!

Her parents had named her wrong. She was not like Odysseus's wife at all, who had waited years and years for her husband to come home. Penelope had waited almost five years for her friend, Aaron, and it was much too long. They had both been sixteen when he had gone away—and he was her best friend, her only real friend.

Penelope bit her trembling lips and sat down on the boulder, tilting her face up to let the sun fall fully upon it. Now she didn't care whether she freckled or not, did not care if the face tanned. She blinked at the hawk that floated high, high up on the air currents. Oh, it was what she longed to do.

Memories came flooding back to her of a small boy with straight brown hair and huge brown eyes and a small girl with pinafore and puffed sleeves, running about on the ridge, meeting in secret like forbidden

15

lovers and playing like the young children they were; wonderful games: hide-and-seek, catch-the-butterfies, wash-the-kangaroo-rat-from-his-burrow. And there was always poor Mark intruding, chasing her with a centipede, offering her flowers, always lurking about interfering.

And Aaron had kissed her once. Only once, just before he went away. That last day. A quick, sixteen-year-old, red-faced, damp peck on her cheek and he was away, running down the ridge for home, with Mark loping behind him saying, "I saw you kiss her."

"I did, but she liked it."

"She didn't."

"She did."

"She didn't."

Penelope smiled now remembering, for she *had* liked it.

"Gotcha!"

With a shriek Penelope threw up her hands and jerked around to face him. *Aaron!*

With another shriek she jumped up and threw her arms around his neck, and he lifted her up, swung her around laughing, then released her. As she backed away from him flushed with delight and excitement, and gratitude to God and anybody else responsible for his being here, she watched his laughing eyes darting over her face and down to her bodice, back up, saw the touches of color on his cheeks, his smile waning—and she knew why.

They had both been sixteen when he had gone away and now they were twenty. And they had changed.

He was taller, taller than her own father, lean, hard muscled, broad shouldered. His large brown eyes glinted with a mixture of mischief, shyness,

boldness, and . . . experiences she had not shared with him.

"Oh, Aaron. You hid from me to frighten me. I should have known. But look at you. You've gotten so tall!" She laughed, clasping her hands. *And so handsome. So awfully handsome*, she thought.

His admiring eyes grew shy. "And you've changed, too."

Feeling her blood rise to flood her face, she dropped her gaze. "For the better, I hope."

"Oh, aye. Much better." His eyes, the same soft chocolate-brown as his hair, dropped briefly to her breasts, then came up quickly to her face.

A kookaburra laughed in the nearby young forest as she looked at him. As children of ten they had stolen moments of play together because they were the same age and few children were closer for them to play with. The fact that it was forbidden by their parents had only made the secret meetings better, and they had grown fond of each other, shared their deepest secrets and dreams.

The fact that he was a boy and she a girl had not mattered much then.

"Your Aunt Fran told me you were coming home this summer. You're early."

"Aye. We, Mark and I, took earlier passage than we had thought. One hundred twenty-three days it took us to sail from Mother Bank to Sydney."

"Such a long time to be away. Are you glad to be home?" she asked, then turned to look down upon the Aylesbury-Crawford farms to hide her blushing.

"Aye, a long time. And I could not wait to get home."

She felt his eyes upon her as she smiled and strolled away from him, heard his step crushing the grass and rotted twigs beneath his boots, felt a thrilling surge

17

rush through her body, thrilling because he had become even more handsome as a man than he had been as a boy. He had changed, and yet he was the same.

"I suppose now you have many beaus," he said, coming to stand beside her.

"A few." She glanced at him, blushed as she had never blushed before. And she had always prided herself because she did not blush. "You read my letters?"

"Aye. Few as they were," he teased.

Her glance at his half-amused, half-amazed expression made her bolder because she saw the lad Aaron in it. "It's not easy to post letters without the parents' knowing, or receive them, either."

"Luckily we had my Aunt Fran to send and receive for us."

Penelope had taken her letters to Frances Aylesbury, dressmaker, and that kind, practical spinster had mailed them for her, received Aaron's and given them to her. "Mum thought I was becoming such a fashion-conscious lady because I was making so many trips to the dressmaker."

Their laughter relieved the peculiar, unexpected tension between them, and they sat down upon their favorite half-buried boulder to gaze out over the Hawkesbury flood plain where alluvial soil was rich and productive, where Aaron's maternal relatives, the Crawfords, cultivated and grew livestock, and where his father's holdings, the Aylesbury farm, stretched in a checkerboard as far as the eye could see. Aaron remembered the early years of poverty when they had lived in the old wattle and daub hut with its drafty lean-tos. His mother had worked in the fields with his uncles, and his father had gone to and from the hospital at Parramatta on the old horse, Gray.

Then Lachlan Macquarie had arrived in the colony as governor, and things had changed for the better, just as Aaron's father had predicted. The past twelve years had seen phenomenal growth in the colony, the building of roads and public buildings, changes in government, and, under Macquarie's benevolent rule, the poor Hawkesbury farmers at last realizing profits from their crops and livestock.

"I can't stay long, you know," Penelope said, casting him a sidelong look. "Mum expects me for tea."

Aaron tossed a pebble down the slope of the ridge. "Aye. And father will be home soon. I haven't seen him yet."

"Is he still expecting you to take a position in one of the hospitals?"

Aaron's handsome face darkened. "I suppose."

Penelope observed him. He had gone away to school in England, and then to medical school in Scotland, only to please his father. Dr. Matthew Aylesbury did not seem to notice that Aaron had no interest in medicine, and only Penelope knew what Aaron really wanted to do. Only *she* knew.

"I'm so glad you passed your exams, Aaron. I tried to think of something wonderful to give you to celebrate your receiving your doctor's certificate. But I couldn't. You'll have to tell me what you want."

He studied her now, his brown eyes shining with admiration and joy—and something else, too. As she looked into her best friend's eyes she thought she could drown in them as easily as she might drown in the muddy, sparkling waters of the Hawkesbury. "Then I'll tell you," he said softly. "A kiss would do it."

Penelope's heart stood still. She had loved him forever, since the first time she had seen him with her

mother in Mr. Campbell's warehouse store. She had loved him as a child and the love had grown and matured, and she wasn't surprised to realize she loved him still.

His face came close to hers and she leaned slowly toward him. His eyes focused on her lips and then she shut her eyes, felt his lips cool and moist on hers, then warm and moving. A great, aching pain gripped her abdomen, and her hand went trembling to the place.

Then she felt him lift his lips from hers and opened her eyes, seeing the change in his face. In that moment, she realized that he had kissed girls in England, and she was at once jealous and angry. "What makes you think," she said softly, "that you have the right to kiss me without permission?"

"You are my girl, Penelope," he reasoned softly, his eyes still caressing her face. "Have always been my girl, my lass. I have always thought—"

"A penny for your thoughts, mate."

The couple started and turned to see him standing, one boot propped on a log, arms folded, hair shining like gold fleece in the afternoon sun.

Penelope rose abruptly because girls did not behave in this manner; it smacked of—of Parramatta Female Factory behavior. Or convict prostitutes. "Oh, Mark," she exclaimed. "We were just talking."

Mark Aylesbury grinned, but his blue eyes were still narrowed with what Penelope knew was jealousy. "Extremely interesting conversation," he said, withdrawing his boot from the log. "May I join in?"

Penelope cut her eyes over at Aaron. It was like always. Mark intruding. And she still resented his calling himself an Aylesbury. He would always be Mark Troop to her.

Aaron had risen slowly and good-naturedly

20

hooked his thumbs in the waist of his trousers. "He's Solicitor Aylesbury now, Penelope."

Penelope smiled. "You passed your exams too, Mark?"

"I did."

Her gaze dropped before his steady scrutinizing one. Mark was a few months older than Aaron, handsome and built like his father, Dr. Aylesbury—tall, broad shouldered, sturdy. He was dressed in a white shirt with full sleeves, and tight breeches of brown sailcloth. And he had always loved her. She knew that and had hoped that it would change. She could see now that it had not.

Aaron saw it, too. He sauntered to Penelope's side, his half-smile never leaving his face as he observed Mark's hopeless worship of the girl they both loved. "Father home yet?"

Mark dragged his gaze from Penelope. "No. But Mum sent me to fetch you for tea." He looked at Penelope again and all three young people were silent as Mark's lips opened then shut, opened again. Then, "Penelope, I have to say that you have grown from a charming young miss to a beguiling young woman."

Penelope's chin came up slowly. "Thank you," she replied trying not to appear cool, then turned to Aaron. "I must go too, before Mum and Father start hunting for me."

"Yes," Mark said steadily, "you must not be found speaking with one of us currency lads."

A tiny frown formed on her brow as Aaron took her elbow. "I'll help you on your horse," he said.

Penelope allowed Aaron to assist her onto Bayleaf although she could mount a horse as well as he, and then sat looking down at the half-brothers as they stood side by side looking up at her.

Aaron was the image of his mother, though taller. Mark looked very much like his father and seemed to have taken on a rather urbane demeanor because of his education in England. They were two young men, handsome and agreeable, and two whom Penelope had been forbidden to see.

"I shall see you again soon?" she asked Aaron as the breezes from the west off the Blue Mountains, which he had sworn to conquer, chilled her bare arms and stirred the stray wisps of dark hair at her temples.

"Aye. Soon."

She did not miss the tingling brush of his hand against hers as he relinquished the reins to her, and Penelope turned her horse about to begin her way through the infant forest and home.

But not before she caught the glint in the eyes of Mark, a glint that told her more than Aaron's last words had. *Aye. Soon.*

Chapter II

The brothers stood together watching Penelope turn her horse about, nudge him with the heel of her dainty slippers, and trot into the trees. As they watched, Mark's eyes narrowed, and Aaron placed his hand on his shoulder.

"Go easy on the lass, Mark. It's not her fault."

Mark's wide mouth twitched at one corner. "I know." With a sigh he dragged his gaze from the deserted path to look at Aaron. "Mum says Father will be home early for tea."

Aaron's smile ceased, his eyes dulled. "We'd best get back, then."

Going down the faint path that led from the top of the ridge to the wheatfield, the brothers breathed in the cool air that was so familiar, that stirred more than the infant grain heads of wheat or the grasses and nodding fragrantless flowers. It stirred memories of their boyhood. Here the air was cool, but the sun warm; the air was dry and easy to breathe, unlike the air in England, which was damp and heavy. England, where everything was backwards, like the sun, which moved across the southern sky instead of the northern sky where it belonged. Both felt the joy

of returning home after five years of being away, aware of the unique importance of their position, belonging to the first of those native-born Australians to go abroad for their education.

Aaron had long ago ceased to ponder the fact that Mark was his father's bastard son, born of a prostitute in Sydney, a golden reminder of his father's first years in the colony as a convict exiled from his home in England. Aaron's own mother had discovered Mark, and his father had brought him home one day at the age of eight and introduced him to Aaron as Mark Troop, Troop being Mark's mother's last name. Matthew Aylesbury had adopted his illegitimate son, and his legal name was now Mark Troop Aylesbury.

Matthew and Milicent Aylesbury had brought Mark home with them during the "poor" days, when the farm was struggling for survival, when the uncles all lived with them in the wattle and daub hut, now destroyed. Days when a single bout of wheat blight could endanger the very existence of the family, even of the entire Hawkesbury settlement. Those were the days before Macquarie. Governor Macquarie had marched into Sydney from his ship, the *Dromedary*, twelve years before, in 1810, with all the pomp and circumstance of a king. As governor, he had immediately ridded the colony of its worst blight, the Rum Corps. He had befriended and upheld the social rights of the emancipated convicts, attempting to establish a middle-class society. He had erected fine public buildings, with his name forever carved on the cornerstones, built roads, named towns, encouraged the settlers to improve their farms, to build better dwellings, to add barns and fences.

Aaron's mother's brothers, the Crawford men, had prospered under Macquarie rule, as had the Aylesburys. Uncle Tad owned his own horse farm now

Uncle Owen had expanded his riverboat trade. Uncle Buck was a legend, a bushman—he had been one of those who had advised William Cox in building the road over the mountains the year after the way through the mountains had been discovered.

Aaron's countenance darkened with resentment. He had wanted to be, dreamed of being, the one to cross the mountains first, but William Wentworth, son of his father's friend D'Arcy, and two other men, Blaxland and Lawson, had beaten him to it. Aaron had been only twelve at the time, but—Aaron took a deep breath, a deep, fresh, exhilarating breath of cool New South Wales air. There was a vast world south, north, and west that had not yet been explored, mysteries of the rivers to be solved. *Was there an inland sea? Why did all the rivers west of the mountains flow away from the coast?*

"—decided yet what you'll tell Father, Aaron?"

Aaron and Mark had been half-walking, half-sliding down the faint path from the ridge. Aaron's mind was on the fading horizons, the sapphire mountains, the gray-green forests to the west, and he heard only the last half of Mark's question.

"No," he answered.

Mark placed a hand on Aaron's shoulder. "He'll be asking. I'll explain, if you want me to."

"No. I'll fight my own battles, Mark." Perspiration began to bead on his forehead. "Thank you for offering, though."

"If you need me—"

"I won't."

Mark squinted across the wheatfields. No. No one ever needed him. Not his real mother or his stepmother or his father or Aaron. And certainly not the lass he loved. Only the colony. The colony needed him, needed men like him, educated for a purpose, a

25

man of ambition, a man with a cause. The colony of New South Wales needed Mark Troop Aylesbury, by God.

But it needed Aaron too, and men like him. Aaron, too, had ambitions—of a different kind. But were they really different, or was it only the means by which he would try to fulfill them that were different?

They were skirting the wheatfields now. One could not see the borders of the property anymore from this ridge. The Aylesburys and Crawfords and other settlers with their convict laborers had pushed back the brush, the waves of forest that stretched on and on for who knew how many miles to the north, to the south, on to the Blue Mountains in the west, over and beyond them.

In the gum tree forests the Crawfords had begun their farm, had spread out, and had been joined later by Matthew Aylesbury's land. Like dividing cells, Aaron's uncles had left home, had taken up adjoining lands and spread out. Thaddeus Crawford had moved east buying up land, Owen had moved north to the river and across, each man clearing the land of the bush, spreading a checkered blanket over the land, planting the low fertile places in wheat, rye, oats, Indian corn, vegetables, and orchards.

They had left the rolling hills of grass for graze, and sheep and cattle now grazed on them. The nucleus of the cell was the house, a rectangular, two-story brick built with convict labor, the brick made on the spot by convicts. Like most every other house in the colony, the Aylesbury house had a veranda all across the front and back, to shade the inside from the glaring, merciless summer sun. Matthew Aylesbury had tried to match the grandeur of the Cranstons' house at Cranhurst, for reasons of his own. And both

Mark and Aaron had guessed what the reasons were.

The Crawfords and Aylesburys had prospered under the regime of Matthew Aylesbury's old friend Macquarie, who had arrived in Sydney on that bright January day in 1810, his regiment preceded by a band playing drums and bagpipes. Macquarie, who was now sick and broken and disillusioned, had begged for a replacement. The colony did that to men, especially to its governors.

Aaron and Mark did not say much more. They were admiring the fields, the new barns and paddocks below, and were awesomely conscious that to their right were three graves on the side of the hill. One was Silas Crawford's, the other was old Davie O'Shea's, and the third was their sister Jessica's. To the north, they could occasionally glimpse the wide, deceptively peaceful Hawkesbury River through the trees that followed its banks. It looked blue from here, but the men knew it was a muddy gray-brown up close.

"After my freezing to death all winter in Scotland and your continuous colds in England, Mark, doesn't New South Wales feel like heaven?" Aaron grinned as he looked up at the opal-blue sky in which white clouds of cockatoos winged chattering. They were coming into the dooryard of the house now; it was bare of grass, but within the new picket fences Mum and Grandmum had begun to grow flowers, English flowers.

"Aye. The sun feels good," Mark said, flashing him a grin, "but I think our parents and all the other first-generation Australians would swear it was the other way around."

"That they would. But then I was afraid *you'd* stay in England and practice law there."

"I knew you better than you knew me then, mate; I

27

knew you would come back." Mark smiled wryly. "If not to practice medicine, then to—"

"Shh. Mum will hear."

"I've a feeling Mum knows already."

A stocky yellow cat named Tuff stood up when the two young men stepped up onto the veranda, and observed them with soft green eyes trimmed in black. He arched his back and rubbed a veranda post seductively. Aaron squatted on his heels to stroke him.

Mark hooked his thumbs in his pockets and said, "Have you noticed the cats and dogs here are shorter-legged and stockier than those in England?"

"They're huskier, more muscle-bound. And look at Tuff, his chin even juts out. He is tough too, I'll wager."

"Adapting to a new country, a wild country, just as people do."

Aaron stood up. He and Mark watched as Tuff purred and dropped to the veranda floor on his side. A puff of dust wafted up from the old tom, but he didn't care. He stretched out and finally rolled over on his back to let the sun warm his belly while he kept his scraggly head in the shade.

"We'll be a country in our own right someday, just as ol' teacher Baldwin said."

Aaron nodded. "Aye. We'll have to proceed slowly though, mate, lest we end up in war against the mother country, like America did."

Mark's blue eyes danced as he met Aaron's gaze straight on. "But not too bloody slowly, mate."

Mark's revolutionary ideas were in their infant stages, Aaron realized, but slightly disconcerting, because they were premature. Aaron was uncomfortable looking into his half-brother's eyes and hoped that Mark possessed the wisdom and self-

control it would take to nurture his maturing ideas. "Let's go in to tea."

It had taken two years and four months to build the house. It was located on Crawford property that was owned by Grandmother Crawford. One hundred acres had been allotted to Silas Crawford when he had arrived in the colony as a free settler from England in 1801, and an additional ten acres for each of his five children was allotted to him. Before his death the same year, Silas had told his children that upon their coming of age, each child could claim his ten acres and do with them as he or she wished. Since then, each one had added many more acres to the original allotment—all except for Buck Crawford, who had given his acres back to the family and taken to the bush.

Since it had been Silas's daughter, Milicent, Aaron's mother, who had taken over the running of the farm, it was understood that upon Mrs. Crawford's death the farm would become Milicent's. Matthew Aylesbury's nine hundred acres were adjacent to it on the southeast, and both farms were run together.

It was upon this assumption that someday Silas Crawford's property would become Milicent's and Matthew's, that Matthew had built the house on the site of the old Crawford wattle and daub hut. For financial reasons, Matt had been unable to finish the house once it was started, but when Governor Macquarie became governor the economy had improved and Matt had finished the house, adding more and more to his original plans, even before it was finished.

Aaron remembered why, too. He was trying to build a house as large and fine as his old foe Oliver Cranston's, and he had succeeded. Except for

the furnishings.

The men stomped their feet and went in. There was a wide central hall, at the end of which the stairway to the second floor began, going up to turn at a landing before reaching the second floor. But the men entered what the colonists called the "living room," on the right side of the central hall.

Milicent Crawford rose smiling from her lady's desk in the far corner of the room and held out her arms to them. She had embraced them once already, upon their arrival home that morning, but Aaron knew she couldn't resist doing it again. He also knew that he was special to her, though she treated each lad exactly alike. It was singularly remarkable that she could do it and not appear partial. For Aaron was hers and Matthew's child, while Mark was Matthew's son by a prostitute in Sydney. Aaron loved her all the more because she was able to accept Mark as one of her own, because of her perfect love for her husband.

She was shorter than Aaron remembered, coming up just to his chin now. Her rich brown hair was shot with gray on the sides and on one streak above her forehead. She was a handsome woman, still beautiful, and poised, self-confident, and in perfect control of everything she undertook.

"Your father will be home shortly," she said, still holding both their arms. "I'm glad you're home. He'll be surprised—no one expected you until summer. What did you think of the farm?"

Since it was on Aaron that her eyes rested, he replied, "We've spread out, haven't we? How many laborers do we have now?"

Milicent smiled gently, brown eyes dancing. "Twenty-two," she said, and turned away to stroll to the living room window. There, she drew back lace curtains—an enormous luxury, sure to strike envy in

30

a Cranston breast, if one were to ever enter the house—and peered out. "Remember the years we had only one servant?"

Aaron nodded. "Aye. Rolph." His father's cousin Rolph, who had come over on a convict prison ship with his father and been assigned to the Crawfords. "Has anyone seen Rolph lately, Mum?"

She sighed. "No. As I wrote you, he came by twice in one year three years ago, but we haven't seen him since." She turned to look at Aaron. "He roams about, you know, doing odd jobs."

Aaron remembered Rolph well, lackadaisical Rolph, who had taught him to fish, who had taken the place of his father, his father who was too busy and too preoccupied to play with him during his difficult younger years. "I wish he'd come home for good."

Milicent Crawford smiled. "So do we." She turned back and let the lace curtains fall back into their place. "Here comes your father."

In the years to come, Aaron would always look back on this moment and wonder why he had been seized with the urge to urinate. The urge grabbed him and threatened, even while he took deep breaths and squeezed his thighs together. *God, I'm going to wet my trousers.* As a cold sweat broke out on Aaron's forehead, Mark turned toward the door and said, "Aaron? After you."

"Go on, Mark."

Mark had always deferred to Aaron and Aaron had always relinquished it, so no one thought it strange that Aaron hung back, allowing Mark to greet their father first. The lord of the manor cometh, Aaron thought. Mark hurried outside and Aaron fought for courage. Just as he thought all was lost, his mother touched his arm. When he turned to her, he saw her

31

eyes bright with tears.

"Aaron, my son, I'm glad you're home at last," she whispered.

And he experienced a whole new sensation in that moment. He embraced her and held her close. "All is well, Mum. We're home." He had not been as tall as she when he had left for England. Now she seemed small in his arms. And what was this other sensation, the need to weep? My God, he had been home less than six hours and he'd gone back to being two years old. Oh, wise woman. She had somehow sensed his consternation about meeting his father and had offered him this time to gather his wits. Mum, Mum. It was heaven to be home again.

Matthew Aylesbury was forty-five when his sons came back home from England. He no longer thought about those first three years when he and Milly had sacrificed to pay the boys' passage to England, and their room and board there, the costs of sending Aaron to Edinburgh to study medicine and Mark to Cambridge to study law. Because the last two years had been enormously prosperous for him, the farm, and the trade. Benevolence had smiled down at him in the form of his uncle's old friend, Governor Macquarie, who had taken him and Will Redfern and others like them under his wing, seen that they prospered and that they were included often at his own personal dinner table. Matthew had spent the last two years in preparing the way for his sons in New South Wales.

Riding tall on Pompeii, his favorite gelding, his blond hair straighter and whiter at the temples than when the boys had left for England, Matthew squinted when he saw Mark standing in the doorway near the gate, but he didn't believe his eyes at first. No, it was a lad who resembled Mark, only taller.

Matt rode easy. His torso had thickened slightly through the chest, waist, and thighs in the past five years, but he was still solid and hard muscled. He was just as strong as he had been in his youth, he told himself, and his mind was keener and quicker than ever. Being a doctor, he was never ill. Nature didn't allow it, but now his heart did funny things in his chest when Mark raised his hand in greeting.

Matt's wide mouth stretched slowly into a grin as he kept the little bay at a walk. He rode up to Mark, looked down at him as Pompeii blew and stamped one hoof. "You're early."

"Aye," Mark said, his eyes shining, but the shine dimmed when Matthew's gaze slid to the door of the house.

"And what about Aaron?"

"Home also, sir."

Matt nodded to himself and dismounted. Father and son clasped hands and Matt's left hand went to his son's shoulder. "Welcome home, Mark. I hope your return early doesn't bode ill . . . for either of you."

The five years of growing up and maturing since he had left home had not dimmed Mark's awe of his father, the awe and the love. The awe had been born out of Matthew's being the only adult male Mark had ever been close to, his only adult relative. The love was because his father had claimed him immediately, sought him out as soon as he had learned his existence, taken him home, reared him, and sent him to school. But Mark loved him for the man himself. To Mark he was the king, he was God, the most beautiful man in the world. His love for his father was his most priceless agony. He longed to embrace him, but there was that reserve between them, invisible but real.

Matthew released his hand. His greeting had been genuine, his grip affectionately firm, but Mark did not fail to see his father's eyes stray to the front door again, once, twice, three times, to brighten at last, and to mist almost imperceptively. "Aaron," he whispered.

Aaron was smiling, approaching his father, moving with that easy male grace that Mark envied and admired. With a fixed smile Mark watched his father and Aaron clasp arms, saw his father's hand tremble on Aaron's arm as it had not done on his own.

"Son. Aaron. You're home early."

"Aye."

"Why?"

Aaron released his grip on his father's hand. There was the old stern demand, already, his father demanding to know the whys of everything. Ire leapt into his eyes despite his joy. "Mark and I both were top students, sir. We received good marks in our studies. I wrote you that. So we were able to take exams early. I waited a week in Cambridge for him, and we booked passage together."

Matthew Aylesbury nodded and turned away, gathered Pompeii's reins in his hands and handed them to their black groom. When he turned back he looked at Mark, then Aaron. "I . . . am . . . glad you're home."

Both young men smiled, and glanced at each other. It wasn't often Matthew Aylesbury expressed his approval, his appreciation, or his love for his sons.

Matt saw their reactions and became embarrassed. "Let's go have tea," he said huskily.

The three men entered the central hall of the house, which had been built employing the European architecture of the day, except for the two

verandas. Inside, it was furnished almost entirely by furniture made by Owen Crawford. Except for six old pieces which the Crawfords had brought over with them from England, the entire house was furnished in Crawford furniture, an adaptation of Old World styles to Australian casualness.

On a couch that vaguely resembled those in English parlors—a provincial adaptation of a European provincial adaptation—Matthew sat down after tea and began to fill a long-stemmed clay pipe with precious tobacco, which only a man involved in trade could afford.

Mark sat down in a chair that vaguely matched the couch. Milicent was sitting in a chair at the hearth, and her mother, Elvira Crawford, sat in an American invention, the rocking chair, across a rag rug from her, knitting. Aaron felt more comfortable sitting on the raised hearth. There was a fire in the hearth because spring nights tended to become cool. Soon lamps fueled by whale oil would illuminate the rooms until the family went to bed.

Matthew lit his pipe and puffed twice. Then his blue eyes flashed from Aaron to Mark. "Now then," he said. "D'Arcy Wentworth's son, William, has gone to England to study law with the intention of practicing in Sydney along with others whom you'll recognize, Mark."

Mark nodded. He could feel his heart thudding in his chest as his father puffed twice, his father so handsome, so distinguished, so . . . almost beautiful. Milicent Crawford kept sewing, not lifting her eyes to them, but listening. This was man's business, which most businesses were, but Mark and Aaron were well aware that the women in this household managed the family affairs, controlled them, and made certain adjustments to them when it was

necessary to do so. Matthew knew it, Aaron knew it, Mark knew it, the uncles knew it. But not a soul would admit it, not on penalty of death.

"I've spoken with John Fitzhugh. You remember him, Mark, he was a partner of Sebastian Darby."

"Aye. I remember." Mark felt the hair on the back of his neck stand up. Fitzhugh and Darby were big men in the colony.

"Darby died about a year ago and Fitzhugh needs a partner. He has agreed to take you on as an assistant."

Mark leaned back abruptly. "But he's one of the top solicitors in the colony," he blurted.

Matt puffed and said softly, "Aye."

Mark caught only a glimpse of the mischief in his father's eye. It was a favor of some sort. Fitzhugh owed Matthew Aylesbury for something—or they were making a trade of some sort. Mark saw it in the arrogant lift of his father's formidable chin.

"You approve?" Matthew asked, raising his brows.

Mark jumped up. "Approve? Approve!" He slapped his forehead with the palm of his hand as he strode quickly to the front window, which over-looked the front veranda. "Father, it's a dream come true! So soon, too!" He turned toward him. "When may I start?"

Matt nodded, shrugged. "Tomorrow, if you like." He watched Mark approvingly, puffing on his pipe, another invention of the Americans that D'Arcy and several of the other surgeons had taken to. It soothed. How it soothed. Yes, Mark was an intelligent young man. He would do well. He was a hard worker and dependable, a credit to the family, indeed. "There is a fund set aside for you in the bank, Mark, enough to buy a place of your own plus expenses until you

begin to earn a living."

Mark smiled slowly, his blue eyes shining from the dimming light coming in at the multipaned window, and from some inner light, which until now had been only a flicker. Matthew recognized that light for what it was—ambition. Fierce ambition.

"Thank you, Father."

Matt inclined his head. "And please, thank your stepmother, who saw to it that a certain percent of the farm profits went to it."

Mark went to her slowly and she lifted her gaze to him. "No need to thank me," she said.

But Mark dropped to one knee and caught her hand, kissed it. "Mum," he said. "Thank you very much."

"And thank your grandmum," came Matt's voice from behind him.

Mark rose and turned to Elvira Crawford, who smiled and pointed to her wrinkled cheek. Smiling, Mark went to her and planted an affectionate kiss on her cheek, for he loved this old woman. She was a white-haired saint with a gentle smile and a gentle voice, who never scolded or complained, who loved Aaron boundlessly, but never showed partiality for him. She, like the others, had always treated Mark as an equal to her real grandson.

"And you must thank your real mother," Matt said. "She left you everything she had, and we'll discuss it later."

The pain hit Mark in the chest, a real sorrow made worse by guilt and regret. He had left his mother's house at the age of eight to live with his father because she had wanted him to, and he had not expected to enjoy living away from her as much as he had. She had died while he was away at school

37

in England, at the age of forty-two. Mark nodded.

"You're pleased?" asked Matthew, removing his pipe.

"Yes. Thank you," Mark said politely, for he had learned his lessons of gratitude well. All of them.

Matthew nodded and turned his eyes upon his other son, Aaron.

Aaron had been peeling the bark off of a log in the log box and now looked up slowly to meet his father's gaze. Matthew Aylesbury's eyes glinted with ill-concealed eagerness. His chest expanded every so slightly, his mouth softened at the corners.

"So. Aaron," he began. "And what prospects have we for you?"

Aaron smiled slowly and met his father's gaze straight on. "I'm sure one of us knows," he said gently, aware that Mark was fading into the growing shadows in the corner of the room.

As usual, Matthew did not quite know how to reply to his son. "And so we do," he said. "Of course, there is an opening at the hospital in Parramatta. But I'd much prefer that you worked in the one in Sydney. They need civilian surgeons there desperately."

Aaron drew in a deep breath. His father's friend D'Arcy Wentworth, who was now principal surgeon in the colony, and two other men had made a bargain with Governor Macquarie the same year Macquarie had arrived in the colony as governor, to build a hospital in Sydney with their own capital—in exchange for a monopoly in the rum trade. The hospital had been built, D'Arcy had realized an enormous profit, and all were happy. Folks called it the rum hospital. It was a huge rectangular building, a center block with two long wings, and it was so large that there were never enough patients to fill it.

Consequently, there were differing opinions about whether to use the extra rooms as law offices and various other utilities.

When Aaron did not reply, Matthew asked, "What do you think?"

Aaron glanced at his mother, whose eyes came up slowly to meet his, then at his grandmother, who had compressed her lips and fixed her eyes steadfastly on her sewing. He took another deep breath. This was it. The moment he had been dreading for fifteen years. "I . . . don't want to begin practice yet, Father."

Matthew's expression did not change. It froze. He took the pipe out of his mouth slowly. "What did you say?"

Aaron's gentle brown eyes held his father's staring blue ones. "I'm not ready to begin practice yet, sir."

Matthew said, "Well, I suppose you are weary from your studies, Aaron, but I should think five months aboard the ship on your voyage home would have been rest enough. But if not, I can use another hand on the farm for the summer to—"

"It's not for the summer, Father."

Matthew stared. His pipe had gone cold, as cold as this moment. That something that his insight had shuttered from his conscious thought for over fifteen years was suddenly before him, forcing him to see what he did not want to see. He looked at his wife, and her brown eyes, so much like Aaron's, met his with the same gentle defiance, the same love. "What?"

Aaron stood up slowly. "I want to . . ." He choked on his own words. "I want to do some exploring before I settle down to my life's work."

Matthew stared. He did not explode. He began to simmer slowly. He kept staring wordlessly because his mind had set up a blockade between his brain and

his speech. Then, without his mind directing it, his lips whispered, "Explore?"

"Aye." When his father's eyes darkened with inner fury, Aaron went on gathering momentum for his explanation as he gathered a few more threads of confidence. "We live on a vast island continent, Father. We know that now, thanks to Flinders's explorations of the coasts. But we don't know anything about it but what's along the east coast and that island south of it, Van Dieman's Land." When Matthew did not reply, but just kept staring, Aaron went on. "Explorers found a way over the mountains and opened up the Bathurst plains for settling. But what's beyond that? What's to the north, to the south? The colony's running out of land, Father. We need—"

"Dash the land!" Matthew roared suddenly, his pipe clattering onto the table beside him. "You were sent to medical school, Aaron. Let somebody else look for land."

"For which I am truly grateful, but—"

Matthew leapt to his feet. "You always knew you wanted to go off like that on your own, didn't you?"

Aaron said, "Yes."

"Then why in hell did you go to medical school?"

"Because you wanted me to."

Matthew winced as if he had been slapped. "Because *I* wanted it. Because *I* wanted it. My God, Aaron, I didn't send you to medical school to become an explorer. You can't make a living exploring." Matthew was shouting and Milicent had risen and gone quietly about the room gently shutting the parlor door and the two windows one by one so that the servants wouldn't hear.

"Father, it's only for a while. It's something I have to do. And when I am through, I'll settle down

40

somewhere to hospital work, or to private practice some—"

"You have to do it? You have to throw away your young years?" Matthew shouted.

Aaron's mind went blank in an abysmal quicksand with only occasional words surfacing, like hands grasping for something to hold on to. He stood, his face burning, his frame trembling with his own anger and hurt. Words from his father like "shirking responsibility . . . a world of people needing medical help . . . your mother's hard work . . . your grand-father's legacy . . . my boasting to the medical department about my son who was studying to become a doctor . . . how can you do this . . ." kept slapping him in the face.

"What are you going to end up being, for God's sake, Aaron? A bushman like your Uncle Buck?" Matt shouted.

By now Matthew's shirt was unbuttoned at his throat and he had thrown off his coat. His hair was standing on end, and Aaron swallowed, hurt to see that so much of it was white now. "I hope that I can have Uncle Buck's understanding of what a man must do," Aaron replied softly, trying not to drown in the anger and hurt.

"Or are you going to be like Rolph, a swagman?" Matthew hissed. "A drunkard."

"Your Cousin Rolph is a gentle man. A kind man. A man capable of compassion," Aaron said steadily. "And he understands the needs of somebody besides himself."

Matthew rocked back on his heels. Speechlessly he stared, the nostrils of his fine nose flaring. "And I am not?"

"I'm sorry, sir, but I haven't seen it in you."

For a moment Aaron thought his father was going

41

to strike him. The room was oppressive with fury and agony and the smell of perspiration, of women's soft tears and trembling. And Aaron could bear no more of it.

"I am going soon, Father. I don't know where or how or with whom, but I'm going. Give me a year. Maybe two or three, but I must do this. I must do this for the colony, for myself."

"I gave you four years of formal schooling so that you could do something for the colony, for yourself," Matthew breathed shakily.

"But I must do this first. And soon."

They stood motionless. Then Aaron turned away, turned and strode to the living room door, went out into the hall, out the door into the cool spring air of dusk, leaving his father standing in the center of the living room floor with fists clenched and his face tragic to see.

Mark had at first leaned against the wall in a corner listening, but he had slowly sunk, out of horror and fear, to the stool beside the window, shrunk into the shadows like a forgotten ghost. He didn't even think he was breathing. His own emotions were cyclonic. For he feared what his father would do to Aaron; yet his father's disapproval of his brother gave him a secret pleasure. He did not want to see the hurt and anger in his father's face, but he struggled with a perverse delight that it was Aaron who had caused it. And in spite of himself, he envied Aaron's courage to defy his father, though he himself would never dream of it.

"Mark!"

Mark jumped up from the stool so fast it toppled over. "Yessir!" he said breathlessly.

Matthew's anger still simmered, but he was able to sit down again, and after passing a trembling hand over his face, he said, "Your mother left her house,

her merchandise, and all her savings to you."

Mark crept toward him slowly.

"I was appointed her executor, and I sold the goods and the house and put the money in the bank, which was one of the first accounts in The Bank of New South Wales, by the way. It has been drawing interest since then, of course, and you will be able to take over the account when you are twenty-one."

Mark watched as his father massaged his eyes with his hand, disappointed that he seemed to take no more interest in telling him this than he would have taken in playing cribbage with a witch. "How did Mum die?" Mark asked softly.

Matthew looked up slowly, wearily. "It was consumption. She died gently, suffering very little. And she told me to tell you she loved you."

Just like that. Matter-of-factly.

Mark summoned every ounce of courage he had to ask, "Were you there?"

Matthew looked away from him. "Yes."

And that was all. His father's mind was elsewhere. For all practical purposes, Mark was dismissed. "May I go now?"

Matthew nodded, but Milicent rose and went to Mark. "Come to the kitchen. I've tea made and tarts."

There, at a polished round table made by Owen Crawford, Milicent gave him the details of his mother's death, what had been done for her, how she had wanted her son to be a good solicitor. Mark sat and admired his stepmother, grateful to her for taking this gentle moment for him. But then he was grateful to his father too, and his mum—everybody. For no one in this family had ever treated him like what he was—his father's bastard.

Aaron walked fast, walked fast down the garden

path and out the gate, across the grassless dooryard toward the paddock. Beyond the paddock was a little creek where water ran most of the year, and a little place where it deepened, where its bed was gravel and the water was clear and good for swimming and bathing. He pushed through the brush, beneath the giant gum trees, and it wasn't until he sat down beside the creek that he realized that the roaring fury in his ears had become the deafening, prehistoric churr of cicadas. The sound rose and fell in intensity, and beetles clicked and rattled in the brush. The rustling in the grass revealed the secret stealth of some small creature, a kangaroo rat, probably. Not a snake, he hoped.

A snake. Aaron shut his eyes. When he and Mark were nine years old, their little sister, Jessica, had been bitten by a deadly black snake in the east field where the three of them and cousin Deen had been playing. They were farther from home than they should have been. Deen, the son of Uncle Buck, a half-native boy, was only seven then, but he knew what to do. He had cut the wounds on Jessica's tiny leg with a knife and sucked the blood from the wound. Then he had screamed, "Make her run! Make her run!"

Aaron had grabbed Jessica's hand and run across the field, pulling her behind him. He had run, pulling her along, until she stumbled again and again, crying and exhausted, and Mark had run to catch her other hand, while Deen ran ahead to tell those at the house.

"Run, Jessica, run!" Aaron and Mark had screamed to the little girl as they dragged her along. "Run, Jessica, run," until they reached the house. His mother had sent a convict for their father in Parramatta, but until he arrived they had tried to

make Jessica run. But how do you make a four-year-old run?

They had put her to bed, applied warm cloths to the wound on her leg. His father arrived angry and panicked and began working over her. He worked on the little girl and called in his friends Drs. Redfern and Wentworth to help. Day passed into night. By the next morning, Jessica was dead.

Now Aaron bit his lip and leaned his forehead on his knee. Deen had suggested the only cure for snakebite, a native cure that had proved to work in some cases. For death from snakebite always came because the venom paralyzed the lungs and the heart, and people who were bitten ran to keep their hearts pumping and their lungs working, and to sweat out the poison. It was a native remedy, and it was the only thing that worked. But little Jessica couldn't run long enough.

That had been Aaron's first encounter with death, the first time he had witnessed the failure of medical science, the first time he had questioned the ways of God. In medical school he had seen worse things, much worse. *From boyhood a man is taught that God is love. As a man he wonders if God isn't also a monster.*

Aaron raised his head and looked up at the stars. They were closer here than in England. Aaron had never gotten quite used to the sun's moving across a southern sky there. The moon here was closer, clearer. These night sounds were real; the countryside sounds of England were like a fantasy. He was home at last, and glad of it. Only he wished there was not this antagonism between his father and himself. But then, it had always been there.

Hey, Aaron, are you a currency lad?
Nay, I ain't.

45

My mother says ye are like the rest of us, 'cause yer father was a convict.

Aaron could still remember the shock, the anger, and the humiliation of learning at school that his father had been a convict. Before that, he had thought only those miserable wretches in chains who worked on the roads were convicts.

A convict he learned, was a person who was convicted of a crime. *A crime.*

His father had been a convict. Humiliation wrestled with him, in bed, at school, even at play. But the family had never spoken of it. Never.

And pretty Penelope Cranston, six years old, had asked, "Are you a currency lad?"

How had his convict father dared to marry his "free settler" mother, and worse, after having sired a bastard son of a prostitute convict woman? Even now he raged at his father's arrogance, his selfishness in pursuing and marrying the innocent daughter of a free settler.

At the age of eleven, about the time Aaron was beginning to forget that his father had been a convict, Aaron had run into the new house one day from playing and into his parents' bedroom. And before his shirtless father could turn around, Aaron had seen the white puckered scars of old lashes lacing his father's broad back. Aaron had stared, and Matthew had turned to see his shock and horror. Aaron had turned and fled, had run away to this very spot and had cried long and hard. *His father had been a beaten convict.*

He gnawed his fist now, thinking how thoughtless his father had been to subject his mother to the humiliation of being the wife of a convict.

Aaron stretched out on to the soft, cool grass and propped his head on his hands. Solitude. Solitude

was what he needed. A long time of solitude, away from the crowds of medical school, away from family, away from everything. He was even thankful for this place where he could come and be alone with his thoughts and his private wars.

He did not know that this was the place of his conception.

Chapter III

"I say, I have heard it told that somewhere on this continent there are alligators and crocodiles. Tell me, are there any in this river?"

Deen Crawford never batted an eye as he considered the pompous young Englishman with barely concealed amusement. "Oh, aye, sir. A small mob of them stays near Owen's Landing where we'll drop anchor. But don't worry, they aren't hungry. We feed them a few Limeys from time to time to keep them happy."

As the women in the boat giggled, Penelope watched Sir Henry Braxton raise his brows and nudge his son, who had asked the question. "There you are, Weldon. He put you in your place, did he not?" Then he haw-hawed aloud as Weldon's face turned red with embarrassment.

Penelope could tell that her father was enjoying Deen's quip, because she knew he had been disappointed in Weldon Braxton, whom he had been considering as a prospective son-in-law—until he had met him for the first time yesterday in Sydney.

"Of course," Deen went on, "our alligators are as big as elephants, so it takes several dozen Limeys a

week to keep them content."

"Haw-haw-haw," laughed Sir Braxton.

The entire voyage from Sydney had been like this, with Deen Crawford, who was captain of the sloop, *Milicent*, entertaining them all the way. Deen, whom everyone knew was Buck Crawford's son, was a favorite in the colony, especially with the settlers along the Hawkesbury. For, like most of the natives the settlers saw in the colony, Deen had a prodigious sense of humor. Deen was tall, very lean and hard muscled, with curly black hair that tended to show streaks of red in the sun, and black eyes, always glittering with amusement. Though he was half-native, Deen's nose was not wide with large nostrils like the natives'; his was like his father's, narrow and straight, and his lips were full, but not wide. The settlers often laughed about the fact that Deen was not as dark-skinned as many of the white farmers in the district.

On the Cranston party's trip from up the Hawkesbury River, Deen had entertained them with a potpourri of historical rhetoric and amusing anecdotes, but it was his spontaneous quips that caught his rapt listeners by surprise every time. The party, including the Cranstons, the Livingstons, and the Braxtons, had left Sydney in the sloop sailing out of Port Jackson, through the heads, and up the coast into Broken Bay, the mouth of the Hawkesbury. Oliver Cranston had decided to make the journey from Sydney to Cranhurst by river rather than by land, giving the Braxtons the best view of the river's rich alluvial flood plain on which the Braxtons were contemplating settling—if they decided to stay in New South Wales—and the Cranstons thought they would.

The Braxtons were among the new immigrants

who had responded to the English government's recent campaign to encourage immigration to New South Wales. They had written the Cranstons of their plans to tour the colony with prospects of settling, and had been expected sometime that summer. When they had arrived two days before, they had gone to the Livingstons' estate just north of Sydney to stay until they could find a residence, and had sent word to the Cranstons that they had arrived.

The Cranstons had immediately gone to Sydney by boat and were bringing back both families for a brief stay at Cranhurst, giving Henry Braxton a chance to see the country.

Meanwhile, all the Braxtons could talk about was Sydney.

The cheerful English family called Sydney a penal settlement. Penelope smiled to herself, for Sydney was no longer a penal settlement. It was a town. As Governor Macquarie, whom she secretly admired, had said, "I found New South Wales a jail and left it a colony."

The Braxtons thought otherwise. Nowhere else had they seen such swarms of convicts, both in shackles and out, mixing and mingling with free people. And they had marveled that even most of the free people were pardoned prisoners—emancipated convicts. And they exclaimed that the town itself was just emerging from colonial primitiveness.

"I say, Mr. Crawford," said Braxton now. "When did you say this river was discovered?"

Deen grinned. "My mother's people say 'sometime long ago,'" he returned, reminding them cheerfully that the black natives had been here long before any whites. "My mother's people call it the Deerubbun. But my father's people first came to it in seventeen-eighty-nine, one year after the first fleet landed in

50

Sydney Cove and settled there. The expedition was headed by our first governor, Arthur Philip, who called it 'so noble a river.' That was thirty-three years ago." A gleam of mischief appeared in Deen's eyes even before the quirk appeared on his mouth. "That was back when Mr. Cranston was about—let me see—fifteen? Sixteen?" Deen's grin broadened as his eyes slipped to Elaina Cranston. "And Mrs. Cranston would have been about . . ." He paused.

There were astonished gasps from Lady Braxton and Mrs. Livingston, and Deen grinned and said, "Three? Four?"

Everyone laughed, relieved. One didn't speak of a lady's age unless one gave her the advantage of being several years younger than she was, which Deen had done.

Penelope laughed outright. Only Deen Crawford could get by with calling Englishmen "Limeys" to their faces or guessing the ages of the ladies aboard his boat. She loved it. She liked Deen, and he knew it and liked her, too. This was the first time she had been around him since Aaron Aylesbury had gone away to England. As a small lad, Deen had sometimes joined in Aaron and Penelope's play. She especially remembered how Deen had come upon them one day up on the ridge while they were chasing a kangaroo rat. Deen had joined in the fun, using his native expertise, and they had trapped the little animal, inspected him, prodded him, and finally released him. She was sure the glint in Deen's eyes now when he looked at her was because he knew of her love for Aaron. And he seemed to approve.

"I lied," Deen was saying. "There are no alligators in this river." He let the ladies laugh, then added, "Just crocodiles." Then he said quickly, "No. Seriously. Those are in the ponds and lakes in the

51

northern part of the continent, in the tropical rain forests. Absolutely no alligators here." He paused again. "Of course, I don't recommend hanging your hand over the side of the boat, Lady Braxton, just in case."

Lady Braxton gave a startled chirp and jerked her hand up, to the delight of the others.

Penelope laughed again. She liked Lady Braxton, whom her mother claimed had been her only real friend back in England. And she liked Sir Braxton, knighted by King George III for distinguished military service in India. But she could not abide their pompous son, Weldon. Because he was haughty and a braggart and, as far as she could tell, had, at the age of twenty-two, accomplished nothing. And perhaps she detested him worse because her parents had viewed him as a prospective son-in-law.

"All land you will see along the Hawkesbury from here on is rich bottom land," Deen went on after his brief diversion from the serious. "The Hawkesbury flood plains have been called the breadbasket of the colony. In the early days, settlers along the river raised crops and livestock and sold them in Sydney to the government commissary from which convicts, settlers, and the military drew their rations." With a smile, Deen gave the rope of the mainsail a tug and shouted commands to the four men managing the sails. "And *my* breadbasket tells me it's time for tea," he said, patting his abdomen. "It will be two hours yet before we reach the landing." Indicating the entire river with a sweep of his hand, he added, "Enjoy." With that he swung down from the little forecastle to the deck and down into the small hold.

Elaina had come prepared with baskets of food for the noon meal. So the men waited while the women handed squares of linen to them and then pieces of

bread, wedges of cheese, and grapes, which she explained came from a lower Hawkesbury farm.

"I say," began Weldon Braxton to Penelope when the ladies had settled upon their benches again with their meals. "Is that chap, Crawford, really half-savage?" He had sat down close to her, something he had begun to do more frequently the farther upriver they sailed, though Rodney Livingston had glared at him, letting him know that his attentions toward Penelope weren't to be tolerated. Penelope was well aware that handsome Rodney, the son of her parents' longtime Sydney friends, had marked her for his own years ago. Rodney had been sulking all the way from Sydney, because he didn't like Englishmen in general, and Weldon in particular, especially since Weldon seemed to be attracted to Penelope.

"No. He's not savage," she said, dropping her gaze to the bread in her hand. "At all."

"I meant native. Is he really half-native?"

"Deen Crawford is half-native, yes. His mother was a native, his father is Buck Crawford, the brother of the man who owns this boat."

Weldon pulled a face. "Oh, I hope such an arrangement isn't common in the colony. I mean, a white marrying a native."

Cranston spoke up. "As a matter of fact, it's rare. Buck Crawford took to the bush early in his life, trapping and hunting for a living. Sells skins for a good price and leads hunting parties into the bush. Buck fathered Deenyi of a native woman, and when the boy was five or six years old he brought him to the Crawfords' farm to be brought up."

Sir Braxton was leaning toward Oliver Cranston, his eyes intent upon Oliver's face. "He seems intelligent enough, though I have heard the natives here are quite primitive," he said.

53

"They are. You see, Deenyi had an excellent teacher," Cranston replied.

Penelope looked quickly at her father. Deenyi had not gone to school at all. Macquarie had started a school for native children, but Deenyi did not fit in. After all, he was half-white. And neither had the lad fit in with the lads at the private boys' school in Parramatta. It was Aaron's mother who had taught Deen to read, write, do sums, to appreciate the white man's history as well as native customs and myths. Everybody in the colony knew that.

Penelope watched her father's expression closely. For several years now she had suspected that her father admired Mrs. Aylesbury more than was ordinary. As her gaze slid slowly to her mother's face, she had to bite her lip. For Elaina Cranston had her nose in the air and her mouth drawn tightly into a small pucker. "Humph," Elaina Cranston said.

Oliver Cranston gave her a wry smile and said, "Of course, he *must* have learned something from Dr. Aylesbury, too."

Penelope saw their eyes meet, hold briefly, their gaze darting away like bees who had lit on a flower and found no nectar there.

The Braxtons had seen nothing. "Aylesbury. Aylesbury," Sir Braxton said after he had swallowed the bite of cheese in his mouth. "That name—"

With a strange, brief glance at Penelope, Oliver Cranston explained, "Matthew Aylesbury and his kinsman, Rolph Danbury, were two of those we arrested for burning my corn cribs, Henry, shortly before we decided to sail for New South Wales back in eighteen hundred. Remember?"

Sir Henry Braxton threw back his head, letting his mouth fly open. "Oh, indeed I do. Indeed, yes. It was during a ball given by you. Yes. It was a sort of riot of

the small farmers, wasn't it? And Aylesbury and his kinsman were sentenced to hang, but his father's solicitor got the sentence commuted to transportation." Braxton nodded. "Yes. And he's here?"

With a snort, Rodney Livingston spoke up. "Not only is he here, he and Danbury were given full pardons by Governor King, and Aylesbury has prospered under the benevolent rule of our former, misbegotten governor, Macquarie. Dr. Matthew Aylesbury, physician, farmer, and merchant."

"Indeed!" exclaimed Braxton amazed. He pondered, smacking his lips a little as he nodded. "Well, it could only happen in New South Wales, what?"

"And America," Weldon said, sniffing.

Penelope's face was suddenly burning, and she pressed her cold hands on each of her cheeks. She had heard of Dr. Aylesbury's background, but not from her parents. It was from Frances Aylesbury, the dressmaker in Parramatta. But Miss Fran had not told her that it was Penelope's father who had arrested him back in England. Now, at least, she knew why the Cranstons and the Aylesburys hated each other—and why her love for Aaron Aylesbury was so forbidden.

She was suddenly remembering something else Frances Aylesbury had said to her once. *You musn't forget Rolph Danbury, Dr. Aylesbury's cousin, who was pardoned at the same time Matthew was. He went away when you were very small and we've seen him only twice since. You must meet him, someday.*

Penelope had always wondered why she must remember that vagabond man. Now she thought she understood why. Her father had arrested that man, too. She raised moist eyes just in time to see Rodney Livingston smile at her cynically.

But as Deen Crawford came bounding up out of

55

the hold of the boat to direct the steering of the sloop toward the bank with its wooden pier jutting out over the water, Penelope lifted her chin and rose to lean against the boat's rail. *I won't let their hate dissolve my love. Never. It can't, no more than water can dissolve a stone.*

"I take it that you never heard the Aylesbury history before, dear Penelope."

She did not look at Rodney, who had come to stand beside her. "What is that to you?" she said irritably.

"Mark Aylesbury used to brag that he would marry you someday."

Penelope turned and glared at Rodney, aware that any time she happened to look at him, he seemed upset about something. "Rodney, I can truthfully say that I have absolutely no interest in Mark Aylesbury."

Rodney's glittering dark eyes searched her face, and his lips stretched into a smile without mirth. "But what about his brother?"

Penelope felt the slow blush creep up from her breast into her face, and she knew Rodney saw it.

Anger flashed in his eyes. "Ah. I had guessed. A triangle of affection. How romantic. How disgusting. How could you, Penelope? Aaron is as beneath you as the other one."

She looked away. "As I said, it's not any of your affair."

"I'll make it my affair."

Penelope pressed her lips together in fury. Rodney thought he owned her, because the Cranstons and the Livingstons had been friends for years and Rodney had been born only weeks before her, born in Sydney of parents who had come from England, and they had been thrown together since childhood every time

the families got together. He was good-looking enough, but she couldn't forget things like the time he overturned James's bucket full of pollywogs and stomped them just for fun, or the time he threw a kitten into the hole of a privy. Or the time he attempted to entice her into his father's barn, for whatever reason.

"I won't go away, Penelope. Ever. Because you seem to attract undesirable boobs—like that Weldon over there, for instance. What a pompous ass *that* would-be suitor is."

"Hush. He'll hear you."

"Good. He's more obnoxious than a currency lad."

By the time the little sloop *Milicent* slid slowly toward the pier at Owen's Landing, Deen was at the helm singing something about the river and his love, his strange profile with its slightly sloping forehead silhouetted against the blue-white sky. As she watched him in one of his unguarded moments, when his eyes went to the east bank and a hint of melancholy seemed to come upon him, Penelope was remembering a bit of young people's gossip that claimed that Deen Crawford was in love with a white girl. No one knew who the white girl was or where the gossip originated. Penelope ached for him, for to her his plight was even worse than hers, and so painfully sad.

Since his father had announced that he was not going to make Aaron's trust fund available to him until he was ready to "settle down," Aaron had to work at something else to make money for the venture he hoped to undertake. He would not have accepted the trust fund money anyway until he

finally began his life's work. Labor in the colony was plentiful and confict labor was cheap, but even so, there was always an odd chore or two to be had, which a vagabond, an extra hand, or a penniless nephew could do for a few shillings.

Aaron had spent his second day home from England visiting his uncles in search of chores. Uncle Thaddeus had allowed him to break a couple of his young horses for riding, which had taken a full day. Then Owen, who was short of labor at the moment, had allowed him to help at the landing. After spending four years at hard study and hospital work, Aaron thought it felt good to be doing physical labor again.

The day was warm and the sun was burning his skin, but his soul was luxuriating in the warmth like an eel floating in the backwaters of the river. After four years of freezing in Scotland, the New South Wales sun was a balm. But the task Owen had set him to warmed him more than he wanted—forging iron nails, for use in building boats, making iron pins larger in diameter than a man's finger and twice as long. It was hot, tedious work and did not require much skill. It was a task Owen often set young blacksmith apprentices to, or young lads wanting to make an extra shilling or two. Aaron had to melt down each chunk of iron in the open-air forge, keep it there until it was white-hot, then take it out with tongs, place it on an anvil, and strike while the iron was hot, fashioning it into the correct shape and size. When the pin was eight inches long with a sharp point on one end, he would plunge it into the wooden tub of water to cool and harden. Steam would roll up with a great hissing sound, and then Aaron would toss the pin into the crate nearby with the hundreds of others he had wrought that day.

Occasionally he had to pause and shove more coals into the forge, and even more often, he had to pump the bellows to fan the coals. He was pumping the bellows when Annabelle Moffett rode up to the forge on her horse.

"Aaron!" she cried as she dismounted.

He greeted her with a grin, and tolerated her jostling him when she threw her arms around his neck, but he did not pause as he pumped the bellows with all his might.

"Aren't you going to greet me at all?" she said, stepping back with her arms still in the air.

"Greetings, Annabelle," he said as he pumped.

Almost in tears, she watched him and finally said, "You didn't come by the farm. I almost died when I heard you had come home."

He glanced at her now, seeing a taller Annabelle, though she had always been tall for her age, not much different than she had been at fifteen when he'd left for England. Tall, angular, hazel-eyed, freckled-faced, and plain, Annabelle hadn't changed much in the last five years. He smiled to himself, thinking again she'd make a handsome boy. Besides Mark and Deen, Annabelle had been his only playmate except for the lads at school, and except for occasional stolen moments with Penelope. Glenn Moffett was the nearest neighbor who had children, except for Uncle Ben, but Ben had kept his boys always at work on his dairy farm.

"When you didn't come to see me I decided to come to see you. I rode to your house this morning and your mother said you were here."

"And very busy at the moment," he told her.

She watched him as he pumped the bellows causing the coals to glow, precious coals Owen had hauled from up the coast, which Aaron felt obligated

59

to get the most use out of, keeping the charcoal glowing at optimum temperature.

"I can see that. Where's Mark?" Annabelle asked, folding her arms across her breasts as she watched him.

Aaron glanced at her, hoping to see in her face some real interest in Mark. But it wasn't there. Her eyes were devouring himself. "Sydney."

"Already?"

"Already. Taking up his new position as assistant solicitor." A lock of hair had fallen over his glistening forehead as he set the bellows aside and pulled the padded glove onto his left hand. "Stand back, Annabelle."

"Some greeting you gave me, Aaron. Haven't I changed much? Or grown—or something?"

Aaron picked up the tongs and looked over at her, his eyes flicking over her body briefly. Then his mouth stretched into a grin. "No." He heard only a small sigh from her as he took a lump of white-hot iron with the tongs. "Now go away, Annabelle, I have work to do. I have to make five hundred of these wretched pins."

But she stood by and watched him beat the red-hot iron—*clang, clang, clang, clang* and—turn the metal—*clang, clang, clang*—turn—*clang, clang, clang*, sweat dripping off his chin, his lips stretched against his teeth, feeling the tearing grueling work of the muscles in his right arm, shoulder and back. But the heft of the hammer and the pounding did not cause his muscles to ache as badly as holding the tongs just so.

"Can't I help? Five hundred of these? You'll never be finished. And I've a million things to tell you. If I wait, I'll die."

Aaron plunged the pin into the tub of water, the

hiss and the steam encouraging more perspiration. His shirt was already soaked down the front, back, and under his arms. He'd take the damned thing off, but Owen wouldn't allow it, since there were women always coming and going on the landing.

"You can pump the bellows and keep the coals glowing," he said, tossing the new iron pin into the crate with a clank. "What things can't wait or you'll die?"

"My new mare, for one. Father bought a carriage. And a fascinating story that one of his farm laborers told about building the road over the mountains and of finding something unusual." With a smile on her boyish lips, Annabelle took the heavy bellows in her hands.

"What did he find?" Aaron asked, frowning.

"I'll not tell you until you finish."

"What did he find, Annabelle?" He had no patience for games at the moment.

"Gold."

He snorted. "That's nonsense."

"I don't think so."

Aaron took another piece of iron from the fire. "Don't bellow while I'm striking iron—it's dangerous. Stand back. Do the bellows when I'm through pounding."

Aaron beat the iron, a large piece this time, separating it into two smaller pieces, then he threw one piece back into the coals and began forging the other—*clang, clang, clang.* When he was through, Annabelle determinedly pumped the bellows while Aaron cooled the new pin in the tub of water. It was when he finished cooling the pin that he noticed the sloop, the *Milicent,* he thought, just coming toward the landing.

"I guessed something about you before you went to

61

England," Annabelle said, pumping the bellows. "I know you wanted to be the first explorer over the Blue Mountains."

Aaron smiled crookedly. "I was just a boy," he said, but his mind went back to the day his father had announced that the expedition party that had gone to find a way across the mountains had returned with news that they had found a pass over the mountains. Aaron had wept and raged, and he was remembering now Penelope Cranston's sweet words of comfort when he had vented his rage and hurt. *Don't worry, Aaron. The mountains are just little things. It's a whole lot of big things like plains and rivers on the other side that you'll explore someday.*

A lad's dream. Aaron beat the pin into shape and smiled to himself, for he realized that he had not changed any more than Annabelle had.

"—and talk about the new governor," Annabelle was saying.

He listened to some of her chatter and didn't to the rest. Annabelle spoke in a monotone, and what she had to talk about was boring. She droned on. Bothersome as she was, she was a friend, and he was determined to put up with her chatter until the five hundred pins were forged, or until she left—whichever came first.

Finally, her voice took on a different pitch when she said, "If you haven't seen your pretty merino friend, Penelope Cranston, since you returned, Aaron, you shall now."

Aaron glanced at her and plunged the pin into the water, then followed her gaze to the party just making its way up the slope from the pier. Ahead of the party came Deen, striding with his quick, long-legged, bobbing stride. Deen grinned, showing two rows of white teeth as he opened his arms wide.

"Annabelle. Did he hire you to keep the forge going? They pay lads a shilling a day for such work," he shouted.

Annabelle straightened and wiped her hands down the side of her dress. "I volunteered, but I'm sorry I did. He's no fun to talk to. He hasn't heard a word I said."

Aaron had noticed something about Deen a long time ago. He worshipped Annabelle, but one could only glimpse that worship in unguarded moments, in instances when Deen did not think anyone was noticing him. The adoration was there now, just one flicker of his gaze, briefly, almost imperceptibly over her body, a slight inflation of his chest, the bobbing of his adam's apple as he swallowed. "Ah, don't you see, Annabelle," he said. "His mind's on his work . . . wondering how he can get out of it."

Aaron was thinking that if Deen was in love with Annabelle as he suspected, it was a sad and impossible situation. But he had to smile at Deen's quip. His own eyes went to the Cranston party as they moved up the slope from the pier—ten of them, including Rodney Livingston, the bloody larrikin. "I'll not get out of it till I'm finished," Aaron said. "I need the money."

"If it were me making things and I had a pretty girl like Annabelle to keep the heat up for me, I'd do it forever," Deen said jocularly, and Aaron had to study him for a moment to decide just what Deen would do forever. But Deen had pulled the jester's mask over his face, and all Aaron saw there was an innocent grin.

Aaron grunted in reply and tossed the pin into the crate. Then he paused to flex his arm and shoulder.

"Arm weary, mate?" Deen asked.

"Sore."

"Physical exertion doth not a physician make?" Deen clicked his tongue. "Plan to work at this long?"

"Long enough to make enough money for an exploration party, provided I can find your father."

Deen shrugged and hung his thumb in the pocket of his trousers. "He's out there, God knows where. But he's been gone three months now, so he's about due in any day. Word is the hunting's been good lately. Roos coming up from the south to forage because of the drought. Father Buck will have every mule burdened down with hides."

Annabelle exclaimed, "I feel terrible about the kangaroos and wallabies. I wish your father wouldn't hunt like that."

Deen's expression sobered momentarily. "Sorry," he said, and took his eyes from her face to watch the party as it went by. Then he leaned close to Aaron. "There's Limeys amongst 'em, so fresh they're tangy." He grinned at Aaron, winked at Annabelle, and then went away from them with that quick, energetic, bobbing walk that was so characteristic of him.

Aaron had not missed a step of the Cranston party. Straightening now, he watched Penelope as she noticed him and raised her hand in greeting. He watched as she started walking toward him. He was still watching when her father caught her arm, said something, drew her gently back to the group. Penelope looked over her shoulder at Aaron, but the party was approaching the waiting carriage and horses, and the man handed the women into the carriage and then began to check cinches and saddles on their horses. The carriage was too small for all of them, so apparently Cranston had instructed old Cricket, his groom, to have the horses ready for the men.

64

While the Cranston party was still getting settled in the carriage and on the horses, Rodney Livingston broke from the group and strode toward Aaron.

A kookaburra laughed insistently in a tree nearby as Livingston came to stand beside the forge. Aaron observed him narrowly, and for a moment Livingston did not speak. Then, "Penelope Cranston sends you her congratulations for earning your doctor's certificate."

Aaron smiled hugely. If only the bludger knew she had already delivered that greeting in person!

"And the Cranstons congratulate you."

Aaron inclined his head with a mocking smile.

"So now that this has been said, there will be no reason for Penelope to speak to you . . . will there?" Rodney's eyes were darker than the coals that Aaron had earlier shoveled into the forge.

Aaron regarded Rodney Livingston contemptuously. When they were boys, Livingston had tormented him and Mark continuously . . . as long as he knew he was backed by his friends. "There might be," Aaron replied steadily, not taking his gaze from Rodney's.

Rodney's eyes flashed. "Here's my advice to you, Aylesbury. Remember your place, and Penelope's, so that we won't have any unnecessary . . . conflicts."

Aaron grinned sardonically and said, "My place?"

"You know what I mean, currency lad."

"Maybe I do. Maybe I don't. Maybe tonight you'd like to meet me somewhere and make it plainer, Livingston."

Rodney glared silently. Then he said, "There'll be a time, Aylesbury. Never fear." He started to walk away, but paused, turned back. "When the time comes, by the way, bring your brother." And then he strode away.

Annabelle took a deep breath. "Well! Whoever would have thought that you would fight over Penelope Cranston!" She was staring at him, and he thought that her face had gone slightly pale.

Fury engulfed him. He had a sudden urge to run after Livingston, grab him, and knock hell out of him. But that was when Uncle Owen came strolling toward him wiping his dirty hands on a rag.

Owen Crawford's eyes were quick to take in a scene and assimilate it, and he approached smiling, dispelling the tension with his singularly relaxed and congenial manner. Owen had never spoken a cross word in his life. Short, built muscular and solid, Owen had built up his businesses from nothing, with his own hands. When he was still a lad, Owen had built one large sloop using convict labor, and had begun to carry the Hawkesbury farm goods down the river and down the coast to Sydney, to bring back supplies for the settlers. That was during a time when even rags for wiping one's hands on were scarce. They were worn instead.

As a boat builder and freighter, he had invented some techniques for bending wood and for managing the intractabilities of the ironbark tree, which made him one of the best boat builders in the colony. Once Owen had mastered the craft of boat building and had captured the Hawkesbury River trade, he had set his convict laborers to building farm wagons, farm implements, and household furniture. Owen had never had an enemy, as far as Aaron knew, and he did not acknowledge the personal feuds of his family with the Cranstons.

Owen's curly, dusty-blond hair was beginning to grow over his ears and down his neck, a little longer than was the fashion. He was dressed in white shirt open at the neck, brown Parramatta cloth trousers,

and matching vest. "That was the Cranston party, wasn't it?" he asked taking a stand near Aaron as they watched the carriage move away, flanked by Cranston and the other men on horseback.

Aaron turned abruptly toward the fire. "Aye."

"That's strange. Oliver Cranston is supposed to pick up the finger protectors for his daughter."

Aaron frowned as he picked up the tongs. "Finger protectors?"

Owen nodded and stuffed the rag he had been wiping his hands on in his back pocket. "That little lass came into the furniture shop with her parents to order a stool and easel made. I noticed then that the tips of her fingers were calloused and—"

"Penelope's fingers calloused?" Aaron exclaimed.

Owen nodded. "From playing the harp. I suggested thin copper finger protectors and had ten made for her." Owen shrugged. "Well, they'll come later and get them, I suppose." He walked around and looked into the crate of newly made pins. "You've about three hundred pins to go. You're slow, Aaron." Owen looked at Annabelle nearby and winked. "I might have to dismiss you if you're not finished before dark."

Aaron smiled wryly and did not answer.

"You'll come back tomorrow I hope?" Owen asked, grinning.

"I won't be able to lift a hammer tomorrow."

"You'll lift one," Owen said, watching Aaron take the metal out of the fire. "There's one thing about you, Aaron; you never give up."

Aaron smiled, and Owen raised a hand in farewell and walked away.

"Oh, pooh."

Aaron glanced at Annabelle.

"Three hundred more to go? You won't get

through before dark. Now I'll have to tell you what I really couldn't wait to tell you. Father gave me a message for you. He wants to see you to discuss an exploration expedition with you. And you won't even finish here—"

Aaron stared. He dropped the tongs holding the white-hot metal, and as it bounced and fell into the dust near his feet he danced a jig to avoid it, swearing under his breath. Then, furious, he stood, arms askew, glaring at Annabelle. "Damn, Annabelle! Look what you caused! What? What about an expedition? Why didn't you tell me?"

"I was saving it for tonight."

"Damn, Annabelle!" Aaron raged. "That's the most important thing in my life, and you were saving it!"

The girl stared at him, her hazel eyes misting over. "It really is, isn't it?"

Aaron's eyes flicked to the hill south, then back to her. "At the moment, yes."

Annabelle had seen the direction in which his gaze had gone, and she pressed her lips together briefly. "Is it really?" When he didn't answer, she said, "What about your doctor's certificate?"

"To hell with that." Aaron beat the glowing metal with renewed vigor, beat it, then plunged it into the water, tossing it into the crate. When he went to the forge again, he saw that the rich glow of the coals was waning. "Can't you do anything right, Annabelle? You're letting the coals cool off."

"Well, you can bellow your own coals, Dr. Aylesbury. Or why don't you have Penelope Cranston come back and pump the bellows for you?"

Aaron shut his eyes and between clenched teeth swore again.

Annabelle watched him pick up the bellows.

"You'll be going away again," she said, and when he pumped it to fan the fire she added, "And my own father will be the cause of my losing you again."

Aaron straightened and eyed her angrily. "Annabelle, you can't lose something you never had."

He was surprised at the hurt he saw in her face at that moment. It was as if he had crushed something she loved under the heel of his boot. He had not known the depth of her feelings for him until now. Well, better she understood how he felt now rather than later. "Sorry," he muttered as he took the tongs in his hand. "I have to get these done now."

He barely noticed when she turned and ran away, barely glanced when she mounted her horse and rode furiously from the landing in a cloud of black dust.

His thoughts were on only one thing. To finish making the five hundred pins before dark.

Chapter IV

Fitzhugh had him doing a dozen menial tasks at once, but Mark figured that the quicker he proved efficient at doing the mundane, the quicker he could proceed to the more important. But he was piqued because he'd been doing these bloody clerk's tasks now for five days, filing deeds of trust, property claims, and land grants, copying in triplicate every bloody abstract that had come into the office, and balancing ledgers—all clerk's tasks, not the important legal work of a solicitor, even one fresh from college.

And what a dismal hole of an office this was. Mark looked around him. The eighteen-by-eighteen-foot room was plastered inside and painted pee-yellow, smelled like it looked, too, because it was located in a wing in Sydney Hospital—the rum hospital built by convict labor with the funds of three wealthy men in exchange for a monopoly in the rum trade. The room was bare, except for the fireplace, two clerks' desks, two high stools, one chair, and a coat rack that leaned toward the door because part of its base was cracked. The shelves lining one side of the room that held the dusty law books, records, and ledgers smelled like a

chicken house. Fitzhugh had one of the most respected and profitable solicitor's trades in the colony, but he didn't believe in extravagance. Maybe that was why he was considered the best, or next to the best, in the colony.

On Saturday night Mark would be going home to spend Sunday with his family, and what would he have to tell his father that he had done the first week as Fitzhugh's assistant? That he had filed papers and copied legal instruments? Made tea for John Fitzhugh and himself? Swept the floor each morning and each evening and replaced the fly paper daily? Bah.

He was impatient. He was having to stifle his overwhelming desire to make money, to make a name for himself, to show the colonists here and the Limeys in England that an Australian-born man *could* make a name for himself, that he could rise above his birth and the stigma of being a currency lad. And to make his father proud of him.

Only during the past five days, since Mark had been back from England, had it become clear to him that he had for years been formulating a plan in his mind of rising above the social strata to which he'd been born. He would make the Aylesburys as prominent in the colony as the Macarthurs, the Marsdens, the Campbells, the Cranstons. The Cranstons.

Mark's gaze lifted from the copy and drifted to the nearby window and out, to the west and north, and in his mind and to a high ridge and a pretty girl with the wind blowing her flimsy dress against her trim body. And if one caught the light just right, one could see her ankles through it. He shook his head. But those were the thoughts of a larrikin, not a gentleman— even a gentleman who loved her, desired her, and had desired her since the first day he had seen her. The day

71

Governor Macquarie had arrived in Sydney in his carriage from the pier in all his pomp and glory.

"Hello," Mark had said to the pretty young thing Aaron had been talking to in the crowd that day.

A puffed sleeve had come up to hide her chin. "I don't know you."

"I'm staying with Dr. Aylesbury. My name's Mark. Mark Troop."

She had looked at him from under lowered lids. "What is that to me?"

"Nothing, I guess. Yet."

Mark Troop. What is that to me?

It will be something to you, Penelope. It will be something to everybody in this country soon, as soon as I can—

Someone rattled the knob on the door of the office and Mark jerked his head back around and bent over his desk quickly. Wouldn't do for Fitzhugh to catch him stargazing.

Whoever it was came in and shut the door behind him. Mark took his time looking up, as if he couldn't tear his attention away from the copying he was doing. But he needn't have pretended. It was Aaron.

"Aaron!" He jumped up. "My God. What are you doing in Sydney?"

Aaron moved with that easy grace Mark so envied, coming toward him, offering his hand. "Begging money," he said. "How is it going with you?"

Mark seized his hand. "Well, Fitzhugh already has me—uh—lets me do the ledgers for the firm, and I have drawn up a few legal instruments. Sit down. Care for a cup of tea?"

Grinning, Aaron held his hand under his chin. "I'm up to here in tea, coffee, sarsaparilla, and Madeira."

Mark laughed as they sat down, Mark on the high

clerk's stool at the desk, Aaron in the Morris chair near the window. "Father still angry at you? Or should I ask?"

Aaron's smile waned. "He hardly speaks to me at breakfast before he leaves for Parramatta. Is grumpy at dinner, but I try to stay away from him."

Mark grunted. "Still working for Uncle Owen?" Uncle Owen wasn't Mark's uncle at all; he was a Crawford. The thought depressed him briefly.

Aaron held up his hands, which were red and calloused with burned places on them. "I made five hundred pins the first day and a half. Then he had me doing iron braces."

Mark laughed. "Why are you up to your chin in tea, coffee, sarsaparilla, and Madeira? Has it something to do with looking for money?"

"It has everything to do with it."

As Mark listened, noticing that Aaron's skin had tanned deeply, that his hair had bleached out in streaks from the sun, that his movements were stiff from sore muscles, Aaron told him about Glenn Moffett's plans to approach the new governor, Brisbane, about funding an expedition to explore the country around Bathurst, the only frontier settlement beyond the Blue Mountains. There was a great rumbling in the colony for more land, and since Wentworth, Blaxland, and Lawson had beat Aaron to finding a way across the mountains, and Macquarie had declared the Bathurst district a town, stockmen were wanting to drive their stock over the mountains to the plains there. Already there were a few farms and cattle stations in the district, including the government's own cattle station. And now the English government was beginning to encourage Englishmen with capital to migrate to the colony. Graziers and farmers were becoming restless and

eager to seek better lands beyond the mountains. Soon even the Bathurst district would be filled up. Then what? Where were other plains suitable for pasture? Did they have adequate water year round? Where did those western flowing rivers lead, those that flowed away from the coast inland? Was there an inland sea?

Glenn and Aaron had approached Sir Thomas Brisbane first. Brisbane was residing at Government House in Parramatta, while Macquarie, who had handed over the running of the colony to him in December, remained at Government House in Sydney getting his affairs in order, selling his furniture, packing his belongings in preparation to leave the colony forever to return home to England. They had spoken to Brisbane yesterday.

"I cannot at this time offer government support for your expedition," Brisbane had concluded.

"In truth," Aaron said, shifting his weight in the chair as he related it all to Mark, "I don't think he believes Glenn, Buck, Jack, and I can handle such an expedition."

"Why?"

Aaron spread his arms wide. "We're Australians, not Englishmen."

"The hell, you say," Mark breathed.

"So he refused to lend government support to it."

Aaron went on to tell how they had approached Macquarie then, earlier that very day. The man was tired, sick, drawn, depressed. "Macquarie said he had no influence in the colony anymore. Said Father did, though. You know how Macquarie loves Father."

"Yes."

"And, of course, Father won't lend us support or influence anyone else to, because he has no interest in land other than his own. Besides, *I* would be part of

the expedition."

Mark studied Aaron, swallowed some gorge, and said, "Father sets great store by you, though, Aaron."

Aaron's expression darkened and he replied, "Yes, but only in what he wants me to do, to be." Aaron smiled quickly. "Well, I won't keep you any longer." He rose and hooked his thumbs in his coat. "Just wanted to see my brother in his first law office."

Mark stood, saying, "I'd lend you the money, my part of the trust fund . . . if it weren't all tied up at the moment. You know I would."

Aaron shook his head. "I wouldn't ask that. You need that money. Bought a house yet?"

Mark shook his head. "I'm staying at the inn, but I'll find a house soon and furnish it."

"Macquarie is holding an auction for some of his furniture, mate. You should look into it."

"I will. But what are you going to do now, Aaron? Scrap the expedition plans?"

Aaron's brown eyes glinted as he pondered telling Mark what his last resort was. Finally, he decided to tell him. "Macquarie made another suggestion. He said that Oliver Cranston has been hounding governors for years to fund expeditions to open up new grazing land for cattle. We won't approach him, though; we want him to come to us. We want the gossip to get around that we are preparing for an expedition, but need money for it. Glenn thinks Cranston will help fund it and influence maybe Macarthur or Marsden and a few others to help."

"Why don't you just ask Cranston for help?"

"Because he and Father . . ." Aaron made his hand waver in the air.

Mark nodded. "Well, I wish you good fortune in obtaining the funds."

Aaron smiled. "Thank you. Coming home for Sunday?"

Mark nodded.

"See you then, mate. Maybe we can play some cricket."

"I'll look forward to it." Mark closed the door behind his brother and smiled at Aaron's sense of honor. He needed money, knew Cranston would give it, but wouldn't ask for it because Cranston was his father's old foe. Cranston had had his father arrested in England. Cranston and his father had even dueled once, wounding each other. The men avoided each other, envied each other, tried to outdo each other. But neither hated the other. If it wasn't hate, then what was it?

Sauntering back to his desk, Mark pondered the fact that Aaron could have punished his father for shouting at him and refusing to release his trust fund by going to Cranston for help, but he had not. How he could have hurt his father, had he wanted to. His father, who approved of Mark and didn't approve of Aaron . . .

Mark picked up his pen, examined it. It was a wooden pen fixed with a delicate silver point, given to him by his father. A beautiful pen, and costly. Mark liked it very much.

But there was that other pen, that "fountain" pen, the pen the sea captain had given his father years ago on the convict ship when he was sailing from England to New South Wales. The pen that was so dear to his father's heart. His father had given that one to Aaron.

"Mercy sakes an' the saints preserve us if it ain't the spirit of me own 'osband, God rest 'is soul!"

76

Penelope plucked the strings of her beloved instrument, the harp, unhappy with the sounds it made. Why couldn't her chords sound like the masters on this piece?

"Ee-ee-ee! Look at it!"

Penelope looked up at the maid who was standing in the middle of the ballroom with her hands on either side of her face, watching a spot of light dancing around on the far wall. Penelope's mouth came open, then she jumped up. "Oh, Abigail! It's only the reflection off some piece of metal, or off a pond of water," she said, racing to the window that faced north.

"Not dancin' the way it is, it ain't, it ain't. 'Tis like some restless soul's sendin' us 'is message from beyond," Abigail said, backing against the far wall, watching the light dancing across the ceiling.

Red-faced, Penelope jerked the draperies shut over the window. "I tell you, it's just a reflection," she said, but she thought: It's some restless soul sending a message, right enough, from beyond the ridge. "I just remembered something I have to do," she said to the maid. It was a weak excuse to leave the room, but the maid was still so shaken she wasn't listening anyway.

Penelope rushed out of the ballroom—her mother still called it a reception hall—and once out of sight she ran up the stairs to the second-floor landing, flew into her room, grabbed her hand mirror off the dressing table, and ran to the north window. *Flash!* Aaron's mirror caught the sunlight and reflected it back expertly into her window. Bottom lip between her teeth, Penelope flashed her reply, the signal that she had seen his and would go to the ridge as soon as possible. Then she ran to her armoire, flung open its door, and found her riding habit, a two-piece affair, and threw it onto the bed.

77

In ten minutes she was out of her morning dress and into the skirt, a plain brown muslin, and the cream-colored silk shirt. Quickly, she pulled on her boots and rushed out of the room. Her mother was taking her nap, her father and brother, James, were in the west cow pastures. Now if she could just get past Greta—bah, she would tell Greta to mind her own business. She was a grown woman now and need not fear the old maid's tattling on her to her mother.

Penelope need not have worried, for Greta was nowhere in sight as she hurried down the stairway, through the central hall, and out into the dooryard. The little groom, Cricket, who had been in her father's employ even as a convict laborer before his pardon, cheerfully saddled Bayleaf for her, winking his rheumy eye conspiratorially, and soon she was riding north up the well-worn path to the ridge. Even in her delight and impatience, Penelope noticed again how worn the path was on this side of the ridge, while she remembered that the path was faint on the other side, on the Aylesbury side. She knew why, too. Her father, and sometimes even her mother, often rode to the top of the ridge to spy on the Aylesburys. But the Aylesburys couldn't spy on the Cranstons even if they wanted to. Her father had planted trees on his side so that the Aylesburys couldn't see anything. But Penelope knew they wouldn't, anyway. She had noticed for years how when the two families attended the same functions, which was rare, or happened to be in town at the same time, which was often, the Cranstons always looked at the Aylesburys, but the Aylesburys only looked at each other.

The breezes were warm today, the grass jade-green and whispering, the sky bleached white by the

morning sun. The Blue Mountains in the west were violet and the young eucalyptus forest, which she now approached, was a treasure trove of sapphire, emerald, and ruby-colored birds flashing amongst the branches. New South Wales birds did not sing as European birds did; they squawked and chirped instead, but their plumage was breathtaking and there was nothing that made the spirit soar like watching a flight of pink-breasted galah against the blue sky.

The flowers in the pastures and on the hillsides were riotous with color, seas of azure, rose, and gold, but they had no fragrance. Butterflies with painted parchment wings flitted everywhere. Penelope absorbed it all as she plunged into the forest and urged Bayleaf forward.

When she burst out of the forest at a gallop exactly on the Cranston-Aylesbury property line, there Aaron stood, hands on his hips, watching for her.

Laughing, she jumped off the horse and was in his arms, breathless. She had not seen him since the day at Owen's landing. "Oh, Aaron. I thought you had forgotten me."

"I was working, and then I went to Parramatta and Sydney on business." He released her and reached into his pocket and brought out a small parcel. "I didn't have much money, but I passed a bakery and had to buy these."

She clasped her hands and watched him untie the string around the parcel, marveling that as children they had never embraced, never touched, but now, now it was so natural that neither had to think about it. To a stranger with a head for propriety, their behavior might have seemed outrageous. A gentleman did not embrace a lady unless he had paid court to her formally and acquired her parents' permis-

sion. And certainly a lady would never behave as she did, embracing a gentleman in such a manner. Oh, but this was Aaron, and they had known each other for years and years.

He handed her the pastry and their gazes met, held like butterflies in midair, then flitted away.

Suddenly shy, she took the tart he offered and he took the other. "Strawberry," he said.

Laughing, they went to their rock and sat down. Strawberry jelly got mixed up somehow with his quips about her matching cheeks, the flaky pastry became confused with his brown eyes laughing at her, and the sweet taste merged with the sweetness of the moment, and then he had stopped eating and had caught her hands in his and his laughing eyes roved over her face. He kissed her fingers where the callouses were from playing the harp, and murmured, "Penelope. Penelope, I dreamed of you last night."

Her heart ceased beating and she was somehow suspended above the earth, hovering, looking down upon them both.

"I have no right to call you mine, but I can't bear to think of you in the arms of another," he said.

"And neither shall I be," she whispered.

When his mouth touched the palm of her hand, and then his tongue licked the sticky strawberry filling from her fingers, a great, hot cramp gripped her lower abdomen and left her short of breath, paralyzed her until all she had strength to do was watch. Then he raised his head, and she felt his eyes were dissolving her, and then he bent his head and his mouth found hers. Penelope thought she was dying.

Suddenly he was setting her from him. He stood up, turning his back to her. "I have no right to do

that," he said hoarsely. "But you see, Penelope, I . . . care for you very much." He turned back to her and she saw the wars going on behind his eyes.

"And I love you, Aaron. I always have," she said.

He looked at her soberly for a moment and said, "Then I will speak to your father."

Penelope's eyes misted. "Yes, Aaron. When?"

He shook his head. "I don't know."

"I do. When you get your medical practice set up, that's when."

He winced visibly. "Ah," he said despairingly.

Penelope's smile faltered as he looked at her, his face showing a turmoil of emotions as his eyes came to rest on her face. "That . . . won't . . . be for some time yet, Penelope."

Then she remembered. "You want to do some exploring first, don't you."

He nodded. "Aye."

"It was a boyhood dream and I thought—"

"That I had outgrown it?" He smiled. "I haven't." He came to her and took her arms. "I believe that it's vital for us to find new lands. To expand this colony is every bit as important as my working in a hospital in Sydney or Parramatta, treating convicts."

"There are not three doctors in the entire colony for the rest of us—"

"Even as important as setting up private practice in a small town to treat the rest of the colonists." He released her and turned to look out over the Aylesbury and Crawford farms, propping his foot on the rock. "The colonists are running out of pasture. Besides, I have to do this. I must."

"My father would agree with you. He wants to raise cattle." Penelope frowned and wanted to go to him, to make the seriousness of his tone go away, but he was a man now and she a woman and she must

81

behave like a woman. "Other men say the future of New South Wales is in sheep, in the wool industry, but Father hates sheep and only keeps a mob of them for food."

"I agree with your father. I hate sheep, too."

"And I despise cattle."

He turned and looked at her amused. "Why?"

"Why do *you* hate sheep?" she asked.

"For one thing they're stupid and a nuisance."

"And cattle are unmanageable beasts."

"Nevertheless. We need new lands opened up, and nobody seems to be doing any exploring. No one's gone beyond the Bathurst district since it was opened up for settlers."

Penelope was fighting tears, but she was telling herself that she had known, had known for a long time what Aaron wanted to do, since the first day she had seen him, when they both were six years old and their parents had gone into Sydney to Campbell's warehouse store.

. . . But do you know what you're going to do when you're grown up as tall as your father?

Yes.

What?

You wouldn't understand.

But I would. I'm very good at understanding.

I'm . . . I'm going to be an explorer . . . I'm going to find a way over the Blue Mountains.

Oh Aaron. I'll keep your secret forever.

And she had kept his secret. But all along she had dreamed of his returning, establishing his medical practice, of building a little house, of their marrying. But she smiled now, for above all else, Aaron must be happy. "Then you must do it, and it won't take a lifetime, anyway, will it?"

He smiled again. "No. If it took a lifetime I

wouldn't have just spent four years learning a profession."

The sun came out again in Penelope's soul, and hers was a sunny one anyway. "Then we won't talk any more about . . . other things. You will go soon?"

"Hopefully."

"In the meantime, we shall have adventures as we used to." She tossed her head and enjoyed the feel of his smiling eyes upon her as she went to the rock again and sat down. "I've not found any more wombat holes lately." She turned her head and looked at him.

He smiled, observing her exquisite beauty. Her flawless skin was lightly tanned, but his imagination suggested that underneath her dress that skin was the color of alabaster. Her dark hair, her green eyes made his heart stop beating, and all he could think about when he looked at her was kissing her sweet, pink mouth. "That's terrible—not to find any wombat holes. Perhaps we should look for gold in the creek again," he teased.

They stared at each other and both read the other's thoughts. Childhood was gone. They were adults now. Wombat holes and pretend gold was no longer any fun, nor hunting wallabies or kangaroo rats, nor making huts out of wattle branches. Nor anything else they used to do. They smiled at each other, knowing the other's thoughts, and laughed.

"I know," Penelope said, springing to her feet. "While you were away, I was riding back on the far side of our property where the bush hasn't been cleared and I came across a little cottage, all dusty and boarded up. Isn't that a mystery? But even more mysterious was this awful-looking greenish . . . thing, this metal thing that stood off in the bush a little ways from the cottage. I couldn't make out what

it was."

Aaron's smile grew as he became entranced with the movement of her ethereal body. "What sort of thing?"

"It was as big as a horse, with all these pipes and things sticking out of it, and the pea vines had grown all over it, and horrid creatures skittered out of it when I went near."

"It sounds like a still."

Penelope's hands went to the side of her face. Stills were illegal. Absolutely illegal.

"Is it on your father's land?"

She looked at him round-eyed and nodded.

Grimly Aaron said, "Let's go see. Come on, we'll have an adventure."

Aaron had walked to the ridge and had no horse, so they mounted Bayleaf together and rode through the back path onto a narrow trail skirting Cranston land. Aaron was riding in front and Penelope behind him, clasping her arms around his chest, resting her cheek on his hard back, smiling, enjoying the smell of him, the hardness of his body. A delicious kind of pleasure flowed over her like syrup as they rode through tangled brush and forest, amongst fat, high trees, until at last they came to a small clearing. There in the middle of the clearing stood the small cottage she had found. It was made of brick and had two multipaned windows blinded with decades of dust and cobwebs. It seemed abandoned, but had been kept in good repair.

"The still's through that scrub," she said softly.

Aaron was off Bayleaf in a flash. He helped her down and could not help but hold her close for a moment as he looked about.

"It's as if spirits were about," Penelope said, looking at the cottage out of the corner of her eye.

"Nay, I've been in places in England that were very, very old where I could swear spirits hovered. Whatever beings were in this place were very much alive."

"Still, I feel strange."

"Where's the still?"

She pointed.

Aaron placed her behind him and crouched a little as he began to make his way through the underbrush. Vines clung to the smooth trunks of the gum trees that he had to sweep aside while bees in the scarlet pea blossoms threatened him, buzzing angrily, then giving up the vines for others farther in the forest. "I don't see a still," he said, turning back to her.

"It's a little farther, I think. On the side of a slight rise in the—"

An animal scurried through the brush beside them and Penelope's hands clasped his arm. "What was that?"

"Kangaroo rat, probably." Aaron stepped over small wattle bushes and held a branch draped with vines as she paused. "One thing puzzles me. What were you doing off in here when you discovered the still?"

Penelope didn't answer and when Aaron looked around at her again she was blushing.

"You shouldn't ask," she said demurely.

"Oh." He bit his lip and turned back around. Almost immediately they stepped into a small clearing.

"There!"

All that showed of the old still was a dome, green and brown with age, and the rest covered in vines. While Penelope stood at the edge of the clearing, Aaron stepped toward the still and began to pull the vines away from it.

By the time he had cleared the bushes away from the still, Penelope had advanced to his side. With her hands on her hips, she looked the still up and down and said, "I don't understand why that's here."

Aaron opened a little door and gasped, stepping back. With a screech and flutter of wings something rushed past their heads. Penelope screamed and in the next minute was in his arms with him laughing at her. "It's just bats," he said.

But they had become aware of each other's bodies, and both blushed, releasing each other. Aaron drew in a slow, deep breath. "You asked why the still is here. Probably your father brought it here during Governor Bligh's administration."

"Why?"

"Bligh tried, more than any of the previous governors, to stop rum trade in the colony, but that's how people paid their convict servants. So many landholders and merchants were sly grogging." Aaron examined a strange protrusion on the side of the old still. "He probably distilled the grog from wheat mash."

"Father knows nothing about making grog."

"Either he did or one of his laborers did." Aaron pulled a pipe off the still, looked at it, tossed it onto the ground.

"I don't like it here, Aaron. Let's go back."

He was wading into the brush around the still and did not reply.

"There could be snakes," she said, then wished she hadn't. For Aaron's little sister, Jessica, had been bitten by a snake and had died.

"There's something in this hill behind the still," he said.

"I hope it's not a grave."

"Rotting timber is exposed where the dirt has

washed away from it," he said, and all she could see of him was his behind as he bent and pulled at the old timber. "Aagh! Termites. Spiders."

"Oh, Aaron, come away. This place feels haunted."

He made a grunting sound. "There's spirits here, all right."

While Penelope hugged herself, Aaron backed out of the tangle of brush carrying two pottery jugs, grinning. "They're full, too," he said shaking the jugs. "If it's been here since Bligh's time, this stuff is over fourteen years old."

Penelope's chin came up. "I'm certain Father doesn't know about this. He would never do anything illegal."

Aaron tossed one of the jugs into the grass beside the still. "I think he would sell grog." He twisted at the cork in the top and it came out with a loud pop. He raised the mouth of the jug to his nose, sniffed, threw back his head. "My God!" Then, blushing, he said, "I'm sorry, Penelope. I didn't mean to swear."

"It all goes together. Swearing, sly grogging, and drinking spirits," she said primly, because that's what she thought a proper lady should say. "And you shouldn't taste it. You and your family are Weslyans, and they don't believe in drinking spirits."

Aaron turned the jug up and tasted the grog and made a wry face. "Whew. Powerful! More powerful than rum!"

"And how would you know?" she said, smoothing her skirt.

"While I was in college I drank wine, port, beer, and rum." He took a swallow, gasped, and frowned. "This tastes like what the Scotsmen make."

"Not like wine? Wine's all I ever tasted."

"In a way it's worse. In a way it's better."

"If you don't stop, you'll get drunk," she warned, noticing a slow flush creep into his face. His eyes were bright as he went over to a clear spot of ground where the grass was short and sparse.

"It would take more than a couple of swallows, love." He said. "Come. Sit. We'll go shortly, but I want to try to understand the meaning of the little cottage and the still."

"Always the adventurer, aren't you? Well, I think we should go. I don't like this place."

"Sit for a while."

Penelope went to him and sat beside him, but glanced about at the shadows in the forest. "I think that whoever ran the still lived in the cottage and died and he's creeping about in the forest looking at us."

"I don't."

"Why?"

"If that cottage was built for a sly grogger it could have been built of wattle and daub, or from bark, or even slabs of wood. Instead, somebody went to a lot of trouble to haul brick here." He shook his head. "A man doesn't build a cottage like that for himself. He does it for a woman."

Now Penelope's eyes widened. "But Father knows his own property. And Mum would never live in such a place." She studied Aaron's face. "Then who?"

He shrugged, but he looked funny, too.

Penelope picked two of the flowers close by and studied them, remembering the softness in her father's eyes when he looked at Aaron's mother. Could it be that they—she looked up at Aaron, saw that his eyes were on her, studying her. She felt that something was going to happen, and she said, "Why don't you throw that jug away. It smells."

"It doesn't taste as bad as it smells," he said. "But if

88

it annoys you—"

She held out her hand. "I want to see if it's worse than wine before we go. And we must go. There may be snakes—"

Aaron held the jug out of her reach. "No. This isn't a lady's brew."

Something was keeping her here. Perhaps it was the heady feeling of being alone with him, so close to him, his lithe body, his handsome face. The mischief in his eyes caused her to feel carefree, and she was a child again. "Please, only a taste?"

"Absolutely not," he said. "I won't be responsible for causing you to become intoxicated. And if all you've drunk is wine, you might, with just a swallow."

His eyes were looking deeply into hers, and she knew she was having some terrible effect on him. She felt shy and bold at once; she wanted him to kiss her, yet she was afraid for him to, and rich, delicious sensations were coursing through her body as his eyes caressed her face and her neck. "You had two swallows," she said softly. "Are you intoxicated?"

Aaron didn't reply for a long moment. His smile had vanished, his eyes had gone soft and deep, the pupils had dilated, and he did not breathe or take his eyes from hers. "Yes, but not from the brew."

Penelope blinked. He had let down his guard, so she snatched the jug from him. Aaron cried, "Hey!" as she sprang to her feet laughing, and he was after her in a second. Away she ran toward the still. The clearing was small, probably about twenty feet across, and she ran shrieking as he sprinted after her grabbing at the jug. Screaming with laughter, she held it away from him, and when he caught her arm, she jerked free and ran away.

Laughing, he caught her again, but she spun out

of his grasp, only to stumble and fall to the ground. In a tumble of pretty skirts and spilled brew, giggles and laughter, he held her down and reached for the jug, wrenched it from her hand, and while she gasped with laughter, flung it into the grass.

He straddled her, held her arms at her sides. "There, impudent lass," he said. "There'll be no drinking from it again. You bewitched me into relaxing my hold on it, but you won't bewitch me into releasing you until I'm ready."

It was an excuse to wrestle and both knew it and both pretended it wasn't, but he was becoming aware of her body again and she was beneath him laughing, her lips red, her eyes very, very green, and her hair had come loose in the tussle.

"Did I, Aaron?" she asked softly, her eyes searching his. "Did I truly bewitch you?"

He swallowed. Her throat looked suddenly warm, and he became aware that her breasts were thrusting up against the material of her shirt. Her hips stirred beneath him, causing fire to shoot into his face. "You are bewitching me still," he said. Her eyes drew him, her lips drew his until he found them, soft and moist, and he was suddenly strangling with desire for her, to touch her body, to crush her beneath him.

Penelope's hands went to his face to be sure that he was real, that his lips were real and not one of her dreams. She wondered vaguely who was bewitched, for his lips moved upon hers, sending great and aching spasms through her body, which at once puzzled and delighted her. His ragged breath upon her face, the trembling of his hand as it moved slowly from her arm to her shoulder, caused her to catch her breath, to hold it.

She was slowly drowning in his kisses, in the feel of his body, as he lowered himself to her side. Penelope

wanted more. She had no idea how people made love, she only knew she wanted more of his mouth, and so she opened her lips and felt his tongue touch hers. With the shock of it, she groaned in an agony of delight and her hand went to his arms. His hand crept slowly to her neck and halted. She waited, wanting him to touch her breast, and when he did not, she slid her hands down his arms, grasped one hand and placed it on her breast herself.

He moaned softly and cupped her breast, caressed it tentatively as his breathing became erratic and quick.

Finally, he lifted his lips from hers and without opening his eyes said, "We'd better go."

"Soon," she whispered and pulled at the collar of her shirt, baring her neck for his lips. He kissed her there, kissed her ear, the hollow of her throat.

"Come. We'd better go, my Penelope. I can't—"

She waited, her breasts heaving with want. "Can't what?"

"Stop."

"Then . . . don't."

His lips came down again, ravaged her mouth, and sensation followed sensation, each better than the one before it as his tongue searched her mouth. Still she wanted more, and she unbuttoned her shirt and pulled down her chemise as his eager hand followed to caress her breasts, none too gently, and his lips left a trail of fire from her lips to her nipple. She cried out with waves of ecstasy as he suckled each breast, groaning with pleasure and hurried desire. And then a rush of frenzied want came over them and her skirt was gone, her pantaloons, gone, and he was beside her naked, shivering, grasping and tasting her body, his hand caressing her breast, her belly, and her thighs.

She could not breathe. Even the air was hot. Her nails raked his arm when his hand cupped her between her thighs, and she gasped, but she was on fire there, swelling and damp, and she glimpsed his erection and wanted it, wanted it there. "Please," she cried. "Please."

His breath was ragged in her ear as his hand massaged her, waiting, waiting.

"I said please," she hissed angrily, dipping her nails into his hips.

She thought she heard him whisper, "Dear God," before he parted her thighs with his knees. She felt him pause, enter her, wait, then push gently and steadily into her.

There was pain, brief and sharp, but it was so exquisite and surrounded by so much pulsating want that pain did not matter. She opened her eyes briefly to see the face of her beloved, flushed, perspiring. He was gritting his teeth, his eyes shut tight, and the vertical vein in the middle of his forehead was standing out. Great waves of love for him flooded her and mixed with her passion and then he began to move in her, to move slowly, then faster, and Penelope gasped because she couldn't believe the delight.

Suddenly a great wave welled up in her, a great ecstasy that rose and swelled until she cried out with its exquisite pain.

He groaned, then stiffened.

Her mouth opened wide and she felt him throbbing inside her, deep, hot pulsations that matched her own, until she thought she would die. And then, slowly, the surges lessened, ebbed slowly, and he lowered his damp body onto hers and she held him to her, held him so tightly neither could breathe.

"I love you, love you, love you," she said into

his ear.

He shuddered on her body.

She held him on top of her for a long time, and when he finally rolled off of her she smiled, for he looked as he had that day when she saw him at Owen's Landing. Red-faced, gleaming with sweat, hair tousled, exhausted. And so handsome. His broad chest was covered with dark hair. His trim waist was almost as small as hers. She placed a hand on his hip and smiled up at him, wondering about what they had experienced together. She had never dreamed of anything so wonderful. And he was looking at her with a half-bewildered, half-apologetic expression on his face. She ran her fingers over his lips and said, "You look like you did that day at Owen's Landing."

He observed her a moment unblinking. "I *feel* like I did that day at Owen's Landing," he croaked. When she giggled, he said, "You are a little witch," and smiled gently. "A sweet little witch. I did not intend to go so far. I—"

"Hush. It was my fault."

"But I overpowered you."

"And I permitted you to. Don't you see, I've wanted you for so long?"

He shut his eyes tight. "And I've wanted you."

"You see? It felt right, didn't it?"

"Agonizingly so," he admitted soberly.

When she giggled again, he grinned and bent down to still her laughter again with his kiss.

Chapter V

He could hear her horse coming up the path through the forest, the horse's hooves striking the stones, stepping softly, and Aaron frowned. Usually she was more anxious to greet him when he signaled and would race up the ridge. Could it be, he wondered, that since yesterday she was hesitant? After having pondered what they had done beside the still? It was early morning yet. The deed was, after all, only twenty hours old.

Aaron passed his hand over his face, mentally chastising himself again for what he had done. His father was right, he was irresponsible. Well, he would get on his knees, beg her forgiveness, beg her forgiveness and tell her he had changed his mind about the expedition. He would go to his father and tell him he was not going to . . . to go on the expedition, that it was just a boyhood dream anyway, and that he was ready to take a position at one of the hospitals. Then he would break it to his parents that he intended to marry Penelope Cranston. Yes, Penelope, it's the only honorable thing to do. Besides, one didn't just decide to go on an expedition and go.

Successful explorers were given land grants for their efforts by the government, and each of them stood to gain from it. But the big picture was, the entire colony would benefit. Only a tiny bit of this continent, which Macquarie disdained to call "New Holland," in favor of "Australia," was explored. Flinders had circumnavigated it the year Aaron and Mark were born, and had discovered that it was large, indeed a continent, an island continent, isolated and unconnected to the rest of the world. Which explained its strangeness to the botanists.

But he, Aaron, had made a mistake and was willing to face it. He must forfeit his right, for the time being, to go on this expedition.

But would she accept him? Would she be angry? Blame him? No, she did not blame him yesterday. *No, Aaron, I knew what we were doing. I wanted you to make love to me. It had to happen because we waited so long.*

She had smoothed his frown with her fingers. *I was a child until it happened. I am truly a woman now. I feel it. I've changed. I must behave like a woman. And I'm glad. So wonderfully glad.*

Aaron looked up at the sky over the Aylesbury and Crawford farms. He loved her. Loved her probably more than his own life. He would ask her, today, to marry him.

The horse snorted behind him and he turned eagerly, smiling, toward it. But his smile faded when he saw that it was not Penelope on the horse.

Oliver Cranston reined the bay and smiled grimly as he sat looking at the young man before him. He was tall and lean, a cornstalk youth like most of the first-generation Australian-born. He was tanned, and there was a certain arrogant tilt to his chin and a slight defiant stance following his first shock and

disappointment. And he was handsome, with Milicent's uncalculated grace and gentle pride. The young man resembled her in coloring and in his eyes, his hair. Oliver had seen the resemblance before when the boy was young. It was even more pronounced in the man. He could have been Oliver's son, if his plans had worked out. This handsome, bold, intelligent youth.

"Penelope won't be coming today," Oliver said, and admired the quick animal alertness that sprang into the young man's eye. He dismounted with deliberate casualness, as if he met this young man on the ridge every day—as Penelope had probably been doing since Aaron had returned from England.

Oliver was dressed in the typical gentleman's town garb, white duck trousers, blue jacket and broad-brimmed hat woven from the fronds of the native cabbage tree. In a few more weeks, Oliver would exchange the blue coat for a white one when he went into town. Normally, however, he would not be wearing the town garb at home, but he had taken Elaina and Penelope into Parramatta early and had ridden back in a hurry after hearing gossip that Glenn Moffett, Jack Summers, and Aaron Aylesbury were talking of an expedition and that Governor Brisbane had refused to give them government support. Having returned home, Oliver had been climbing the stairs of the house with the intention of changing into his fustian brown waistcoat and trousers, when he had seen the reflection dancing around in Penelope's room. One quick glance out her window had revealed the source. It was coming from the edge of the forest on the ridge. And Cranston had known instantly who the signal was meant for and who was sending it. Hmm. Ingenious.

Now he propped his booted foot on a large rock

near where he had reined his horse and regarded Aaron with a sardonic smile. "I escorted Penelope and her mother and James to Parramatta very early this morning. The new toll road makes traveling easier and quicker. But still there are bushrangers and escaped convicts and I dare not let them go alone, even with the driver armed."

Aaron's dark eyes regarded him steadily—as Milicent's would have—and he had not moved. But a slight frown had formed between his eyebrows.

"A pity that Governor Macquarie did not find the colony more to his liking during the last three or four years and stay. Who knows what miracles his wonders to perform? He might—ah no, he *would* have funded your expedition, Aaron. For he respected your father so."

Aaron kept regarding him steadily and did not reply.

"But never fear. You have a new prospective benefactor for your expedition."

One side of Aaron's mouth twitched into a smile. "You?"

"Discerning of you, lad. I've the funds and I'm willing to fund your party."

"In return for—"

"My choice of any newly explored lands that the governor might see fit to have surveyed and deeded to me."

When Aaron did not reply, Oliver turned his head to regard the farm below. With a sweep of his hand he said, "Farmers can spread out along the river; enough land here for a century of farming. But a grazier needs pasture." He looked at Aaron. "I want to start a cattle station in the new district."

"I had heard."

Oliver nodded. "It's common knowledge. I would

97

like to meet with the rest of your party as soon as possible."

"That can be arranged."

"Tonight?" Oliver noticed the joy leap into Aaron's eyes. "Penelope and her mother and brother will be in Parramatta tonight and will go with the Braxton family to Sydney for a fortnight." Oliver smiled. "That will allow us an entire evening and fortnight if necessary, to plan the expedition without interference from the women. They worry so about such things as meals, tea, and cakes whenever I have guests. I would think one evening and one day of uninterrupted planning would do it. And I'll be free to assist in any purchases you think necessary."

Aaron's face was carefully expressionless now. "I will contact Glenn Moffett and see if we can all get together tonight. If so, I'll send word to you."

Oliver smiled. "Good." He removed his boot from the rock and straightened his spine. "I'm sure we can work together splendidly."

"I had planned to speak with you. . . ."

"About my daughter?"

"Yes."

"You should know, Aaron, after spending four years in England, how important class differences are."

"This isn't England."

"It's an extension of England."

"You're wrong, sir. Australasia will never be another England, and you and my father and your generation would fare better if you realized that."

Oliver's black eyes snapped. "Don't tell me about my generation. There are class differences in every culture under the sun. And *you* would fare better if you realized *that*."

"Nevertheless, I will speak to you about Penelope—"

"Not now. The expedition comes first."

"But I think I should—"

"It can wait, Aaron," Oliver said slowly, sternly. "There is no immediate concern about it. Is there?"

Cranston's eyes were so forbidding, so threatening, that Aaron was jolted into realizing that his eagerness to make amends to Penelope had been silly. Adults treated such serious considerations with careful thought and planning. Knowing Penelope as he did, he was sure she would not want to rush about and do anything without a great deal of deliberation. Aaron dropped his gaze from Oliver's. "There is no immediate concern," he said.

"Good." Oliver strode to his horse, which had been nibbling Aylesbury grass at the edge of Cranston forest, and mounted it. He looked down, this stern, handsome man who was Matthew Aylesbury's enemy, at the son of Matthew and the woman he himself loved. Without another word, Oliver Cranston raised his hand in a brief gesture of farewell and reined his horse about to walk him into the trees.

He could have loved Milicent's son had he not been Aylesbury's son, too. Given his daughter to him willingly. But he was an Aylesbury, and that was more despicable even than his having been the grandson of a poor dirt farmer and the son of an ex-convict. And since he was all three, the situation was impossible.

Glenn Moffett was an ex-convict like Aaron's father and had married an ex-convict woman named Sally. The Moffetts had been emancipated and had

married two or three years before Aaron's maternal grandparents, the Crawfords, had settled on their land. Moffett was the Crawfords' and Aylesburys' neighbor, with holdings east of Uncle Tad's horse farm. The Moffetts' house was a typical Hawkesbury house of plaster and lathe, four rooms all on one floor, with windows reaching down to the floor to make the maximum use of any breeze, and with the shingle roof extended beyond all four walls to form a deep, shaded veranda all the way around. Glenn was a crusty farmer and was adept at hunting, as was Sally, his plump and cheerful wife. Aaron had always felt comfortable in their company.

The only thing Aaron didn't like about the Moffetts was that they had always thought he should marry their only child, Annabelle.

Aaron had been at Glenn's twice since he had returned from England, and both times Glenn had teased Aaron about marrying Annabelle. On Aaron's first visit, as he sat sprawled in the Moffetts' parlor, Glenn, grinning, had handed him a mug of port and, chuckling, said, "You marry Annabelle and Sally and me'll be jolly proud, Aaron. But you'd have to learn to drink with the missus and me."

That bit of conversation had disintegrated without comment. But while Glenn plied him with port, Mrs. Moffett had made him stay for dinner, urging great heaps of potatoes, vegetables from the garden, and great slabs of tender veal and sliced ham on him. Grinning, Glenn had poured the wine saying, "Annabelle cooks like this. Can you imagine a life like that, Aaron? Huh?" And he had laughed, and Mrs. Moffett had kept winking, as if to say, "He's just teasing; don't pay any attention to it." But not denying any of it, either. And Annabelle, helping her mother set the table and serve, had kept saying, "Oh,

Pa, leave him be."

"Take Sal and meself, why we were married when we were your age," Glenn had said after the meal. "Life's short, and a man's old before 'ee knows it, so 'ee ought to marry young. Now Annabelle is old for a single woman, so I suppose with there bein' ten men to every woman in the colony she'll accept one soon. She has beaus who've proposed. So you'd better snap 'er up while you can."

The second time Aaron went to the Moffetts' house he had been carrying a receipt from Uncle Owen to Glenn, and again the man had plied Aaron with stringy bark, port, and rum. "You marry Annabelle," he said, "and I'll give you one hundred acres. That acreage next to your Uncle Thaddeus, and a dowry of fifty pounds to get started on."

And now, on his third visit, Aaron was telling Glenn about Cranston's offer to fund the expedition. They were sitting on the veranda and Sally Moffett was trying to force cake and pudding on him, winking and smiling, but Aaron refused to go in lest he get drunk again on Glenn's rum and sick with too much rich food. Glenn was pouring Madeira this time. They were discussing some of the provisions they would need and how many convict servants.

"Aye, we can meet ta Cranston's place. Never been there meself, but Jack Summers 'as. Told me about a big paintin' Cranston 'as on the wall of 'is ballroom. About five feet by six. Picture of a mob of nekkid women." Glenn laughed. "But Jack says the painting wasn't Cranston's but his wife's. Sally don't believe it, though." Glenn nodded. "Jack'll go. And Buck. You tell Buck yet?"

Aaron shook his head. "Haven't seen him. He came in late last night so weary he was still in bed when I left this morning."

101

"Well, we may all be up late tonight, lad, so drink up. That's only your second glass o' Madeira."

If Aaron didn't know better, he'd swear Glenn was trying to get him drunk enough to agree to something now that he couldn't back out of later.

"'Aft ta do better than that if yer going to join this family by marrying Annabelle."

Aaron stood up. "I never gave any indication of wanting to marry Annabelle, Glenn."

Glenn was undismayed. "Them perfessors over in England took some of the Sydney sandstone out of your mouth. You talk almost as Limey as Cranston."

Aaron just grinned and sipped the wine, thinking that the colony had taken some of the Limey out of Cranston and all the English-born in this colony, including his own father and mother, and added a tad of Sydney sandstone. Some had even picked up the lower London street dialect people were calling Cockney, like Glenn. But he had a feeling Glenn had picked up the accent, not in Sydney, but in London itself, long ago. All the English spoken in the colony had changed into a strange amalgamation of Cockney, upper-class English, and an accent he had heard nowhere else—Australia's own, he guessed.

Glenn was eyeing him, red-eyed, but steady. "Took some of the sense out of you, too. Not plannin' to marry Annabelle. Why, you and Annabelle used to play together."

"Annabelle and I were friends. Still are."

"Friends enough to get married?"

There it was, said with a teasing air, but said straight out, nonetheless.

"No."

Glenn nodded and stood up. "Marry Annabelle and I'll give you the hundred acres, fifty pounds, a bull, a Merino ram, and a start of chooks," he said,

leaning toward him. Seeing that Aaron was putting on his cabbage tree hat in preparation to leave, Glenn looked over at Annabelle, who was grooming her new mare in the sun, keeping away from the men, but keeping an eye on Aaron. "Look at 'er. Not a Thoroughbred, but a beauty, anyhow. Trim and well-mannered, too."

"Annabelle?"

"No-oo," Glenn said indignantly. "The mare." He put a hand on Aaron's arm. "But come to think of it, Annabelle's like that. Look at 'er. 'Ow can you refuse 'er? What's wrong with 'er?"

Aaron looked at Glenn steadily a moment, amused. Then he smiled and said, "Nothing." And he turned and strode to his own horse and mounted it.

"Tonight. Seven o'clock at Cranston's," Glenn said.

Aaron touched the brim of his hat, reined the horse around.

"Aaron! Leaving so soon?" Annabelle called in dismay from the paddock.

Aaron tipped his hat. "Almost not soon enough," he answered, then spurred his horse and rode out of the yard.

When Aaron saw his Uncle Buck half an hour later at Owen's Landing where a convict servant was shoeing his horse, Buck had washed up, cut his hair, and was shaving as he looked into a mirror hung on a gum tree outside the forge shed. Under his chin he was holding the barber's basin, a copper basin with a wedge cut out of the rim big enough to fit a man's neck.

Buck was taller than the average man and built as

103

solidly as a tree. His skin was deeply tanned, making his teeth seem unusually white in his face. He wasn't a handsome man by popular standards, but there was something arresting in the expression in his brown eyes, eyes that were crinkled at the corners, a faraway look that was wise and kind, but didn't quite see you, as if his eyes were looking at you but seeing something else. His shoulders were wide, his body muscular, yet his whole frame was slender. He moved with a slow deliberation, but he could move with a graceful quickness, too.

Buck had taken to the bush at seventeen, had roamed and hunted and lived with the natives. His part in helping the Crawfords and Aylesburys to survive those early difficult years was bringing home kangaroo, wallaby, emu meat, and duck for the family. Buck made money by selling skins and guiding hunters in the bush. He was neither rich nor poor, and probably made only enough from his skins to pay for shot for his muskets and pistols and to buy traps, so that he could go back into the bush and do it all over again. He didn't drink because he didn't have to. Adventure was his intoxicant. Aaron had noted before, as he did now, that Buck always looked like he was trying to smile and couldn't.

"Hello, Aaron," Buck said with typical undemonstrativeness. He was seeing him for the first time in five years.

"Buck." Aaron propped his booted foot on the tree stump and watched his uncle, the bushman, scrape his square jaw with the razor. It was difficult because Buck had probably a three-week-old beard to shave off. "Seen Jack Summers?" Aaron asked.

"Came by early."

"Say anything about the expedition we are trying to form?"

"Told me all about it."

"I saw Cranston this morning. He'll fund us."

A slight jerk of the razor as Buck's brown eyes darted to Aaron. An expression of quick alertness, which he covered in the next instant. "That so?"

"You'll do it, won't you Buck? Be our guide?"

Buck scraped and said, "I've never been to Bathurst but once. Been over the mountains only four times, but only as far west as Bathurst."

"We want to go beyond Bathurst. What we need is your knowledge of survival in the bush. Of what to avoid, how to proceed. All of that."

Buck didn't reply for a while, but when he did he said, "You're taller, Aaron. And you look more like Milicent than ever."

Aaron smiled. "Mark's taller too. Looks more like Father."

Buck nodded and went back to shaving. Aaron waited and was just about to press Buck for a decision when the man spoke up again. "I'll go," he said and swished his blade around in the copper basin. "Can't let you get lost in the bush."

And that was all. Whatever Buck's answer was was final. There would have been no arguing with him if he had refused. Aaron had the distinct feeling, though, that the reason Buck had agreed to go was to protect Aaron for his sister's sake.

They met at Cranston's that night. Aaron had never been inside the house before and was amazed at how European it looked inside, furnished with European furnishings, English chairs, Louis XV settees. And there *was* a huge painting of naked women. Aaron's education hadn't taken a turn down the artist's path, and he didn't know who the women

were supposed to be or who had painted it. He only knew that, as he stood in the Cranstons' dining room, with the map spread out on Cranston's dining table, he could look across the central hall into the dimly lit ballroom at the painting. The impression was of lots of flesh. It was all he could do to avoid looking at it, perspiring all the while.

Plans were made to purchase supplies in Parramatta the next day, which was Saturday. With the drought promising fair weather, they decided they had better leave on Sunday, if possible.

Aaron was wild with excitement, but there was only one drawback in the plans for him. He wouldn't get to see Penelope before he left.

So while Buck and Glenn prepared a dray to be taken over the road to Parramatta for supplies, Aaron took Deen aside and handed him a note.

"Mrs. Cranston and Penelope are coming back from Sydney on the *Milicent* with some supplies that Cranston ordered. Would you mind giving this letter to Penelope for me?" Aaron said.

Deen smiled, nodded, and sighed. "Very well."

"I wish you were going with us."

Deen shook his head. "Uh uh. Not me. I've had all of that wilderness I want. 'Sides if I went, who'd give Penelope the note?" His eyes danced with a mixture of amusement and sarcasm. "Annabelle?"

Aaron just looked at him, knowing that Deen approved of his interest in Penelope but didn't understand his lack of interest in Annabelle. Deen grinned and punched him on the shoulder with his fist, then lumbered off with that bobbing, loose-limbed grace meant to show the world that he was carefree. But Aaron sensed that he wasn't.

*   *   *

106

"You want young draft horses," Uncle Thaddeus said. "They're sturdy, hard muscled, deep chested for pulling mountains, and they're sure-footed." He made one expert stroke of the gray mare's side, then looked at Aaron. "These in this paddock are derivations of the Welsh mountain pony and the Arabian. They're sure footed, have strong hearts and lungs. Durability is what you need." Thaddeus Crawford was the youngest of the Crawford clan and probably the handsomest. He was neither tall nor short, but one got the impression that he was tall, because he behaved tall. Thaddeus moved with the grace of one of his finest Thoroughbred race horses and dressed as if he'd never hoed a row of corn or cut a sheaf of wheat. Like now—he was clad in a bright new blue jacket, white duck trousers, brown riding boots, and a wide-brimmed cabbage tree hat. The ruffled shirt wasn't usually worn by a country gentleman while he was out on his holdings, but Thaddeus often wore his and was wearing it now. Thaddeus, like Owen, didn't have an enemy. Yet his cosmopolitan aloofness was more discouraging to close friendships somehow than his brother Buck's bushman reticence. "I'd say," he said, his brown eyes looking straight at Aaron, "that you'll need nine or ten horses. One for each of you to ride and one and a half horses for packing your gear. And even at that you'll ride the horses to death unless you go slow." His eyes snapped as he looked at Aaron soberly. "Go slowly. I'll be willing to buy them back from you when the expedition is over, provided they are in good condition. Draft horses are rare in the colony." He turned his back to Aaron and strolled along the paddock fence with Aaron plodding behind him.

Thaddeus's grounds were extensive. His house was a two-story plaster and lathe painted white with the

typical deep veranda on the lower floor, supported by Doric columns he had imported from France. His farm was fenced and cross-fenced with dog-leg fencing. His stables were better and bigger than the house. Sleek, shining horses grazed in the paddocks and on the sides of the rolling hills. The even texture of grass showed the expertise with which Thaddeus grazed his horses. It was Thaddeus who had taught Aaron that a horse didn't pull the grass up by the roots, but nibbled only the tops of the grass, leaving the rest to grow and spread out. Horses were kinder to pasture than cattle, who wrapped their tongues around the grass and ate it short, sometimes roots and all, or the blasted sheep—which Aaron hated and Penelope loved—whose sharp hooves trod the grass into the ground. Thaddeus's farm, with its fine house and fences and horses and stables and neat rows of convict huts, looked like a design woven into a deep green plush carpet.

"Those are my newest breeds," he said when he noticed Aaron was looking closely at some short-legged bays in the paddock nearest the house. "Trotters. Out of Miss Bailey. I've bred some of the best trotters for racing in the colony. The Americans have the best. I'm presently breeding Arabians and Thoroughbreds that I intend to crossbreed with some American trotters."

Aaron was anxious to get back home before tea. He had to take the string of horses back with him the five miles, but one did not hurry Thaddeus Crawford. On a whim he could change his mind, decide not to sell his precious draft horses, and delay the whole expedition. So Aaron perspired in the spring sun and strolled beside his uncle, and pretended he wasn't anxious to leave.

Thaddeus stopped, propped a boot on the fence

and gestured to a magnificent bay stallion that was capering around his paddock, blowing and arching his neck. "A great-grandson of Rockingham, first breeded horse in New South Wales."

"He's magnificent."

Tad smiled. "I'll have to watch him. Bushrangers like to pick the best horses because they are the fastest for getting away from soldiers."

Aaron nodded, knowing that Uncle Tad had more trouble with bushrangers stealing his riding horses than did any of the others.

"From the riding horse, the trotter, and the draft horse, I intend to breed stock horses for mustering sheep and cattle. The wool industry is bound to expand, so more sheep and more cattle mean more land and more horses that are intelligent, sturdy, and fast—in that order." He stopped, his brown eyes searching Aaron's face briefly, then dropped his foot to the ground. "But you'll want to get back before tea." He gestured toward the house. "Come in. We'll make out a bill of sale. I'll have Cranston sign it tomorrow." The two started toward the house. Tad's stride was brisk and long as he glanced at Aaron. "How does your mother feel about your going on this expedition funded by Cranston?"

Aaron smiled. Every one of his mother's brothers had worried about that. "You know Mums. She hates to see me go away so soon after coming home, but she's excited for me and pleased."

Tad did not look at him or break his stride as he asked, "And . . . your father?"

Aaron took a deep breath before he replied, "He doesn't know yet." But he's about to find out, he thought and expelled the rest of his breath.

*   *   *

Aaron waited until after tea and after his father had gone out to check on his horse's hoof, for the gelding had gone lame on his way home from Parramatta that day. Aaron waited a few moments on the veranda, then took a deep breath and walked to the stable. Dark would fall soon, and "fall" was the right word for it, he thought. There was no twilight in New South Wales as there was in England. Night fell with a soft thump that stirred to life the click beetles in the grass, the frogs in the creek, and the cicadas in the trees. Shadows of the big gum trees in the yard were stretching longer, and all the pickets in the fence were pointing east where the sun would come up in the morning as abruptly as it would fall tonight.

When he entered the slab and shingled stable, his father was squatting on his heels in one of the horse stalls examining his gelding's hoof. The smell that Aaron loved, of gum tree lumber, damp earth, and sweet new hay permeated the stable with its two open ends and its six horse stalls. It was this air that he took a deep breath of before he said outright, "I'm going with Jack Summers and Glenn Moffett on an expedition. Buck's coming too." There. It was out in the open.

Matthew Aylesbury slowly raised his eyes and looked at him, his handsome face reflecting such a mixture of horror, disbelief, and anger that Aaron had to force himself to keep his eyes on his father's face. "You . . . are . . . *what?*"

"I'm going on an exploring expedition with Jack Summers, Glenn Moffett, and Uncle Buck."

The expression on his father's face did not change as he asked, "When?"

"In the morning. We have already bought our supplies. Horses are in the paddock—"

"How?"

Aaron felt the blood beating in his temples. "Mr. Cranston is funding it."

A slow, scarlet flush rose from the base of his father's throat and moved up to cover his face. He rose slowly from his squatting position, glared right into Aaron's face, and said, "Why?"

"He wants first pick of the land we explore."

"And you?"

"We hope that the governor will allot us some of it for our efforts."

"Where?"

"Around Bathurst. It's just an outpost, the only settlement west of the Blue Mountains, and no one's explored the district much."

Matthew stood looking at him, then turned his back. Aaron swallowed. This man had spent all day at the hospital in Parramatta treating convicts, doing experiments, and writing his papers. He was one of the two surgeons who were responsible for the better care that prisoners shipped over from England in convict ships had begun to have in the last few years, and he was responsible for reduced sentences for floggings in the colony. This man was a civilian in a government hospital, and although he was the most educated doctor in the colony, he would never gain anything in the way of public recognition for his efforts other than people's respect. He did not make his money at the hospital; he made it in trade and in farming. And yet, he wanted to sentence his son to the same drudgery. He turned toward him. What Aaron saw surprised him. "You . . . want to live near Bathurst, then?" It was more a statement than a question.

"I've considered it." Then Aaron's own pent-up emotions burst out like water from a broken dam.

"Father, I have never wanted to work in that rum hospital in Sydney. Or in Parramatta. There are settlers all over this colony who have no medical care. They have no hospital, and most of the doctors are military men not allowed to treat civilians. If . . . when I settle down, I want to set up a private practice. In an area where I'm needed. And I'd like to graze cattle while I'm at it."

Matthew was studying his son, all the fury gone now. He would never understand Aaron's total lack of interest in medicine. Four years at Edinburgh and he was no closer to being a doctor than he ever was. He would rather hunt than heal, roam than research. He stared into the steady eyes of his son and saw that he was defeated. And in the muddle of injured feelings, of disappointment, floundering anger, itching frustration, the only thing that surfaced was, "Why Cranston?"

"He was the only man who stepped forward to offer the money."

And I withheld mine, Matthew thought. He squatted back down and took the salve and began to massage it into the horse's hock where the thorn had lodged. He wanted to thrash his son. Wanted to take Milicent in his arms because they had fought over Aaron's trust fund, Milicent wanting him to release it and Matthew refusing to do so. And he wanted to beat the hell out of Cranston. It was damned hard for a man to be strong sometimes for the wives and grandmother and sons. Like the time Jessica died, when a part of him had died, too. What had he done wrong? Had he talked about medicine too much when Aaron was young? Had he said anything to turn him against it? And if Aaron hated medicine, why hadn't he spoken out before now? And Cranston—why was he always around to step in when

something went wrong in the family?

Matthew did not look up as he said, "Then it's all settled. Without my knowledge, without my consent, without my approval?"

This was it. The duel. Aaron's lips had stuck together because his mouth had gone dry, and he pulled them apart and said softly, "Yes."

Matthew rose then, studying him soberly as he wiped his hands on a rag. And then he nodded with finality and said, "So be it."

Fifteen horses stood in the yard early the next morning. Ten belonged to the expedition, four of which were saddled. Six were loaded with equipment. Chaos reigned, and it irritated Aaron a little that the family could not dispense with going to Sunday church at Windsor just this once just to save confusion. And to top it all off, Ben Crawford had come with his tribe. Not that Aaron wasn't glad to see Uncle Ben and Aunt Becky, and especially Benny. But he and Glenn were having a hell of a time getting the horses ready for the track.

Benny, who was Aaron's age and an exact duplicate of his father, Ben, stood dressed like one of Penelope's watercolor paintings of a country gentleman—one that had been left out in the sun too long and had faded. Benny was watching with envy as Aaron struggled with one of the tents, which kept slipping off the horse's back.

Uncle Ben, the patriarch of the family, was the oldest Crawford, graying into his fifties with not a slack muscle in his entire body, except those in his face. If Buck tried to smile and couldn't, and Thaddeus didn't see any point in it, what was Ben's excuse for not smiling?

113

"Are you certain you want to do this?" Uncle Ben asked, coming to stand beside him, sober and subtly disapproving, as always.

Aaron, tugging on the cinch beneath the pack horse's belly, turned halfway around. "I'm certain, Uncle Ben."

Ben stood straight, hands hooked in his pockets, chest out, a fashion mannequin to display Aunt Becky's careful and continuous care of his shirt and waistcoat. His face had never been handsome like Thaddeus's and Milicent's, until his later years. His graying hair instead of thinning, seemed to have gotten thicker. His thin face had filled out. "Your mother would be terribly hurt if you were killed out there. I hope you realize that."

"I do. And I wouldn't be in such great shape myself," Aaron grinned, but he was met with so cold a regard that he sobered quickly. "I'll be careful."

Ben stood like that for a moment, then surprised Aaron by thrusting out his hand. Hesitantly, Aaron took it. "God bless you and keep you, Aaron," Ben said.

"Thank you sir."

Ben turned and walked away, his children, both boys and girls, nine in all, swarming around him.

Benny still stood, envy written all over his face, but he said, "Good fortune. Maybe someday we can go together."

Aaron took the hand Benny proffered. "You intend to be a cow cockey like your father?"

Benny smiled. "No."

"What then?"

Benny's eyes darted in the direction of his father, then back to Aaron. "When you go to get that cattle station going, tell me. By then I'll be twenty-one and . . ."

Aaron nodded and smiled. Benny hurried away.

Becky waved to him now, and the children swarmed into the wagon calling, "Farewell, Cousin Aaron," "Good-bye Aaron," "Bye, Aaron." And little Flossie, waving from her mother's lap, called, "Bye bye." Then Ben flicked the reins of the two horses and the wagon moved forward.

Aaron got the cinch tightened, and it seemed that the tent made of Parramatta cloth with its pots and tins wrapped inside was secure at last. He glanced at Buck doing something with his musket, at Glenn examining his riding horse's hoof. They would lead Summer's horse, and he would join them up the track at his place when they got there.

Rosey, their black stable boy, had brought the carriage out of the barn with the horse that would pull it, and two horses for his father and Mark.

Mark was out of the house now. Then came his grandmother and his mother.

Buck came to him, his brown eyes flicking over the ten horses and their swags and gear.

"Does it look like we're ready?" Aaron asked, trying to remain calm.

"Seems so," Buck answered.

"Then—"

Buck nodded and sauntered over to Glenn.

There was a gentle touch on his arm and Aaron looked down into his mother's pretty face. Her brown eyes moved back and forth, searching his eyes, his face. "You must take care, Aaron. Take every precaution. Listen to Buck. But then, you always have. See it, Aaron. See it for me out back behind the mountains, because I never will. Remember everything to tell me later."

A little surprised, Aaron smiled, then embraced her briefly. "Mum. I will, I will."

115

She released him to his grandmother then. Grandmum's soft eyes embraced him first, then her arms. "God will keep you, Aaron," she said softly. Aaron batted back stupid tears that he didn't understand.

Aaron's mother was speaking to his father, who was testing the cinch under the carriage horse's belly, but he did not answer her. He had not spoken to Aaron since Saturday when he had told him about the expedition.

Then Mark was beside him, and Aaron paused long enough to look him up and down. "Very dandified," he said.

Mark was dressed in a brown frock coat and matching trousers, a cream-colored waistcoat, a ruffled white shirt, brown boots, a beaver hat, looking outlandishly handsome. And he knows it, Aaron concluded with a smile. Mark held out his hand. "Find what you seek, brother. But don't kill yourself doing it." His smile waned a little, "Father needs you."

Aaron grinned. "Aye. I noticed," he said sarcastically.

Mark glanced at their father, then looked back at Aaron. "He's very hurt that you're doing this."

Aaron nodded. This was the first time that Aaron sensed any disapproval from Mark. Mark clasped his arm. "We'll go have a night in Sydney when you return."

"I may need it," Aaron said, grinning.

Both laughed. But as Aaron adjusted the stirrup on his saddle, Mark said, "As for Penelope—"

Aaron paused, and when Mark did not go on, he turned slowly to look at him. Something had gone cold in Mark's face even though he was still smiling. "I think you have known for years that I intend to give you a bit of competition."

116

Aaron looked at him. Then, "Penelope is a free woman. She takes counsel of her own mind."

"Yes. Thank God."

Aaron studied his brother and said nothing.

"No rancor, then. You've had a fair go with her," Mark said. "Now I shall have mine."

Anger flushed Aaron's face, but he turned away so that it wouldn't show. "Fair enough," he said.

Mark slapped his back. "Good fortune. Enjoy your outing."

Aaron looked across the back of his horse and saw Buck mount his horse. Aaron mounted too and did not look at his stepbrother again. There was a chill between them that had never been there before.

The next moments were a blur of stamping horses, clattering gear, good-byes from the women again, the feel of the horse moving under him, the pull of the lead to the pack horses he was leading, one last visual sweep of the house and yard in case they had forgotten something. Buck taking the lead, Glenn following. An unbearable thrill.

Aaron held up his hand in a gesture of farewell to his mother, his grandmother, Mark, and to his father's back.

Swallowing anger and hurt because his father had not said farewell, Aaron rode on up the track until they reached the forest that would close the farm from sight. Then he turned just before the party passed under the branches of the trees and saw the women still waving, Mark still standing. And his father turning slowly to catch one last glimpse of his son.

Chapter VI

Something fell from Deen's shirt as he swung onto his horse, reined him about, and galloped up the track to the south, away from the landing. Annabelle called to him and ran after the horse, but she was too late; her shouts were drowned out by the beating of the horse's hooves and the pounding of carpenter's hammers next to the water. Sighing, she dropped her arms to her side and strode to the place where she saw the paper flutter to the ground and picked it up. It was a folded and sealed letter.

Annabelle looked at it, turned it over. *Penelope C.* was written carefully on the outside—by Aaron Aylesbury's hand. She knew his neat, careful scrawl.

She had been angry with her father for hauling Aaron off so soon after his return from England, and she had been terribly hurt because Aaron had paid her absolutely no attention since he had come home. Indeed, it seemed as if he was trying to avoid her. She had cried every day since he had been so rude to her at Owen's Landing the first day he worked there forging the pins. She had waited years for his return, this childhood friend who was more than friend. Now, the pain of seeing this letter written by him to

Penelope C. was like a knife thrust into her own stomach. Spreading her hand over her abdomen, she stared at the letter. Cold horror twisted the knife in her, wrenched her insides until her hands began to tremble. The letter's sealing wax was still warm from Deen's body and was beginning to soften in the sunlight. Annabelle bit her lip trying to keep it from trembling, her eyes misting over. Penelope C. Oh dear God, and I had hoped— And then a sudden surge of anger flooded her. He took me when we were twelve, she thought, in the grass on a hill near the river. We pretended we were married.

Some little elf in her mind reminded her that Aaron wasn't the first. But he was the last, and he was the one she loved.

Annabelle started walking toward the forge where she had left her horse. She had so wanted to tell her father and Aaron good-bye at the Aylesburys', but her father had forbidden it, saying, "We don't need no more people there, lass. Tell me farewell now along with your good mother." The Moffetts had not gone to church today. Perhaps she should have, for she would not be standing here holding this letter now, paralyzed, in the sun. The sun, which was softening the sealing wax.

A soft breeze fluttered the edges of the letter. Annabelle knew she must not look, must not read the contents, but she was also aware that the message in this letter would tell her the ultimate truth. Did Aaron love Penelope?

The sun melted the wax slowly, and at last a breeze caused the letter to open and flutter in her hand. Annabelle read the neat lines before her.

My Dearest Penelope,
    Your father has probably already told you

119

about our expedition. I wanted to see you and tell you farewell, to kiss you good-bye.

I wanted to apologize too for what happened near the still. Penny, love, I have no excuse for what I did, except that I love you so much. Can you forgive me?

We should return in two months, at which time I plan to speak to your father about our future, if indeed you have forgiven me.

Will you wait for me?

Yours most affectionately,
Aaron

The little whimper was her own. It started deep inside and came up into her chest and throat of its own free will. *I have no right to him any more than any other girl. Why have I always assumed that he was mine?* The tears spilled. *Is this my punishment?*

Aaron had not been the first. Nobody had ever told Annabelle that it was wrong. And nobody thought it was wrong when she let them, either. It had never occurred to Sally Moffett that, at eleven, little Annabelle might have such temptations. After all, her body had only just begun to develop. Annabelle had been friends with Aaron, and they had played being married. She had liked him so much. In fact, she'd taught him what to do. Big-eyed Aaron, blushing and innocent. The others were Mark, Jory McWilliams, some she had forgotten the names of. And only once each.

Annabelle Moffett will let you.

She blushed now thinking about it. Other boys had swarmed eagerly around her for a while, until she had told them all enough times, "No, I can't see you. I like somebody else." That somebody was Aaron.

It hadn't been easy growing up on a farm isolated from other children. And Annabelle had learned early that her father and mother had been convicts. She was what people called a currency lass. The "pure merino" boys in Parramatta hadn't looked at her much until word had got around that "Annabelle Moffett will let you."

She had been born to parents who liked being around other people, who loved life and enjoyed doing things. Annabelle, too, had grown up yearning for someone to play with, a girl to be her best friend. But there were only Mark and Aaron and Deen and Ben Crawford's five boys; the Crawfords did not have a girl until their sixth child.

"You want to know how people make babies?" she had asked twelve-year-old Aaron one day when he wanted to go home before she was ready to stop playing.

He had blushed and said, "I *know* how people make babies."

"But have you ever done it?"

Aaron had blushed again, furiously. "Of course."

She had known he was lying. She caught his half-willing hand and pulled him into the trees where the dappled shade made the tall grass darker. Unceremoniously, Annabelle pulled down her pantaloons and stretched out in the grass. "There. You're supposed to lay down on top of me and put it in."

Aaron had stared at her, and it was the first sexual thrill she had ever experienced—just from his eyes looking at her bare thighs.

"But what if it makes a baby?" he choked.

"It won't," she assured him. "It takes ten times to make a baby."

"But," he gasped, "won't it hurt?"

"Not anymore," she said.

Now, as she remembered, Annabelle shut her eyes. After Aaron, there hadn't been any more. After the wonder of Aaron, she couldn't tolerate anyone else.

I'll kill myself. No man will have me anyway because I am not a virgin. I thought that Aaron loved me. I was wrong. So wrong. So terribly, awfully—

Annabelle took a deep breath, holding it to still the sobs that threatened her. Penelope C.

I wanted to apologize for what happened near the still.

I have no excuse except that I love you so.

But what about me?

Annabelle took another deep breath, threw her head back, and swallowed the sobs. The air was cool and laden with the pleasant aromas of sawdust, damp gum trees, the river, the forge. The sounds around her were busy. Life was going on. And Aaron would come back.

But not to me. Not to me.

She should destroy the letter. Let Penelope C. think Aaron had forgotten her.

No. She couldn't. To hurt Aaron would hurt herself.

Maybe not. Maybe Penelope would hate him.

No. Aaron would only make amends to her when he returned.

Penelope C., the girl who let Aaron.

Penelope C. is no better than me.

In a daze, Annabelle resealed the letter and took it to Owen, saying that it had fallen out of Deen's shirt and that she had no idea who it was from.

Owen looked at the handwriting and said it looked like Aaron's. He said he'd keep it for Deen until he saw him next, and Annabelle mounted her mare,

122

kicked her, and tore away from the landing at a dead run.

Deen hated farewells, so he never said any. But the expedition was exciting, in spite of what he had told Aaron. He would have wanted to go, except for one thing. He wasn't invited. Besides, he had to be there for the wheat harvest. About Monday the farmers would start bringing their grain down to the landing and he'd have to start hauling it down river, and down the coast to Sydney. He was, after all, in Owen's employ. That was why nobody had thought to invite him along on the expedition.

He had had a good visit with his father, though. But it seemed to Deen that each time Buck came in from the bush he was harder to talk to than the time before, as if his long days and nights alone had made him forget how to converse. Maybe even how to feel.

Deen was sitting on a hill near Windsor where he could watch the expedition party go by on the track below. There would be no fanfare with this expedition. Men like Wentworth, Blaxland, and Lawson would go down in history as having discovered this and that, but there would be dozens of others whose names would be lost in a muddle of time and trouble and disinterest, like flotsam in a muddy river.

Here came the Ben Crawfords. A family large enough to fill the largest dray in the colony. Going to church. To be reminded that in the beginning God created the heavens and the earth.

The white man said that his mother's people were some of the most primitive on earth, but Deen smiled because he knew better. For his mother's people taught that in the beginning the earth was in utter

123

darkness and all creatures lay sleeping in the caverns in the mountains. Yhi lay sleeping, too, until Baiame, the Great Spirit, whispered to her to awaken. And she opened her eyes and from her eyes came the first light. And she came down to earth because of her light and her love, and everywhere she walked grass and flowers sprang up and came to life. She entered the caverns, and the creatures came to life and went down from the mountains to spread out over the land and dwell there.

In the beginning was the Word and the Word was with God and the Word was God, began the Gospel of John. *And the Word was made flesh and dwelt among us.* This was what the missionaries were teaching his mother's people.

But his mother's people had for centuries told the story of Baiame, who said, "I cannot appear to my creatures for I am but a spirit. I have a plan. I will make my spirit and my mind flesh." And Baiame put a little part of his power of mind into each creature, but the greater part of his mind he put into a new creature, which he called Man.

These were two of the oft-repeated stories of his mother's people as they squatted around their fires at night. There were a thousand more. Were they much different than those of his father's people?

The Europeans called the natives' stories of creation "myths." The Europeans called their own stories of creation "Genesis." They also called the natives' stories of God's being made flesh "myths," while they called their own story of God in the flesh "the Gospel."

Here they came; Buck in the lead on a gray horse leading a white pack horse. Then came Glenn Moffett leading a pack horse, and Jack Summers leading one horse and Aaron leading two. There was

the familiar clatter and clank of pots and pans, muskets sheathed behind the saddles, at the ready in case of bushrangers . . . or hostile natives. All dressed in moleskin trousers and muslin shirts, high-top boots and cabbage tree hats. Buck had the usual lucky emu feather in his.

They would have an adventure and come home to their women—except for Buck. Deen didn't know what his father did for a woman. Couldn't imagine him with one. Maybe he did what Deen did: visit a native woman when the need was more than he could bear. When the night dreams and day imaginations of his beloved became too insistent and too real.

Annabelle, Annabelle, how blind can you be? Aaron doesn't care for you the way I do. I have loved you since I was seven years old when father brought me to the Aylesburys' from the bush. I was a little savage, but even then I did not miss your beauty. I was enthralled with your golden hair, long and straight, and with the sun that lived in your eyes. You wiped my runny nose and hugged me to your chest. And you were only a friend visiting Aaron, three years older than me.

I suppose I thought you were Yhi. I know I thought Dr. Aylesbury was Baiame for a while. And I played with little Jessica with the sunny smile.

Deen, squatting on his heels, watched as the party passed on and into the town of Windsor. His usual smile had not left his face, because it was a habit to keep it there. One kept smiling because one must. If you weren't a white man, you stayed cheerful to show them you were pleased with their world. He wasn't a native either, so he put on a smile for his mother's people, too. *You belong to neither race and yet you belong to both. But you were raised as a white man and you behave as one, while not forgetting you are*

125

half-native. And because of that you fell in love with a white lass and have no hope because you are half-native. What do you hope for, Deenyi, the Ironbark Tree? To forever ply the river in your barques until you're old? What then, Deenyi, will you join your mother's people on the edge of town and beg for a cup of meal and a bone to boil your scraps with, grinning and nodding your old head of white fleece?

Let them think they are greater, then, for it's true they are more powerful. While I, Deenyi, am caught between. I am half one man, half another, but I am a man. I have a man's heart and a man's dreams and a man's desires. But I cannot claim the dream or the desires. Only the heart. They will allow me that, but not the others. Ah, I wish I could be like Aaron, free to send my love a letter, to court her, to love her.

Misty-eyed, Deen's hand went to his shirt, to his bosom where he had tucked Aaron's letter. He felt for its crispness, and did not find it. Flushing, he jumped to his feet, felt in his pockets, looked around him on the ground. "Damn," he whispered aloud like a white man. And turning, he ran to his horse, mounted, jerked him around, and tore down the hill again going east.

They say that the Hawkesbury begins south and west, on the eastern slope of the Blue Mountains, and that its name is Nepean until it reaches Richmond. Then it becomes the Hawkesbury. It winds like a giant brown snake through the alluvial flood plains, widening as it goes, and then it flows into Broken Bay, and Broken Bay is the sea. The Pacific Ocean, indigo and mysterious and deep. *And that is where my body will go.*

She had ridden her new mare hard, letting the

wind tear the combs and pins from her hair, until it flowed out behind her, letting the wind dry her tears over and over again almost as fast as she could cry them, until she came at last to the sandstone cliffs that rose high, high above the river where it made a bend and cut away the bank beneath the cliffs. There on a grassy place that sloped toward the edge of the cliffs she had stopped and got off her horse. She had walked to the edge, looked down. The river was slow-moving and deep below, sixty feet below.

Now she shut her eyes, lifted her face to the sky. "Aaron . . ." she cried.

Her knees gave way and Annabelle fell to the ground, bent over with the pain in her chest. Jealousy.

She had been in pain before, had known sorrow, hunger, longing, humiliation, embarrassment, but nothing like this. This was the worst. This jealousy was unbearable, the most painful, awful, sickening feeling. Anger kept rising in her only to be overridden by hurt, disbelief. Clenching her teeth suddenly, Annabelle hooked her fingers in the front of her shirt and ripped it open and let the breeze touch her, yes touch her chest where her small breasts were, and her slender neck. And in a fit of rage, she pulled it off, flung it over the cliff and sobbed as she watched it float down like a pink bird, down, down to the water where it floated on the surface for a time, and then was caught up in a current and disappeared beneath the murky water. *And so shall I.*

A numbness began to settle over her now, a mindlessness as she pulled off her boots. Then, standing, she let her skirt fall to her feet. Without emotion now she kicked it over the cliff, peeled out of her underpants, then her chemise, and tossed them over the cliff.

Because if Aaron won't have my body, she reasoned, then the sea shall. I will go to the sea, it can have me. It will take me gladly, let me sleep in its cold arms, wash into me, give me its salty issue. Because if I can't have him, I want no one else. Ever.

Annabelle stood on the edge of the cliff naked as the day Sally Moffett pushed her without a whimper into the world and Matthew Aylesbury, freed only the day before, caught her in his strong hands and stuck his finger into her mouth so that her chest could fill with cool air, shocking her into crying out in rage.

And life had been hard for a while, with Sally's milk drying up because there wasn't much to eat. And Annabelle going without shoes at times and learning at five that she was a currency lass, daughter of ex-convicts. But she'd faced the world with a stubborn cheerfulness, letting others think that Annabelle Moffett was a merry thing even if she wasn't too pretty.

But Penelope C. was pretty. Penelope C. was beautiful.

Mother would miss her, and Father, and instead of gaining a son, they would lose a daughter. But they had each other. Annabelle had no one. Their arms were never empty. *And neither will mine be.*

A crow cawed and soared above her head, and before she walked to the very edge of the cliff, Annabelle thought, Crow, you will not have me. I am a bride of the sea.

Deen's horse had barely stopped in a cloud of black dust at the door of the warehouse where Owen had his office, before he was out of the saddle and running up the wooden steps to the door. He had watched for the letter every step the horse took on his

way back from the hill near Windsor where he had watched the hunting party go by, but had not found it.

Thinking he might have dropped it at the landing and someone had found it, Deen hurried through the door into the warehouse where Owen's convict laborers were sawing wood, hammering, sanding, making someone's furniture. Deen went to the door of Owen's small office and rapped on the door jamb.

Owen was standing at a table, a lead pencil behind one ear, another in his hand, a large paper spread out upon a table, and he was drawing a line with ruler and pencil. He looked up when Deen came in.

Deen lost no time in getting to the point. "Owen, Aaron gave me a letter to deliver for him and I somehow—"

Owen pointed to the windowsill with his pencil.

Deen took a deep breath. "Thank God," he said and took the letter off the sill.

Owen was not one to interfere in anyone's business; indeed he seldom appeared aware of the emotional turmoils of others; he remained always steady, even tempered, cheerful, and minded his own business, but now he looked at Deen pleasantly, his gray eyes steady and unreadable as he said, "Annabelle found it. Rode away . . . rather fast." That was all.

Deen felt the blood drain out of his face. He would have preferred to keep the existence of the letter from her, because he knew her heart. She loved Aaron. He was all she could talk about, wasn't it? Aaron this, Aaron that, until he could pull all his hair out, until he could run and butt his head against a tree because of the jealousy he felt. Because she loved Aaron and not himself.

"Thank you, Owen."

Owen nodded and tipped his pencil toward him in farewell.

Outside the warehouse again, Deen looked at the letter. Penelope C.

On the other side the wax was secure. Or was it? It had melted in the sun at some point in time. But had it melted enough for the letter to come open?

Rode away rather fast.

A chill settled over Deen. Annabelle would be hurt. Hurt terribly. Something warred in Deen, a gladness that Aaron did not intend to claim her, a sadness for Annabelle, a sorrow for her pain. He swallowed, knowing he had no right to interfere. No right at all. He should go down to the river, check the rigging on the *Milicent* and the *Elvira,* and let Annabelle handle her hurt as he had learned to manage his own. Yes, he should.

But . . . something old, something deep, something deep down inside stirred and whispered, made his scalp prickle, caused the pores on his back and arms to open, and a chill settled over him.

Rode away rather fast.

Overhead a crow cawed and flapped its ebony wings and soared on the air currents.

Deen tucked Aaron's letter in his boot and mounted his horse, intending to trot from the landing up the track that led to the Moffetts' farm, but by the time he came to the track, he had set the game little horse at a canter.

"No, Deen. I 'aven't seen Annie since she left this mornin' to carry me message to Owen Crawford down ta the landin'," Sally Moffett said, smiling cheerfully. "She be caught up in the expedition, I think. D'ya know if it left yet, lad?"

Deen was perspiring now as he stood on the Moffetts' veranda. "Yes, missus. They left over an

130

hour ago."

Sally Moffett sighed. "Well, 'twill be lonely, but that's the way of it. We women sit ta home and wait while our men make 'istory, we do. Won't ya come in for a cup o' tea, Deen, lad?"

"No, missus. I—I've an errand to do," Deen said backing off the veranda. "An errand to do . . . promptly."

"Very well, then. Don't keep yerself so scarce, lad. Good seein' ye."

"Thank you." Deen spun on his heel and mounted his horse. What to do now? Where could she be?

Once when they were playing with Aaron and Mark, she had said, "On the cliff overlooking the river, I always feel I can float free, like a bird."

Deen reined the horse around. *God in heaven.*

She was there. He knew it as surely as he knew his horse was under him now. He kicked the horse into a trot until he was out of the Moffetts' dooryard. Then he set him at a gallop, going east down the track. Down the track that followed the river.

He never afterwards remembered the race down the track. He only remembered his tears, his fear, his horror, that *knowing* that was so terrible, so black. He would remember racing the little horse until his coat was lathered with sweat, reining him off the track, galloping up the slope, up, up, ducking the limbs of young gum trees, up to the wide grassy slope that was the top of a ridge that overlooked the Hawkesbury.

He reined the horse and saw her, a flash of white against the blue sky.

"Annabe-e-elle," he cried, jumping off his horse before it had come to a complete halt.

She had vanished. Deen tore off his boots even as he ran, for they said a man would drown in the water

with his boots on. In his horror and blind fear he saw her boots at the edge of the cliff, but his feet did not hesitate. Deen ran in long, smooth rapid strides, the strides of a native, long, swift, and sure, and he did not even hesitate at the edge. He went over in a dive as clear and swift as a seagull. The air whistled in his ears, and even then he sought a sign of her and caught a flash of gold before he hit the water and went under.

Then he surfaced, impatiently slinging the water from his face, searching. One arm and her golden hair were all he saw. He swam for it, long, even strokes, and his hand clamped on cold flesh, which was his Annabelle.

"Baiame, don't let her be dead," he cried, and he locked his arm under her chin and swam through the slow water to the edge. When his feet touched bottom, he drew her into his arms and carried her to the bank, up into the grass where he laid her down.

"Annabelle," he panted hoarsely. "Annabelle!"

Her face was white and still. But then she came to life in a sudden spasm of coughing. Coughing racked her body as Deen gathered her into his arms, feeling the warm water from her mouth pouring down his heaving chest. "Annabelle," he whispered, and smoothed her hair.

He held her close as she coughed, coughed and gasped, and then, after a while, lay against him shuddering. Her eyelids fluttered. She looked up at him, recognizing him even as she shuddered, her breathing coming in quick, jerking gasps. It was then that the full impact hit him that his love was naked. For an instant he glimpsed her white body, her long white arms and legs, the flat abdomen, and he shut his eyes against it, tightly.

"Why didn't you leave me alone," she said hoarsely.

Deen could not speak. Gratitude overwhelmed him and he was near tears. He dared not speak. She was alive and she would live. And she was in his arms, achingly beautiful.

"I wanted to die. I wanted to, Deen," she said and caught her breath sharply. "Oh dear God, Deen. The pain is so awful."

He kept his eyes shut tight and lowered his chin to the top of her head. "I know," he said.

She was quiet for a long time. The day was warm and the breezes still. The dappled shade of the nearby grove of gum trees moved away from the water and left them alone in the sun. When she sat up at last, hanging her head over, letting her long damp hair hide her face, Deen unbuttoned his shirt and took it off. With fingers that had never touched a white woman before he pulled his shirt over her bare shoulders to hide her nakedness.

She nodded. "Thank you." Then, "You know that I love Aaron."

"Aye," he whispered.

She turned her head quickly to look at him. "Did you know of his love for Penelope?"

Deen looked away from her pale face and could not answer.

"Yes, you knew. Perhaps everyone knew, but me." She swallowed. "Perhaps everyone has been laughing at me all these years, for loving Aaron and not knowing—"

"Hush," Deen cried painfully and jerked her against his chest, holding her there. "No one laughed, Annabelle. If they had, I would have beaten them." Hadn't he fought with some of the other boys enough times because of their hints that "Annabelle Moffett will let you"? Aaron had fought them, too, for the same reason. Yes, Annabelle had "let" maybe

133

three, maybe four. He knew that, but what did it mean? Nothing, only the breaking of one of the white man's multitudinous rules, rules that made little sense and caused a hell of a lot of trouble.

"You?" she said softly. "You would have fought for me?"

"Don't you know yet that I've loved you since the first day I saw you?"

Annabelle sat up slowly, frowning. "But you were a baby. Five years old, and I was eight."

Deen's mouth quirked into a smile. "Is there a particular age when it's permissible for a man to fall in love?"

His light answer made her smile. Deen had always made her smile. Her hazel eyes, not quite green, not quite blue, the only thing besides her hair that she considered beautiful about herself, searched his. "You risked your life for me."

"Nay. I know the river and I'm a good swimmer."

Annabelle knew she could never love anyone but Aaron, but he was lost to her. His going had left a great gap in her life, his lack of love a great gulf in her soul. The pain of loss was terrible, but the pain of jealousy was worse. She could bear no more, and flushing, she picked up Deen's brown hand off his knee and took it to her breast, placed it there, arranged the palm of his hand over it, spread out its fingers.

"No, Annabelle," he whispered.

"Yes, Deen." She wanted only to reward him. If he loved her, this would be his reward for it and for saving her life.

"Please no. No, no, no. We can't."

She held his hand to her breast, bent her head over it. Her damp hair fell over his arm. "Who says we can't?" she said tremulously.

"The gods!"

Annabelle was weeping when she tossed her head, letting her hair fall away from her face. "We've defied the gods once today, why not again?"

Deen's eyes were swimming in tears as he reached one trembling hand and slowly pulled his shirt from her shoulders. He looked at her then, the sprinkling of freckles over her straight nose, her thin but perfect lips, her trembling chin, her neck, her firm breasts with their pink nipples, her abdomen, the wedge of golden fleece where her thighs came together, her straight, slender legs. His hand spread out over her abdomen first, as she lay back onto the soft grass. The other hand went to her forehead as he stretched out beside her, and then he lay looking at her, the wonder of her, marveling at the magic of this moment, this dreamlike moment. His hand moved down her abdomen and paused when it touched the curling hair at her thighs.

"I want you," she whispered.

Something came apart inside him and he was kissing her lips slowly and then her neck and her breasts, pleasuring each with a restless moan, as his hand felt and caressed her between her thighs.

He raised up on his knees long enough to undo his trousers and get out of them, then he bent again to caress her body. With deliberate slowness, he kissed her breasts, her belly, and then her thighs. Moaning, he savored her, tasting her body, searching, demanding.

"Ah yes. Yes that's good. Oh . . . Oh . . ."

She gasped when his lips and tongue tasted her between her thighs, a soft moan coming from between her clenched teeth and increasing to a cry of ecstasy. When her body convulsed, he raised himself over her and slid his hands beneath her hips to bring

135

her up to meet his thrust. He slid inside her, a slow, deep penetration, then moved in her. Annabelle's mouth came open in paralyzed pleasure, her eyes shut tightly.

And Deen loved her, gave her all of himself, everything he had to give, hard, deep, slow, sure, knowing even as he tumbled over that cliff in his mind to float like an eagle in the air that, with her eyes closed, Annabelle was pretending that he was Aaron.

He knew it, but loved her still.

Chapter VII

Dr. Matthew Aylesbury gazed around him with an air of proprietary pride. He had always dreamed of his son's working in the "rum" hospital in Sydney. But— His eyes rested on Mark. This was not the son he'd been thinking of, nor the part of the hospital he had dreamed of, either.

When Lachland Macquarie had arrived in the colony as governor, the old hospital on Dawes point had been a stinking collection of dilapidated huts. Good-hearted, charity-minded Macquarie had accepted three men's offer to build a new hospital with their own resources if Macquarie would grant them a monopoly in the rum trade. Since rum constituted almost all currency in the colony at the time, Macquarie hesitated. After all, the rum trade was one of the main evils that he had been sent to New South Wales to abolish. But he relented and accepted the proposition. D'Arcy Wentworth, one of Matthew's good friends and associates, was one of the men who built the hospital, using convict labor and paying for labor and materials in rum. As a result, D'Arcy and the other two men involved had realized a good profit. Gossip claimed that D'Arcy's profit was, in

fact, enormous.

The hospital was huge, and time proved that it was much too large. There were not enough sick convicts in the entire colony to fill it, and the medical staff was inadequate to take care of them if they had filled it. So at the moment law offices and courtrooms were set up in one of its wings. John Fitzhugh's solicitor's office was one of them.

Matthew jerked his thumb over his shoulder. "That was Samuel May's son," he said, indicating the young man who had just spoken to him as he went out the door of the office.

Mark replied, "Yes. Stuart's his name. He graduated a year before me at Cambridge. We became friends there. He's in law too."

"Yes, I heard. A rather radical fellow. Best you watch your associations, Mark. Stuart's the son of an ex-con—" Matt stopped short, seemed slightly abashed. When Mark smiled, Matthew smiled too. "Well," he said, changing the subject. "You seem to be busy enough."

Mark had stood when his father entered and he had noticed with satisfaction that Matthew flicked an approving gaze over his dress. Mark was wearing the gentleman's summer suit of white linen waistcoat and trousers, white ruffled shirt, and brown boots. He had been sitting at his tall clerk's desk on a tall stool, with law books and courtroom records spread out on the desk before him. Yes, he must have looked every inch the solicitor to his father. "I *am* busy, sir."

Matthew's blue eyes flashed as he nodded. "I saw Fitzhugh up the street. He told me that he is having you work up your first case. Anything interesting?"

Mark grinned. "Routine and boring to Fitzhugh, exciting for me. I've been in New South Wales two weeks and this is my first case, a civil suit."

138

"Ah. Some poor laborer was hired for a certain wage by a big landowner, but when it came time for the landowner to pay him, he offered less than he had promised for the job?"

"Aye. An old story. And landowners always win because they or their friends run the judicial system in this colony. But I intend for our client to win."

Matthew studied him approvingly with a father's discerning eye. "Good luck."

Mark was standing at attention, just as he had done as a lad, wondering to what he owed the honor of this visit from his father.

"This is your birthday."

Mark grinned again. "Today I am a man."

"I spoke with Fitzhugh about your having a tankard of stringy bark with me at the wharf house tavern. I've business to talk over with you. *Your* business."

Mark hated to relinquish the time. Getting into his first case had whetted his appetite for success, and he hated giving up even an hour of time on it. But it wasn't often he got to talk with his father, and at the thought his face flushed with pleasure. "And Fitz said?"

"That indeed you may come along with me. He told me to tell you to take your time, and to lock the door, please, when you leave."

Smiling, Mark walked over to the crooked coat tree by the door and removed his white linen coat. He shrugged into it, buttoned the front, took his cabbage tree hat down from the coat rack and put it on. Another flicker from Matthew's eyes showed that he approved of his son's appearance. He approved but would never voice it, of course.

Matthew put on his beaver hat and waited on the street as Mark locked the outside door to Fitzhugh's

Law Firm. Father and son walked in silence down Macquarie Street. This was the first time Matthew had treated Mark as a man. And he was a man now, for today Mark Aylesbury was twenty-one.

As they walked, Mark caught a glimpse of the look on his father's face, one he had seen there before—his pride and satisfaction in how Governor Macquarie had come in and set things right in the colony. The dirt streets had been straightened, the tree stumps pulled out, holes filled in. Fine brick and stone buildings had been erected. The hospital was one of them. And there were dozens of others, many built by Macquarie's favorite architect, an emancipist named Greenway.

"Good day, Dr. Aylesbury, sir," greeted a passing gentleman.

"G'day, Mr. Farnsworth," Matthew replied.

Mark nodded to the man and felt his chest swell a little at the look of respect the gentleman had given his father. He longed to receive that same look of respect. And vowed for the thousandth time that someday, he would.

They paused where Hunter Street intersected with Macquarie and let a carriage pass.

"I never told you about the small legacy your mother left you, Mark."

Mark jerked a look at his father. "Legacy? That little hut she lived in?"

"She left you everything she owned."

Mark felt ashamed he had spoken so quickly and nodded.

"With what I was able to get out of selling the hut and the inventory plus the interest it has accumulated in the bank, the entire sum, including the trust fund I set up for you, amounts to a little over five thousand pounds."

"Five thou—" Mark stopped and gaped at his father, who kept walking without breaking his stride. Mark caught up to him again, controlling his surprise and delight with effort. "It's much more than I thought."

"Until Simeon Lord started up his hat factory, your mother was the only person in the colony who made hats. And once Macquarie arrived and got rid of the barbarous rum corps, your mother did very well as a milliner. You aren't rich, but you have enough for a good start. Buy a house first, Mark. Fine homes are being built in the colony now. If you can't buy one someone has built and abandoned, have one built for yourself. But on several acres. I think Sydney will continue to grow, but in case we have currency problems again, you should have land. You can't fail if you have a few acres for farming or grazing."

They stopped in front of the Bank of New South Wales. "Let's go in. I've a release to sign so that you can draw on your trust funds, and you must leave your signature."

Mark was almost dizzy with delight. He had had no idea the little hut that had contained his mother's millinery shop would bring more than a few pounds. It probably hadn't, but the interest had accumulated, and with the fund his father had set up also drawing interest—

They signed the release before the grinning banker. Mark left his signature beneath his father's.

Dr. Matthew Aylesbury
Mark Troop Aylesbury

And soon they were back out on the street again.

"G'day, Dr. Aylesbury," said a passerby as they stood in front of the bank.

"Morning, Mr. Rucker," Matthew said.

141

As Mark nodded to the gentleman, it occurred to him for the first time that a doctor received a great deal of respect from people, once he had established his practice. Jealousy reared its ugly head. "I had no idea you were so prominent, Father. Perhaps I should have been a doctor." Like Aaron.

A sudden flash of anger flushed Matthew's face, but it subsided quickly. "A solicitor such as yourself, or a barrister, as Dr. Wentworth's son is to become, receive recognition much more quickly, Mark. A doctor has to prove he's not a quack first. Besides, being a nongovernment doctor in a government hospital treating no one but convicts is *not* how people came to know me. It was from my trade. And my friendship with Macquarie."

Mark blushed and felt ashamed. Mentally he kicked himself for not realizing that. It seemed no matter how much he tried to show his father how he respected him, it just never turned out quite right. But he was feeling the warm glow of currency in his purse on the inside pocket of his coat and pressed his hand there. In the bank, *five thousand pounds.*

Matthew looked around him. "Mark, I really didn't want a glass of stringy bark. While I'm in Sydney I need to get down to Campbell's and go over some receipts for cargo that came in yesterday. And you really should get back to work."

Mark looked at his father, feeling a sudden sting of disappointment. For the first time his father had treated him like a man and he had been looking forward to taking slops with him at the tavern. "Yes. I suppose I should." Disappointment choked off his words, but his father didn't seem to notice.

Instead, Matt held out his hand and Mark took it. "Have a pleasant birthday, son. Your mum and grandmum are planning a feast for you Sunday."

"Thank you, sir."

Then he left. Mark watched him, a tall handsome figure of a man dressed in blue coat, white trousers, a beaver hat on his head, nodding to everyone he met on the street.

Mark took a deep breath of the damp salt air of the sea. The street where he stood sloped down to Sydney cove, Port Jackson, the indigo sea. Sydney had grown since he was a boy. Bark, slab, and wattle and daub huts had been replaced by white rectangular houses with red-tiled or shingle roofs. Some houses had two stories, others were built on one floor. The larger houses sported verandas across the front, just as most of the farmhouses did away from the city. Macquarie had encouraged fences both in the towns and in the country. He did not like animals wandering about the streets to trespass into gardens and orchards or to pollute the tank stream, so Sydneyites and farmers along the Hawkesbury built fences. In town people had built picket fences, and in the country they had built dog-leg fences for their livestock.

Sydney was built on low hills, and on the top of three of them brick windmills turned in the breezes off the cove. Nowadays one could tell the convicts from the settlers and emancipists; for the newly arrived convicts wore canary-yellow uniforms, while ticket-of-leave convicts or those well cared for by their employers wore gray. From where Mark stood now, he could count six different types of uniformed soldiers, some wearing red coats, others wearing blue, both wearing white trousers and tall beaver hats. An occasional bushman appeared on the streets dressed in coarse cloth and sporting a kangaroo-skin hat. There were more carriages on the streets than had been there before he and Aaron left for England, though not as many as they had seen in England.

When they had left five years ago there had been only four or five carriages in the entire colony. Mark had even seen a coach and four the day before.

Mark nodded to a gentleman who passed by. "G'day, sir."

The man was obviously a gentleman of high breeding and he simply gave Mark an indignant look and passed on without speaking.

Mark smiled. One didn't speak to people one did not know. One might be a convict. His smile turned to a grimace as he realized for the first time that the upper-class exclusionists in the colony, those who had never been convicts, were much more snobbish than the upper-class citizens in England. Well, la-de-da, you bloody bludger, he thought. Someday, you'll look at me and either cheer or cross the street to the other side to avoid me, but you *will* notice me. You *will* recognize Mark Aylesbury.

Sydney. Mark spread his large hands over his breast where the forty pounds were that he had just drawn out of the bank. He would take his father's advice. Look for a house that was appropriate for a young solicitor. One with land, though he had no interest in land, either to farm it or graze it. He would purchase clothing, good clothing, the kind that distinguished a prominent citizen. He would set about conscientiously establishing his reputation as a gentleman and a solicitor in the colony. He would be rich someday. For he had an excellent start: an education given to him by his father, an excellent financial legacy given by his mother.

And . . . his blue eyes traveled north and east. He would attain—no, *obtain*—the thing he wanted above all else, she whom he had desired from the first time he had seen her. He would have her for his own, take her to himself where no man, including Aaron,

144

would ever be able to have her. Mark smiled to himself and nodded. The time had finally come—and not a moment too soon, either. He would immediately begin a campaign to win her. She of his most exotic dreams. Penelope.

Elaina Cranston's gown made swishing sounds as she walked. Normally she would not be wearing this brocaded silk from India, so easily obtainable in New South Wales, but today she was feeling poorly again and she did not care to waste one of her better afternoon gowns by wearing it when she didn't look her best. The messenger had delivered a letter and Elaina hoped it was what she thought. As she broke the seal she approached the drawing room where Penelope had moved her harp, and read the note.

"Ah. Just as I had hoped."

Penelope looked up from her harp strings. They had moved her harp into the living room because the dancing master was using the ballroom. Penelope was having trouble adjusting to the copper tips on her fingers. Perhaps she never would, for a harpist felt the music through her fingertips, and though they did not hamper her playing, she fancied she could not get into the mood of her pieces when playing with the copper tips. Her disgruntled thoughts focused on her mother who was smiling her strange smile. Elaina Cranston had a strange mouth because her upper lip did not move, giving her an elfish smile. But she was still beautiful, with her green eyes and dark hair, where secret red lights shone. Penelope had a distinct feeling that her mother had many secrets. Mother and daughter were not much more familiar with each other than strangers. Penelope had been nursed and raised by a

convict nurse, a woman who had lost her own child and had been assigned to the Cranstons shortly after for the purpose of wet-nursing the infant Penelope. The woman had been Penelope's nurse for five years, until she died. Elaina regarded her daughter with resigned tolerance, and Penelope sensed she was somehow a weapon that Elaina held in readiness against her husband.

Elaina's beautiful eyes lighted on Penelope now. "The Phyfes are giving a ball in honor of the Braxtons. We are invited, of course."

Penelope smiled a little. Perhaps a ball might break the boredom, after all. Aaron had been gone now for two weeks. The time had sat upon her heavily, insufferable as the dry heat of summer.

"I hesitate to go because the Phyfes tend to invite emancipists to their doings. However, a ball doesn't roll around often enough in the colony for one to be very discriminating." Elaina tapped the note on the palm of her hand. "Besides, the Aylesburys will be going, no doubt, and—" Her eyes cut over to Penelope, and she paused. "And I do wish the young Australians wouldn't take over everything these days. They crowd the reception hall floors and start arguments with their elders. Our friends' sons and daughters aren't a bit more respectful than the emancipists' offspring." Elaina sighed for the days gone by, the days of her youth. "Well, I've the new satin from London to wear, and if I don't attend a ball soon it will be out of fashion."

"It probably already is," Penelope said. "By the time gowns arrive from London, the fashions have changed. That's why I prefer Frances Aylesbury's gowns."

Elaina looked at her and her peculiar smile widened. "I know the *real* reason you prefer

146

Frances Aylesbury's gowns."

Penelope might have blushed two weeks ago, but now her chin came up, softly defiant. "Five years ago you and the rest of the colony's elite preferred her gowns also."

"That was before ships arrived as frequently as they do now. Five years ago we were also wearing these gowns from the Orient while we really longed for the French fashions. We were also at war, if you'll recall. But now it's the London label we want." Elaina's eyes flashed. "It would serve you well if you used Miss Aylesbury only for your riding frocks and everyday gowns. And while we're discussing Aylesburys, I might remind you that Mark Aylesbury is beneath your station."

Penelope could not contain the smile that crept to her own mouth. It was just like her mother to guess wrong.

"It's not Mark whom I admire," she could not help but reply.

Snap went the cold eyes of Elaina. "Surely not the other one, the one who looks like his mother."

"His name is Aaron." Penelope watched her. She had seen her mother looking at Dr. Aylesbury when they were in town, and she wondered if there had been something between them long ago. If there had been, Dr. Aylesbury had certainly forgotten about it!

Elaina Cranston's mouth turned up at the corners. "I swear, you've as much taste as your—as Oliver. If you must dream of a gentleman who is beneath you, Mark is the handsomer of the two."

Penelope stood up abruptly. "Because he resembles his father?"

Elaina's mouth flew open in horror and was still open when Penelope walked past her to leave the living room. Two weeks ago, I wouldn't have spoken

147

to her like that, Penelope thought as she entered the hallway. But I am no longer a girl. I am a woman. Aaron made me a woman with his love, and I'll not be a child again.

Penelope intended to go out, to have Cricket saddle Bayleaf and to ride to see her father's shaggy, hairy sheep, but the barely controlled exasperation in Mr. Pettybone's voice caused her to pause, to turn and approach the ballroom—the reception hall, her mother persisted in calling it.

"No, no, no, Master James," the dancing master wailed. "A gentleman does not touch his heels on the floor at all, like a—like a—"

"Hawkesbury duck?"

Penelope bit her lip to keep from laughing. Quiet, thoughtful Jamey conserved words like a miser, then played them like cards in a game of cribbage at just the right time. She watched as Mr. Pettybone made a show of pulling his own hair out.

This was the trait in Jamey that dismayed her parents, this quiet disdain for anything that smacked of "culture," to which he somehow did not belong.

The dancing master gestured to his assistant, who prided himself on his patience. After all, if one assisted the only dancing master in New South Wales in teaching the currency lads and lassies to dance, those sons and daughters of ex-convicts who had been transported here at one time and now wanted to become cultured, one had to be patient. But he had not dreamed that teaching an exclusionist's son to dance would be so devastating to his good nature. The assistant placed his bow on the strings of his violin again and began playing the waltz for the fifteenth time as Mr. Pettybone tutored. "One, two, three. One, two, three. One, two, three. Now, please turn, one, two, three—" Mr. Pettybone stopped. "No,

no, no, no. One cannot rock back and forth like a—
a—"

"Abandoned boat in the river?"

Pettybone nodded vigorously. "Exactly. A gentleman must turn, whirl the lady 'round," he said
twirling. "A dip and a sway would not break your
back, either. Master James. Da, ta, ta, da, ta, ta," sang
the dancing master, in his old-fashioned knee-length
breeches, stockings, and swallow-tailed coat, as he
dipped and swayed.

James Cranston, aged twelve, stood with a slight,
lazy smile on his lips, his light brown eyes glinting
with some inner thoughts no one would ever hear
spoken.

The master stopped abruptly when he saw Penelope in the doorway, his angry, panicked expression
changing to sweetness. "Miss Penelope!" he said,
gliding toward her. "Miss Penelope!" he said again
and captured her hand, planting a chaste kiss upon
it. "Oh *do* speak to your brother about his steps. He
cannot seem to learn them, and if he doesn't learn to
waltz he'll never learn the minuet!"

Penelope was already smiling at her old dancing
teacher, and she truly felt sympathy for him.
Teaching Jamey to dance must be like teaching a
kangaroo. "Minuet? Why not a quadrille?" she said
teasingly.

Mr. Pettybone held his head in his hands.
"Quadrille! A peasant's dance. And he would not be
able to do that, either. Master James has no rhythm."

Laughing, Penelope went into the room smiling
at her brother, her friend and confidant. "Rhythm?"
she said. "Jamey," placing her hands on her hips,
"Are you a gentleman?"

James Cranston was not slow. He bowed deeply.
"Miss Cranston," he said. "May I have the pleasure

of this dance?"

"Certainly you may," she replied.

James grasped her waist and hand, and the assistant to the dancing master began the waltz for the sixteenth time. Jamey proceeded to steer his sister back and forth, back and forth, turning her once like a bullock turning a millstone, his expression extremely grim.

Penelope pressed her lips together to keep from laughing, but finally exploded. "Jamey. It's a matter of rhythm and it's a matter of relaxing, too. You're so intense. You have rhythm when you ride a horse, don't you? Your body movements match his gait, and you are happy when you ride. Oh!" Penelope clenched her teeth from the pain in her foot upon being trampled by his boot.

He released her. "I'm sorry, Penelope," Jamey said, abashed. "I'm sorry. It just won't work. I can't dance, don't even want to."

Penelope paused and released him. "It will work, and you must learn." She turned to the assistant to the dancing master. "Please play a waltz that's just a bit faster, something by Weber, perhaps."

Mr. Pettybone, with tight lips to show his intense disapproval, ordered his assistant to play a vigorous waltz from *Invitation to Dance*, by Weber. Without hesitation, his assistant rolled his eyes up into his head and began.

Penelope looked at her handsome young brother with his bushy black brows, his blue-black hair, and saw her father as he might have looked as a boy. Her father was a graceful dancer, and so could Jamey be. "We shall begin again."

With the expression of a chained convict, Jamey took his sister's hand and placed his other hand on

150

her waist.

"You are riding, Jamey," she said. "You are riding far and away, perhaps across the Blue Mountains, and before you is a great wide plain with only a few trees. There are no stumps, no wombat holes, nothing but smooth grass as far as you can see."

Jamey frowned, shut his eyes, and began to move.

"One, two, three. One, two, three," Mr. Pettybone called.

"And you are riding a magnificent horse, sleek and shining. One of Thaddeus Crawford's best. You are cantering. Cantering, Jamey, across that flat, wide, open country beyond the mountains."

"One, two, three. One, two, three . . ."

As Jamey waltzed, his body changed. It loosened, his feet became pounds lighter. Yes, and he could feel the wind in his face, the rhythm of the horse beneath him, a slower canter than usual, but sailing over a hill, turning into a draw. He whirled Penelope, his eyes shut, a slight smile on his face.

The assistant played and Mr. Pettybone called out, "One, two, three. Dip, sway, *lean.*"

Jamey's horse ran into a dry creek and up on the other side. And there was nothing but rolling hills and grass. *And on a hill stood a beautiful woman, the wind blowing her blue-black hair. . . .*

Penelope laughed. Jamey's eyes flickered open. He stared at his sister.

"I do believe you thought you were riding across that plain, Jamey," she said as they waltzed.

He was frowning in bewilderment as his eyes focused upon her face. "I was," he said. He did not tell her about the beautiful woman he had imagined, with dark, dark hair and shockingly blue eyes. "I will ride there someday," he said. "I'll ride and ride, after

Father's cattle, perhaps, somewhere where I don't have to dance." He smiled. "Yes, Penny. I was on the other side of the mountains, riding."

Penelope kept smiling, looking beyond his shoulder dreamily. "And so was I, Jamey, and so was I," she said.

Awesome quiet. A sapphire haze. A chasm deep and wide bristling with thick forest. The brilliant yellow shock of wattle blooming like paint spattered on a carpet of green. Perpendicular cliffs, white and gold and forbidding. Above, the sky was azure blue, with clouds like shredded fleece. God's breath blew cool here.

Aaron longed for Penelope to see this sight. As children they had played the explorers and fancied they climbed these mountains, even as in reality they gazed upon their hazy ridges. Then, no white man had found this treacherous pass through the Great Dividing Range, and in their fantasy he and Penelope had thrilled at being the first. Only now men had found a way. Convicts had built a road through it, treacherous and steep, so precipitous that the horses had to be let down by ropes to keep them from slipping on the steep road with their heavy packs and falling into the chasms below. She must see this wild beauty, their wild fancy as it really was.

The expedition party would be through the mountains tomorrow, Buck had said, to arrive in the Macquarie plains. Their progress had been a little slower than usual because Buck had insisted on hunting along the way to supplement their provisions. Finding mobs of kangaroo or wallabies or emu on the other side of the mountain was not guaranteed

at all, he had said. So when a small mob of rock wallabies appeared near Springwood, he shot several, and the men dressed them and cut the meat into thin, narrow strips, which they hung on small racks upon the pack horses to dry. All of it took time.

The ascent into the mountains with its wild wilderness beauty had taken two days. Winding over the road, stopping at Springwood and Blackheath, and hunting and dressing the wallabies all had taken time. On their fourth day, they saw the Vale of Clwyd, with its wild, breathtaking beauty. Aaron had drunk in the wilderness scenery and became intoxicated by it. His awe was accompanied by the echoing clatter of hooves on rock, the clanking of rigging and provisions, the occasional blowing of the horses, better to him than any music, and he knew Buck felt the same, had seen it in the near-fanatic gleam in his squinting eyes.

Now as Aaron stood with boot propped on a boulder and looked down into the vale below, he was thinking there was only one thing wrong with this savage beauty, and that was that other men had seen it before. To him it was no longer virgin country.

That something within him that wanted to see country no other white man had seen rose up in him like passion for a woman. The country, the vast country beyond these mountains and beyond the explored areas around the Bathurst district, drew him, drew the soul of him like a siren song.

He liked being alone like this, though he knew the others were in the camp just several hundred feet away. "Don't go wandering off in ta bush, lad," Glenn Moffett had cautioned. "A man can get lost not fifty feet from camp."

As a child Aaron had wanted to explore this realm,

which Matthew Flinders had first called Australasia and Macquarie had insisted on calling Australia. But now, as a man, Aaron had an even bigger reason for wanting to participate in an expedition into the lonely wilderness, to go into the wilderness where no white man had ever gone before. His soul needed healing.

He needed desperately to immerse himself in the purifying silence, to smother in nature, to try to discover God again, the God who had vanished in the hospitals of England amongst the cries of dying children, the warping, twisting diseases of old people, the stinking sicknesses of mankind. He had not been born to become a doctor, because he had not been born to accept disease, dying, and death.

"No one has," his professor, Dr. Radcliff, had told him. "That's part of what you're being trained for."

So they had baptized him in the hell of other people's misery. He had emerged shaken, but he had emerged. Many had not. But in his soul there still festered the wound in his faith, the faith in his own immortality. So he must come to these mountains, to that vast thing beyond them that Glenn called "outback," seeking a cure.

He had not told anyone of that festering sore in his soul, not even Penelope. Nor would he ever.

"Coo-ee-ee-ee!"

Aaron, smiling a little, turned, looked up the slope toward camp. Above the camp, towering cliffs reflected the dying light of day.

"Coo-ee-ee-ee!"

It was Buck calling the ancient call of the natives. It meant, "Come here." He must learn to do it like Buck. It was an untamed sound, a sound that carried far and when heard caused the pores to open and the

heart to beat faster. Aaron tilted back his head and cupped his hands around his mouth and called back, "Coo-ee-ee-ee!"

The cliffs echoed back his call like impatient spirits. Aaron felt a knifeblade thrill slice through his loneliness. His boyhood dream was coming true.

Chapter VIII

Mark had never forgotten his position in the New South Wales society, but two things would have reminded him had he forgotten: his fanatic friend Stuart Mays, and balls such as this one, where the host and hostess had friends from both social strata.

"Look at 'em, Mark. It's been this way for thirty-two years. The pure merinos keep carefully to themselves," Stuart said.

Mark was watching. The Phyfes' was an enormous house, with a large ballroom. Tonight the ballroom was crowded, lit by chandeliers holding dozens of candles and by lanterns in sconces along the walls. Ladies dressed in high-waisted pastel dresses danced on the polished floor like pieces of fruit bobbing in a punchbowl.

The Phyfes had hired the band, an amalgamation of members from the military band, who volunteered to play at parties for a fee. They were dressed in their uniforms, blue coats with white trousers, eight in all, sitting on a platform the Phyfes had made for this affair.

Mark had just arrived with Stuart and Jory McWilliams. They had been greeted formally at the

156

door by the Phyfes' doorman and then announced. No one but a few tittering currency lasses sitting against the wall waiting for an invitation to dance paid much attention to the young currency lads' arrival. Someday they would notice, Mark was thinking irritably. Someday when Mark Aylesbury's name was announced, they would stop and look at him. Some would cheer. Someday.

Now he stood with the young men he had gone to school with in Parramatta as a boy. As young tradesmen and apprentices in the colony, they had gravitated to the taverns together since his arrival from England. They were standing with him now. Mark Aylesbury, solicitor, one of the only currency lads in the colony to have been educated abroad.

The emancipists called the upper-class English-born of the colony who had never been convicts "pure merinos," the Merino being the favored sheep in the colony, the blue bloods of sheepdom. The pure merinos referred to themselves as the exclusionists.

"We segregate ourselves," Bob Olsen said. Olsen was another young man in the huddle of young men standing near the door that opened out onto the front veranda. "We are as loath to mix 'n mingle with them pure merinos as they be with us currency lads and lasses."

"What else can you expect?" Stuart said after tasting the glass of ruby-red punch in his hand. "They are full citizens of Britain and our parents aren't. And neither will our parents ever be, unless we fight for it."

"Ah, it galls me soul to think we shall live all our lives in another Britain," put in Jory McWilliams. Jory's father was an ex-convict who had participated in an Irish rebellion near Castle Hill eighteen years before and had only recently been pardoned, after

spending the eighteen years at Newcastle on the Hunter River.

Mark was observing how the English-born swells kept carefully aloof from those men and women who formed New South Wales's middle class—the emancipists—even though many of the emancipists had risen to prominence and wealth greater than some of the pure merinos. And from where the group of young men stood, if one did not know the people involved, one could not tell one class from another. Most of the emancipists who had been transported for crimes in England to New South Wales had earned their pardons, then gone on to make a fortune in trade, farming and stock raising. But they had no voice whatever in government. They had no say in politics. This had irritated Mark for years because it galled his father so.

There on the ballroom floor currency lassies danced the minuet with currency lads and emancipists danced with their own or another emancipist's wife. No pure merino's son deigned to dance with a currency lass and no currency lad dared dance with a pure merino's daughter. Mark's face burned with indignation.

"Phyfe has a powder keg here tonight," Stuart said, amused. His black eyes glinted with barely suppressed eagerness—for what, Mark wasn't sure.

Mark's eyes had never left Penelope since he entered the ballroom, though his mind was a muddle of thoughts at the moment. His gaze moved slowly over the guests in the room. He knew that none of the Crawfords had been invited, though, amusingly, the Crawfords had never been convicts and were actually pure merinos themselves. But they had one black sheep in their flock. Deen Crawford. If someone like the Phyfes were to invite a Crawford to their party,

they would have to invite all the Crawfords and they would have to invite Deen. And whoever heard of a native—even a half-native—mingling socially with the colonists, except in the capacity of a servant. Such as the grinning young natives who were working in the Phyfes' kitchen serving refreshments.

Only Milicent was invited—having married Matthew Aylesbury, she was now an Aylesbury. Mark's face burned again. Still he did not take his eyes off Penelope Cranston for long.

"Wouldn't New South Wales quake if one of us invited a pure merino to dance?" Stuart said close to Mark's ear.

Sometimes Mark thought Stuart was the devil in himself. He looked at him slowly.

"You've eyes for no one but the Cranston lass, Mark, but you've no chance. Between Weldon Braxton and Rodney Livingston, she's well occupied."

Mark looked at Penelope again, gowned in a white dress made of some sort of floating material gathered just beneath her breasts, trimmed in ribbon the color of emeralds. Her dark, lustrous hair was caught up in folds at the crown of her head, showing a neck of exquisite alabaster, with wisps curling round her perfectly shaped face, which was now flushed with the exertions of the minuet. The bodice of her dress was scooped low, just enough to show the beginning of the cleavage of her breasts. And she seemed exquisitely happy. Laughing, cheeks pink . . .

"There's only one man truly paying court to her," Stuart observed. "Livingston. Braxton is only interested in demonstrating himself. All dash and verve, isn't he?"

Mark smiled wryly. The party was being given for the Braxtons and much of the guests' attention was

on the Braxton's handsome, pompous son. In England, Weldon Braxton might not have elicited more than a glance, but he was cutting a dashing figure amongst the young ladies here, as he danced extravagantly in his beautifully tailored suit. He dipped and swayed and postured, all calculated to attract attention to himself.

Jory McWilliams nodded his reddish-blond head. "Ain't 'ee gorgeous?"

"He thinks he is," said Gib Riley.

Mark smiled then, noticing his father cutting a handsome figure of his own, dancing with Simeon Lord's wife, as a good emancipist should. He looked at his stepmother, Milicent, still beautiful in a striking dark brown gown sewn, no doubt, by Frances Aylesbury. There was Oliver Cranston too, keeping to his crowds of merinos and talking business, probably about the expedition. And Mrs. Cranston dancing every dance with other pure merinos. She was a beautiful woman, too, and Mark hadn't missed her look of approval when he entered. In fact, she was about the only other merino woman who had even looked at him.

Macquarie was responsible for the rise in prominence of the emancipists. He had invited pure merinos and emancipists both to his own dinners and balls. Phyfe had taken the ex-governor's admonitions to heart that the colony must socially recognize the emancipists who had risen to some sort of prominence in the colony. Matthew Aylesbury had risen to that prominence because of his success in trade, his selfless devotion to Parramatta hospital—and because Governor Macquarie had boosted him there.

It exasperated Mark that men like his father were considered unacceptable to sit on any judicial court

160

and incapable of electing their own legislators. They had absolutely no voice in their government, and in the courts were completely at the mercy of the upper social strata. The exclusionists—the pure merinos—were the ruling class who were trying to make a new England out of New South Wales, a class system of lords to rule over the peasants. Mark was damned if he'd not put up a fight against them.

"Don't you see a lass who strikes your fancy, Mark?" Stuart asked, his black eyes gleaming with mischief. "A currency lass, of course. You wouldn't dare dance with a merino."

Mark looked coolly at Stuart. "I'm waiting for a waltz," he said. He couldn't do the minuet. That was a dance for old, upper-class Englishmen.

As if in answer to his statement the minuet ceased. Livingston, with whom Penelope Cranston had been dancing, escorted her to the refreshment table. The band rearranged their music and began a waltz. Mark didn't know the name of it; he was no musician, but he saw Penelope refuse a dance with one of Livingston's merino friends. Mark straightened, handed his glass of punch to Stuart, and said, "Excuse me."

Then, as his twelve friends stood watching, Mark, with eyes wide and mouth tight, began to make his way through the crowd of guests saying, "Pardon me. Pardon me. Thank you. May I pass, please? Thank you," and came finally to stand before Penelope. Out of the corner of his eye he saw the young merinos step back as he bowed to her. "Miss Cranston, I'm sure minuets are very tiring, but this waltz is a slow one and I'd be pleased if you would share it with me."

It was as if a light had been turned on behind Penelope's face.

161

"Mark!" she exclaimed delightedly. "Yes, I'd love to."

And he was leading her to the center of the floor, leaving the huddle of shocked pure merinos to gape and glower behind.

Mark had no illusions about Penelope's delight. He knew she preferred him over the other young men only because he was Aaron's brother. He had no intention of changing the delight, only the reason for it. Aaron had had his chance; now he would have his. Who had said, "Love sought is good, but given unsought is better"? Shakespeare, probably. Shakespeare had said everything else that made any sense, and a lot that didn't. Mark liked the way she was looking at him, liked it very much. But—

Penelope felt like embracing Mark. He had delivered her from another dance with Weldon Braxton and Rodney Livingston or one of the other boring young men. "Have you any word of Aaron?"

"Eleven."

Penelope raised her brows as he swung her around between the crowd of waltzing gentlemen and ladies forming a kaleidoscope of pastel colors, brown and black suits, blue and red uniforms. "I beg your pardon?" she asked. "Eleven what?"

"Seconds. It took you eleven seconds to ask about Aaron."

Penelope laughed delightedly. "Why, you counted!"

"Yes, I did."

She smiled up at him. His was a handsome face, broad, pleasant. And he was dressed in the latest fashion in men's evening wear, black frock coat, black trousers, white ruffled shirt, cream-colored waistcoat. He looked good and danced well, but Penelope was noticing the look of shock on the faces

162

of young and old alike when they saw her dancing with him.

"No, we've not heard from Aaron," he said. "He's been gone only a month. We expect him to be gone perhaps two or three more weeks yet."

Penelope's face smoothed out. "I know. I just thought that Deen—"

"Deen hasn't heard either."

They fell silent and it occurred to Penelope that she and Mark had never had much to say to each other. He had never seemed interested in the games she and Aaron played, had never seemed interested in tracking and trapping and playing with the little wild creatures they found. He had seldom joined them in their play, but had often watched with a detached interest. He had always been on the fringes of their activities, as if he were . . . waiting.

". . . lovely tonight, Penelope."

Her attention came back to the present. "I'm sorry. I didn't hear what you said."

"Your mind was many miles away. I said you're very lovely tonight." Mark grinned quickly. To-night? You have always been beautiful to me, he thought.

Penelope smiled. "Thank you. May I return the compliment?"

"If you return that exact compliment I would certainly take a better look at myself in a good mirror at the first available moment and have some alterations done to my appearance."

She laughed.

"But now the waltz is ended. Do you care to dance again?"

Penelope was feeling the effect of dancing every dance and said, "Please. I would like to sit a while and I'm awfully thirsty." But placing a hand on his

arm she added, "But I'd like to sit with you."

Mark kept the delight out of his face as he gestured gallantly toward the long linen-covered table near the veranda door.

Once he had gotten them both a glass of punch, Mark escorted her to a chair and sat down beside her.

"It's terribly selfish of me to take up all your time, Mark. I know you must have a special lass you want to dance with, but if you'll sit with me through this one dance, I shall release you and not claim any more of your attention tonight. I promise."

Mark stared at her incredulously, his glass of punch poised in midair. "I have a lass, yes. And I'm pleased to sit with you, Penelope."

"Wonderful." This was as close to Aaron as she could get, and although she was feeling a little guilty for taking so much of Mark's time, she just could not let him go yet. He was Aaron's brother, and she did not want to relinquish even that. Also, she had not missed the glares the young "pure merinos" crowd were giving Mark. It had not occurred to her when Mark asked her to dance that he was crossing a social barrier. She had only been glad to see him.

She looked across the ballroom floor at the dancers dancing the new waltz. She smiled delightedly. "Oh look, Mark. You seem to have set a precedent."

Mark followed her gaze with his. They watched amazed and amused as Penelope's father asked Milicent Aylesbury to dance, relinquishing Penelope's mother and virtually leaving her in Matthew Aylesbury's arms.

"My God! Oh, sorry, Penelope," Mark said grinning quickly. "But I've suspected for a long time that your father . . . uh . . ."

Penelope laughed softly. "That he admires your mother? So have I. And look at your father's face. He

164

doesn't like my mother much."

Mark and Penelope laughed conspiratorially.

"I have a theory," Penelope said. "Something happened back in England between your father and my mother."

"What do you imagine happened?"

"We'll never know, but this I do know. My mother nearly swoons when anyone mentions your father's name."

"Ah, but it's all for nought. I have never seen two adults so smitten with each other as my father and stepmother. You'd think by now they would have grown just a little tired of each other."

Penelope gasped. "Oh no! If two people love each other, how can they ever grow tired of each other?"

Mark looked at her steadily for a long time, but she had turned to watch the dancers again.

Penelope delighted in watching her father as he swung Mrs. Aylesbury about. He was talking to her, the admiration—no, it was love—was evident on his face. Mrs. Aylesbury smiled politely, seemingly unaware of how she was affecting him. And Dr. Aylesbury, so handsome for an older man, had a smile on his mouth that was more of a grimace than a smile, and there was thunder in his eyes. Her mother had gone simpering and silly.

"Oh it's so silly," Penelope said. "They're too old to play such games."

"They're forty-five and more," Mark agreed. "You'd think they would have more dignity by now."

"I don't think older people feel love with as much intensity as younger people do."

He was looking at her, the pupils of his eyes dilated, gone dark. "Neither do I."

It was then Penelope saw it, what Mark was

feeling, saw how much he loved her, and it came as a complete surprise. Her lips parted as he took a sip of his punch, not taking his eyes from hers. It was a moment of shock for Penelope as she stared into his eyes. Mark stopped breathing, the glass still on his lips. Then something jolted him, causing him to spill the punch down the front of his coat.

Rodney Livingston regained his balance and said with a smirk, "Sorry, Aylesbury. I must have stumbled." He bowed to Penelope. "So clumsy of me." And he was off.

Astonished, Penelope whipped the handkerchief from her sleeve and wiped the punch from Mark's coat and waistcoat while he glared after Livingston. "Oh, how awful. I hope it doesn't leave a stain on your waistcoat, Mark. That's strawberry in the punch and sometimes it doesn't come out. If we had water, I would—"

His eyes left Livingston and came back to her. Her touch had awakened something in him and he clasped her wrist. Both froze, smothering in an avalanche of emotions as he held her. Mark's heart began to thud in his chest. "Penelope, I—"

Quickly she stood up. "Mark, please." She did not want to give him the impression that she cared for him. Not in *that* way. "You must know—"

He stood up and looked down at her. "I know nothing that I don't want to know," he said breathlessly. "But I must warn you, I am going to—"

"And I don't want to hear this. Father—"

"—speak with your father about allowing me—"

"He will never allow you—"

"—to see you."

She looked at him, a tiny frown lining her brow, her eyes searched his face. Oh it was there, twelve years of love were there, and she was sorry. So sorry.

166

"Oh, Mark," she whispered. "You *must* know that I—"

The face of Stuart Mays appeared beside Mark's. He inclined his head politely to Penelope, then said to Mark. "I need to speak with you, Mark. A matter has just come up that needs your expertise."

Stuart's words barely touched Mark's consciousness. She had touched him, brushed his waistcoat and shirt with her handkerchief, and it had been like setting the bush on fire. He wanted to breathe her in, into himself, this essence that was Penelope. Some old unspoken resolution hardened in him at that moment.

"You must go," she said.

"No," he answered, not taking his eyes off her, irritated at Stuart for interrupting.

"We need your advice," Stu said. "It's a matter that concerns you . . . personally."

Slowly, Stuart's words sank into his foggy brain. Mark dragged his gaze from Penelope's face to Stuart's. "What?"

Stu's eyes flashed with secret meaning and he said nothing more.

Mark bowed to Penelope. "If the lady will excuse me."

"Of course, of course." Her answer was more a sigh than words.

Mark followed Stuart through the crowd of guests to the door of the veranda where their friends stood—twelve of them now, all currency lads. "It seems that we have a problem." Stuart's dark, conspiratorial eyes flashed around the room and came back to Mark. "We need to discuss how much currency it would take to purchase a mob of sheep."

Mark caught his meaning. "I did not intend to involve you chaps."

"Never mind," Stu said. "What's done is done. And this isn't the first time, as you well know."

"But this will be the best time," Jory McWilliams said, furious. "As for me I ha' been waitin' for this day."

"And I," said Olsen.

"And I," agreed both Herb Jenson and Bob Blake.

Mark looked around at the currency lads. All twelve of them with fire in their eyes. His smile grew in spite of himself. Shades of old Sydney. Shades of school days in Parramatta. "Then let's be negotiating, you blokes," he said.

They moved one by one through the crowd toward the side door of the ballroom, which opened out onto the veranda, leaving the gaily lit ballroom behind. Outside, the stars were fireworks frozen in the sky and the parchment moon was full.

The currency lads found the young merinos waiting in the back dooryard together. Fifteen of them. Beyond the dooryard were fences and cross-fences. Stock penned in their separate paddocks stood or lay drowsing. Horses whinnied when Mark and his friends came to stand before Rodney Livingston and his mob of merinos.

For a moment no one spoke, then Livingston said, "Trying a little taste of forbidden fruit, weren't you, Aylesbury?"

Several in Livingston's crowd jingled coins in their pockets to deride the currency lads.

"Baa-aa-aa," taunted Mark's friends softly.

Mark hooked his thumbs in the pockets of his trousers and put all his weight on one foot. He had known there would be hell to pay for daring to dance with Penelope.

"Forbidden?" he said. "By whom?"

Livingston sneered and turned his head to look at

young Macarthur who stood beside him. "I told you he would pretend innocence. An English education, while advantageous to us, is deleterious to a currency lad's memory." He looked at Mark again. "That's why it is an abomination to send one of them to England for an education. It gives them subliminal ideas."

"It might alter your philosophy a bit to know," Mark said steadily, "that I bloody well had subliminal ideas before I ever went to England for an education."

"All the more reason for us to show you the error of your ways, Aylesbury. To remind you that one of our lasses is off limits to the likes of you."

"Baa-aa-aa," offered someone behind Mark.

The merinos jingled the coins in their pockets.

"Who's going to set the limits?" Mark asked.

"I am." When Livingston began to peel out of his coat, Weldon Braxton, who had been standing wide-eyed on the veranda, stepped toward Livingston saying, "Oh, now! See here! We must not engage in fisticuffs over this. There are other ways to negotiate—"

Mark had his coat half off when Livingston's blow caught him in the jaw and sent him flying backward into Stuart's arms.

Stuart said in his ear, "Go at him, Mark."

In a second Mark was out of his coat and at Livingston's neck. As Mark grabbed him to set him up for a blow to the face, his memory was doing some flashbacks through the prisms of time. He had fought Livingston and others before as a lad at school in Parramatta. He and his friends, the currency lads against the pure merinos' sons. And always Aaron had been in the fray, fighting with him, the two of them side-by-side.

169

The blow to Livingston's grimacing face sent a thrill of pain through his fist, up his arm, into his chest to his gut. A blow to his abdomen knocked the breath out of him, but still he was aware that the others had exploded into the fray. Scuffling, grunting, and sounds like rocks hitting fence rails came to him. White shirts flashed in the moonlight. Mark grimaced and hit Livingston a blow that sent him sprawling onto the ground. But someone grabbed Mark, spun him around, and landed a powerful blow on his jaw, sending him tumbling into the dust beside Livingston, his legs higher than his head.

Then Livingston was on him again, grappling for his throat. Mark threw him off, sprang to his feet, blocked a blow aimed at his abdomen, and threw one of his own, sending Livingston crashing through a fence. Goats ran and leaped from the paddock bleating past the men as they struggled, fighting sprawled in the dust and grunting with their blows.

Somebody crashed into the water trough. But now the convict servants had heard the ruckus and had poured out of their huts to urge on the fight. They stood well to the edge of it, backing up as the fighting area spread out, shaking their fists and shouting.

Mark delivered Livingston a solid blow in the face and Livingston staggered back, then regained his footing. His eyes were black, his face smeared with blood, his teeth flashing in a grimace of pure hate as he crouched and gasped, "Bloody frigging bastard."

Bastard was the key to the dungeon of Mark's deepest fury, because it was true. He was the bastard son of Dr. Aylesbury, and no one had ever tried to protect him from that truth.

Blind rage took over as Mark went at Livingston again, and when the latter finally lay sprawled on the dust of the goat pen, Mark turned, caught Macarthur

as he flew by backward, and gave him a blow to his
face over and over until he did a somersalt in the dust ·
and fell over the fence into the chicken yard. Mark
was on him in a flash. He hit him again and again.
Macarthur's father had caused hell in the colony for
every governor they had ever had, and for that Mark
beat him. Not that he needed an excuse. His next
blow was weak. Exhaustion threatened him now, his
lungs screamed with pain, and a paralyzing stitch
stabbed his side.

Macarthur came at him. Mark caught a blow that
sent him crashing into the chicken pen, and
Macarthur came at him again as he slid down the
wall, half unconscious. But someone came up and
pushed Macarthur aside. A well-aimed kick caught
Mark in the thigh, and that was all it took to revive
him. He was on his feet in a flash. Livingston
pummeled his face, but Mark sent him crashing into
the chicken house again. White bodies exploded
squawking from the chicken house, feathers flew like
flurries of snow.

"Stop! Stop!" someone was shouting. "Stop this at
once!"

Mark caught a glimpse of the older men pouring
out onto the veranda and into the yard. No one paid
them any mind.

Someone beat Mark on the back. Someone threw a
bucket of water on two grappling youths in the dust
of the chicken yard. "Stop! Stop this!"

In a fraction-of-a-second lull, Mark caught a
glimpse of his father on the veranda, hands on his
hips. Not trying to interfere. Mark staggered with
clenched and bloody fists after Livingston. Goats ran
bleating and leaping over wrestling men in the dust,
chickens squawked and fluttered between the feet of
the fighters. An enormous hog with six piglets raced

171

squealing through the yard, and a goose was running after Gib Riley with its wings spread and its neck stretched out.

"Stop! Stop this fighting!"

Someone prodded Mark in the side with a walking stick. "Stop this at once." Mark glanced at Cranston, who was glowering over him, and he remembered that once before, on his first day at the Aylesburys', when he and Aaron had gotten into a fight on the ridge between the Cranston and Aylesbury properties, Cranston had come upon them and had prodded them both with his boot, shouting, "Stop. Stop at once!"

Mark stood up, his chest heaving from his exertions. The cool night air made him take note that his shirt no longer had a right sleeve. Furthermore, what there was of it was blood-spattered and filthy. He had a tear in his trousers at the knee. Panting, he looked with one eye into Cranston's black ones.

"Who started this?" Cranston demanded.

Mark opened his mouth to reply, but Stu was there. "Nobody. We came out for a breath of air and it just happened."

Cranston knew it was a lie, but he saw that none of the youths was going to confess about who had started it. The young men might be on opposite sides of the social barrier, but they would never tell on each other. Cranston stared furiously at Mark for a moment. Mark became aware of the young men rising off the ground wiping blood and dirt from their faces with handkerchiefs or the backs of their hands. It was then he heard the frantic gallop of hooves. Mark turned to see a shadowy figure on horseback riding into the dooryard.

"Dr. Aylesbury! Where is he!" the rider demanded.

The voice was Deen's.

Matthew Aylesbury was already striding across the yard and taking hold of the horse's bit as Deen cried, "It's Grandmum, sir. Something's wrong. I think you'd better come home immediately."

Mark was walking toward him, horror replacing the aches in his body, his head. He saw Matthew turn, saw his eyes fix on his own. "Mark, I'm going with Deen on his horse. You bring Mum with you in the carriage."

Mark nodded dumbly.

Since the fight was over, the young merinos were scattering slowly, the currency lads remaining to ponder their glorious retribution. Milicent Aylesbury was at Mark's side, having heard Deen's shout and Matthew's command. Mark said, "I'll take you home right away, Mum. It's a two-hour drive, so we'd best get going."

Milicent nodded, her face pale, "Yes, Mark, hurry!"

Chapter IX

Mark stood long after the others had left the hillside. The hill was part of the north slope of the ridge separating the Cranstons' and the Crawfords' properties. Overhead the sky was cloudless. A flock of pink-breasted galah winged noisily by chattering among themselves about the stubble field they would settle down in just beyond the ridge.

A breeze came from the west, stirring a curl of hair which fell on Mark's forehead. He raised a hand to his throbbing eye, forgetting that its itching was part of the healing. He touched his split lip and lowered his hand to his side again. Today Elvira Leah Crawford had joined her husband on the hillside, lying beside and beneath the granite marker that read:

Silas P. Crawford
1756-1801

Beyond the new mound of black earth was a smaller marker where a tiny grave, sunken a little now, was lovingly tended. The marker read:

Jessica Rebecca Aylesbury
Our Beloved Daughter
1804-1810

Farther down the slope looking north was another marker, where old Davey O'Shea, the Aylesburys' friend and faithful servant, lay.

Mark could feel Penelope's presence still, though she had departed with the others twenty minutes before. Mr. Cranston and Penelope had come to Grandmum Crawford's funeral, which had surprised Matthew Aylesbury, until he realized that it was for Milicent that Cranston came to pay his respects. So Matthew Aylesbury compromised his own inclinations by ignoring his old foe, instead of ordering him off his land.

Deen had been the last to leave before Mark, and now even he was gone from the hill. Mark let the memory of Penelope's soft green eyes wash over him. "I'm so sorry, Mark. Mrs. Crawford was a lovely lady," she had said.

Yes, she had been a lovely lady, and the only grandmother Mark had ever known, though she was no blood kin of his. He loved her, too. It was Aaron who would grieve the most, though, when he heard of her death. Aaron, whom she had loved more than anyone else on earth. And Buck would grieve when he returned to find his mother gone. But it would be Aaron who would grieve the most.

A little mole of curiosity surfaced cautiously and nibbled at Mark's grief. Grandmum had left a will and testament. He knew that she had named each of her children in that will, and she must surely have named her grandchildren: Ben's children, Aaron, and Deen. But—no. Mark was no blood relation to her at all. Not at all. He was, after all, the bastard son.

Fitzhugh had called the family to meet back at the house after the funeral. They had all gone down the ridge to the house. A glance at the dooryard now showed Mark that they had gone inside. Friends still stood about in huddles in the yard, but the Crawfords had gone into the house; Milicent Crawford Aylesbury, Ben and Becky Crawford, Owen, Thaddeus, Matthew Aylesbury, and even Deen. Even Deen had more right to a portion of the will than Mark. He ran his hand under his nose, blinked back tears, tears of grief and of self-pity, then took a deep breath of early summer air to dilute the depression that clouded his brain. He was remembering the night they had come home from the ball. By the time he and Mum Aylesbury had reached the Aylesbury house that night, Grandmum had been beyond help.

Deen, outside the house, had told Mark, "I had just brought in a load of kindling for the fireplace and Grandmum was sitting in her rocker chair as always. She told me that she needed to go to bed now. I went to help her up, and when she stood up she clutched the front of her gown and frowned. Then I saw her go pale. I carried her to her room. By then her lips were blue. The convicts were abed so I called Mrs. Lacy to stay with Grandmum while I went for Uncle Matthew."

By the time Matthew had arrived, Grandmum was gasping for air. Deen had told Mark that when Matthew went into the bedroom to her, she had been only half conscious, and had confusedly asked, "Is the baby a boy or girl?" Grandmum had given birth to her six children and to numerous other babies who had died at birth or shortly afterward.

Mark had arrived moments later with Milicent and had watched her go to her mother. By then Grandmum had only had strength to reach a hand to

176

her. She had clutched her daughter's hand, but it was to Matthew Aylesbury she had whispered, "Aaron . . . is a good boy." And then, as Mark had watched, she'd seemed to sink deeper into her pillow, and her eyes . . . her eyes had dilated incredibly fast, and became fixed on the ceiling of the room.

Mark blinked back tears again. He had never seen death. Jessica had died with only her mother and father in the room, for he and Aaron had been whisked outside and kept there. He shuddered a little now. Aaron had seen plenty of people die, but he wouldn't talk about it. Mark knew that death wasn't pretty, but for Elvira it had been peaceful, and for that he was thankful.

"Ma-ark!" drifted a voice on the breeze. Dare he look? The little mole nibbled again at his grief. "Ma-ark!" He turned to look down the hill. It was Deen coming up the hill toward him. "C'mon along. It's time."

Time for the reading of the— He pointed to himself. *Me too?*

Deen nodded. "Your father says."

Your father says. Mark turned away from the mound of black earth and put his hat back on. Going down the hill was easier than it had been going up, carrying an incredibly heavy coffin with Grandmum inside.

Aaron . . . is a good boy. It was the last thing she had said. Mark ground his teeth together.

Aaron was a good boy, but Aaron wasn't even home when she died.

Bathurst isn't even a real town, Aaron had written. Macquarie had placed the flag of England there and declared it a township seven years before, but it was

177

only a scattering of sheep runs and sod huts on a wide, undulating plain. The expedition party had come down the western slopes of the Blue Mountains five days after they had left the Crawford farm, then down out of the wild treacherous, breathtakingly beautiful slopes of the Great Dividing Range where the O'Connell plains opened up in a violet mist of morning.

We saw an enormous flock of emu today, Aaron wrote next, *and had a merry chase. Many of the birds are more than six feet tall and they are faster than any horse, but thanks to Buck's unfailing aim, he brought one down with one shot and we had emu leg for tea near the track on the Macquarie plains.*

Then came the wider Bathurst plains, watered by rivers, undulating grassy plains like English parks. They had arrived in the Bathurst district and camped on the property of a man named John Webb, where they stayed for five days letting the horses rest and graze while they rested and attempted to find out about the land to the west and south. Neighbors, the original settlers of the district, came to call on the party, offering food, advice, directions, and rum. The explorers found out that the settlers didn't have the time or the money to go much beyond the district. Besides, there was thick bush all around, and the natives were wild, untamed, and treacherous. This side of the mountain barrier nomadic natives existed who had never seen a white man, and unless a man were well armed, well provisioned, and well accompanied, going into that unknown bush could be fatal. The settlers advised the explorers to hire convict laborers to go along, to help hack a trail through the bush in places where it was too thick for a man and a horse to pass.

Glenn and Jack went to Government House in

Bathurst and hired four convicts whom the super-intendent swore were reliable, while Aaron and Buck took stock of their gear, their provisions, and the condition of their horses. Aaron was pleased that Thaddeus Crawford's sturdy draft horses had stood the trip over the mountains well.

Now, the waiting was unbearable to Aaron. They were about to go into the unknown. Bathurst was the starting point of all the exploring that had been done on the west side of the mountains. For after Bathurst had been declared a town in 1815, a party of explorers led by the Surveyor-General Oxley had followed the Lachlan river westward until it became lost in marshes to the west. They had turned back and gone more south, only to cross land that they had already explored. They had declared the area "desolate, melancholy, and desertlike." Furthermore, he had declared that all the land south of that was useless. His expedition had not solved the riddle of the rivers.

Why did the rivers flow west toward the middle of the continent? Settlers and citizens of New South Wales had concluded that the rivers flowed into a vast inland sea. "Yup," said one of the settlers in the Bathurst district, "them marshes Oxley found was probably the edge of the sea."

Glenn Moffett didn't believe it, nor did Jack Summers. How could Oxley declare all the land south beyond that which he had explored useless until he had seen it? Aaron agreed.

On the fourth day after their arrival at Bathurst, on the ninth day of the expedition, the party trailed west along the Lachlan River. Oxley had followed the Lachlan downriver going west. But Aaron's expedition had turned and followed it upriver going south-southeast, toward its source. On the eleventh day, they had crossed valleys and plains worthy of

179

Cranston's praise. And one wide plain, not far from Bathurst, Aaron marked in his mind as his own. It was vast and wide and full of the parklike areas that were so beautiful, undulating hills carpeted with grass, flat grassy plains with groves of trees following promising creeks, still running water in spite of the drought. Aaron set a stick in the ground with a piece of kerchief on it, then, in case the stick blew down, he mounded up a pile of rocks. This was his.

He would recommend to Cranston the land north of it, nearer Bathurst. To establish a cattle station as soon as Cranston wanted to, it wouldn't be wise to get any farther away from the military post at Bathurst than this.

But there was other unknown territory to the south, and it was toward this that the expedition party moved on.

By the sixtieth day, Aaron had become apprehensive about their course. The country was too full of grassless slopes and rocks. He had been contemplating suggesting a change in their direction, when Jack Summers did it for him.

"We didn't come on an expedition to climb mountains. We're supposed to look for plains."

"Buck wants to stick as close to water sources as possible," Aaron said. "He says in drought you may go hundreds of miles and never see a drop of water. Conditions are drier here than on the east side of the mountains."

As if to confirm Aaron's answer, Buck, who always scouted a little ahead of the rest, came through the trees on his horse and reined him in front of Aaron, Jack, and Glenn. "There's a falls up ahead about a mile, at the convergence with a creek that seems to go due south."

"Well, good," Glenn exclaimed. "Goin' east is

only goin' to lead us into the mountains again. We'd best be campin' for the night. And come morning maybe we should follow the creek south."

Aaron turned about and looked up at the sun behind him. Only late afternoon, probably four hours before dark. Tonight he would describe this quiet land that made a man feel melancholy because of its sameness, remoteness, its *waiting*.

Aaron turned back to see that Buck was still looking at the men silently. Though he was expressionless, Aaron noticed his restless eyes searching the bush on either side of them, his head tilted slightly, as if listening.

"What's wrong, Buck?" he asked, barely above a whisper.

"I don't know." Because Buck did not move, Glenn and Jack stared at him, their backs stiffening. The hair on the back of Aaron's neck stood up. The convicts' eyes widened, and all their heads turned as they scanned the woods on either side of them.

Finally Buck turned his horse around and advanced along the trail the convicts had cut through the thick underbrush. Glenn shifted the rifle in his arm and nudged his horse. Jack and Aaron followed, glancing on either side of them as they went.

They heard the splashing pour of the falls before they saw it. The bush stopped and left a clearing about twenty feet in diameter where a creek trickled from the south, probably coming from a spring somewhere in the foothills and rushing its way toward the Lachlan River. The water in the falls was meager, but it was a welcome sight. Aaron smiled as he rode to the falls, which split into three forks and flowed from an embankment about twenty feet high into a still pond flanked by grasses, nodding ferns, and wild flowers. Some of the melancholy and

181

apprehension vanished at the sight, for it was an oasis of movement and sound in a desert of still and quiet. He dismounted and looked about. The others dismounted as the convicts set about to make camp.

Aaron led his horse to the edge of the pond to let him drink. After a rest in the still pond, the water overflowed into a creek again and trickled over smooth stones on its way north. Aaron's horse sipped the water as Aaron squatted on his heels to look into the pond where he glimpsed silver fishes drowsing, fish as long as a man's arm. There would be fish for tea tonight, he vowed, roasted over a fire with dampers, a flat bread made from flour, water, and salt, and billy tea.

This afternoon we camped beside a pleasant creek where there was a beautiful falls, and I speared four fish for our meal, he would write to Penelope.

In the journal he would write: *Day Twelve: Followed the Lachlan to convergence with a northern flowing creek, the bed of which is about six feet wide. Followed creek going south for two miles until we came to a falls about twenty feet in height at the bottom of which there was a deep pond where there were codfish in abundance.*

Something caught his eye along the pond's bank, and he stared agape at a creature sleek as a seal that came waddling low to the ground from the base of a gum tree. Its beady black eyes were on the pond and it did not see him. It was an animal, but it had a bill like a duck. With the ease of a seal it slid into the water, and as Aaron watched it swam to the bottom and began to catch its dinner. He could not see what the creature was finding to eat, though he strained his eyes watching.

He would write to Penelope: *Also this afternoon I watched a duck-mole come from his lair and slide*

into the pond. Duck-mole. That was what the settlers had named the animal, an animal like none that existed anywhere else in the world. No telling what the men who studied animal life would call it once they had decided what species it was, mammal, bird, fish, or reptile.

"Don't move."

Aaron gave a start and looked up to see Buck standing beside him. He cut his eyes around to see Jack and Glenn frozen in the act of unsaddling their horses. The convicts were building a campfire, but the tone of Buck's voice had caused them to pause.

"There's natives," Buck said gently.

Aaron's eyes came around again. "Where?"

"Across the pond."

He looked and did not see them. "How do you know?"

"I know."

Glenn and Jack led their horses slowly over to Aaron and Buck, pretending to adjust the cinches and bits. Glenn's broad, ruddy face was beaded with sudden perspiration, and his blue eyes were wide as he asked, "What do you think, Buck?"

"Just go about your duties, but keep your eyes open. I doubt I can speak their particular language."

"I thought native talk was native talk. All alike."

"They have different languages. Jack, go tell the servants and tell them not to make any threatening gestures. No matter what happens."

When Jack had walked off Glenn asked, "Think they would steal the pack horses?"

"I doubt it. They wouldn't know what to do with a horse."

"Eat it?" Aaron suggested.

"Easy. I think they are about to make our acquaintance," Buck said steadily.

The hair on the back of Aaron's neck was bristling, and, frozen to the spot, he slid his eyes toward the forest across the pond.

The natives did not emerge from the trees, but seemed to materialize, one by one, two by two, natives more dark-skinned than those around Sydney and Parramatta. Aaron had seen natives from Africa, but the natives of New South Wales were not as black. They were the color of strong coffee, and as they stood with spears, boomerangs, and clubs in hand, Aaron was able to observe them thoroughly. He noticed that their heads were a little too large for their bodies, bodies which were muscular, wide shouldered. Their broad chests tapered to small waists and narrow hips. Their foreheads protruded at the brow line, their eyes were black, their lips thick, and they had the same wide, bridgeless noses that the natives who hung about Sydney and Parramatta had. All were bearded. Their bodies were coated with mud, which Aaron knew was their way of keeping the flies and mosquitos from biting them. It also conserved body moisture, but God, how it lent a grotesque, sinister quality to their appearance. The natives stared without moving, their black eyes going over each man, taking in his physical features just as thoroughly as the white men were taking in theirs.

Slowly now, Buck raised his hand in the native gesture that meant: Who are you?

A black who seemed to be the leader stepped cautiously forward, made a motion with his hands, then asked in the sign language: Who are you?

Still in the sign language, which was understood by all tribes, Buck answered, "We are from across the mountains. We come in peace," speaking aloud as well for the other explorers to hear.

The natives muttered cautiously among them-

selves. Then the leader called across the creek a jumble of words that Aaron could not understand, though he knew some of the native language of New South Wales, which Deen had taught him. "What did they say?" he asked Buck.

"I don't know." Buck signed to them, but they muttered amongst themselves again, gesturing toward the men.

Perspiration was running down the side of Jack Summers's face as he leaned toward Buck and asked, "Think they're figuring on having us for breakfast?"

"Or are they figuring on massacring us?" Glenn said out of one side of his mouth.

Aaron smiled nervously. Buck had claimed that natives were not cannibals, but . . . there were rumors. . . .

"What are they going to do to us?" the convict named Ames asked.

Buck held up his hand to still the verbal speculation. After watching the leader gesture, bringing his cupped hands from his chest and casting something invisible toward them, he said unemotionally, "They think we are women."

Glenn let out a hiss of air. "Jesus," he breathed.

"That's in our favor," Buck said.

Glenn Moffett's face was ruddy, but he was white around the mouth when he said, "You've had too much sun, Buck."

"It means they've never seen white men before. Which means they have not been exploited, chased, shot at, or massacred. So it's possible they aren't hostile."

As the men watched from their huddle, the four convicts having come close to stand with them, the natives filed along the far edge of the pond toward the falls, where they climbed agilely as cats up the rocky

sandstone sides to the top. Then, as they continued to watch, the natives waded one by one thigh-deep in the water to arrive on the same side of the creek with them.

"Just stay calm," Buck advised. "Jack, now's the time to get out the beads and tomahawks."

Somehow, incredibly, Aaron was not afraid. He was aware of his lack of fear and realized it was because he was fascinated. Here, before him, were primitive men, a race who still hunted with spears tipped with stone points and tomahawks made of quartz, a race who had never discovered metal, who had never seen a white man before.

Today I thrilled deep down inside because we witnessed the shock and fear and curiosity of natives who had never seen a white man before, he would write to Penelope. In the journal he would describe the natives in detail.

The natives came to stand cautiously at the edge of the camp and looked the white men up and down while the explorers stared at them. At last the leader advanced a step, handed his spear to a native behind him, and proceeded to gesture in sign language.

All eyes were on Buck as he said, "They think we are women because we have no beards."

"Well hell, Buck, can't you tell them otherwise?" Jack said angrily.

"I did, but they don't believe me."

"Well, what the hell difference does it make?" asked Ames.

"Are you jesting, Ames?" Jack said.

Suddenly the natives seemed more menacing than before. Somehow their viewing the explorers as women was more frightening than their seeing them as breakfast.

They watched the natives gesturing frantically.

"They say they have plenty of kangaroo meat, much fruit, but they have not had women in many days." Buck turned around and looked at the others, his face as expressionless as ever. "I think if we can prove we are men, we can form a friendship with them."

All eyes went back to the natives. "Hell," Glenn said. "What are we gonna do, Buck?"

"We'll have to prove we're men."

Their grizzly faces reddened as the men glanced at each other. After a few moments of shuffling and glancing at each other, Glenn said, "Maybe if we open our shirts . . ."

"You can try," Buck said.

Glenn Moffett was not as tall as Buck or Aaron, but he was built square, muscular and deep chested. Thrusting out his chest, he unbuttoned his shirt slowly, then took it off, rubbed his hairy hand over his chest.

The natives stared, then muttered among themselves. Then the leader signed to Buck.

Without even a hint of a smile, Buck said, "I think the leader says many women have flat breasts, and seeing Glenn's chest proves nothing."

This brought some appreciative chuckles from the other men as they looked at Glenn, and Glenn growled an oath under his breath.

The leader startled them by stepping closer and shaking his fist, uttering sounds that to Aaron sounded menacing. Then he signed at Buck.

Buck signed back. "They want more proof." He turned slowly to the others. "And they're becoming impatient."

The men stared at him, then Glenn asked, "Wh-what proof, Buck?"

Without batting an eye or changing expression,

Buck answered, "The ultimate proof. It's the only way to settle this so that we can get down to serious parley."

"This ain't serious?" Ames asked in awe.

"Well, I bloody well ain't goin' to do it," Jack said. "I'd rather be skewered on a spit 'n roasted."

Buck narrowed his eyes at Jack. "And there's no guarantee we won't be."

"What's the matter, Jack?" Glenn asked. "You ain't ever had no qualms about doing your business in front of us before."

Jack reddened. "That's different. What they want us to do is . . . indecent."

Grinning, Aaron said, "Glenn, they didn't like your chest, why don't you see if the other part will convince them."

Glenn eyed him maliciously. "You young pup. You . . ."

A shout from one of the natives startled the men and Aaron said, "Look, Buck. Why don't we just draw straws."

The men glanced at each other, nodded one by one, and Glenn bent down and picked up a few twigs, broke off eight exactly the same length, then shortened one. He held them up for everyone to see. Then he took off his hat, dropped them inside, and shook them up. Meantime the natives were watching, entranced by the white man's strange ceremonial. Then, without looking, each man drew his twig, Aaron going last.

Blushing a little, they brought their twigs together. Aaron's hand was trembling as he held his up against the others. And well he might have, for his was the short straw.

Aaron exploded. "Damn, Buck. I'm not going to do *that*," he shouted.

Buck hooked his thumb in the waistband of his trousers and eyed him soberly. There was that almost-smile on his mouth as he said, "It was your idea."

Aaron's face burned. Out on an exploring party in the wild, trying to think God back into existence, bringing his mind round to exalted things, and instead he was going to have to expose his most private parts like some London sodomite. Perspiring now, he looked at Glenn. "Glenn, you're my friend. You do it."

Glenn grinned. "Promise to marry my Annabelle and I will."

Desperately, Aaron looked at Jack. "Jack?"

"Not me," Jack said, shaking his head and grinning. "Mine would just tend to intimidate 'em."

Aaron appealed to Buck. "Buck. Uncle Buck. Can't we make one of the convicts do it?"

Buck shook his head. "You drew the short straw, Aaron."

In a fit of rage Aaron snatched off his hat, threw it on the ground and stomped it. Curse words came easy and he spat out every one of them he knew as he turned his back to the natives to unbutton his trousers.

"Turn around, Aaron, so they won't think you're playing a trick on them," Buck said.

The world was on fire. Aaron hated everybody. He hated Buck, Jack, and especially Glenn, Glenn who stood there grinning and chuckling wheezingly. Perspiring, face burning, Aaron took out those parts which, at his birth, had proved to the world that he was a male, and held them in his hand. He had proved it other times too, with Annabelle once, with a maid in England, with a courtesan of a friend in England, with a girl at the female factory in

Parramatta, and finally with his love, Penelope. Maybe it was for that last that he was being punished like this.

The natives had approached hesitantly but eagerly. They peered at his most private parts as if they were examining a new weapon. But they must have concluded that the weapon was very common, for they grinned approvingly and jabbered enthusiastically amongst themselves. Even in his rage and embarrassment, Aaron realized that their enthusiastic response was a greater one than he had ever received before about his manhood. He looked at Buck. "Now can I put it back?"

Buck nodded somberly, but Aaron did not miss the amused glint in his eye.

Aaron's face burned with indignation, fury, and embarrassment as he buttoned his trousers. As he finished, Glenn sidled up to him and said, "I'm havin' second thoughts. I've always wanted a grandson, but now that I've seen the instrument which could make it happen, per'aps I'd better look for another son-in-law. Why Annabelle—"

Aaron exploded and with one motion hit Glenn a cracking blow on the jaw that sent him staggering backward into Jack's arms.

Raging, Aaron crouched, fists clenched waist-high. "Anybody else want to make any remarks?" he challenged through his teeth.

Nobody did, but they were grinning. The convicts were grinning. Even the natives were all grinning. The whole damned world was grinning. God, he'd never live this down!

For the rest of the evening, as Buck displayed their gifts of beads, tomahawks, small mirrors, and brightly colored handkerchiefs, Aaron sat off by himself. The natives carried parts of kangaroo to the

190

campfire and the convict cook roasted them. Potatoes were roasted in the hot coals and damper was brought out, enough for all. Aaron ate and drank his billy tea, smiled a little when a native grinned and nodded to him trying to be friendly. And as he wrote in his journal and drew on his map, the natives peered over his shoulder in fascination at the marks he made on the parchment.

After the feast the natives entertained their white friends with a corraboree, dancing around the campfire and employing incredible movements with their spears and weapons. Buck explained that their dances symbolized the hunt. The fire flickered against the black night as the explorers and their servants alternately gaped with fascination and laughed at the antics of the natives, who were masters at mimicking kangaroos hopping, koalas crawling up trees, emus running. Glenn and Jack joined in the dance once, much to the natives' delight.

Finally, when all were exhausted, the natives made their beds out of bark and leaves at the edge of the clearing, and the explorers spread out their blankets and mosquito netting on the ground. Jack stood watch with a brace of pistols in his belt, a rifle nearby, and every man lay with his weapons close to his side. The natives kept spears near them as they slept.

Before dawn the natives took their leave. Ames began boiling billy over the campfire while Aaron saddled his horse and cinched it, placing the pack behind the saddle.

Buck came to stand beside him when he was buckling the cinch and said, "Best I could understand, the natives say there is good land to the south. They saw the sea south of here. There seems to be a large river south, which Oxley must have stopped just short of. There are also high mountains with

191

'white rain' to the southeast. Snow, I guess. Directly south there's rolling hill country. Valleys and rivers. To the west is 'small tree' country. Beyond that, many days away is 'no tree' country. Sounds like Oxley was wrong about the land south being desolate wilderness unfit for grazing. I think the land south of here is what we are looking for, unfortunately."

Aaron was still smarting from his embarrassment of the day before. The men would carry the tale back with them, and every man and woman in New South Wales would hear about it. But he did not fail to catch Buck's note of disappointment. "Unfortunately?"

"Our provisions won't last more than ten more days. That means in four days we'll have to turn back."

Aaron was silent a little longer, then turned toward his uncle. "Why are you telling me this?"

"I'll be telling all of them at breakfast. Aaron, I like this country. I'd like to keep going."

"Why can't we? We could hunt for our food. You know how to find water."

"Dangerous. Water is scarce, and where water is scarce so is the wild life. Besides, the horses can't take it. Two are already going lame." Buck leaned against a tree and regarded Aaron. "I'd like to see the map."

Aaron pulled the rolled-up map from the swag and handed it to Buck. In addition to writing the details of the journey in his journal, Aaron had carefully drawn a map, adding to it each evening, showing rivers, streams, hills, and other landmarks.

"Reason I want to check it is to be sure we got all the landmarks down. I intend to come back someday. I believe we'll find rich grazing land from here all the way to the sea."

Aaron lifted his gaze and looked south. With

indignation still fresh in his breast, he had a great desire to leave his heartless comrades and go on by himself. But he was wise enough to know going alone in the bush, unless one was a skilled bushman, was dangerous folly. Almost sure death.

Still . . . Perhaps just to wander a little way. On a plain where he could not lose his sense of direction. To get away from the conversation of the others, to feel alone. Just for a short while.

He tightened the cinch under the pack horse's belly. He'd mention it to Buck before they had to turn back. Work something out. *Today I rode off on my own,* he'd write Penelope.

He was certain it would be the most important experience of his life.

Miss Frances Aylesbury rose from her chair next to the window and came to greet her patronness. "Penelope," she said. "I got your note yesterday."

Penelope inclined her head to Fran Aylesbury, then curtsied to the gentleman who had been sitting on the sofa in front of the window. He was Mr. Francis Baldwin, the schoolmaster in Parramatta, Aaron and Mark's old teacher, who ran a boarding school for boys and was reputed to be the best teacher in the colony, as well as a poet with revolutionary ideas. He bowed with grave dignity and said in a deep voice gone soft with sixteen years of lecturing, "Miss Penelope," he said, "How do you do?"

"I am fine, Mr. Baldwin. And you?"

"Fine. Fine. How are the harp lessons?"

"Boring," she said, smiling.

He bowed again. "A sign that you have learned all you wish to know about the harp."

Penelope managed a soft laugh. She had always

193

thought that Mr. Baldwin was very tall. But either he had shrunk a bit or he only seemed shorter because she was taller. His long, thin face was lined with a few wrinkles now, his black hair brushed with white. Rumor was that Mr. Baldwin was the one who had dealt the old vicious rum corps a lot of misery by drawing and writing lampoons and circulating them in the colony anonymously. No one knew for sure, though. One thing they did know: Mr. Baldwin had set his cap for Frances Aylesbury a long time ago, but rumor also said that Miss Fran loved someone else. No one seemed to know who.

"I'll be leaving, Miss Fran," Baldwin said. "And I'll return for my shirt on Tuesday."

"It will be ready by then, Francis, I promise," said Fran.

When she shut the door behind the schoolmaster, Penelope began taking off her gloves, searching desperately for something to say, knowing she must concentrate carefully on keeping her expression and voice cheerful. "Your names could get rather confusing, both of you being named Frances and Francis."

"It's confusing only to others," Miss Fran said, smiling. Dr. Matthew Aylesbury's sister had none of the doctor's handsomeness. She was tall, slender, straight as a tree, with a plain, honest face, brown hair, and direct hazel eyes. Dr. Aylesbury had come to the colony as a convict, but Miss Fran had come over with a family servant and her own mother. After Matthew had been transported, financial reversals in England had caused Fran and her mother to have to take work in a clothing manufactury in England, which had promised to be a blessing. For when Dr. Aylesbury sent for them, Miss Fran came with a trunkful of garment patterns of the latest fashions. In

194

Parramatta she had set up a shop in a small hut and was the first dressmaker in the colony. Her trade had flourished from the very beginning and was still flourishing, only now the rich settlers came to her only for their most mundane clothing needs.

Now Frances Aylesbury was mistress of a dressmaking manufactury. Her brick building was long and narrow, and the room in which they stood now was furnished like a living room, complete with brick fireplace, oversized chairs, sofa, paintings on the wall, and even a harpsichord. A patronness could sit on the burgundy brocade sofa by the elegantly draped front window and have tea while one of Frances's clerks showed the lady the newest fabrics and patterns.

The west wall of the living room was lined with shelves where Frances kept her bolts of fabric neatly arranged according to fabric content and color. In front of the wall was a long table, built and polished to a sheen by Owen Crawford, on which the clerks could spread the fabric for a lady's perusal.

Behind the living room was the manufactury, a long, narrow room painted pale yellow, where eight girls hired from the Parramatta Factory sat sewing on frocks before long, broad windows that faced east. The effect of Frances's manufactury was one of light and color. The pleasant aroma of new fabric permeated the place. No one frowned or wept here; it was a pleasant, exciting place.

Penelope came here for all her gowns and undergarments because she liked Fran, liked her fashions, and because, during Aaron's long stay in England, Miss Fran might have a letter from him to her. But Penelope had come here today for a very different reason. Keeping a smile fixed on her face, she turned to Aaron's aunt.

195

"It was a large order," Penelope said. "I hope you don't mind."

Frances Aylesbury dealt with many women daily, and she knew women. She had developed an instinct for their moods, problems, and needs and knew exactly how to behave accordingly.

"Oh, not so large that I wasn't able to find the fabric we'll need," Frances said as she bustled behind the table near the wall of fabrics, where she paused and looked at Penelope.

Their eyes met and Penelope dropped her gaze. "It's just that I feel that I'm older, that I need gowns that are more sophisticated," she said.

"Old so soon?" Fran said, taking bolts of material from the shelf that lined the wall. Seeing Penelope was not in the mood to be teased, she added, "Ah, it's time, I suppose. You are all of twenty."

Penelope smiled. "An old maid, too. In just a few months, I shall be legally a spinster."

Frances expertly flopped the bolt of material onto the table, so that it fell in folds that displayed the highlights and texture of the fabric. "I'll be showing you what I have new myself. Priscilla is ill today."

"I hope it's not anything serious."

"Matthew—Dr. Aylesbury—says not. Now that you need gowns more sophisticated, we shall start with fabrics of a darker color, but let's not get into browns or blacks yet. But we will abandon our passion for pastels, except for summer evening wear, and go to dark muslins, lame, and plain cotton."

Penelope had written a note saying she needed several morning and afternoon gowns. Perhaps six or seven. And two or three for evening wear. Father would think she was silly, and Mum would be too wrapped up in herself to care. And what good fortune that was. *Good fortune, indeed.*

Frances sensed Penelope's pensive mood and did most of the talking. "You realize that the waist is dropping? We are no longer receiving fashions with high waists, and women are wearing corsets, as you know. Your last six gowns required corsets. It's on pretty, slender girls like you that these *Gigot* sleeves look best. Short, plump women do not look as well in the leg-of-mutton sleeves, and I tell them so." Frances had displayed six fabrics, which had elicited a small smile and nod from Penelope. "What do you think?"

"I like them all. You know what I like and what looks best on me. And you've such good taste."

"Wonderful. There'll be no need to measure you . . . unless you feel you've put on a little weight."

"Oh, I have. And you must measure me," Penelope said breathlessly.

Frances met her gaze again, then turned away. Dear Lord! Don't let my suspicions be true. "Well, unfortunately, all of us put on weight as we get older." When Penelope did not answer Frances turned back, avoiding looking at her. "Come. Let's go back to the sewing room and I'll measure you, child." Frances called one of her clerks to come out into the living room to wait on any patrons who might come in, and motioned smiling, for Penelope to precede her into the sewing room.

The girls in the sewing room spoke to Penelope, glancing up from the frocks they were working on, each dress in various stages of construction, from pieces fitted to wire dressmaker's dummies to pieces on which they were sewing finishing touches of lace, ribbon, and rosettes.

The measuring room was the most charming room in Fran's manufactory, a small ten-by-ten room with one long window draped in gold velvet, tiny white

Louis XV chairs with gold cushions, a glass-top table, an elegant coat rack, a gorgeous multicolored carpet from India on the floor.

As Frances draped a tape measure over her shoulder, she asked, "Shall I call for Martha to help you? Or would you rather undress yourself?"

"I . . . I'll undress myself today, thank you."

"Fine. I'll be back in shortly."

Trembling now, Penelope removed her morning gown and petticoats and stood in her pantaloons and chemise pressing her hands to her bosom waiting until Frances came back into the room to measure her.

"Arms up, Penelope. We'll do a complete measurement on you, for I'll wager you've grown a few inches in height, too."

As Penelope held her arms up, Fran measured her bust first. "Mmm. You've gained some there. Busts are certainly in fashion."

Penelope thought she would smother. Just die. But something must be done. Must be done . . .

The tape went around her waist. Frances remained silent. Then the tape went around her hips. Then she jotted down the measurements on a slip of paper. "You are an inch larger in the bust. And three inches larger in the waist," she said softly.

Penelope's chin came up slowly. "I . . . obviously . . . need fullness in front—"

"Yes. We'll fix that. The high waist isn't out altogether yet. We can do one gown in a high waist with gathers in front, but with the new mantle draped from waist to hem on one side, as is the newest fashion. On others we can add the pelisse, and huge bows and ruffles to the gathers." Frances paused. "You can put your arms down now, Penelope. And . . . I advise you from now on not to tie the corset

so tightly."

Their eyes met again, and this time Penelope's eyes filled with tears that did not spill. "I love him," she whispered. "I love him more than my own life, Miss Fran."

Frances stared for a moment, then her thin hand went to shade her own eyes. "Dear God," she groaned and did not look at Penelope for several moments. She was not pained at what she had already guessed, she was pained because of the suffering this girl might have to endure at the hands of the gossips in the colony, and that her nephew might be the man responsible. Frances lowered her hand and looked at Penelope. "Aaron?"

Penelope said steadily, "I cannot say."

Frances was suddenly furious. "What are you going to do?"

"Wait."

"Until he returns?"

Penelope bit her lips, unable to betray Aaron. "I cannot say."

Frances took a long, shuddering breath. "Child, the expedition was due back over three weeks ago. They may never—" She dropped her hands and gathered her tape, her slip of paper. "I . . . I'll do something to hide your condition."

"Yes. If you can just add fullness to the front of the gown—"

"I'll do that. With gathers, flounces, ruffles, bows, mantles, and shawls, a lady can go almost a full nine months without showing. Yes, I can do wonders with fabric, but—" She looked at Penelope directly now. "Eventually—"

"I alone must worry about the eventualities, Miss Fran," Penelope said, smiling through her tears as she gathered her dress to her bosom.

Frances studied her, thinking, My God, Oliver Cranston will kill Aaron. This scandal will ruin Penelope, shame the Cranstons and the Aylesburys and even the Crawfords. And there will be hell to pay. Somebody could get killed. *Damn.* What a mess.

Penelope saw the stern emotions in Frances's face. "I know what you're thinking," she said steadily, looking at the dressmaker now. "I won't let anyone get hurt because of it. I know what you must be thinking of me, too, Miss Fran, but I must tell you that I'm not sorry it happened. And if I had it to do all over again, I'd do it again."

Fran observed the pretty thing standing before her bravely bearing up to a horrible misfortune. And the girl was determined to see it through. Penelope in that moment grew ten feet taller in Fran's estimation. "Penny, don't you worry. I'll fix these gowns, and see what else I can do."

"There's nothing else for you to do, Miss Fran. This is a problem only Aaron and—" Her fingers came up to her lips.

Fran nodded. "Never mind. I knew who the man was anyway. Who else could it be?" Patting Penelope's arm, she said, "Put on your dress, love, and when you're done, come to the living room."

Fran left the measuring room and noticed that her newest girl from the Parramatta factory, Betty Scoggins, was walking away from her, glancing over her shoulder, and it occurred to Frances that the girl was awfully close to the measuring room when she was supposed to be at her station by the window. "Finished with your gown, Betty?" Fran asked with a frown.

"Yes'm and I was comin' to tell yer, but saw yer was in the measurin' room, so I didn't bother yer, Miss Aylesbury," the girl said smiling, her huge brown

eyes wide with innocence.

Fran had just acquired Betty from the female factory. The girl was due to be pardoned any day, at which time Fran would either choose to keep her on as a hired seamstress, or let her go. She sensed that the girl had no intention of staying on at the manufactory once she was pardoned. It seemed that her interests leaned more toward prurient matters. Fran mentally shrugged and went on into the living room.

Penelope pulled the gown on over her head. She had told no one else, no one at all. For surely Aaron would return soon and then—and then what? Would she tell him? No, because she did not want to trap him into marrying her. She would only hope that he would ask to marry her once he returned, for she hoped that by then his wanderlust would be satiated and he would want to settle down and start up his practice.

At the front of the shop Penelope pretended to be her old merry self, and Fran pretended to be thrilled at the large order for gowns.

But when Penelope shut the door behind her, Fran turned frowning toward the window. *Damn.* What was she going to do? Could she betray Penelope's secret? The Aylesburys were responsible for this girl's plight, and she was honor-bound to see that the Aylesburys took that responsibility. But she would wait a few days before going to Matt and Milly with this. Wait and see if indeed Aaron did return soon. For, as she had said, the expedition party was already over three weeks late coming home.

Chapter X

After office hours the day before, Mark had ridden to Parramatta and stayed at Webster's Inn because he had to deliver a letter to Fitzhugh's friend. Then, today, he had started out on the Windsor road, now a toll road, carrying a court summons for, of all people, Oliver Cranston. But despite the summons, Mark hadn't stopped smiling since yesterday when Fitzhugh had slapped him on the back and handed him a sealed letter saying, "You did an excellent job on the Perkins case, Mark. It was your good research into Hamilton's background that brought to light how he had often failed to pay his hired help when he lived in England. I think that fact alone made the magistrate rule in favor of Perkins."

Mark was not one to pretend modesty. He believed in accepting credit when it was due. "Thank you, sir." He had worked hard on the case, gone over the details with Fitzhugh, and Fitz had presented it to the magistrate. There were so few barristers in New South Wales that solicitors—who normally only worked up a case and hired a lawyer to present it in court—had to present the civil cases themselves.

"It's rare the judges rule in favor of an ex-convict.

It's a mark—pardon the pun—in your favor," Fitz had gone on to say.

Mark guessed that within a year ol' Fitz would make him a full partner. In the meantime he had a deal worked out with a man named Epps concerning a house he had been building south of Sydney beyond the brick fields. Epps had contracted and begun building a house on forty acres, until recent financial reversals had caused him to abandon the project. And there was a contingency in Mark's favor. The contractor was suing Epps for expenses, and had asked Stuart to take the case.

When Mark had found out about it, he and Stuart Mays had put their heads together. If the contractor would take so many barrels of rum instead of currency, the case could be settled out of court and Mark could have the house for nothing. For Mark and Stuart and several older men in the colony had rum on a ship that was already anchored in Sydney cove this very moment. Mark had invested one hundred pounds in the rum and could sell it in the colony for twelve times as much as he had paid for it.

And Stuart would see to it that his client, the contractor, took the rum instead of currency—with just a little arm twisting. For Stuart's sly investigating had revealed that the contractor was married to three women at the same time. One in England, one on Norfolk Island, one in New South Wales. All Stu had to do was mention this fact to the contractor and he was certain to agree to taking the rum instead of currency.

It would be slightly unethical of Stuart to do that, but it was fair to all concerned. The contractor would receive the rum in payment for building the house, and since he had hired convict laborers to build it, the rum would be better appreciated by the workmen

than currency. And Epps wouldn't have to pay the contractor. All he would lose was his time and planning on the house. Mark would have the house and land free and clear, Stuart and he would both have won their cases in that they were settling out of court, and all would be happy. Jenkins, Stu's senior solicitor, and Fitzhugh needn't know about the rum's being involved at all.

The only thing that bothered him was that trading in rum was slightly illegal. Well, it *was* illegal. But everybody with the money and the guts did it at one time or another; the principal surgeon, the colony's most affluent traders, and even some of the magistrates. Everybody knew it was going on and everybody ignored it. If the governor ever happened to find out, whoever was trading in rum would get thrown in jail for a few days, much to the delight of the man's friends, and then he'd be out boasting about it.

At the moment Mark was riding a pacer he had bought from Thaddeus Crawford, a sleek sorrel gelding with a gait as smooth as a rocking chair. Dressed in a white linen suit, Mark was feeling on top of the world. The day was bright, too bright. The road from Parramatta was dusty, despite the gravel that had been hauled in to pave it when Macquarie was governor. Droughts were easy on the roads but hard on people and crops. But nothing could dismay him today. He was carrying a court summons to Cranston, and when he delivered it, he intended to speak to Cranston about Penelope. The only misgivings he had about that concerned his father's disapproval. Mark could not think how to change that. Perhaps when he told his father what Fitzhugh had said the day before, he might be in a good enough mood that he wouldn't shout when he heard about his intentions toward Cranston's daughter.

With a fine house and forty acres just outside of Sydney, Mark would be well on his way to becoming a respectable citizen himself. Like his father. Like Cranston. A man worthy of Penelope.

His conscience itched him again, because he knew Aaron cared for Penelope but—*but what, Mark?* But if Aaron had cared for her very much, he would have taken the trust fund and settled in Sydney or Parramatta, taken a position in a hospital, perhaps even become one of the two or three physicians in the colony who had a private practice, and he could have begun to court her properly, as a gentleman should. Instead, he had turned his back on all their father had planned, and gone off on an expedition that not even the governor recognized. God only knew what he would do after that.

Mark came to the track that led from the road through the bush skirting Ben Crawford's property to the Cranstons'. He was barely aware of the blazing sun, unusually hot for this time of year, and not even the insane cry of the kookaburra bothered him, even when it caused a dozen others to call and laugh in the bush on either side of the track.

When he topped the rise and looked west, Cranston's house looked like a doll's, for the track dipped down, crossed a wide creek, and the land lay green like a carpet, with patches of cultivated crops. The house was made of rose-colored, handmade brick, and Cranston had imported six of the strange pine trees that grew on Norfolk Island and planted them in front of it. Mark remembered when Cranston had planted them. Mark's father had scoffed and snorted and called Cranston pompous. How Mum Aylesbury would have liked a few pines in their dooryard, but Matthew Aylesbury had shouted, "Not as long as I live. They remind me of my stay on

Norfolk Island."

Mark shuddered at the thought of his father's having been sent to that penal settlement, and he wondered vaguely how long ago that had been.

Now he noticed as he approached the dooryard that Oliver Cranston was in the pasture beyond the south side of the house. He was walking among the jumbucks. Jumbuck was the native word for sheep and also meant white clouds. Mark reined his horse and waved away the scrawny little groom who came to take the horse. "I'll only be a moment, Cricket."

The groom clicked what was left of his teeth and said, "J-just tie 'em to the fence, then, M-M-Mr. Aylesbury."

Mark dismounted, looped the reins over the fence, and struck out across the dusty dooryard toward the parklike rolling pasture, which was dotted with a few huge gum trees. Grazing on the slopes of the hilly pasture, like clouds drifting in a green sky, was a mob of Cranston's sheep. Not pure Merinos, Mark noticed. He wondered why.

He gazed around him. Cranston's property, as far as his eyes could see, but not a great deal larger than the Aylesburys' now. Milicent Crawford had inherited Grandmum's land, which made it Aylesbury property, and, together with what Mark's father had been allotted upon his pardon in 1802, plus what he had purchased, Aylesbury property was considerable. Several hundred acres was a lot of soil. Of course his father had been farming the same acreage for years, but now they were actually his. According to English law, Mum owned it, but whatever came from the land was her husband's. That was the law. Even though Milicent managed not only her own land, but his, too. Remarkable woman! But give *him* a woman like Penelope. Not only beautiful, but

206

tutored, trained, and polished in the ways of a lady. A lady.

Oliver Cranston looked up as Mark approached, and squinted as he came to stand before him.

"Mr. Cranston, sir, good afternoon," Mark said, extending his hand.

Oliver looked at him, at his hand, and finally took it briefly.

Mark gestured toward the grazing sheep. "Very profitable-looking mob, sir. What breed are they?"

Oliver glanced at his sheep, then brought his gaze back to Mark. "You don't know much about sheep, do you? These are direct descendants of the Dutch breed of sheep our first governor brought from the Cape of Good Hope on the first fleet. They aren't profitable at all. Just edible."

"Oh," Mark said, coloring. "Well, at least they seem to be proliferating. One can tell you certainly enjoy raising sheep."

"I hate sheep," Oliver said, causing Mark's jaunty smile to cease. "However, at the moment, wool seems to be the only commodity in the colony that England is interested in, so my daughter is urging me to try breeding a few."

In a third attempt to impress Oliver Cranston, Matthew offered, "But the colony is doing well exporting sealskins and whale oil too, sir."

On Cranston's face was that unsmiling, penetrating stare again, which almost unnerved him. "Unfortunately, Mr. Aylesbury, I can't raise seals and I can't catch whales out here in the pasture, can I?"

Mark swallowed. "No, sir."

Oliver eyed him a moment and reached down to scratch the head of a ewe nuzzling his foot. "What brings you 'round here, Mr. Aylesbury?"

"Sir, I wish you'd call me Mark."

"Mark, then. I like that better, anyway. It's less irritating to my constitution."

"Sir?"

"Never mind."

Mark brought the letter out of the inside pocket of his coat and took a deep breath. "Sir, I hope you don't think I personally am responsible for the matter contained in this letter, just because the party which we—Fitzhugh—will be representing is—well, I was asked to deliver this to you."

Oliver frowned at him, then took the letter, which was his summons to appear in court. Studiously he broke the seal and read it. He looked up at Mark sharply. "Thaddeus Crawford can't do this."

Mark's mouth went dry. "Sir, let me assure you that I *personally* knew nothing of this matter until yesterday when I was apprised of it by Mr. Fitzhugh." Mark was wishing at the moment that Thaddeus Crawford was no kin to anyone in his family. Why did he have to hire Fitzhugh to represent him in a lawsuit against, of all people, Oliver Cranston?

Oliver's face reddened with fury. "When Crawford came to tell me that my sheep had broken through my fence and gotten into his pasture during a rainstorm, my groom and I went immediately to view the— Forty pounds is absurd. No meadow is worth forty pounds, imported grass or not."

Mark was bound by ethics not to comment one way or another. Actually, Thaddeus's pasture *was* expensive, and Cranston's sheep had surged through the broken fence, trampled the grass Thaddeus had planted, all forty acres of it, and what the sheep hadn't nibbled down their hooves had beat into the grass. A brief, heavy rainstorm had come, the last the colony had had in months, and had washed a great

deal more of the grass away. Thaddeus had demanded restitution. Cranston had refused, claiming it was Thaddeus's stallion that had broken down the fence trying to get to one of Cranston's mares—which he had. "I'm sorry sir."

"Yes. I'm sure you are," Cranston said in his mounting anger.

"Sir, I— The Crawfords are no kin to me."

"Unfortunate for you," Oliver said and turned to walk away.

Mark fell into step beside him. Cranston ignored him, his anger carefully contained in his tall, dignified manner. Mark was torn between his duty and his desires, which were both his destiny. "Sir, I hope that my part in this suit will not color your attitude toward me as a suitor for your daughter, Penelope."

Oliver stopped short and stared at him, his black eyes boring into him like one of Owen's awls. "You too?"

Mark's chin lifted a little. "Yessir," he said, his throat clicking with a dry swallow.

"My dear . . . Mark. Let me assure you that your part in this lawsuit is not the part in you I detest."

"Sir—"

Cranston quieted him with a flutter of his hand. "I will tell you exactly what I told your brother. Or to be more exact, your *half*-brother: that you are forgetting your social status."

"My status is as stable as any pure—I mean, any son of an exclusionist, sir."

"But your family's is not."

Mark opened his mouth, shut it, opened it again. "Our family is quite well to do now, sir, all of them. And respectable—"

"I'm aware of that." Cranston studied him again.

209

Apparently he didn't like what he saw. "Don't come around here, Mark. I'll have none of you or your half-brother, and never mind the reasons." He started walking again with that long stride of a man proud of the land on which he walked.

Standing still, angry and frustrated, Mark watched him go, then, in a sudden fury, hurried to catch up to him again. "I *shall* come around, sir. I'll come around again and again until you consent—"

"You will be turned away at the door again and again. I'll never consent to your seeing my daughter."

Speechless now, Mark fumed. It was unfair. Bloody *damned* unfair. "Sir," he gasped, "you have—have always attempted to—to overwhelm us Aylesburys and Crawfords."

Cranston's mouth jerked into a sardonic smile. "Don't be absurd. Your family has overwhelmed me for twenty years, if not by their common ways, at least by the sheer weight of their numbers."

Cranston was right. How many Aylesburys were there? Four, counting Mum. How many Crawfords? Counting Ben's nine children, fifteen. Nineteen in all. They had come before the gate to Cranston's dooryard where Mark's horse was tethered. "Sir!"

Cranston stopped, scowled at him.

"Sir, I *wish* you would forget my family and regard me as an individual."

Cranston said gently, "Not likely," and with that turned on his heel, went through the gate, and strode toward the house, leaving Mark standing red-faced with fury.

Bloody damned merino. Mark turned and unwrapped the reins from the fence, swung into the saddle, and reined the horse about, setting him down the track again. When he was out of sight of the

house, he reined him off the track and through the bush going up the gentle slope of the east end of the ridge that separated the Cranstons' property from the Aylesburys'. And all the while he was vowing that he would see Penelope Cranston. He would besiege the Cranston household with himself until Oliver gave in. Perhaps he would wait until Cranston was gone. But there was still that haughty mother of Penelope's to contend with. That haughty mother who had a penchant for his father . . . his father, who looked like Mark . . . that woman who had stared at him approvingly at the Phyfes' ball. . . .

Mark's scowl smoothed out. He threw back his head and took a deep breath, then shouted, "All's fair in love and war, Aaron, my *half*-brother. Wherever you are."

Tonight Aaron would write: *Buck told us yesterday that we must turn back tomorrow. Our provisions are running out and we have barely enough to get us back to the Bathurst district. It's true that we have crossed, charted, and mapped some excellent grazing country, but Glenn and I agreed that just beyond our present location to the south, or to the west, or both, that there is grazing land superior to any we have seen yet.*

So as not to waste this last day, we decided that we could cover more ground if we spread out. Buck was against this, but we took a vote and it was Jack, Glenn, and I for it. But with Buck's urging we consented that we would go out alone only until noon and then we must turn back on our own trail and meet at dark at today's camp. A signal was agreed upon if we encountered trouble of any kind. One shot from a musket followed by one shot from a pistol.

Each of us had both. And at dawn we each struck out on our own, Buck going east, Glenn southeast, Jack going northwest, and I going due west. The convicts went with Glenn and Jack, who also took with them the pack horses.

Penelope I can't tell you how exciting this was. I write you these things rather than waiting to tell you later for fear I might forget the details, though I don't believe I will ever forget any of it.

Alone. That was the greatest thrill. Going west was easy. The bush was not as thick as it had been earlier in their journey. He had gone through large stands of gum trees and red cedar and now came to an open, parklike area where nothing grew but tall, gray-green, luscious grass and wild flowers, where butterflies with wings of stained glass fluttered like flowers blown apart by the wind. Overhead, wedge-tailed eagles soared, motionless against the bleached blue sky. Dangerous to go out alone, Buck had said, but they were all men and each knew the ways of the wild, had learned the elements of survival in the bush, which began with caution and learning how to mark the trail.

In the forest Aaron cut a notch in a tree every few feet. In the clearings he stacked stones to form pyramids and knew the others were doing the same. In addition, he was mapping his way on paper, noting every hill, ridge, creek, river, every landmark, as he had done for the entire expedition. He had mapped, charted, and kept a journal. Except for Buck, his was the only literate hand in the expedition, which was the main reason Glenn had asked him along. He felt that he had done his part well.

This back country! Undulating hills, forests of tall gum trees thick with wattle, and clearings like this, as

if human hands had prepared it for the plow. And the forests were growing more sparse, the trees farther apart, and there was shade, dense enough to shelter cattle or sheep from the searing sun of summer, but not so much that grass couldn't grow beneath the trees. Only thing was, most of the creeks were dry. The rivers must have been deep and wide during some seasons, but they must have rushed out of the mountains at their source and tumbled over rocks in the gum forest, then trickled through ridges and clearings only to disappear at last into the sand. Every creekbed had gone dry.

Strange country. It was as if it were showing the explorers what could be someday, but wasn't yet. Or, it was a lure, a siren song. The country beckoned one with its strange beauty, leading one on with trickling streams of crystal water, forests and grassy hillocks, breathtaking with splashes of blue, yellow, and red wild flowers. Flocks of birds with plumage of unbelievable colors suggested paradise just ahead, perhaps over that sapphire ridge or that haunting violet mountain. But as one went on, the streams sank into the earth, the birds vanished, the wild flowers disappeared, and one was left with little more than silence and the sun. He was beginning to wonder if Australia wasn't what the rest of the world looked like thousands of years ago.

Aaron reined his tired but faithful horse on the top of a high ridge and looked down on the vale that seemed more like a dream than anything else. He took the copper flask that held his drinking water from his saddle bag, removed the stopper, tilted his head back, and drank its sweetness. Water from a spring at their last campsite, the campsite to which he must return soon. He tapped the cork back in, looked up at the sun. Almost noon.

213

But below the vale was thick with trees, probably following the creek, which might or might not be dry. On either side of the vale were forest-covered hills, mountains the settlers called them. But in England they would be called just hills, and he had less than an hour before he must turn back.

After Aaron had marked the top of the ridge with a pyramid of stones, he rode down into the vale. The forest grew thick, the pea vines twined through wattle and gum trees and bloomed blue and pink. He slashed his marks in the trees as he passed, even as the bridal veils of sunlight filtered through the trees enchanting him, and blue, green, and yellow birds flashed chattering through the rays. After an hour's ride, he came to a stream trickling through the forest, probably from the nearby mountain, and he dismounted, letting his horse suck the water as he sat down in the grass to drink in the primeval beauty that no white man had ever seen. I am supposed to be hunting sheep country, he thought. Sheep do not drink from a running stream, they prefer still water. *He leadeth me beside the still waters. He restoreth my soul.*

But He hasn't revealed to me why a tiny babe writhes in pain, or why old folks who have worked hard and led good lives must die such long and lingering deaths. And why man made in His image rots in the grave like an animal.

Today, I asked some questions of God and received no answer. I'll not write that to Penelope, he thought.

And Aaron knew he must be getting back.

He rose from his place by the creek and went to the horse, which was cropping the sweet grass near the stream, took the map from the saddle, and looked around for a place to spread it out. He would chart

214

today's progression, mark this spot well. He spied a large, flat boulder and went to it. There he spread the rolled map out and looked around for something to weight it down. He found a stone for one end and reached for a stick for the other.

At first, the shock of pain did not register in his brain. Aaron jerked his hand back with an "Agh!" The writhing, ropelike snake was what registered.

Aaron cried out. His body convulsed in horror, propelling him backward into the creek. Gasping, he fought the shallow water as if it, too, were a giant snake, and he heard himself crying out, "Agh! Agh! Agh!" Through a haze of pain he saw the horse rear and scream, rear again. Then it leaped and bolted through the trees. Aaron struggled up onto the bank, slipping and sliding. His panicked eyes sought the grass for the snake, but it was gone. He was terror, and he was horror itself as his eyes searched for his musket. Must give the signal. Must give the signal. Must give the signal. Must . . . but he saw that he had knocked the musket into the creek. Moaning with horror, he splashed back into the creek, pulled it from the water, hefted it to his shoulder, pulled the trigger. Muskets do not fire when the powder is wet, he reminded himself. His hand grappled for the powder horn hung on a leather strap from his shoulder. Dripping wet. Then his hand clawed for the pistol in his belt. Wet. Soaking wet. He pulled the trigger anyway. The hammer snapped and that was all.

Only then did he dare look at his hand. There they were, just above the wrist, two puncture wounds. Swelling had already begun. The poison would be coursing through his veins already, and it would paralyze the muscles that caused him to breathe.

Run, Jessica, run. Words from an earlier tragedy

echoed in his mind.

Gasping with panic, his mind a jumble of horror, Aaron clawed at the leather scabbard that held his knife. The native treatment—cut the wounds, suck out the poison, then run, run, run, to keep the heart pumping, to keep the lungs pumping. *Run, Jessica, run.*

Shaking violently and moaning like a woman in childbirth, Aaron slashed the puncture wounds without feeling the pain and sucked his own blood, spat it out, heard a groan and a whimper from himself. Does a man whimper when he is dying? He tried to remember.

Run, Jessica, run.

Aaron sucked the wound and spat out the blood and poison, sucked and spat until he gagged. He must run back. Must. He grabbed up his musket. No time to waste. He started running back the way he had come. Already the blood was thudding in his head, temporal pulses slapping like waves against a boat. With crazed eyes he sought the slash marks in the trees as he ran stumbling, trying to keep his mind focused on the trail he had just blazed and in holding on to his musket. His powder horn slapped his breast, his boots squished with every step he took. He had no choice. He must run, run, until he could not put one foot in front of the other. It was his only hope, and it was only a faint hope. The tiger snake was deadly. Rarely did a man survive the bite of a tiger snake.

Bitten. My God, bitten, cried his brain. Aaron ran stumbling over dead branches. His feet became tangled in vines and he fell. He clawed at the vines that held him, his hand and arms growing numb. "God, I'm dying," he gasped. "I can feel my arm dying." *Run, Jessica, run.*

But a man's energy gives out and the poison's still there and he dies. He asphyxiates.

Asphyxiates. I will die because my lungs will not function anymore. The muscles for breathing become paralyzed. Asphyxiation. Aaron fell again, scrambled up, knowing he must run. He ran and some part in his mind, an area clear of the confusion of pain and horror, told him that if he found the horse, he must mount it and ride toward camp. He did not want to die alone.

But I did everything I knew to do, Mum. I cut the places, sucked out the poison, and then I ran, I ran, and I ran, as we were taught to do. I was scared, Mum. Anyone would be. Bitten by a snake is a terrible thing. Being shot by an enemy, speared by a native, drowning, these aren't fearful deaths. But being bitten by a snake, like Jessica . . .

Run, Jessica, run.

The boots grew heavy. Perspiration soaked his shirt, the sun came out—where had it been? The sun burned him. His head pounded with pain. Slap, slap, slap, the hot poisoned blood thudded in his temples, but he looked for the slash marks on the trees and there were no trees. Only waving grass on hills as far as he could see, the dwarfed gum trees dotting the hills. *Coolabah*, Buck called the tree, dwarf gum trees called *coolabah*. But a man has to look for his trail, the pyramid of stones with which he blazed his trail.

But there were no coolabah trees on the trail you blazed, Aaron.

But they will find me, and it's more important that I keep running. For death from the snake is imminent, death from the bush is not.

Then look at the sun. It is behind you. You are running away from it. No. It can't be. The sun is in my head.

But he must run. He turned back in the direction he thought their last camp was. Aaron ran, his lungs ached for air, his side slit open with pain, and the pounding blood thudded in his head, his heart thundered in his chest, his eyes glazed over with pain and exhaustion and he did not see the gully. He tumbled down, down the hill. Stones clattered and dashed against his face. Trees swayed overhead and he came to rest with his face in the sand.

Run, Jessica, run.

He rose to his feet and climbed out of the gully. Splat, splat went the blood in his head. His arm was bursting. The pain wanted out. Breaths were coming in loud gasps, like a man dying. He ran for the blue hills in the distance, ran while the air closed in around him and shadows crept over the earth. The sun was vanishing. He had run for half a day . . . or was it death creeping close? Was death a shadow?

Yea though I walk through the shadow of the valley of death . . .

The shadow crept into him, seeped into his blood. He was a shadow himself now. He could no longer feel the pain or the pulse. He could no longer even feel his own body. He ran in the air, his movements light and slow. He barely touched the earth anymore. The day was darkening around him. His body was the earth. His blood was the sea. And when he fell and rolled down, down, down, and looked up at the darkening sky, the drum of the heart drowned out the ringing in his ears, the ceaseless roar of the sea.

He knew that soon the earth would cease to exist, for there would be no more air upon it.

But he, Aaron, would never know when it happened, because he would be asleep, with Jessica in his arms.

Chapter XI

Fitzhugh had made him sweep out the office, and now he was having to sweep the board walk in front of the office before he could go home for the weekend. Damn him. Fitz's office was one of the few in this wing of the hospital that had an outside entrance. Lucky for him. Mark had not been going home every Saturday night these past few weeks, because on Saturday nights he and Stu and Jory and the others always had a fine time in the taverns together. They ate and drank and talked and jested, played games, did a little gambling—all the things young men did for entertainment.

But today his father had sent him a message by courier. It seemed that Jack Summers and Glenn Moffett had returned from the expedition, but Buck and Aaron had not. It seemed everyone was trying to find out why Buck and Aaron hadn't returned, but Jack and Glenn weren't telling. So he, Mark, was expected home. Why, he didn't know. What the hell could *he* do about it? Was he expected to hold his stepmother's and father's hands? Damn! A man works all week and—

"Charmin'."

Mark paused with broom in hand and turned scowling to see who spoke. Before him stood a buxom girl with wide brown eyes, full lips, and curly brown hair.

"Do yer 'ire out as a cleanin' boy?" she asked with one hand on her hip, "or wot?"

Mark's face flushed before he realized from her stance and her forward manner that the girl was just another prostitute. As she smiled flirtatiously and moved her body provocatively, Mark's eyes were drawn to the cleavage where the scooped neck of her bodice stopped just short of revealing the plump rise of her breasts. Prostitutes badgered the men of Sydney constantly, by day and by night. They came in boatloads from the jails of England and plied their trade openly and lucratively in the colony. But this one was prettier than most, and though Mark wasn't above giving one a brief tussle for a few shillings occasionally, he turned many more of them down than he accepted. He felt himself getting an erection immediately.

"I don't hire out to sweep walks, or anything else," he told her. "Be on your way. I'm not interested in what you have to sell."

The girl was undismayed. "From where I stand, Mark Aylesbury, I'd say yer lyin'." Her eyes swept from his face to his engorgement and back up to his face.

Mark's face burned. "How did you know my name?"

The girl shrugged and smiled. "A little bird told me. Actually, I've seen you on the street and asked a friend wot yer name was. When I 'eard the name Aylesbury I figured I'd 'ave more to sell you than the obvious."

Mark stared at her. "Why?"

She smiled coyly and strolled to the building, swaying her hips the way prostitutes did, and leaned against it, pressing the palms of her hands against the wall, which caused her breasts to strain the fabric at the front of her dress. "I'm disappointed, because it was Aaron I 'ad somethin' to tell."

Mark's face burned even more, this time with anger, which served to take the pressure off his loins. "Aaron is gone."

"Aye. I 'eard. 'Tis a shame, too, for 'e'd want to 'ear wot I know."

Glowering at the girl, Mark went to her slowly, glancing around to make sure nobody was noticing them. "Why do you want to see Aaron?"

Smiling she said, "My name's Betty. Betty Scoggins. I worked for yer Aunt Frances in Parramatta. A seamstress 'ears lots of lady gossip." She lowered her eyes to the front of Mark's trousers and back up to his face. "I 'ave a place all me own. And I'm emancipated, too. No disease, neither. And I've been watchin' you. I think yer the 'andsomest man in Sydney. And I don't take to a man personal much, either." Her brown eyes seemed to dissolve like two pieces of chocolate, and her breasts swelled with each deep breath she took.

Mark observed her and decided that she was attractive enough to interest him temporarily, better than the odorous hags he usually ended up with. He smiled slowly. "Why did you want to speak to Aaron if you like me?"

She dropped her gaze. "I'm not one fer gossipin' in the street."

Anger flushed through him, and Mark hefted his broom and gave the girl as contemptuous a look as he could manage, then turned away. All she wanted was to seduce him for a fee.

She called after him, "It's about a girl yer know."

When he turned back, he saw that the girl's eyes were wide with some hidden truth. "What girl?"

Betty's eyes cut first up the street, then down. "Penelope. Penelope Cranston."

A snake of horror slid down his back, horror that Penelope's name should be on the lips of a girl like this one. He took a step toward her. "Damn you. You'd better tell me what you have to say about her that concerns Aaron."

Betty smiled. "I will. At my 'ut. Tonight."

Mark glowered, then said, "Where is it?"

"South. Near the brick fields. The white one with the thatched roof and two chimneys."

He nodded, not taking his eyes from her face. "What will it cost me?"

Betty Scoggins smiled. "The gossip or the pleasure?"

"Both."

Her breath was deep now as she replied, "I've a cravin' for you, Mark Aylesbury. I've 'ad it since the first time I saw yer out walkin'. I seen yer often and I asked yer name. Yer can 'ave it free. Anytime you want." She placed her hand on his arm and moved closer, but Mark stepped back, striking her hand away from his arm, and glanced around. "Not here," he hissed. "I've a reputation to maintain."

"Tonight?"

He glared at her, then nodded.

Betty Scoggins smiled slowly, and Mark recognized raw passion in her face. "You won't be sorry," she said searching his face, and then she turned and moved down the street away from him.

The next day was Sunday and Mark rode to

Parramatta, then took the Windsor road going northwest. He was slightly sore, and riding horseback didn't help. What Betty Scoggins hadn't squeezed, probed, and used, she had kissed and bitten. It inflamed him to think about it now, but at the time he had actually had trouble getting an erection because of what she had told him before her incredible lovemaking began.

She had been sitting on her bed dressed in a satin wrapper when Mark arrived at her hut. He had no sooner shut her door than he demanded her to tell him what gossip she had about Penelope.

"I only 'eard Miss Cranston say somethin' about fullness in front. Then I 'eard Miss Fran ask her wot she was gonna do. Then I 'eard her say, ''ide yer condition,' and then the name Aaron."

Mark had glowered at the prostitute, ignoring the glimpse of her breasts as the wrapper she was wearing fell loose in front. "Is that all?"

Betty had shrugged. "To a man it'd mean nothing. To me it meant lots." She had risen from the bed, and stood smiling as she untied her wrapper. Mark had felt his face crease with the horror of what Betty suggested about Penelope, and even as the wrapper floated to the floor at the whore's feet, leaving her standing naked before him, he was asking, "What does it mean to you?"

She shrugged. "Means the girl's knocked up, it does."

Mark's hand had shot out and slapped her before he realized what he was doing. He had never struck a woman before. "You scurvy wench. You lie."

Betty Scoggins pressed the back of her hand to her cheek and never took her eyes from his face. "I don't let men beat me, Mark Aylesbury, but if yer want to play rough, I can."

Next thing he knew she was grinding her mouth against his and her loins against his own, and his mind had stood aloof and pointed out to him how incredible the moment was. There he stood all alone in a pretty prostitute's hut, the woman had it going hot for him, was naked and climbing his frame for want, and all he could think about was how stupid she was. He, who usually got an erection just *hearing* the word "whore."

He had pushed her from him. "Penelope Cranston wouldn't be that—that— She would never do that. She couldn't," he snapped.

Betty Scoggins's eyes were glazed by then. "Whatever yer say, love," she whispered as she nibbled his lips.

"How could you come to such a stupid conclusion when all you heard was what you told me."

Betty had shrugged. "Per'aps I was hot or somethin' at the time and just made somethin' out of something that wasn't there, love."

Still frowning, Mark had let her unbutton his trousers, and soon her skilled hands were fondling him, cupping him with one hand as the other went to the button of his shirt. "Oh, I've upset ye and you've got a frown now, love. But I'll 'ave ye crying out for wot I 'ave, and when it's all done there'll be a smile on yer 'andsome face."

There still was.

And he had put the whore's ridiculous fabrication about Penelope out of his mind.

Mark arrived at the farm early that afternoon, handed the reins of his horse to Rosey, then gave Mrs. Lacy his hat as he entered the house. The short guinea hen of a woman was the wife of the Aylesburys' emancipist overseer, Hiram Lacy, and was the only maid the Aylesburys had. Because of

Mum's excess energy, there was really no need for more house help, for she oversaw the cooking and cleaning, doing part of it herself, as well as managing the farms. Hiram had proved efficient, and over the past nine years he had acted as overseer of the hired laborers.

The Aylesburys had hired the Lacys four years before Mark left for England, and he knew and liked them well.

"Oh, it's glad I am yer home, Master Mark," Mrs. Lacy said, taking his hat. "Yer father and mum are so upset about Aaron's not comin' home. Ye'll be a comfort to 'em, you will."

"I see that Aunt Fran's gig is parked out front."

Mrs. Lacy always had a ready smile. "Aye, Master Mark. Just arrived she did, from church. She's in the livin' room with yer father and mum, but they said they couldn't be disturbed." Mrs. Lacy nodded vigorously as she hung his hat on the coat rack near the door. "Somethin' mighty mysterious, methinks. Would ya care for a cuppa tea, Master Mark? I can serve it to ya in the dinin' room. Or if ya please I can take it up ta yer old room."

Mark's eyes went to the closed living room door. He could hear Aunt Fran's voice coming from the room. "No, Mrs. Lacy. No tea. I'll go up to my room and wash, if you don't mind."

The woman bobbed her head. "I'll be comin' up with a pitcher o' water then, Master Mark."

"Thank you."

The maid left, hobbling toward the back of the house where Mark knew she would draw water from a well behind the house and carry it in a pitcher to his room. Just as he was about to mount the stairs that rose from one side of the hall to the first landing, he heard the word "Penelope" come from the living

room. Mark paused, turned his head, caught the word "problem."

Betty Scoggins's words came back to him and that cold reptilian horror slid down his back again. His scalp crawled and then an unexplainable anger possessed him as he stepped to the door and paused to listen.

"What kind of problem?" Matthew Aylesbury asked. Only it was more a demand than a question.

Frances folded her hands in her lap. "The girl came to me a week ago to be fitted for several gowns." Frances had deliberately waited until Sunday when Matt would be home. She had considered telling only Milicent, but that would have been shirking part of her responsibility. No, she must tell Matt herself.

He had been standing with his back to the wide living room window and was only a dark figure against its blinding glare. Milicent had sensed something was amiss and had sat down in a chair next to Fran's. Fran loved Milly, a woman so strong, so sensible, so straightforward, so very like the woman Fran wanted to be. It was not Milicent who caused her to pause to seek the wisest words. It was Matthew, her own brother, so volatile, so easy to anger when it came to problems involving his sons.

"Penelope Cranston is going to have Aaron's child," she said outright at last. Fran caught only a glimpse of Milicent as she shut her eyes, then opened them. Matthew seemed to materialize out of the glare of the sun and she could see his expression now. It was blank, but even as she watched her brother's handsome face, his eyes dilated and grew hard, the lines on either side of

226

his mouth deepened, and a vertical crease deepened in the middle of his forehead. He said nothing.

"She did not name Aaron. I simply guessed." Fran looked at Milly. "Penelope and Aaron played together as children."

"I suspected it," Milicent said softly. "And saw no harm in it. So I never mentioned it."

Fran could see that her brother had not moved, so she went on. "When Aaron was overseas, he and Penelope exchanged letters through me." Fran cleared her throat. "I saw no harm in their exchanging letters, Matt. Don't look at me like I'm a traitor."

"The fight at Phyfes' ball."

Fran looked at him as he came toward her. He was looking at Milicent and his expression was now what Fran expected. Thunderstorm coming up over the mountains.

"That was all over that damned Cranston girl," he said.

"Matt," began Milicent. "It wasn't her fault at all."

"What kind of girl is she? What kind can she be with parents like hers?" he demanded loudly. He turned and glowered at Fran. "She named Aaron?"

"She named no one," Fran said. "She did not even tell me she was with child, Matt, but there were a couple of symptoms. I guessed. I asked if it was Aaron because she loves him, and he recently returned from England and I knew they—"

"God *damn* him! *And* Cranston's offspring, for God's sake."

"They care for each other. Haven't you guessed that, Matt, or have you been blind to everything your son cares about?" Fran stood up and set her jaw, ready to do battle if necessary.

227

Fury flushed his face. "My son, Aaron, cares for nothing but his own appetites!" he thundered. "And no, I don't doubt he got the Cranston girl pregnant." Matt waved away Milicent's shocked protest. "It's exactly the kind of irresponsible thing he'd do." He turned and strode toward the window, his hand going through his hair. "God in heaven! Now what are we going to do?" He turned to Fran again. "Very well, she got her message across to you, however subtle. What does she want us to do? What does she *want?*"

"Aaron," Fran said. "And Penelope is her name. You don't know her, Matt. She's a sensible girl, a good girl."

"She's a whore."

Fran slapped him before she knew what she was doing, but she'd fry in hell before she would apologize. "The girl is a decent young lady, who loves your son."

"Any girl who would allow a man to—" Something checked Matthew and he glanced at Milicent, who was standing beside him, her bottom lip between her teeth, her eyes meeting his in some secret message meant only for him. Matthew blinked, looked away, and heaved a sigh. His shoulders sagged as he looked at the floor and said, "Aaron and Buck did not return. Glenn and Jack won't say why. They lie. They mumble something about Aaron and Buck staying longer to explore a river. But they aren't telling everything. Something is wrong." Matt rubbed his face. "Meantime, for the Cranston girl, time is—"

"Of the essence," Fran said. "She can only disguise the obvious for so long."

Matt looked at Fran a moment. "Do the Cranstons know?"

"I think not."

He bowed his head, shook it.

Fran gathered her gloves. "I can't stay. I've an appointment at three o'clock." She looked at Milicent, who was now standing beside her little lady's writing desk. "I betrayed Penelope's confidence. I told you her secret because it is the Aylesburys' responsibility to do something for her. I waited as long as I could. She won't be able to disguise her condition much longer. Was I wrong, Milly?"

Practical, level-headed Milicent shook her head. "No, Fran. You are absolutely right in telling us. Penelope may not agree with you now, but later she will see why you had to do this, as it is the only honorable thing to do."

Fran nodded. "I waited before telling you. But now—" Her eyes went to the window, beyond the window, then came back to fix on Milicent's face.

"But you sense something is wrong out there, too, don't you, Fran?" Milicent said.

Fran studied her sister-in-law. Women were like that, sensing things about their men, especially when they were in some kind of danger. Fran nodded. "Yes. Something's wrong. I don't know what."

"Something in the bush. Something to do with Aaron."

Fran whispered, "Yes."

Matthew only stood like a big oaf and looked from his sister to his wife. That the hair on the back of his neck bristled, that his face paled suddenly, Fran did not see, for she turned and walked toward the door saying, "I shall be in touch."

When Mrs. Lacy opened the front door for her, Fran bade her good day and walked out onto the veranda into the blinding New South Wales sun, which she could never get used to. On the veranda

229

Mark was standing against a post looking out across the yard. "Good afternoon, Mark."

"Afternoon, Aunt Fran. I'll help you into the gig."

"No need. By the way, your waistcoat is finished. We mended the tear in it, and you'd never know it was there." She smiled at him out of the corner of her eye. "But it won't take any more fights. Best you behave when you're wearing it from now on. That's terribly expensive linen."

Mark looked at her as if he didn't know what she was talking about. Then what she had said registered on his brain. "Oh. Fine. I'll pick it up on my way to Sydney early in the morning." He walked with her to the gig saying something about the drought and how all the birds had vanished. He had aided her into the carriage and she turned to wave to him, and Milicent and Matt on the veranda, then drove out of the dooryard.

"Coming in, Mark?" Milicent called to him.

"I . . . think I'll trip over to the landing for a bit, Mum, if that's all right."

"We'll see you for tea, then." And Milicent went into the house followed by Mark's father. His father, who had not even greeted him, had stood without seeing him. His father, who would have nothing on his mind now but Aaron. Aaron and his problems.

Mark let the anger and hurt and confusion wash over him then. Aaron had—had—had done it. He had—had taken Penelope. Taken *Penelope*. Tears blinded him as he strode for his horse. Bloody damn him. Damn him, like his father had said. Damn, damn, damn, damn!

Mark did not even bother to pretend he was headed for the landing. He rode down the track going west. He would circle the ridge, go around the western edge of it through the bush and to the Cranstons'. *To*

230

the Cranstons' for what? To ask to speak to Penelope. Penelope, who had let Aaron take her and use her? He would shake her until her teeth chattered, slap her, slap her and— Of course, he would not lay a hand on her. But he would— His intentions became suddenly clear, like the sun coming from behind a dark cloud. He would ask her to marry him. He would save her from scandal. Aaron might not return in time before her belly— Mark's face burned and he wanted to vomit. But he would ask her. He would let her know that he knew. It would save the Aylesburys and Cranstons from scandal, and it was the only honorable thing to do, after all . . . and his father would be grateful to him. Besides, he loved her. He wanted her. Even though Aaron had already taken her? Yes. Yes, even now.

"I'm sorry Mahsta Aylesbury, but Miss Penelope is not in," the Cranstons' doorman said.

"I know bloody well better," Mark said heatedly from the shade of the Cranstons' veranda. The doorman was short and fat and, in his black livery, reminded him of the Reverend Marsden of Parramatta, which intimidated Mark somewhat, but did not prevent him from venting his anger. "I've come to see her on a matter of utmost importance. Importance to the lady."

The doorman was undismayed. "I'm sorry, sir, but the lady is not in."

"Did Mr. Cranston tell you to say that?"

"I'm sorry, sir. But now that you have brought it up yourself, sir, Master Cranston *did* give us orders not to admit you to the house, sir."

Livid with fury, Mark was becoming aware that convict workers had begun to appear here and there in the dooryard. That blackguard has warned them all to keep me away, he thought. "Then I must speak

231

to Mrs. Cranston, if you don't mind. Immediately!"

The doorman's hauteur was not ruffled. "I'm sorry sir, but the lady is ill abed and cannot see visitors. Now if you would be so kind, sir, I've matters to attend to in the house." With that the doorman shut the door softly, leaving Mark staring at a wrought iron door knocker, a lion's head with a ring in its mouth. He turned abruptly, looked around at the dooryard. Six laborers had gathered. One was the overseer. Mark had seen him before. A big bruiser with tattoos on his forearms. Boston, they called him in Sydney, where he came occasionally to gad about town with his ruffian friends. A big Irishman who'd been transported to New South Wales for cracking a man's skull. Boston stood with feet wide apart, arms folded over his massive chest.

Mark's anger was so great as he stood rebuffed, threatened, and thwarted that he announced suddenly, "Of course, you do remember that you are still convicts."

If he hoped that they would be as intimidated as he was, he was disappointed. Their expressions did not change. They kept the same sardonic grimace on their surly lips and the same gleam in their eyes. So, with a great show of hauteur, Mark strode off the veranda and down the walk to his horse. He mounted and rode straight for the ridge, following the trail through the young forest of gum trees to the top.

In the clearing that was the Aylesbury side, he reined the horse and dismounted, letting the reins trail in the waving grass. He sat down on a big boulder and propped his elbow on his knee and his chin in his hand. What to do? How does a man get to talk to a lass when the whole household is against him?

How did Aaron get her to meet him here on the

ridge? Mark's head came up. Of course. He should have remembered. He looked up at the sun and judged by it that it was not yet teatime, but he must work fast. There wasn't much of the day left. And he *must* speak to her today. For very early in the morning he had to head back down the track to Sydney.

As Mark hurriedly mounted his horse, he experienced only one flash of conscience about Aaron. Aaron, who was out in the bush somewhere.

Give a recital, give a recital. How many times had Mr. Sheldon urged her to do that? In Penelope's opinion, she had not yet learned a single piece well enough to give a recital. Besides, giving a recital would mean inviting all her friends and her parents' friends to the house for a ball, and before the ball commenced she would be expected to bore everybody to tears with her harp playing, and all eyes would be upon her, and somebody was bound to notice her belly.

Her fingers ran over the harp strings creating a sound like water running in a brook. Did *he* see water running in a brook? Did any raindrops like *these* fall upon his beloved head? She would know soon. Any day he would return. But he would have to discover her problem on his own, for she would not force their marriage by revealing her secret. He must ask her to marry him only because he loved her. He might even be home today, she thought. Her father had been in Sydney for three days, so if there was any news of the expedition, likely she would not hear until he returned.

"Do you know who Father went to Sydney to hire as solicitor?"

Penelope's hands stilled the vibrating strings of the harp and let the instrument tilt back to its resting position. Jamey was standing in the doorway of the ballroom, leaning against the door jamb with his arms folded.

"Ol' Mr. Holt."

"He's not so old, Jamey."

"I meant ol' as in grumpy."

"He's the best in the colony."

"He's an exclusionist, but he has no better character than Crossley, who is this colony's leading legal advisor. And Crossley was disbarred in England because of perjury. Why didn't Father pick someone who at least is honest?"

"He picked Mr. Holt because Holt was recommended to him by the Livingstons."

"Yeah, because Holt is about to make his star solicitor's assistant a full partner in his firm. Your friend, Rodney Livingston."

"Rodney would prepare the case well for Father, and he would be excellent at representing him in court, too. Whatever else Rodney is, Jamey, he's an excellent solicitor."

"The case of Crawford versus Cranston should be an interesting one for you, Penny, especially since your friend Mark is Fitzhugh's assistant and is representing Thaddeus Crawford."

Penelope nodded. "Oh dear. Wouldn't it be terrible if Mark and Rodney faced each other in court with this case?"

"As I said, it would be interesting. Especially since I have just confirmed that our mare Josephine, whom Thaddeus Crawford's stallion visited the night the sheep tore up Crawford's pasture, is pregnant."

Penelope's mouth popped open. "Jamey! Where

did you get such a word?"

"Out of the English language. The same place the words dog, cat, tree, baby, pretty, and manure came from."

"Jamey!"

The handsome, and precocious twelve-year-old smiled. "If I'm going to be a stockman, Penny, I'll be using words like manure often."

"Stockman indeed," she said gathering her skirts as she stood up, trying hard not to laugh. James-of-the-few-words was making them count today.

"Father says if his mare is pregnant, he could file a counter suit for damages himself. He had planned to breed the mare to Chaseman to produce a riding horse. Now he's stuck with a draft horse foal. If it lives. Thaddeus Crawford's stallion was too large for the little mare. Father predicts problems at birth."

Blushing, Penelope hastened to the east window and looked out, making a great show of brushing her curls away from her face. Then she turned to face James. "Then perhaps Father has a chance to win the case."

"More than a chance. He and the Reverend Marsden are friends, and Marsden will be the magistrate hearing the case."

Reverend Marsden was the colony's principal minister and also magistrate of the district around Parramatta. Since the area of the Crawfords' and Cranstons' fence was just in his district, he would preside at the hearing. Poor Thaddeus Crawford wouldn't stand a chance.

"I believe Father should pay the damages to Mr. Crawford's pasture," she said.

"So do I, but I feel sorry for Fitzhugh and Mark Aylesbury, having so much stacked against them before the case is even presented. And speaking of

Aylesburys, Penny, I wish you'd tend to the one on the ridge. His signals are becoming annoying." James grinned then as Penelope stared at him. Then she jerked her head around to stare out the east window, out across the yard, the field, the ridge. There it was. The flash of reflected sun.

"Oh! Oh my *God!*" she shrilled. As she tore past her brother to get out the door, she heard him say something about swearing. Penelope jerked open the door. No time for hat or gloves or boots or proper attire. Barely time for Cricket to saddle Bayleaf. Up she rode like the wind out of a tunnel, up the ridge, beating the horse with the reins, laughing, tears blowing back in the breeze, through the gum trees, up until she galloped into the clearing. She reined the horse and looked about. No one. Her heart was thudding in her breast. He would leap out of the forest grinning and scare her. She dismounted.

"Aaron! Aaron. Come out. I can't stand it!" she cried laughing.

But it was not Aaron who came from the trees.

Her laughter caught in her throat as she swallowed air. "Mark!"

He stood straight, like a young sapling, dressed in a handsome blue coat and white trousers and holding his hat at his side. The hot breeze from the west stirred the curls of his flaxen hair. "I'm sorry to disappoint you."

Penelope's disappointment clouded her manners as she snapped, "Where's Aaron?"

Mark came toward her slowly. "I don't know. No one does. Outback somewhere. He still hasn't returned."

"Outback," she breathed, and tears threatened her, as they did so often lately. "As if he were only in the back dooryard. Oh Mark, hasn't there been any word

236

at all from the expedition? Father has been in Sydney for three days, so we hear no news of the expedition."

His eyes reflected anger just an instant, then softened as he decided to lie. "No. No word."

She turned away and walked to the big boulder where she and Aaron had often sat. "You tricked me," she said, and bit her lips to keep from weeping.

"I tried to call on you properly, but your doorman turned me away and your hired convicts threatened me. I signaled you because it was the only way I could get to talk to you, Penelope."

Her chin came up a little. "What could you possibly want to talk to me about? I thought I made my feelings clear to you at the Phyfes' ball." Now that the threat of tears was subsiding, she turned toward him and was surprised to find him standing so close.

"Marry me."

She blinked. "I beg your pardon?"

"Marry me. It's the only answer, Penelope."

Her face flushed, and embarrassment and dread warred to emerge first in her mind. "I don't understand you."

"We have no idea how long it will be before Aaron returns. If ever."

"Any day. He will return any day now. But what has that to do with you?"

"It has much to do with *you*, doesn't it?"

Her eyes widened as she looked at him. He knew. Somehow, he knew. God in heaven, Frances Aylesbury had told the Aylesburys. "I . . . will wait," she breathed, blushing.

"How long? How long before—" Perspiration stood out in beads upon his forehead. His eyes had gone glassy and his hand trembled as he reached toward her. "Penelope, I love you."

She regarded him, feeling more pity for him than

for herself, and all she could do was shake her head.

"I want you. I always have," he said, barely above a whisper. "I want you to marry me, before there's trouble. Before you cause—"

"Disgrace to my parents?" she said, a smile trembling on her lips.

"And mine."

She frowned. Yes, she had thought about that a million times. "Poor, dear Mark," she said bitterly, "ready to sacrifice himself for his family."

"No. I told you. I love you." Taking hold of her arm, he added, "And you will love me."

"I will always love Aaron."

He released her, turned away. Suddenly his body seemed to swell and he shouted, "Damn!" to the sky. "Why," he cried to the trees, "has he always had everything I want?"

Penelope strode to her horse.

"Stop!" he said, coming toward her, his face damp and red. "Penelope. You must answer me. You see . . . Jack Summers and Glenn Moffett returned Saturday morning, without Aaron and Buck. And they aren't saying why."

Penelope felt a cold hand grip her heart as she stared at Mark. The possibility that Aaron could be in danger refused to surface in her mind. He would be back. And soon. Soon.

"Penelope?"

"I will wait for Aaron." When she saw the pain in his face, she added, "I'm sorry, Mark. I like you, you know. You're a dear friend and—"

"Spare me." He turned away from her. "Spare me, please."

Sick at heart, Penelope mounted her horse.

"I'll come back to your house again," he warned her. "I'll be back to ask you again."

238

"Please don't."

"I'll be back, Penelope."

She turned the gelding, kicked his flanks, headed him into the trees, and even as she nudged him into a gallop going down the path through the forest, she heard him cry, "I'll be back, Penelope!"

Chapter XII

"It's Dr. Aylesbury, Miss Penelope," the doorman said softly.

Penelope's skirt made soft, swishing sounds as she hurried the rest of the way down the stairs into the hallway. "Thank you, Quincy." She came to the doctor standing in the hall and curtsied briefly. "I'm so glad you could come, Dr. Aylesbury. I'm Penelope. I don't think we've actually met."

Dr. Aylesbury, Aaron's father, was an older Mark. He had the same eyes, the same light, curly hair, the same build, but this man seemed larger somehow. A strength emanated from him that caused a rush of excitement to course through her almost as if he were Aaron. She offered her hand.

For a moment he studied her, then took her hand briefly and said, "Miss Cranston."

As they stood looking at each other, Penelope realized that he must know that she was carrying Aaron's child, and she thought she could perceive what he was thinking. But she did not take her steady gaze from his. This was a great man, no matter what her father thought of him. He looked fully into her face, his blue eyes searching hers seeming slightly

startled before they softened. "Your mother is worse?" he said, almost skeptically.

"Yes. And we could not wait for Dr. Bowman, Dr. Aylesbury. She seems suddenly so much weaker. Of course, you know Mother feigns much of her illness, but I—I think she's much worse. Her breathing isn't right, and she swears she's dying and can't wait for Dr. Bowman to come from Parramatta."

One corner of Matthew Aylesbury's mouth twitched into a smile. "She's sworn that twice in the past few months, only to get much better when Dr. Bowman arrived instead of me."

Penelope bit her lips to keep from smiling because it was true. "I wouldn't have bothered you, but since she swears she's dying this time, I couldn't take a chance."

"I understand."

"Will you be wanting to see her now?"

"I think I had better see her now."

As he followed her up the stairs carrying his black case, he asked, "Tell me more about the illness. Your servant said it is a lung ailment?"

"As you know, she has been seeing Dr. Bowman for over a year because of a persistent cough. She's been abed for a week now and we thought she was better. But suddenly today, she seems so weak, so awfully weak." They came to the second floor, where Penelope paused before a closed door. "Father is in here with her," she said, to prepare the doctor.

He nodded without changing his expression and followed her into her mother's bedchamber.

Elaina Cranston lay in the same bed in which she had been born. The thing was a tester bed with ornate carvings in dark woods and draped with cotton damask, the folds of which were tied against each post. Her face upon the white linen of her pillows

241

was pale. At first Dr. Aylesbury did not acknowledge Oliver Cranston, who rose from his chair beside the bed. But as he turned and paced toward the door, the doctor flung over his shoulder, "No need to leave, Cranston."

Oliver paused and said darkly, "I'd prefer it."

Dr. Aylesbury did not reply, but set his bag on the chair and bent closer to peer at Elaina Cranston. Elaina's maid, Greta, was standing in a corner, hands folded before her with a strange look on her face, which Penelope could not interpret. Her mother's eyelids fluttered and her pale lips pressed together before a squeak came from them and the whisper, "Matthew."

Dr. Aylesbury said, "Elaina." Then, slowly and thoroughly, he proceeded to take her pulse, counting her respirations, felt her forehead, then straightened. He stared down at her and took a deep breath before he said, "Elaina, your pulse is normal, there's no fever. Why are you breathing like that?"

The eyelids fluttered, as if she could barely keep them open. "I can't . . . get my breath, Matthew." She shot a glance at him before shutting her eyes again. "I can't breathe. Something in my chest."

Matthew looked at Penelope. "I'll have to listen to her chest," he said morosely.

Penelope nodded and Elaina fluttered one pale hand at her. "Go away, Penelope. You too, Greta. I have to talk to the doctor."

Dr. Aylesbury looked at Penelope and said, "Stay."

Elaina took a shuddering breath. "I said leave, Penelope. Leave me be, Greta."

Dr. Aylesbury frowned at Penelope and shook his head, and only Greta left the room. Penelope clasped her hands and went slowly to the window out of her mother's sight.

"I am dying, you know," she heard her mother say softly.

Turning halfway around, Penelope observed as Dr. Aylesbury grimly put his ear to her mother's chest, over the linen sheet that covered her.

"Matthew," Elaina whispered, and Penelope's mouth fell open when she saw her mother press the doctor's head to her bosom with both hands. "Oh Matthew, Matthew, my love. My—"

"Hush," he said sharply. "I'm listening."

Penelope watched, astonished that her suspicions about her mother's being in love with Aaron's father were confirmed. But apparently the feeling wasn't mutual. The doctor raised his head and looked at her mother unsympathetically. "You're not dying, Elaina," he said.

"I *will* die soon. You must hear me." Although Penelope strained to hear her mother's choked words, she could hear only broken phrases, the words, ". . . Oliver never loved me . . . your wife . . . before your pardon . . . his child . . . illegitimate."

The doctor reared back as if struck in the face. "You're lying, Elaina," he said.

"No. It's true. I swear. I *know* it's true. I swear it on my deathbed."

He stood abruptly, the look on his face so tragic that a raw horror whispered to her with cold lips and bade her understand. *Oliver never loved me . . . your wife . . . before your pardon . . . his child . . . illegitimate.* Aaron?

Penelope stepped back and covered her mouth with her hand and bumped into the wall. *Oliver never loved me . . . your wife . . . before your pardon . . . his child . . . illegitimate.* Aaron. She must be talking about Aaron. Oh, God no.

If Aaron was Oliver Cranston's illegitimate child

by Mrs. Aylesbury, then . . . then . . . the room tilted, swayed. Strong arms came and went around Penelope, helping her to the chair. "You heard?" he asked.

Penelope swallowed the bile coming up in her throat. She mustn't let him know she had heard. She shook her head. "No, I was just suddenly faint."

She did not see his hand as he waved a vial of smelling salts under her nose. Penelope gasped. Her vision cleared, and when she looked up she saw that he was smiling down at her, his eyes searching her face with a bewildered expression. "Better?"

Penelope nodded. After a moment, she managed, "And Mother?"

Dr. Aylesbury straightened with a smile. "The same as always. She'll live."

Elaina Cranston sat up so suddenly that Penelope was astonished because all the color had rushed back into her mother's face and her green eyes were snapping with life. "Damn you, Matthew. I *am* dying. You'll see. I'll die, and you'll see that you aren't half the frigging doctor you think you are."

Penelope shot out of her chair. "Mother!" Mouth open in horror, she stared unbelievingly, then jerked her head around to look at the doctor.

Dr. Matthew Aylesbury had an unperturbed half-smile on his face as he snapped his black bag shut. "Oh, you'll die, Elaina. You've all the symptoms of consumption, but it's in its early stages." He took the bag by its handle and turned to her. "By the way, I don't believe a damn thing you've told me tonight." And he started walking toward the bedroom door.

Penelope was still staring when the medicine bottle, which had been sitting on the table beside the bed, crashed into the wall next to the door where the doctor stood.

"Swine! Pig! Bastard!" Elaina screamed.

Matthew jerked his head toward the door, indicating that Penelope should follow him.

Neither spoke as they descended the stairs; Penelope was too horrified and shocked, but once they were in the hallway, she said, "I'm so sorry! I've never heard my mother curse before."

"Haven't you? I have."

"I've troubled you for no reason."

"You were right to call me. You couldn't have been sure she wasn't dying." He stood and looked at her. "Are you certain you didn't hear the great secret she told me?"

Penelope wasn't very adept at lying, but she could manage when she thought it was best. "No. I didn't."

"It's just as well. Her imagination was running a bit wild." He nodded. "You're a lovely young lady."

Blushing, Penelope replied, "Perhaps you should give Father the news about Mother."

Without a word, Dr. Aylesbury allowed her to lead him to the living room where, in an overstuffed chair, Oliver Cranston sat reading. When he heard them at the door, he raised his black eyes from the book that lay in his lap and burned a hole in the air between them with his glare.

Fascinated, Penelope watched the interplay of smoldering hostility as her father and the doctor looked at each other silently for a moment. It was like watching lightning without hearing the thunder. "There's no change in your wife, Cranston."

"I heard," he replied with a sardonic smile. "Her judgment of character has always been better than her aim."

Horror made Penelope gasp, but again the doctor seemed undismayed as he turned and went into the hallway again. She hurried after him, and as Quincy

245

politely handed him his hat, she said, "I must pay you for the call, Dr. Aylesbury. Please tell me how much."

He shook his head. "Nothing." He looked at her as if he might say something else, but then he nodded and was gone.

But Penelope remained in the hallway alone. And in the quiet of gathering dusk, she let all the things she had heard and seen that evening seep at last into her brain, that part of her mind that sorted out mere words and shaped them into meanings. Trembling, she leaned against the door and covered her face with her hands.

Dr. Aylesbury hadn't believed her mother, but her mother had no reason to lie. *Oliver never loved me ... your wife ... before your pardon ... his child ... illegitimate.*

Penelope sorted through the fragments of her mother's revelation and pieced them together with the suspicions she herself had harbored for years. Something had happened before Dr. Aylesbury was pardoned years ago. Her father loved Mrs. Aylesbury. Penelope thought of the cottage in the woods. And who was the illegitimate child? Not Mark; the entire colony already knew he was Dr. Aylesbury's son by Molly Troop, the milliner. Then who?

There was only one answer. Aaron.

Suddenly, Penelope's knees turned to oil. She slid down the door to the floor, but she barely noticed as her world came tumbling in around her and an avalanche of agony descended upon her.

For if Aaron was Oliver Cranston's illegitimate child, then Aaron was also ... her own half-brother.

Frances Aylesbury cleared her throat as she peeled

246

off her driving gloves in the Aylesbury living room. "Yes, I wanted to see you here at the house. I just drove Sally Moffett and her daughter Annabelle home from Parramatta, so it was convenient for me to come by."

Milicent motioned with her hand for Mrs. Lacy to bring tea, then said, "Sit down, Frances. I perceive you've more good news for us."

Frances's grim smile was quick. She'd always appreciated Milicent's sense of humor, although what she had come to tell contained no humor in it.

Matthew, pipe in hand, was approaching the table beside his favorite chair and he took the lid off his tin of tobacco and said, "She can't bring any more news like the last she brought home."

Fran said, "Sit down, brother, because I've more news for you."

Matt froze in the act of dipping his pipe in the tobacco.

"Sit."

Matthew looked at her soberly, then obeyed. But he had forgotten the cold pipe in his hand.

Frances shifted in her chair, cleared her throat again. "It seems that being an old maid in this family has certainly set me up to become the recipient of all the family secrets."

Matthew was looking at her without a sign of expression on his face. "What secrets?"

"Annabelle Moffett came to me today, Matt. She's—" Fran shrugged. "Oh, why be delicate? She's pregnant."

Matthew just kept staring without moving. "Not Aaron again."

Frances was shaking her head.

"Not Mark, God forbid . . ."

"It's Deenyi."

Matthew swore.

Frances nodded. "This is a real problem."

Milicent shaded her eyes with her hand. When she had assimilated the news and its consequences she said, "Does Deen know?"

"Annabelle says no."

Matthew stood up and strode to the window as he had done the last time, as if looking out the window got him out of the house and away from the initial impact of the situation. But when he turned back to face the women, his face was vermilion with anger. "What the bloody hell's the matter with these young Australians? All they know how to do is fornicate!"

"Never mind that now, Matt. Thing is, Annabelle can't marry Deen. I asked her if she would consider it. She said no, that she doesn't love him, and I agree. It's impossible."

Matthew passed a big hand over his face. "The people in this colony will hang Deen. One way or another, they'll hang him."

Milicent stood up and went to her desk, laid her hand on it, then turned back to face her sister-in-law. She knew from experience that when trouble began it was like the Hawkesbury when the rains came—walls of water thundered down uprooting stable things like trees and destroying good things like land, turning everything into debris and leaving behind destruction, danger, and death.

"Yes, they'll hang him. He's crossed not only a moral and social barrier, but a racial one, as well. Our society barely tolerates the first two, but it will never tolerate the third. Now, I *am* frightened. Because this time there's no solution." Milicent pressed her lips together, and her thoughts went first to Mark. If only Mark cared for Annabelle just a little—but she could remember his telling Aaron

once, "I wouldn't court Annabelle Moffett; she's tainted."

Oh dear, how she was tainted now. Milicent's hand trembled, then formed a fist on her desk. "We must do something. Something immediately."

Matthew's mouth spread into a peculiar smile. "Yes. Shoot the whole damned younger generation."

"It would be one solution."

All eyes turned to the door, which had opened softly, and Deen stood there for a moment framed in the doorway. "I heard my name when I passed by the door in the hallway. I heard Annabelle's name, too." He walked in with his black eyes riveted on Matthew's face as he came to stop before them, the man who had raised him, the good woman who had nurtured him, his uncle and his aunt. They stared at him and what they saw was a young man who had just discovered that he was to be the father of an illegitimate child. Was that a millennium of tragedy they read on his face, a face that was both achingly young and suddenly old?

Deen spread his arms. "I have no excuses. None."

No one said anything, and Deen's quick black eyes flicked first to one face and then the other. "I love Annabelle, for whatever it's worth."

Matthew shifted his weight to his other foot, his face getting redder and redder, and he shook his finger in Deen's face a full thirty seconds before he could speak. "You . . . you . . . you can't marry that Moffett girl. They'd tear you limb from limb!"

"I know."

"You've not only ruined her life but yours, too. There's nowhere you can go. Bathurst is the farthest, but the colony will move out there. Civilization will follow every frontier. And a girl fornicating with a native is unheard of." Matthew took a deep breath.

249

"Goddamn it, Deen, you've managed to perform a first."

Deen ducked his head, raised it quickly, spread his arms, and opened his mouth to say something.

"Just don't talk. Just shut up," Matthew shouted. He looked at Fran. "How far along is this girl?"

"Almost four months."

"Same as . . ." Matthew rubbed his face. "It was a fine spring, wasn't it?" Looking at Milicent, he asked, "What are we going to do?"

Milicent's eyes came away from the window. "If only Aaron would come home."

Matt nodded. "Yes. That would take care of—" He stopped and glanced at Deen. Deen did not know about the other family secret.

Deen stood with his hands at his sides. He was remembering pulling his goddess from the river, loving her. He had made love to her twice on that occasion, and no more. For she had been so hungry for affection, so hurt. Her clothes had been washed down the river, but she had worn his shirt home. Even now, as he raised his eyes to the ceiling of the room, he could see her standing tall, slender, his shirt reaching to her knees, her hair damp, her face dewy as she said, "That's ten times. I could have a child now." He didn't know what she meant by ten times, but—

"I think you should not try to see me again," she had said as they parted on the hill after he had pulled on his boots. "They will kill us both."

They. Both knew who "they" were. "They" was the world.

His hunger had not been abated. Since he had made love to her on the banks of the river, he had dreamed and he had ridden by the Moffett farm in hopes of getting a glimpse of her. He had climbed the

250

trees near their house to spy, and his eyes never stopped roving toward the east from the landing. If she came to the landing, she would come from the east. And when the sloop that he was guiding passed those high, sandstone cliffs where she had dived into the water, his eyes went to them and he lived again the touch of her silken skin, the smell, the feel, the taste of her.

Now this. They had defied the gods and they had lost.

"She . . ." Deen began. "She is in love with Aaron. Has always been in love with Aaron. I will ask her to marry me, but she won't. She can't."

Matthew glowered. "And what is she going to do?"

Fran spoke up. "She says that she will bear the child and keep her mouth shut about whose it is."

Matthew dragged his gaze from Fran and fixed it on Deen. "And you had better keep yours shut, too, if you value your life."

Deen nodded. He shut his eyes for a moment. "It's—it's *hell* for a man not to be able to have the woman he wants and for his child to grow up before his eyes and him unable even to call it his own."

Suddenly, all the pain of the world sifted like dust left over from a storm and settled in Deen's voice as he shook his fists up before him and cried, "I wish to God the raiders on my mother's village had killed me, too." The sudden display of emotion and weakness made him ashamed. He dropped his arms and got control of himself once more. "I've never faced a problem that had no solution before. I'm sorry." With that, he bolted out the door.

The three stared after him. Then Matthew's hand spread over his chest and he lowered himself into his chair, shaking his head. "The only thing we can do," he said softly, "is let the girl bring the child up with

251

our help."

"The Moffetts are well off, Matt. They don't need your help," Fran said.

"Then we'll have them marry and send them to America or Canada or South Africa."

"We can suggest that, Matt, but Annabelle won't do it."

"Then what do you suggest?"

Fran bit her lips. "Is Mark smitten on any girl?"

Matthew looked at her sharply. "I was hoping that if Aaron—if Aaron didn't return, that Mark—there's the Cranston girl, too."

Frances looked at Milicent who she could see was going over all the facts in her mind as she would her ledgers, assembling the figures, the cost, the balance. Milicent Crawford Aylesbury had faced a host of difficult problems in her life and had solved all of them. But all she came up with this time was, "Oh, poor Annabelle. And poor, poor Deenyi."

"Sir, I must talk to you."

"I think I told you once, Mark, that you are not welcome on these premises."

"But sir, it's a matter I'm sure you'll be concerned with."

"I doubt it."

"Penelope is going to have a child."

Oliver Cranston stopped abruptly, his black hair blowing in the stiff breeze as he stared at Mark in revulsion. *"What?"*

"Yes," Mark panted, slightly out of breath from hurrying beside Cranston, who had been striding down the furrows of ripening melons. "She is going to have a baby, and if you don't believe me ask—" The next thing Mark knew he was lying among the

252

melons and there was a terrible throbbing in his head. And Oliver Cranston was towering over him, fists clenched.

"You lie, Aylesbury."

Mark scrambled up, shrugged his coat back onto his shoulders. "I don't lie. And I want to marry her as soon—"

The shock of pain from the next blow was black and sounded like a cricket bat striking a ball. He staggered back, gained his balance. "I love her. I've always loved her. I tried to persuade you to let me pay court to her properly, but you—"

"You slime!" Oliver hit Mark again in the face, causing him to stagger backwards. "Slime!" He hit him again and again, spitting, "Slime! Slime! Slime!" with every blow. Mark staggered with each blow, but he did not try to defend himself. *"Slime!"*

Mark flew backwards and landed on the soft earth. A dullness settled over him and there was a ringing in his head he could not shake loose. He tasted blood and salt, and when the blackness lifted he saw Cranston crouched above him, fists still clenched, his hair in disarray, his face horrible to see.

"You bastard. I should have let them hang your father back in England."

Mark touched his throbbing eye. "Nevertheless, sir," he gasped, "I am here, and Penelope is going to have a baby, and I want to marry her."

"Get up."

Mark scrambled to his feet, reeled a little and stared at Cranston, blinking back the black spots before his eyes.

"If this is true, you'll sure as hell marry her. And as soon as possible."

Yanking his coat down, Mark said, "I've bought a house, sir. And I've thirty thousand pounds in the

bank, including my inheritance from my grandmother."

Oliver's twisted expression turned into a sneer.
"Grandmother? You never *had* a grandmother. And
your mother was a whore."

Mark lunged in a blind rage, but Cranston was
quicker, and with a thrust of his body threw Mark
onto the ground.

Teeth clenched, Cranston towered over him, his
chest heaving with rage. "Now get up, you sick pup.
I'm going to take you to Penelope and if what you
said is true, we've got some planning to do."

Mark got up slowly, and as he began brushing his
new trousers, he caught a glimpse of an indigo skirt
blowing in the breeze just on the edge of his
peripheral vision. His eyes slid to the side and went
up to waist hidden in folds and gathers of material,
up to full breasts, a ruffled neckline that displayed a
slender neck, and to a face as pale as the moon. His
eyes met hers, but he couldn't speak.

Oliver's chest was heaving from exertion and
anger as he looked from his daughter to Mark and
back again. "Penelope, Mark has accused you of
something abominable."

Her green eyes left her father and went back to
Mark. For a moment she did not speak. "That was
playing dirty, Mark."

Mark's hand paused in midair as he was dusting
off his coat. "It isn't playing, Penelope. Not
anymore."

"And you've left me no choice but to marry you,
have you?" She was solemn, coolly angry, more
beautiful than he had ever seen her in his life.

Mark swallowed. He hurt all over. He felt dirty, his
eye was swelling shut, his mouth throbbed. But it
was all he could manage to do to keep from grinning

254

as he jammed his hat back on his head and leaned toward her to reply, "No."

"Do you know, Mark lad, that doctors don't know much more than we do about what goes on in a man's chest when he gets old?" Mr. Fitzhugh reached up from his bed and tapped Mark's chest. "Beggin' your father's pardon, of course. Perhaps he knows because he went to Edinburgh College, but Wentworth don't know or Balmaine or any of the others. Perhaps your father doesn't either."

"Mr. Fitzhugh, Dr. Wentworth said you weren't to talk much," Mark said from his chair beside the bed. There was an underlying panic in everything he said, everything he did. Work was piling up in the office, work he had done that needed Fitzhugh's approval before it could be disposed of, and Fitz was ill. He had fallen ill while eating at his own home, with a pain in his chest that incapacitated him, panicked his wife, and caused Dr. Wentworth to put him to bed with strict orders not to get up and not to have visitors.

Fitzhugh brushed aside Mark's remark. "Bah. If I weren't so weak— But, Mark, you've got the firm all to yourself for a while, lad. Whatever can't be put off until I can go over them with you, will just have to stand as is." Fitzhugh took a deep breath, and Mark broke out in goose bumps. Four months back from England and he had the solicitor's office to himself. The routine paperwork he could handle, but the Crawford litigation was something else.

Fitzhugh tapped him on the chest again. "I know what you're thinking. Rumors are spreading like a bush fire that you asked that pretty Cranston girl to marry you." Fitzhugh took another breath. "When is

255

the date set for the wedding?"

Mark fidgeted. "Two weeks from Wednesday."

"That's rather quick, isn't it?"

"Well, yes. But we saw no sense in postponing it, sir."

"Spoken like a true young Australian. You chaps don't adhere much to tradition, do you?"

"What tradition, sir? English tradition?"

Fitz smiled. "I see your point." He coughed, getting red in the face, which frightened Mark, but he settled back on his pillow and said, "The Quarter Session convenes a week from Monday. Be sure Reverend Marsden has the Crawford case on the docket."

"Mr. Fitzhugh, I've been wanting to ask you about that."

"It's yours, lad."

Mark felt all the blood drain out of his face. "But Mr. Fitzhugh—"

"Aye, I know. Cranston will be your father-in-law, and if the case is set after your marriage we couldn't take it, could we? But Cranston is a man who would understand your position, and if—when—you win, he will hold no grudges. After all, you are simply representing your client. Remember, he was a magistrate back in England."

"But sir—"

"But what, Mark?"

Mark had stood up, cold perspiration breaking out all over his body. Stuart had been hoping for this, that Fitzhugh would turn the Crawford case entirely over to him. What a thing they could make out of it. In the first place he would be a currency lad leading a court battle against a pure merino. In the second place, his client was suing the man who had caused his father to be sentenced back in England to

256

transportation. In the third place, Rodney Livingston had just been appointed full partner to Holt and was, incredibly, going to represent Cranston. Four, every young buck in the colony was laughing uproariously about Crawford's stallion breaking down a fence and raping a Cranston mare. The case was going to be the most interesting in years. It appealed to merinos and emancipists alike.

"But sir, Mr. Cranston has hired Holt to represent him," Mark said in a panic.

Fitzhugh never batted an eye. "So. You prepare the case, Mark, and you present it to the magistrate. And don't be intimidated by Holt's young colt, Livingston, or Magistrate Marsden, either." Fitzhugh drew a deep, tired breath. "You'll do fine, lad."

Aye, he'd do fine, but he wouldn't win.

Fifteen minutes later, after he had left Fitzhugh's house and met Stu on the street, he and Stu went to Foster's Tavern where, over stringy bark, Stu raved, "Mark! Don't you see this is your big chance? If you win this case, your career is *made*, mate. Every emancipist and currency lad in the colony will hire you to take his case. Not to mention that it would be a political victory for *our* side, the first since this colony was founded."

When Mark, nursing his beer, did not demonstrate the least enthusiasm, Stu went on, "God I wish *I* had the opportunity."

"Stu, Marsden is the magistrate."

Stu's eyebrows fell two inches. "Oh. That *does* make a difference." His gleaming bright black eyes flashed, though, as he leaned over the table toward Mark. "All the more you've got to win, mate. What are the issues in the case?"

"I can't discuss a case with an outsider. Ethics, Stu."

"I'm not an outsider. I'm a solicitor, aren't I? And I'm your best friend, aren't I?"

Mark set his tankard down and leaned on his forearm. "In Crawford's favor—Cranston sheep did trample forty acres of English imported grass, which Crawford had been growing as an experiment for the purpose of testing it for climate and soil conditions. It was an experiment graziers were watching with interest."

"That's something. What else?"

"That's all Crawford has in his favor."

"What are the issues against him?"

"As everybody knows, Cranston claims Crawford's stallion broke down the fence and proceeded to impregnate his prize Thoroughbred in one fell swoop, a mare he had been waiting to come into season so that he could breed her with one of his trotters."

Stuart was the only young man in the colony who saw no humor in the situation about Cranston's mare. His mind wasn't turned that way unless there was profit in it. "What else is in Cranston's favor?"

"Marsden is an exclusionist, and Cranston is one of his parishioners." Mark smiled wryly. "Shall I go on?"

Stu rested his chin in his hand and studied Mark's face. "We liberals have got to win this one," he said. "You still tend to think only of yourself, Mark, while I'm thinking of the future of the emancipists and currency lads of this colony. Of our rights."

Mark leaned back in his chair. "I want to win this. I want it very much," he said, and thought, I want it for Penelope's sake. I want to show her and Father what I can do. I want both of them to be proud of me. I want to *be* somebody.

"Then you'll win. What you must do is sit down,

take pen in hand, and list all the issues for Thaddeus Crawford and all those against him. You've got to exaggerate the facts in Crawford's favor and demean those against him. And Mark, we've got to find something that will influence ol' Marsden. Something that will influence him in Crawford's favor. For no matter what we learned in our law courses, a solicitor or barrister *must* consider the magistrate's turn of mind. We'll have to dig for it. Do a hell of a lot of research.''

As Mark stood later and watched the hired convicts swarming over his house with brick and mortar, stone for the chimneys, and paint for the inside, he listed the facts for Thaddeus Crawford in his mind.

For: Number one. Thaddeus's forty acres of English-imported grass had been destroyed by Cranston's sheep.

Against: Number one. Marsden, the man who was going to judge the case, was an exclusionist, as was Cranston. Number two. Cranston's mare had been impregnated by Thaddeus's stallion, a sire not of Cranston's choice, and that meant an entire foaling season lost. Number three. It might have been Crawford's stallion that had broken down the fence in an effort to get to the mare. Number four. Both Cranston and Marsden raised sheep, knew their worth. Number five. Cranston and Marsden were of the same religions. Number six. Both raised and bred cattle. And the worst thing against Thaddeus Crawford was number seven. Mark Aylesbury was going to represent him. Fear paralyzed Mark.

"Uncle Thaddeus, since Mr. Fitzhugh is too ill to

present your litigation against Cranston and the responsibility has fallen to me, I'm offering you a chance to withdraw and hire a more experienced solicitor," Mark said as he leaned on the paddock fence. He had been watching Thaddeus train a gelding to pull a chaise.

Thaddeus pulled off his calfskin gloves and narrowed his eyes slightly. "Why?"

"Well—first of all, I'm an emancipist's son and the magistrate, Marsden, is so prejudiced against emancipists he won't even sit on committees or even at the dinner table with one."

Crawford propped his expensive boot on the lower rail of his fence. "Go on."

"I'm a Wesleyan like you are. Cranston's a member of Marsden's church in Parramatta, the Church of England."

Thaddeus studied Mark carefully and said, "You are telling me that just because you are a currency lad and a Wesleyan that Reverend Marsden would be influenced against *me?*"

"Well, it's a consideration."

"Balderdash."

"Sir?"

"I certainly am not going to take my suit to some other solicitor. Cranston's sheep trampled my grass, which I valued at a minimum of a pound an acre. My servants and my neighbors are witnesses to the damage. That is all the evidence I need to win this suit."

"Uncle Thaddeus, this case isn't that simple."

Thaddeus slapped his gloves against his thigh and pinned Mark with one of his incisive gazes. "Probably not. But you'll find a way, Mark. You'll win."

Mark felt a rush of pleasure. "I hope so, sir. I hope so."

Going home, though, he wondered. Everything was stacked against him. Everything, even his birth. Stuart had offered his assistance, but when it came right down to it, Mark had no one to rely on but himself. Was Mark Aylesbury, alone, enough, he wondered. He smiled finally and reminded himself that he had won hard cases before. Penelope was one of them.

The day he had told Cranston that Penelope was pregnant, Cranston had stalked off in a rage and Penelope had stood with the wind blowing her dress against her legs and said, "Your methods rot, Mark."

He had nodded. "I know."

"And I couldn't tell Father the truth."

He had taken his one open eye from Cranston's back to fix on her face. "Couldn't?"

"No."

"Why?"

She seemed about to speak, but looked away from him instead.

"Tell me, Penelope," Mark said. "Did Aaron ever ask you to marry him?"

She had replied, "No, but he implied it."

"Not admissible evidence," Mark had said. "Case closed. I'll speak to you tomorrow." And he had climbed on his horse and ridden back home.

Case closed. But he knew Aaron had the power to open it again. If he returned home in time.

Chapter XIII

The sword was hot in his left hand. He knew that he must shift it to his right hand but he could not. If he were to fight that dragon as he should, the sword needed to be in his right hand.

"Men don't fight dragons in heaven," the light reminded him.

But the dragon came down from the black rocks on the side of the mountain grinning, grinning because it knew he could not fight if the sword was in his left hand. *But it won't take me, not without a fight.* Aaron lifted the sword and swung, even as the tongue of the monster licked out at him, its tongue flicking between its bloody fangs.

"I know you. You're the Rum Corps," Aaron accused. "But Governor Macquarie came and you were disbanded."

"But some officers of the Rum Corps stayed and became free settlers in the colony," the light reminded him.

The dragon laughed, its laughter like the howls of dogs, dogs baying at the moon.

"Not dogs," the light said. Dingoes. They are dingoes.

"Dingoes are wild dogs and they are carnivorous," Aaron said. "They are the only large carnivorous animal we know of in Australia, but they never attack man."

"Not unless they think that man is dead," the light said.

I am not dead. I'm sick, but not dead, not dead, not dead—

The sun stabbed its rays into his eyes and someone groaned because of the pain. The globe that was his head rocked back and forth and suddenly the trees were there in front of him. Aaron's leg kicked involuntarily. Two bristling dingoes yipped in fright and loped away into the brush. He tried to raise his head, but it was too heavy and the dragon was still there when he shut his eyes. But the light was too bright. Too bright . . .

He hurried up the stairs, running because he was already late for his examination. But he could not remember what room the examination was to be held in. He could not remember the room number. The stairs were familiar, but he could not remember this part of them. There were ten feet of space between this step and the next. He wondered frantically how everyone got over the space.

Over here, he must go up this ramp. Aaron ran up the ramp, but it bent the wrong way. So he leaped over the side of the ramp and reached the other part of the stairs just as he heard the clock in the tower gonging. The examination would be starting, but in what room?

All one had to do was look for the professor who was giving the examination. It was Dr. Bright. He must look for Dr. Bright. Aaron ran down the

sloping corridor and looked into every room until he recognized Dr. Bright, recognized his white hair and his spectacles. He ran into the room and saw that the other medical students were already taking the written examination, but Aaron couldn't remember what chair he usually sat in, or at what table.

Never mind. He'd take the first empty one. He sat down, picked up the paper and pencil. "Number four," Dr. Bright said.

Had he missed three problems already, because he was late?

"What is the minuscule vitreous abomination to the venom of the tiger snake?"

Aaron stared at the professor. The question did not make sense. He began to perspire as he looked around him. Other medical students were writing on their papers vigorously, as if they understood.

"Number five," Dr. Bright said. "Green bile is the poison that flows in the veins in the form of maps. Maps that are lost. Where are the maps found?"

Aaron clawed at his face. What was the professor saying? He had never heard of such a thing. He felt his lips trembling in fury at not being able to understand. The students around him were writing down the answer without hesitating.

"I can't understand the questions," he cried to the professor. "You're being unreasonable, sir."

Dr. Bright looked at him, but it was not Dr. Bright at all. It was his own father.

"Father. No. Something's wrong. I think it was the snake."

"The venom of the tiger snake comes up as bile in the throat and because of a map," his father said angrily. "Were you irresponsible enough to lose the map?"

It comes up in the throat as bile and—

Aaron's eyes fluttered open. It was night. But a

person could drown in his own vomit unless he turned his head to the side. Aaron rolled the big boulder that was his head to the side. "Ah, ah, ah," he gagged, and then his abdomen sank in and the warm fluid flowed out of his mouth and down the side of his face. He heaved again and again. Once he made an effort to roll over on his side, but he could not. He coughed and breathed. His breath rushed in and out loudly. The night air was cool, but he was too weak to shudder. His breath roared in, roared out. But it must. Or else the earth would cease to exist.

Water. He couldn't drink it because it was frozen solid and it was green. Green like eyes. But it was not cold like ice, it was warm.

So Aaron took a string and baited the hook on the end of it with a worm, a worm that looked like a human appendix, and cast it into the pond. It sank, though the water was hard. If he could just catch a fish he could drink it. He felt the string jerk and he pulled in a fish, a fish as big as a sheep. But it had fangs, and the pupils of its eyes were vertical slits. He screamed and backed away, but the fish came after him on flippers like a seal. He tried to run and could not and suddenly the fish was on him, smothering him, its cold, slimy body smothering him, and he could not push it off, push it off.

Moaning, he awoke. It was dawn . . . or dusk. He did not know which, but he breathed in the air, breathed it in and felt his whole being shuddering. He was cold and he was warm and he was wet all over, but he could breathe, and so, as the day darkened again, he slept.

He became suddenly aware of looking at a black

spider above his face. The fishing spider, which botanists said was exclusive to Australia. It had spun a single thread from one branch of a wattle to another, and from that thread the spider dangled another silver thread in a circle, making it go around and around, with its single drop of moisture on the end. Aaron's mind did not stray from concentrating on that spider making his thread go around and around. Finally, a gray moth ventured near, flew around, darted, attracted by something, probably the drop of moisture on the end of the thread. Then suddenly it became entangled in the thread's sticky substance. The moth struggled for its freedom even as the spider hauled in his thread and proceeded at last to pierce the struggling body and to dine on the juices of the moth.

Then Aaron became aware of a kookaburra close by laughing raucously. It was answered by another and another, until the treetops above rang with the crazy laughter of dozens of kookaburras. The treetops, he noticed, were overhead. He lay in a forest?

He turned his head to look about him. It was a forest, but not a dense one. For the sun was slanting through the leaves, dappling the grass around him. It was either morning or evening. He moved his hand. He was alive. He had been dying, but he was alive. What was it that had tried to kill him?

Snake. The tiger snake. He moaned with revulsion.

But he was thirsty. He tried to raise his head, but could not. He rested, already exhausted. If only he could have just one sip of water, he might regain some strength. But he was tired. So tired. . . .

*   *   *

266

He awoke again. The sun was bright. Aaron bent one knee, then the other. Something stirred near him. A wallaby. A rock wallaby. It peered at him from about five feet away, then, bounding on its incredible hind legs, it vanished into the trees. Aaron ground his teeth together, and using his arms, sat up. Pain shot through his left arm, but he would not look at it. His chest heaved with his exertions and black spots danced before his eyes, but he kept his consciousness and looked about him. Nothing was familiar, and yet it was all familiar. Groves of gum trees close by, wattle, airy vines, and farther away rolling hills with grass and a few trees.

The silence was awesome. And it occurred to him that he was alone. Alone in a wilderness where no white man had ever been. With no musket, no pistol, no knife, no horse, no tent, no provisions, nothing but himself. Aaron wondered if himself was enough.

"Buck will find me," he whispered, his throat clicking because of its dryness. And then he sank back onto the ground and let the healing sleep overtake him again.

"You sent for me. Isn't that a risk?" Deen asked.

Annabelle smiled, squinting a little against the midday sun hovering in the northern sky. Her plain green skirt was blowing against her legs, her hair was drawn back, tied at the nape of her neck and tucked under. To Deen her lips seemed fuller. Her breasts stretched the front of her bodice until one button seemed about to pop off. Not that she was much larger there, for she was still slender, her breasts small. An ache like the undertow of the sea welled up and tugged at his insides, trying to pull him down from his self-imposed aloofness where there were no

emotions, to this goddess-girl whose eyes were as changeable as the earth.

"Everything is a risk, Deen Crawford."

He smiled gently, trying not to let his eyes move down to that swell at the front of her bodice, or to the hidden swell below where his child grew.

"I was surprised to hear that you were still working at the landing," she said, turning away from him to look down from the hill above the sandstone cliffs and across the river to the rolling hills thick with trees that had never seen knife or plow.

"I will always work for Owen Crawford, I think."

"Yes. But I thought perhaps you had gone to help find Aaron." When she turned back to face him, he saw that her eyes were oceans of unshed tears, tears of misery, hope, dread, bewilderment.

He frowned slightly. "Me?"

"I don't understand my father or Jack Summers or Mr. Cranston or you. I just returned from seeing Governor Brisbane with a petition requesting that he form a search mission for Aaron."

Deen did not reply, simply listened.

"A man is lost in the bush. Certainly troops should be sent out to find him," she went on.

A smile crept across Deen's wide mouth betraying his suspicion about the reason she had summoned him to this hill overlooking the river. "And the governor said?"

Annabelle's lips tightened. "He said that he could not spare the troops, with such an influx of convicts coming into the colony from England, more than has ever arrived in such a short time. And besides, there are not nearly enough men who know the bush, he said." She frowned at him, seeking his agreement or disagreement with Brisbane's reply.

Deen nodded. "It's true. Ninety men in a search party in the bush is no better than one man. They

268

couldn't spread out and search because they have no knowledge of the bush, of survival in it.'' He jerked his head toward the west. ''Out there are hundreds of miles of the same thing, with little change in landscape, no landmarks, nothing but—''

''Yes, I know.'' She smiled. ''How many men in this colony can go out there alone? Two? Three?''

The light of assurance dawned in Deen's brain and he knew for certain why she had sent the message to him at the landing by the Moffetts' convict laborer. He raised his hands and let them drop to his sides. ''You want me to go. You want me to look for Aaron.''

She stepped closer to him, her eyes beseeching him. ''Yes. And I'm surprised you aren't looking already.''

Deen let his eyes wander over her face. ''I suppose I thought Father Buck would have found him by now. And it *had* begun to bother me.'' He nodded. ''And I've recently discovered a reason why I *must* go and help find him.''

Annabelle smiled quickly and turned halfway away from him, glancing at him out of the corner of her eye. ''Then there's no need for me to offer you a bribe.''

White-hot iron stabbed him in the groin and its heat rose slowly, like steam, to choke him, to bead his face with sweat. ''No need,'' he said.

She turned back to face him. ''I haven't forgotten the day you saved my life. The hour we spent down there below. Together.''

He was Deenyi, the Ironbark Tree, with a skin that broke the ax's head, straight, still, tall, impenetrable. ''Neither have I.''

''I think of it often. What we did.''

''You shouldn't, if you love Aaron.''

''I do love Aaron. But you helped me. You saved me. You loved me.'' Annabelle's long, slender hands

269

went to her bodice. "I want Aaron. I want you to go. Bring him back. Please. Please bring him back." Her fingers had undone her bodice, and as he stood transfixed she let the dress fall to her feet.

She wore no undergarments and he knew that she had planned this, to persuade him, to bribe him to go to the bush and search for Aaron.

"You needn't do this, Annabelle. I'll go without it."

"I want to be certain that you do."

In his mind Deen went to her and brought her body against his, held her close, ran his hands over her back, pressing her to him, feeling her buttocks and then her breasts, kneading them. And in his mind he kissed her, plundered her sweet mouth and sucked her breasts and cupped her between her thighs, his fingers touching, caressing, searching. He lay her down in the grass and kissed her body and then slid his burning erection inside her. But only in his imagination.

He wanted her, ached, desired, burned, and even wept for her. "You can rest assured that I will find Aaron, dead or alive," he said steadily. Then he turned away from her and mounted his horse.

With only one last glance at Annabelle, he reined the horse on the ridge overlooking the river and rode away.

To the world he was Deenyi, the Ironbark Tree. But inside, he still dreamed as Malie, a man.

Penelope heard the carriage rigging passing by the north side of the house and hurried through the hallway to the back door. She opened it and saw that her father was just getting out of the gig, leaving the reins in Cricket's hands. His face was unreadable as he came upon the veranda and embraced her briefly.

270

Deep down inside, Penelope was marveling that he loved her still, for not only did he think the child she was carrying was Mark's, but he now knew that she and Aaron had been meeting on the ridge since his return from England. And he must think that the moment Aaron left for the expedition, she had begun to see Mark. Penelope grieved that she must appear a fallen woman to him, and a disloyal one as well.

"You did make it home in three days," she said smiling and walking with him into the house. They had always been friends, her father and she, but since her mother was abed so much these days, they sought each other's companionship more often, including James only when he wanted to be included. "I never heard such talk. Everyone who comes by is talking about the trial. You won, didn't you?"

Cranston smiled and gave Quincy orders for wine to be brought to the living room. When they were seated, he asked, "How's your mother?"

"She has been much better, but she's taking her nap at the moment."

"James?"

"Off with the cattle. You had a new calf born this morning."

"The Cape heifer?"

"Yes."

"Good." Cranston waited for his daughter to be seated before he sat down in his favorite chair by the front window, which faced east. She looked across the tea table at him until his dark eyes came away from scrutinizing the draperies that were Elaina Cranston's pride and joy, and watched as Quincy sat the silver tray with its decanter and wine goblets before them. After Quincy had poured the wine and left the room, Oliver looked at Penelope for a few moments and smiled.

"It goes against my grain, but I am compelled to

drink a toast to a young man who did a superb job of preparing a case, and of presenting a speech that would have swayed the devil himself to his side." With a wry smile her father raised the glass of wine. "To Mark Aylesbury. God rest his soul."

Penelope's eyes widened and her glass paused halfway to her lips. "God rest his soul!"

Cranston sipped the wine and nodded. "He and his motley crowd of plebs have probably been murdered by now." He saw her consternation and smiled. "The currency lads and young merinos were exchanging pleasantries outside the courtroom when I left. You see, Mark won his case."

Penelope shook her head. "Mark won the case? With everything against him?"

"As you know, solicitors for the plaintiff and the defendant prepare their cases for their clients and present them to the judge, who studies them before the trial. Then during the trial each lawyer gives a speech on behalf of his client. In this case neither of us were represented by a lawyer, because New South Wales doesn't have but two or three. We were represented by solicitors, Rodney and Mark. After their speeches, witnesses were called to testify, and then each solicitor made a final speech.

"Mark presented a rather picturesque case. He explained how Crawford had sent for grass seed from England. He presented the document that gave the cost of importing the grass and described in rather picturesque detail how much trouble Crawford had gone to, to plant it. Then he waxed eloquent as he described how, during a rainstorm, my inadequate fence was forced down by my fat and heavy sheep, who, with their exceedingly sharp hooves, proceeded to trample the newly germinated grass into the ground, spreading out over the entire forty acres of

pasture. Then the rain came and flooded the pasture, and all Thaddeus Crawford was left with was a lob-lolly." Cranston smiled at Penelope. "That's what he called it, a lob-lolly."

Penelope smiled a little and set her wine glass on the table.

"His speech took all afternoon Monday, so Marsden adjourned until the next morning. Next came Rodney Livingston. With a swagger and a smirk, he pointed out that my sheep did not tear down the fence at all, that the fence was knocked down by Crawford's oversized stallion, who subsequently jumped my paddock fence and proceeded to impregnate my mare. And he elaborated on all the details of that, and you'd have thought he was speaking about Attila the Hun attacking an innocent maiden." Cranston smiled again.

"In the meantime, the galley was packed with spectators, most of them young bucks from both levels of our society. Reverend Marsden had refused to allow women to be admitted, and it was a wise decision. The ribald comments and guffaws from the gallery occasioned more than one reprimand from the august reverend."

Penelope could just imagine.

"After hearing Rodney's long and melodramatic speech, Marsden adjourned until the afternoon. Then he heard witnesses; my overseer, Boston, explained how the fence appeared in its broken state, how he had to drive the stallion back into Crawford's pasture. Then Crawford's overseer explained what the pasture looked like. By then Marsden was concentrating more to keeping from yawning than on what the witnesses were saying. His mind was already made up, I could see that. He was with me all the way. Until he called for the final statement

273

from Mark.''

Penelope's eyes were resting on her father, surprised that he was enjoying the telling of his own lost case.

Oliver leaned forward and poured a half-glass of wine for her and one for himself. Not until he had leaned back in his chair again did his eyes raise to meet hers.

"What was it that Mark did that won the case for Mr. Crawford?" she prompted.

"A piece of sod."

Penelope raised her brows. "A piece of sod?"

"When Marsden asked for Mark's final statement, he did not say anything until he had placed a foot square of sod upon the table in front of Marsden. In that sod was growing an unwilted sample of the grass that Thaddeus Crawford had been sowing in his pasture, which my sheep destroyed.'' Cranston's eyes flickered in the light coming from the window. "You should have seen Marsden come alive then.''

Bewildered, Penelope frowned.

"You see, your young solicitor fiance knew that civil magistrates—and perhaps higher court judges, too, who are human, after all—are very often influenced by anything that might benefit them personally. Before Mark presented the piece of sod, he managed to inform Marsden that he had taken his law courses at Cambridge, which is where Marsden studied for the ministry. But the clincher was when he showed Marsden the succulent grass. You see, Marsden was the first man in the colony to plant a strain of English grass in an effort to find some that would grow well in our climate and soil. His grass had done well and he had even made hay. But when he saw the square of Crawford's grass—well, like a skein of yarn, he came unraveled. He became so

engrossed in questioning Thaddeus Crawford about the strain of grass and how he had dressed it, etcetera etcetera, that he forgot he was presiding in court. The result was that he ruled in Crawford's favor. I had to pay Crawford forty pounds for his grass. But, being a just man, after all, Marsden made Crawford pay me for my fence."

Penelope was smiling. "And the mare?"

Cranston coughed. "Well, he says Crawford's accommodating stallion saved me a stud fee, and—" Oliver paused. "I can't tell you the rest. Suffice it to say, Marsden used stockman's terminology and the gallery exploded. Crawford was pleased as a peacock. And I—" Oliver shrugged. "I had to go to the bank and pay Crawford. After which he kindly offered me the services of his groom, a man well-trained in animal husbandry, should my mare experience difficulty birthing the foal."

Penelope smoothed the skirt on her knees. "And Mark?"

"Mark set off from the courtroom to the taverns with his mob of friends, all in very high spirits. Followed by Rodney Livingston's crowd who were shouting obscenities and the like at them. I wouldn't be surprised if the whole bunch doesn't end up in jail, the young montebanks."

"You don't like Mark do you, Father."

Oliver looked at her steadily. "No."

She nodded and stood up. "Because he looks like his father?"

"I don't know." When Penelope did not reply, Cranston rose and went to the window looking out over the front dooryard. "I don't know," he said again.

Penelope waited for him to finish. Then she saw that he wasn't going to say more and finally asked

softly, "Has there been any word from Buck Crawford and Aaron?"

Oliver Cranston turned from the window slowly and looked at her for a moment without speaking. Then, "Strange you should ask. John Webb, who owns a sheep station in Bathurst, was in Parramatta and approached me after the trial. He talked about Aaron's being lost in the bush and Buck Crawford's staying to find him. He— Penelope? Are you all right?"

Penelope held tight to the back of the sofa with both hands. Her mouth was open, but words wouldn't come out.

"Penelope?" Cranston put his arm around her shoulders. "Penelope!"

"I . . . I'm all right."

"Are you sure?"

"I just felt faint for a moment."

He released her, frowning. "Can I get you anything? Water?"

"No, thank you, Father. I must go up to my room now and freshen up for tea."

He was watching her closely as she walked past him and she felt his eyes upon her as she went into the hallway and up the stairs.

She kept her poise until she shut the door of her room, then went to the opened window and looked out across the dooryard toward the ridge. Dark had fallen quickly and softly. The ridge was but a dark rise in the land, dwarfed by darkness and distance. For a long time she stood with her fist clenched upon the windowsill. And at last she whispered, "Aaron, you must, you must, you *must* come home to us."

Only the distant churr-rr-rr of the cicadas came back to her on the western breeze.

Chapter XIV

If Grandmum will go with you, Aaron, you may play in the water in the creek.

Grandmum! Grandmum! Mum says if you go with me I can play in the creek. Grandmum? Where are you? I *need* to play in the water. *Please.* Oh, pul-ee-eez.

The water in the creek was dappled with sunlight filtering through the branches of the gum trees, and where the sun was the water sparkled, seemed to twinkle, shimmering. He went to it and tried to drink, felt its coolness on his lips, but it did not wet his mouth. The water was like tasting sand.

Grandmum, please don't hide. Where are you? I have to have water, Grandmum.

He opened his eyes and for several moments no thought registered in his brain. Then he saw a black ant marching past his face carrying a piece of something gray, almost touching his nose as it crawled resolutely past. Then came another carrying a similar burden and another and another, trudging along one behind the other on a tiny trail they had made in the gray dust on which he lay.

Aaron's gaze moved up the trail where the ants

disappeared out of sight in the brush. He thought, I am alive. I survived. At least, until now.

He looked down seeking whence the creatures came and saw only his own arm lying purple and swollen alongside his body, the arm covered, covered with tiny black bodies, working, working.

Aaron cried out and sat up, brushing frantically at the ants, brushing over and over even after every creature had fallen away. Moaning in an anguish of horror, he examined his arm. It was edematous, discolored all the way up to his elbow. The puncture wounds had swollen and split the skin, tissue had necrosed, and it was this dead flesh the ants were carrying away. Shuddering, he crushed the insects and scattered their scrambling bodies, obliterating their trail. Shuddering again, he squinted up at the sun. Noon.

But of what day? How long had he been unconscious? Trembling with weakness, he touched his face and felt a beard, four days' growth. Weariness followed his meager efforts and he lay back down, aware now of the full, bursting throb of his arm.

If it had not been for his racking, grating thirst, he might have lain on the soft, sun-dappled grass and died. But instead, he became aware of a fierce, driving passion that nudged him over on his side, shoved him to one knee, then to the other, and jerked him, swaying, to his swollen feet. Then it pushed him forward, staggering, his arms spread wide for balance. He was aware that his eyes were only swollen slits in his face and that the venom of the tiger snake had caused every tissue in his body to swell. Dehydration had set in, too, shriveling his skin like an old man's.

Standing on top of the low hill, he squinted about him. Small groves of gum trees shimmered in the

near distance in patches, and grass-covered hills rolled away into a sapphire haze.

At the bottom of the hill where he stood, short gum trees and wattle grew. Buck had said always to stay where the trees grew. Water seeks the lowest level and vegetation grows where water is or should be. There could be water below.

Aaron started down the hill, but the muscles of his legs were weak and he staggered forward faster and faster down the hill, until he pitched headlong into the dust and rolled over and over until he came to rest against a stunted wattle. His pulse thundered in his ears for a few moments, then slowed. He rested until his thirst drove him to his knees again. The creekbed he sought lined the bottom of the hill, and he crawled on hands and knees to it.

There's water here. Has to be, else I'll die. He frantically brushed aside the pebbles of the creekbed and began digging into the silt with both hands. He dug, knowing that sometimes there was moist sand or water a few inches below the sand. Finally he sat back on his heels panting, shaking his head. He had dug a hole a foot deep in the sand and it was as dry there as on top.

Aaron looked around frantically. The creekbed was shallow, just a draw between low, rocky hills that caught runoff from the hills when it rained. *But draws run down to larger creeks and creeks run to rivers, and rivers run to the sea.*

But a man had to survive long enough to reach the creek or the river.

Aaron stood up, his weak legs shaking beneath him. His fevered eyes searched the distance—grassy hills rolled, sometimes covered with groves of gum trees, into the distance. No sign of water. None.

In his feverish state, Aaron began to think he was

279

ten years old and that Penelope was beside him, and seven-year-old Deenyi, and they were exploring a dry creek bed that ran into the larger creek on the Crawford property. Deen, grinning mischievously, picked up a stick in the creekbed, dug into the cool sand and came up with a frog. Then he thrust it at Penelope, hoping to make her scream, but she did not run or scream as most girls would. She said, "I like frogs."

Deen's mischievous smile changed then to one full of young wisdom as he said, "My mother's people say in times when the rains don't come, when billabongs dry up and one cannot find water, you can dig up a frog and squeeze the juice out of him—"

Yes, yes. Aaron fell on his knees now, turned over a stone. The water-holding frog had adapted himself to a climate that often saw prolonged drought, preparing himself in the wet seasons by drinking water until he was bloated, engorged with it, so that when drought came he could hide in the sand beneath a stone and live through the drought by absorbing his own body fluids.

Aaron had turned over six stones and dug beneath them and found nothing but sand.

But beneath the seventh stone, as gray and black dots danced before his fevered eyes, he unearthed a fat, bloated frog, cool and somnolent. Chuckling frantically, Aaron tipped back his head and squeezed the cold body in his hand. A brief chirp came from the frog as it gave up its life to save that of its captor. From the frog came fluid, a gush of it that wet his tongue and the inside of his mouth. Two swallows of fluid, tasteless and cool.

Aaron cast the crushed body aside and dug for another, the fluid having only served to make him crave more. Time got mixed up somehow with stones

and cool sand. And time produced four frogs before exhaustion overtook him again.

He crawled to a stunted gum tree in the creekbed and stretched out on his abdomen, giving in to the exhaustion, letting the soft shadows of summer steal over him as he rested. But even as he rested, thoughts of Penelope came to him. He thought of her soft white thighs as he had parted them, he felt her silken breasts, and in his fever and sickness, he desired her.

"I love you," he whispered to the soft warm sand.

As his body began to relax and his thudding heart to slow, he knew sleep would soon be upon him, but that when he woke he must follow the creek north in search of water. Water came first. Then food. Food.

A dispossessed centipede scurried past his face seeking another cool stone sanctuary away from the sun and Aaron was too weary to watch it. His eyelids lowered, then closed. And Penelope's soft fingers brushed his cheek once before he slept.

He woke with a start, knowing exactly where he was and what his predicament was. He rose, noticing that he was a little stronger than he had been the last time he got to his feet. But he swayed, and it seemed the earth undulated beneath his feet for a moment as he climbed out of the creekbed. He peered down the slope to where a gum tree forest began. The last time he was awake the forest had seemed impossibly far away. It appeared closer now.

His throat and mouth were parched and his eyes felt like balls of fire in his head, but he staggered forward toward the forest. Because Buck had said to follow the trees. The trees.

Aaron staggered into the forest farther because the hill slanted down now, his befuddled brain telling him that possibly there might be water in a creek at the bottom. Vines impeded his halting progress, but

281

he mindlessly brushed and clawed them aside, baring his teeth, plowing ahead. He came to another shallow creekbed, but there was no water.

There's water here. Has to be. Else I'll die. He fell on his knees in the creekbed, and though he was weakening, dug into the silt with his hands, grunting, digging, flinging the silt aside. But there was not even moist sand beneath the dry silt. With the last of his strength he turned over stones and dug beneath them for the life-giving frogs. But there were none.

His chest heaving, he rose and looked about. Eucalyptus trees everywhere. Koala. Koala. *Koala* was the native word for "no drink." Because the little bearlike animals did not drink water. They lived exclusively on a type of eucalyptus leaf, which supplied their entire diet and their water.

Aaron stumbled up out of the creekbed and clawed handsful of leaves from a tree and stuffed them into his dry mouth. He forced himself to chew and swallow the leaves, forgetting that the koala had a special digestive system for digesting the leaves.

No sooner had he swallowed the leaves than they came back up again, and when he was through heaving the last of his stomach fluids, Aaron leaned his back against a tree. If he just had a little more strength he could search for water, but he had no more strength left. His knees buckled and he slid down the trunk of the tree and sat looking up, up through the leaves to the pale blue sky of midday.

In the back of his mind, he knew that he had lost his horse, his swag, his gear, the carefully made map, the journal, but right now his mind could only handle the reality of his dehydration, his need for water. He rolled his head back and forth against the trunk of the gum tree and shut his eyes.

As a gray haze settled over him, Aaron thought of the beautiful falls where their camp had been, the pool with its silver fish and the methodical, single-minded duck-mole as it waddled to the edge and slid in. The falls were like Grandmum's silver hair when she brushed it out and parted it into three long tresses in order to braid it. I'm dying, Grandmum.

Listen, Aaron.

Aaron opened his eyes and looked around. Who had whispered? The leaves above stirred in that relentless western breeze. He put his hands on the grass and tried to rise, but there was no strength left in him. He gave up. In a moment he would try again. But it would be no use. No use. His eyes shut again, his mind drifted in that mental dusk just before sleep.

Listen, Aaron.

Again he opened his eyes. The silence was what he heard first. Then, "Carp?"

He frowned and blinked back the grayness shading his eyes.

"Carp?"

"Carp."

"Carp?"

"Carp."

He sat up, listened. The sounds came again. "Carp? Carp."

Frogs.

Groaning with pleasure, he staggered to his feet, cocked his head to listen. There, through the trees where the rays of sun were streaming through. He rushed forward, carried along by the momentum of his thirst and his relentless drive for survival. He stared at the dry creekbed, but his eyes moved up the side of the rocky ledge and focused on the stream of water oozing from the rocks, dropping and disappearing into the damp sand. He grinned and

stumbled forward, fell on his knees as frogs scattered around him, and licked the damp stone. Cupping his hands, he held them where the oozing water dripped from the ledge. A pool of it formed in his hands. Chuckling, he drank it. Then, grinning, he scurried around looking for a stone with an indentation and placed it under the dripping water. Already his mind was reeling with possibilities. He could make basins out of the bark of the gum trees. He could bathe his arm, his face. Soon the stone bowl was full and he drank more.

Smiling, he leaned his head against the rocky ledge letting the water wash his face, and shut his eyes against the unbearable delight. Water. Just a trickle, but it was water. Food.

He opened his eyes. Game always came to water. Food would come to a pool of water.

Strengthened by his new revelation, Aaron crawled frantically searching for a larger rock that would hold water, found a large flat stone with an indentation and dragged it beneath the dripping ledge. In the bed of the creek he proceeded to gather wattle and other shrubs to form a shield, wondering as he did so what he could do to catch game if it came.

Trembling, he unlaced his shoes and found a sharp stone. With the stone he worked feverishly, sawing the tongue off his leather boot. With his leather shoe strings and the tongue of his boot, he would fashion a sling. As children at play, Deen had taught him many things: to throw a boomerang, to make and use a spear for both animals and fish, and to make and use a sling.

Aaron settled down behind his wattle screen and made the sling, boring holes into the tongue of the boot with slivers of stone. And once it was fashioned, he settled down exhausted to wait.

Only as he waited did reality pause to sigh and

point out to him that an animal or bird might never come. And if it did, would his aim be as good now as it had been when he was a boy?

Aaron dozed and when he woke the sun was going down. His efforts had exhausted him, but he gave his swollen arm careful scrutiny. It was discolored, edematous. The slits he had cut over the fang marks oozed a yellow exudate that stank. With his physician's eye he examined the wound. Infection had set in, but the oozing would aid healing. Tomorrow he would wash and dress it. If only he could kill an animal and lay its liver over the wound to draw out the infection. Or if only he had fire. His eyelids drooped. If only he had fire.

Something disturbed the stones nearby and Aaron's eyes flew open. It was early morning. The sky was gray with gathering light. Soon dawn would explode into the sky in the east. He listened. Something was drinking at his stone basin. He turned his head slowly and lifted it, peered through the wattle shelter. At the basin sat two kangaroo rats, creatures the size of a small cat. Aaron had never given a kangaroo rat much thought, but now as he watched the pair, he began to wonder why kangaroos and wallabies and wombats and duck-moles were only found in this country that people were beginning to call Australia, where most things hopped, even the rats.

He was on his knees, expecting the creatures to run when they saw him, but knowing too that the animals in the outback had not learned to be afraid. He raised up, and with one rapid flick of his wrist released the stone. The kangaroo rat sprang up, the dull thud of stone on its body knocking it tumbling into the creekbed. Its mate shrieked and disappeared into the rocks overhead, and Aaron sprang to claim his prey.

285

There was no fire, but it had been four or five days since he had eaten and he barely comprehended that he was eating raw meat. Gorging himself on it, he peeled the skin with its soft fur as he ate. At first his stomach rebelled, threatened to regurgitate the bloody meat, but he lay down with eyes closed and willed his insides to accept his bloody offering.

At last, the nausea passed, Aaron sat up with his back to the cool rocks and considered his options.

He knew this: that he must follow this draw, keep following it, and hope to God it did not end—as so many did—disappearing into the sands of some dry plain. He must methodically find food, fashion better weapons, learn to make fire, and work his way back to civilization. He did not know how far he had run in the wrong direction after the snake had bitten him, or even if he *had* run in the wrong direction. But he knew that the mountains lay east, that the expedition party had traveled south, so he must eventually bear northeast.

As his mind cleared, he smiled, thinking of the game he and Deen and Mark used to play as children. "Lost in the Blue Mountains" was their favorite, and it was young Deen who had taught them the ways to survive in the wilderness. Aaron had learned and practiced their game well. And he had never known until now that those childish games would be the secret of his survival.

Frances Aylesbury always attended the last fitting of a lady's gown herself. But she would have pinned Penelope Cranston's wedding dress herself anyway, for several reasons, the first being that she would not have wanted anyone else to notice the girl's protruding abdomen. The other reason was that she maintained a special affection for Penelope; for the

girl should have been her own child, not Elaina Cranston's.

"Turn toward the window now, please," she instructed the girl as she crouched at her feet in the measuring room. Hemming gowns with trains was tedious business, but she bloody well aimed to do it right.

Penelope sighed softly, and one glance told Frances what the girl was thinking. God help her. She was surprised the girl had decided to marry Mark. Somehow, her decision just didn't seem right. Of course, the consensus of opinion with everyone but the Aylesbury family was that Aaron was dead by now. He had been lost for two months, and few men ever survived in the bush alone with no food and no supplies. She understood that Penelope must marry before her pregnancy was detected, but knowing Penelope, she had thought the girl would have thumbed her nose at the rest of the world and waited for Aaron anyway. What had changed her mind?

Frances glanced at up her. Mark? No, she did not love Mark. She loved Aaron. God help her.

"Now turn toward the table, Penelope."

The dress was an exquisite white satin, so expensive and so white that it was almost blue. Penelope had not cared whether it was lovely or not, had begged Frances to choose the material, the pattern, the veil. Frances had done it all, designed the dress and the veil. She had brought out the expensive lace and satin she had been hoarding to make the dress with. Because . . . her eyes misted over . . . Penelope should have been her own daughter.

For Frances Aylesbury had loved her own cousin Rolph Danbury since he had come to live with the Aylesburys back in England, when he was just eight years old, and Matthew was nine, and she herself was only five. She and Matthew had grown up with that

handsome rogue, that lackadaisical lad who flirted with and conquered much more than his share of the shire lassies, that larrikin who ultimately and unintentionally got himself and Matthew arrested, convicted, and transported to New South Wales.

After his pardon, Rolph had stayed on with the Crawfords as a farm laborer. But twelve years ago, when he had decided to go off on his own, he had come by Frances's cottage to tell her good-bye. Frances had done everything in her power to make him stay, but he would not. And in the course of their brief visit he had told her—she remembered the words perfectly: "The little Cranston lass, Fran. Watch her. She's my child. Her mother told me. It happened during a flood of the Hawkesbury. Elaina and I met accidentally on the road from Parramatta and we were caught in a torrential rain. We were caught in a flash flood. I pulled her from a flooding creek. Afterward, I took advantage of her. I took her against her will. The little girl is a result. Oliver Cranston doesn't know. Neither does Matt or anyone else. Just Elaina, you, and me."

With that burden of guilt weighing heavier on him than the swag on his back, Rolph Danbury had taken to the track and become a wanderer, a tramp, what the people of New South Wales called a swagman.

So Penelope was Rolph's child, not Oliver Cranston's, and so she was Mark and Aaron's second cousin. And no one on God's green earth knew it but Elaina Cranston, Rolph, and Fran. What a shame Rolph couldn't see the wedding.

Frances's eyes misted over again. She hadn't seen Rolph since the day he left, but occasionally Matt saw him, when Rolph would drop in at the hospital all ragged, bearded, and dirty. Once Francis Baldwin had heard that Rolph was mustering sheep on a sheep station south of Sydney. Again, she had heard

that he was chopping wood for a widow, and again someone had seen him mixing mortar at a building site in Sydney. Fran kept turning Francis Baldwin's proposals of marriage down because of that one, distant, faint hope that someday Rolph might want to settle down. And she . . . she, Frances Aylesbury, would be waiting.

Fran pinned the last inch of hem and rose to her feet, noticing a slight pain in her knees. She put her hands on her hips and tilted her head to view the gown.

"Absolutely beautiful," she mused aloud. "What a lovely bride you'll be."

Penelope looked at Fran and smiled, thinking that she should be happy, that in just two days she would be a bride. And Mark was a handsome fiance and becoming so popular with . . . with at least one faction in the colony, anyway, both young and old. She shut her eyes tightly. But half-brother or not, she still loved Aaron. She loved him. God might strike her dead for wanting her own half-brother, but she didn't care. She loved him and she always would.

"I always will," Mark said as he ran his fingers over the lapel of his magnificent dark suit coat. He had just had it tailor-made and it fit perfectly. "I will always envy my brother."

Stuart Mays was sitting in the large suite that was Mark's bedchamber, in an Owen Crawford chair, his long, slender legs stretched out before him, his dark eyes glinting with delight.

"You shouldn't. You've won a major battle, you know."

Mark smiled at his own image in the mirror and pulled down the front of his cream-colored waist-coat. "For the currency lads or for me?"

"Both," Stuart said. "And I think it timely that you were able to persuade your lovely merino fiancee into having the largest wedding possible." Stuart sprang from his chair, unable to sit still for very long, and crossed his arms over his chest.

"I'm leaving it up to you, Stuart, to keep the peace at the wedding. No fighting. If the merinos try to pick a fight, ignore them."

"Are those your orders, sir?"

"Aye."

Stuart threw back his head and laughed one "ha" at the tall coffered ceiling before he crowed, "Think of it. Matthew Aylesbury's son marrying the daughter of his father's worst enemy. I can see it now, one side of the church will be filled with pure merinos, the other with emancipists and currency lads and lassies. I love it, Mark. A lot. You did it, mate, you're going to rub their noses in their own dung. You, Mark Aylesbury, bastard son of the man the merinos fear the most."

Mark's smile waned and a flicker of something flashed in his eyes as he turned from the looking glass to regard his friend. "I suggest that you measure your words, Stuart."

Stuart kept his arms folded and shrugged. "You're a bastard, I'm a bastard, most currency kids *are* bastards. That's one thing that makes this situation rich. We're a whole generation of bastards, and the continent of Australia, which, mark my words, will someday be a nation, will be founded by the bastard sons of a generation of English felons. Not by the legitimate sons of pure-bred English gentlemen."

"My brother is no bastard." Mark was feeling pangs of guilt again about Aaron and felt compelled to defend him somehow.

"But is Aaron alive?"

"Last we heard, Buck Crawford had hired a tribe of

natives to comb the bush. Deen Crawford went off to search, too."

Stuart unfolded his arms, his dark eyes searching Mark's. "You seem afraid that he is alive."

Mark's mouth tightened. "I didn't say that." In truth, Mark had been experiencing many things when word had reached him that Aaron was lost. Penelope's sudden acquiescence to marrying him made him wonder if she sensed something about Aaron, if she sensed that he was dead. And Mark had experienced envy at his father's hollow-eyed appearance lately, his worry, his talk of financing search parties even though everyone knew search parties would be ineffectual and terribly dangerous. And guilt. Mark felt guilty because he was glad Aaron was out of the way.

Yes, he admitted it. He was his father's only son at the moment. And Penelope was his.

He turned his back to Stu and pulled off the coat. Yes, he was a bastard son now, but Fitzhugh's practice was growing, mostly because of Mark Aylesbury. He owned a house and land, he was marrying the girl he loved, who happened to be the well-trained daughter of the colony's best hostess. And the daughter of one of the wealthiest men in the colony. He was on the threshold of realizing an improbable dream. Of being somebody.

"You are our champion, Mark," Stuart said as he watched his friend unbutton the cream-colored, satin waistcoat he had been trying on. "Every currency child in the colony is already looking to you to lead the way to complete freedom." Stuart smiled quickly. "We must obtain the right for emancipists who have full pardons to be able to sit on juries. We must obtain the right to have trial by jury. We must be able to sit on legislative councils, as W. C. Wentworth said in his book. Isn't William Wentworth's father a

friend of your father's?"

"Yes, D'Arcy and Father are friends."

Stuart spread his hands. "See? It's written in the stars. Mark T. Aylesbury, Father of Australia."

Mark's eyes left the ceiling and came back to rest on Stuart's face. He wished instead that the stars read: father of Penelope's child. Although he had no desire either for that child or for one of his own.

But no one need ever know Aaron's child was not his. No one. And least of all Aaron. If he lived.

On January 6, 1823, Aaron Aylesbury drew back the spear he had fashioned of red gum wood and stone, threw it expertly, and brought down a kangaroo doe. Moaning, he fell to his knees and cut the still-quivering flesh with a sharp stone knife, hacking at the bleeding meat and bringing it up to his mouth where he tore and chewed the flesh and drank life. His animal-like eyes went to the trees along the creek where water trickled from a spring in the side of the mountain into a streambed that trickled northward. Gone was any vestige of the educated physician he had been. But he was alive, and beside him lay a primitive spear, a handmade ax of gumwood and stone. His feet were encased in boots fashioned out of the hide of a wallaby. In his pocket was a sling made of leather and the tongue of his boot. His left arm was pale, the skin having peeled twice and become reddened with the sun.

And on that same morning in Parramatta, outside St. John's Church, the Reverend Samuel Marsden stood in his flowing black robe, surreptitiously watching the guests with one eye and the couple standing before him with the other, his plump, round face perspiring even though he stood in the

shadows of the gum trees.

Two hundred people were standing outside the church, too many for the wedding to be held inside, and they were parted by an invisible aisle. On his right, behind the bride, stood her father and mother, the John Macarthurs, the Frank Livingstons, the Henry Braxtons, and all the so-called exclusionists in the colony, and their irreverent sons and disobedient daughters.

On his left, behind the groom, stood Matthew Aylesbury and his wife, the Crawfords, and a host of emancipists, with their troublesome currency lads and lasses. It was like mixing oil and gunpowder. Any spark could ignite it. The reverend mopped his perspiring brow and continued with his prayers and blessings.

Directly before him, luminous in a billowing white gown and flowing veil stood the most beautiful bride he had ever seen, with a sweet smile and sad eyes. And beside her, cocksure and out-rageously handsome, stood that ingenious young solicitor from Fitzhugh's firm, the groom. At last the reverend required that the bride and groom repeat their vows, and then, by the power vested in him, Reverend Samuel Marsden pronounced them man and wife.

Mopping his brow with relief, the reverend smiled, though dubious of his accomplishment, and in-formed the groom that he might kiss the bride.

The reverend then rocked back on his heels, thankful that his part in the affair was over, and fixed a smile on his round face as the groom lifted the bride's veil. But he was not prepared for what happened next.

For the bride burst suddenly into bitter tears.

Chapter XV

Mark did not shut the door behind them. Still dressed in the black coat and cream-colored vest he was married in, he stood and watched his lovely bride as she moved slowly to the bed, where she removed her gloves and laid them on the counterpane that his housekeeper, Mrs. McWilliams, had purchased for him. She looked up at the coffered ceiling and went to the window where the light filtered through bare panes, panes he had paid dearly for.

She was a slender vision, dressed in a rose-colored gown of some light material that floated when she moved. The rounded neckline gave him a glimpse of her tantalizing neck, and the puffed sleeves gathered just below her elbows reminded him of how slender her limbs were. The waist of the dress was gathered under her breasts, emphasizing their perfection, the skirt falling in sheer folds to her ankles. She turned, smiling gently, and said, "The house is lovely, what I've seen of it. Though I think there's much to be done with it yet."

"There's tomorrow to see the rest," he said steadily, then, seeing the flicker of distress in her eyes, he hastily added, "Tea is waiting, and by the time we

294

have it, the sun will be down." Again the flicker of distress in her eyes, and Mark felt his damnable face flushing with embarrassment. God, he thought, does every man feel like a fool on his wedding night?

Penelope reached up and took the wide-brimmed bonnet from her head and placed it on the counterpane. The light coming from the window gave a luster to her dark hair, highlighting it with secret streaks of copper. Her eyes today were darker green than he had ever seen them, and her skin whiter, her lips pinker. Penelope had never been more beautiful. Mark had suppressed the growing desire to have her all day as they had traveled by carriage from Parramatta to Sydney, then to Penmark.

Penmark. His father had called the naming of his estate pompous. But Penelope had seemed to like it, because it was a combination of their first names, Penelope and Mark.

Weary as they were, he had taken her on a brief walking tour through the dooryards, bare of anything save a small stable, a carriage house, a small paddock for the two horses, and dust. Mark had only lived here three weeks and he had no crops planted or stock bought and no plans for any. He hadn't even known where to begin. The house itself was a two-story rectangular structure of white painted brick, with front and back verandas.

Inside, the house was almost bare. He hadn't any idea what to buy for it, besides a bed for each of the six bedrooms, a table and chairs for the dining room, a desk and two chairs for his library, and a living room suite. Owen Crawford had helped him with those few selections by looking at a copy of his house plans. Mark was completely baffled by the huge ballroom. It was the only room that was absolutely bare.

As for draperies and carpeting? Well, he had left

295

the purchases of those incidentals for his wife to take care of.

Mark's hands ached to touch her. He had admired her with his eyes all day, but had not touched her and had not allowed his growing desire for her to show. Now it hit him, like someone had broken a cricket bat over his head, that he had pursued, schemed, and won this woman, this exclusionist's daughter. He, the bastard son of an emancipist. She was his. After all these years, Penelope was his. Not Aaron's, not Rodney Livingston's. His. Perspiration broke out all over his body at a sudden disquieting thought. What if, for some ungodly reason, he could not perform?

Nonsense, his confidence told him. Of course you can perform; you haven't failed yet have you?

But this is Penelope.

So?

I am only Mark Aylesbury.

Only? Only? You are an educated solicitor. You are Dr. Matthew Aylesbury's son.

Bastard son.

Nevertheless, you are his son.

What do I do, then? This is a lady. She is not Betty Scoggins or Jill Jones or any other Sydney prostitute or Parramatta factory girl.

She is still a woman.

Yes, yes. She is that. Mark turned slowly and placed his hand upon the door latch. "I'll go to my own room now and leave you to dress for tea." He smiled at her when he saw her relief. The Aylesburys, his father and stepmother, slept in the same bedroom, but upper-class people, like Mr. and Mrs. Cranston, had separate rooms—at least theoretically —at least, they kept their clothing separated.

"Thank you," Penelope said, her face still inscrutable.

Mark left the room, and outside the door took a

deep breath and let it out slowly before he paced to the adjoining room to change from his wedding suit to something more fitting for a Sydney solicitor at home for the evening.

In her own room, Penelope shut her eyes and sat down on the bed with its counterpane. She was married now. Mark was behaving like a gentleman. He was her husband and she had to behave like a wife. She would be his hostess, run his house, and do all the things a wife did. She would forget—she would pray for the safety of his brother. But she must forget that she loved him. Penelope was resolved. She would be Mrs. Mark Aylesbury, but she would be Penelope, too. She smiled, feeling affection for Mark. He had furnished this potentially beautiful house with the barest essentials. He had been telling her about the house and the acreage surrounding it, during what few moments they had spent together since she had agreed to marry him, about how close to the Macarthurs' southern property it was. But he had not prepared her for how beautiful it was, with its rolling hills and its excellent pastureland. Perhaps he did not even know that it was beautiful.

"Oh," she had cried as she viewed the pasture from the back dooryard just minutes before. "I shall raise the best sheep in New South Wales!"

"Sheep?" Mark had observed her with bewilderment etching his brow. And had that been a flash of jealousy she had seen?

She would breed those sheep and tend the property just as Mark's stepmother tended the Aylesburys' farm. Yes. And I shall try very, very hard to be a good wife.

But how will I explain this to Aaron?

The table was beautifully set for tea, with the rare

297

China trade porcelain, a Wyndham heirloom that Penelope's mother had relinquished as part of their wedding gift. She had sent it over only two days before the wedding. The fine linen tablecloth with its fancywork edges and corners was a gift from Frances Aylesbury. The table and chairs were a gift from Owen Crawford, a highly polished teakwood set with straight lines softened by rounded edges, and stained dark. The furniture intrigued her. It was like no other furniture anywhere, for Owen Crawford had lately abandoned any pretenses of incorporating European design into his pieces.

Penelope sat down in the chair her husband held for her and watched as he took his own place at the other end of the table. He was dressed in a dark brown suit and white linen shirt. His hair was carefully combed, but its natural curls had rejected the smoothing and had recoiled at the thought of staying that way. Penelope thought he was very handsome. His broad face and blue eyes were so much like his father's, but where Matthew Aylesbury's smile was warm, Mark's was not. It was as if his mouth lacked the generosity his father's had.

Penelope knew that Mark had attended enough formal teas in England and at Government House with his father as a child to know the formalities involved. She knew he was born of a convict woman and that the Aylesburys and Crawfords with whom he had been raised were anything but formal. Good people, but they had been extremely poor before Governor Macquarie had come on the scene in New South Wales. But Mark appeared every bit the born gentleman at this moment.

Penelope spread the square of linen in her lap and raised her eyes to look at him. He was smiling and his eyes were crystal blue, flickering with some inner

thought, and from the light coming from the candelabrum in the center of the table—a gift from the Livingstons, begrudgingly given, she was sure.

"Why did you cry when I kissed you at the wedding?" he asked gently. A flash of anger shot in his eyes when the words struck the air between them, and then the flash was gone like some falling star.

Penelope's straightforward gaze did not falter. "I suppose it was the ceremony itself, and a girl doesn't get married every day."

"Nothing else?"

She did drop her gaze briefly, but brought it up to meet his again. "What else would it be?"

He did not reply for a moment as he studied her face. "Nothing, I suppose."

"May I ring for tea?" she asked.

He inclined his head graciously toward her.

Mrs. McWilliams came in carrying the steaming bowls of soup, her apple cheeks glowing from the heat of the fireplace. Mark had introduced Penelope to the housekeeper and the butler, their only servants, when they had arrived earlier that afternoon, and she had liked the short plump woman with the perpetual smile and Irish accent.

"There's beef pie on the fire, Master Mark and Missus Penelope, and I'll be bringin' it in when yer through with yer soup," the woman said.

Penelope smiled and said thank you, and when Mrs. McWilliams had left the room again, Mark said, "She was convicted in England six years ago of stealing a silver candelabrum from her master."

Penelope frowned as she took up her spoon. "But she couldn't have, such a lovely woman."

"I think the master tried to take . . . prurient advantage of her, and when she refused him he accused her of stealing the candlestick."

Penelope began tasting the delicious soup. "Is she your friend's mother?"

When Mark did not answer, Penelope glanced up to see him staring at her.

"Why do you ask?" he said.

Penelope blinked. "I remember your friend Jory McWilliams, whom you introduced me to at the wedding."

Mark stared at her, his eyes catching the light from the candles again. "Yes. She is Jory's mother."

"A wonderful cook!" Penelope said truthfully. "We're fortunate to have her."

Mark bent his head to taste the soup and paused. "Yes, although I could have obtained numerous housemaids and cooks, you know. Convict labor is cheap. But Mrs. McWilliams's former employer died. You remember the Adamses? Jory's father died two weeks ago and Mrs. McWilliams needed a position. And I like the fact that she is emancipated."

"I'm glad you hired her, Mark. You made a wonderful choice."

"I'm relieved that she pleases you."

Penelope continued to eat her soup in silence. The conversation made her uneasy. It was as if Mark was defending himself at her every word. She shut her eyes tightly. Dear Lord, don't let it be this way forever.

Later, while Mark was working on some papers in his library, and Penelope had discussed menus and housekeeping plans with Mrs. McWilliams, she went to her bedroom. It was dark out. The stars seemed close enough to pick out of the sky. The distant chur-rr of cicadas and the clicking of summer beetles stirred the night air as she stood at the window looking out. Her mind went, as always, to Aaron. This could have been us, she thought, and then

berated herself severely, turning away from the window as if doing so could put him out of her mind.

She dressed carefully for bed in an immaculate white cotton gown with long sleeves and a high neck trimmed in blue ribbon. Standing before the crude mirror on the wall, she placed her hands over her protruding abdomen and mouthed the words, I love you. Then shook her head again in dismay.

There was no dressing table in her room. A man wouldn't think to buy one. She sat on the edge of the bed and unfastened her hair from its pins and let it fall to her shoulders. Then took her brush and brushed it until it gleamed, and all the while tears kept welling up within her, threatening to spill. She dared not admit to herself their cause.

Her hand shook when she drew back the coverlet from the bed and placed her knee upon the mattress covered with white linen sheets.

It was then she heard the roar. Quickly she scrambled out of bed and went to the window. Below was a mob of young men. She could see their faces upturned in the torchlight. They were shaking their fists and she could not make out their words. Penelope's hand flew to her mouth in horror as she wondered if the merino lads had come to protest Mark's marrying her.

Then she heard the laughter and recognized Jory McWilliams and Stuart Mays as they dashed onto the veranda below, followed by several of the others. The currency lads had come to carry off her husband.

Penelope smiled and opened her window and a roar of appreciation came up from the mobsters below when they saw her.

"Begone, scoundrels," she cried, as was expected of her.

"We've come to take your husband away," some-

one shouted imaginatively.

"The better to give you a good night's sleep, milady," somebody else cried. The mob roared with laughter.

There was a commotion in the house downstairs and Penelope had to lean out the window to see her husband, hands bound behind his back, propelled from the veranda out into the dooryard. He was allowed only one glance up to see his bride silhouetted in the window above, before he was manhandled into a waiting carriage. Four of the men packed into the carriage with Mark, while the others mounted their horses, torches in hand, and the entire mob rode off in a roar of shouts, laughter, and dust.

Penelope was left alone. She knew that her lady friends would not chivaree her tonight. For she had broken an unwritten code and had married a currency lad, and they would not dignify it by recognizing her marriage other than by attending her wedding. Even her best friend, Betsy Livingston, wouldn't. Sadly Penelope wondered if she would ever be able to win her friends back again, if they would ever set foot in her house or speak to her on the street.

Mrs. McWilliams came to ask if there was anything she needed before she went to her own room behind the kitchen. Penelope only needed quiet, and she welcomed the aloneness.

But in the dark her eyes stared as she remembered Frances Aylesbury's offer when she went to her dress shop to try on her wedding dress the last time.

"I'm a spinster and know nothing of wedding nights, Penelope. But I know women, and I know men pretty well. If you have any questions . . . but, of course, your mother would have talked with you about the wedding night."

Penelope had smiled and replied, "Have you forgotten the shape I'm in? What can I learn now?"

Fran had finished adjusting her veil and said, "The ways of a man."

The ways of a man. His ways. The ways of Aaron, his brown eyes softly caressing her body, his hands on her breasts, more with love than with lust. His soft kisses, his exquisite gentleness, his whispers of love in her ear. His lean, hard body, and the mat of dark, curly hair on his chest. Strange that Fran had not said the ways of a gentleman. That was Aaron. His ways were the ways of a gentleman.

But what were the ways of a man?

The soft silence of summer soothed her. It had been a hard day. Up at five A.M., to bathe and dress and travel to Parramatta. To be dressed by Fran and Betsy at Fran's dress shop, to travel by carriage to the church. To stand beside her handsome father beneath the arch made of wattle branches and woven with the flowers from Parramatta gardens. To tremble before the enormous crowd, to avoid the dark, hating eyes of Rodney Livingston. To smile at handsome Dr. Aylesbury, whom she liked so much, and at Mrs. Aylesbury, who was the most beautiful woman in the colony. To remember that that woman had been seduced by her own father. Yes, she saw his eyes again when he looked at her, and yes, that was what the little cottage in the woods was. These two people had created Aaron.

Penelope's thoughts were drawn to that cottage, so dusty, so unused, but kept in good repair. And the place by the still. And Aaron. Always Aaron.

Her breathing came in deep, even droughts, and it was not until the soft glow of dawn woke her that she knew she had gone to sleep.

Mark was standing beside the bed, rumpled suit,

rumpled hair, red-eyed from lack of sleep, with the faint smell of spirits hanging about him.

Penelope sat up quickly. "Mark!" Her hand went to her head. "They kept you until dawn. You must be exhausted." In her sleepy state she had thought first of his condition. Then . . . then the cold thought of what had not been accomplished the night before settled upon her as the dew must have settled on the grass and trees outside.

"Are you glad?" he asked, as his eyes moved to her lips and down her neck to her breasts.

Penelope did not blush. A cold sliver of dread slid down the ridges of her spine. "I'm sorry they took you away so roughly. What did they do to you?"

"Kept me in Foster's Tavern. Bound up. They poured stringy bark down me. And then the merinos came. We had a slight disagreement in the tavern. The soldiers came, and half the mob was thrown into jail. I happened to escape." He smiled lopsidedly. "I am not intoxicated. Not by the stringy bark. Only by your beauty."

She saw the quiet, almost-fearing lust in his eyes and could not meet his gaze.

"I want to come to you now, Penelope."

She looked up at him and said, "Then you must."

Slowly, Mark unbuttoned his rumpled shirt and removed it, not taking his eyes from her. Then he turned his back to her, unfastening his trousers before she looked away. When she felt his knee press the mattress down, she looked back at him. Men did not go about shirtless, seldom even coatless, and she had never seen a naked man until the day she saw Aaron. Therefore, she compared them now almost with a cool aloofness.

Mark's shoulders were a little broader than Aaron's, his chest and waist thicker. He was built

more square, his skin was paler, and the gold, curling hair on his chest was not as thick as that on Aaron's chest. But he was solidly built, and muscles rippled as he reached out to her, his face flushing, his eyes gone deep indigo with desire. The evidence of his desire did not frighten her, and he seemed to want her to look at him.

His fingers brushed her cheek. "May I re—remove your gown?" he whispered.

She opened her mouth for a moment before she said, "I shall help you."

Mark sat back and watched as Penelope crossed her arms, gathered the gown in her hands, and pulled it up over her head. Men did not often have their wives take off everything, she had heard, but some did. She had known Mark would. Her eyes flew to his face when the gown was gone, seeing his eyes slowly moving over her hair, her neck to her breasts, to her abdomen, to the patch of dark hair below. But his eyes came back to her abdomen and she watched as the lines of his face deepened slowly, his eyes filling with pain, his mouth turning down in a grimace of anger. He whispered, "Goddamn him, Penelope. He even comes between us on our wedding night."

He turned abruptly away from her and ran his fingers through his tousled hair. "Oh, God help me. What are we going to do?"

There was so much pain in his voice and he was so vulnerable, so pathetic, that she reached out to him, touched his bare shoulder. "We shall try to make a go of it, Mark," she said softly. "We must."

He turned back to her, and she could see that he had become flaccid. It occurred to her, comically, that she had never seen a naked man who was not hard and firm with desire. She whispered, "I'm sorry," before she realized what she was saying.

305

His eyes were swimming as he looked at her, his grimace deepening, and he looked at her for a long moment before he said, "Touch it."

Penelope knew she must, somehow, and reached out slowly, hesitantly.

"Penelope, please," he whispered hoarsely.

She watched as the miracle of manhood happened. It grew, lengthened, and fattened itself on his growing lust, until it seemed that it would split its skin. The musky smell of man came to her then.

"Hold it," he said, and when her small hand encircled it, he shut his eyes and groaned. Then he turned to her, pushed her gently back onto the pillows, and stretched out beside her, his mouth coming down on hers. He was gentle, as if fearing he would hurt her, his mouth working upon hers as his hand went slowly to her shoulder and then moved with agonizing slowness to her breast. Penelope shut her eyes and forced her mind not to think of his mouth on hers, wishing she could feel the exquisite pleasure she had experienced with Aaron. But it was not to be. His hand could have been the brush of a gown on her body, his lips a drop of water from her bath. His growing desire deepened her distress, but she bore it and made do for him with a touch on his arm.

He took his lips from her and said, "I want to feast on you, Penelope, my wife, my love."

So these are the ways of a man, she thought.

He had taken women many times before, young and middle-aged, but her body was exquisitely white, her eyes forest pools of shimmering green, her hair dark against the pillows. Her skin was unbelievably smooth, silken under the palms of his hands. Her warm woman smell made his mind rage like a bush fire, and the feel of her under his hands sent great

surges of heat through his body, causing his erection to throb painfully as if it would burst. He drank in her beauty, feasting on her with his eyes and his mouth, tasting, feeling. This was Penelope, the girl he had always loved, and she was his.

He buried his face between her full breasts and moaned with unbearable pleasure. Then he kissed first one rosy-brown nipple, then the other, as his hand moved with a will of its own over her abdomen to the place he had dreamed of touching most. He felt the crisp, curling hair of her under his hand and moaned with pleasure at its warmth and at the hot thrill that passed through him. He massaged her thighs as his mouth forced open her lips and teeth, and he drank the sweetness of her mouth, tasting her tongue, sucking it. His hand caressed her and his fingers went to the warm, moist place that was his. His to love, to caress, to pleasure, to enjoy.

Aaron's first. Aaron's first. Aaron beat you. Aaron beat you. Suddenly he could hear the laughing voices of the currency lads at school when Aaron won the foot race.

Aaron was here first. Aaron runs faster. Mark winced, and pain came to lie beside his lust.

He felt his wife sigh beneath his hands. Was she comparing his lovemaking to Aaron's?

He raised his face to look at her, saw only her serene face, eyes closed, lips parted and moist from his kisses. Perfectly submissive. Anger flared in him, for other women had wrapped passion-spasmed legs about his waist and screamed for release, had clawed his back to bloody ribbons, had thrust their hips up to meet his thrusts, had even taken his erection into their mouths. But she—his beloved—

He parted her thighs, since she seemed disinclined to do so herself, and he massaged the outer lips of her

307

with both his thumbs until moisture came in spite of her. Lie there, then, he told her in his mind, and I will take my pleasure. He delighted in gently running his finger in and out of her as she gasped, and though she seemed hesitant to open to him, she did, and he slipped into her with ease.

Ecstasy overwhelmed him. The screaming and clawing and begging of passionate whores had never given him the pleasure of this passive wife. Never. He gasped like a man drowning, gasped again until the first hot waves subsided. Then he began to move in her. His lust grew unbearable. Sweat poured from him, and her sweet body grew damp with his ardor, not hers, and he pumped until her body drew the fluids from him. He stiffened, swelled, and burst.

Mark threw back his head, opened his mouth, cried out a garbled cry, and released himself in her again and again until he was sucked dry and spent.

Trembling, he lay down on her, wanting to melt into her, disregarding the lump against his own belly, nuzzling his face against her neck, whispering, "I love you."

For a moment she did not move, then he felt her soft hands on his hips. His senses were departing from him, his thudding heart slowing, sleep threatened to overtake him, but he distinctly heard her say softly, "Please? Your weight . . . on my stomach . . ."

Chapter XVI

His eyes fluttered open. They focused on a cynical, old wizened face. Wisdom observed him from small brown eyes. Its patient smile caused Aaron to smile, too.

He did not move. He had learned from several months' experience that the ground in the bush was not the best place for a man to sleep, so he had learned to sleep in the trees. He kept his face against the smooth bark of a stringy bark tree and did not draw away from the close scrutiny the koala was giving him.

It peered at him curiously, black nose twitching, then, curiosity satisfied, the koala reached up with its foreclaws and began climbing the branch above Aaron's head.

From out of its pouch a tiny head peered, a duplicate of the mother's, and seeing the bearded man on the limb below, the baby koala jerked his head back into the safety of his mother's bosom, the pouch door closing him gently from sight.

Aaron laughed softly. Aside from the koala's offensive smell and cranky disposition, it was a likable animal. He had killed several for their skins

because his shirt had worn out, and he had sewn a sleeveless shirt out of soft koala hides.

From the kangaroo he had made a swag for carrying his weapons and fire-starting tools. The swag now hung from the limb at his feet. He had cut strips of kangaroo meat and dried it in the sun on a ten-foot-high rack that he had made from Y-shaped poles stuck in the ground across which he had lain a horizontal pole. He knew that the higher off the ground he could hang the meat to dry, the fewer flies there would be to blow it.

From a wallaby hide he had fashioned his second pair of boots, using sinew for thread and the thorn of some strange bush for needles.

Aaron did not kill unless it was necessary. The creatures in this country were almost tame. The kangaroo and wallaby were more cautious than frightened of him, the koala slow and disinterested, the emus had rather tease or chase him than flee, and even the smaller birds were more curious than alarmed.

Strange land.

Aaron unlooped the kangaroo-tail strap of the hide swag and slung it down, dropping to the ground after it. He had learned to keep everything made of hide or sinew off the ground because of the pesky dingoes. He stretched now and yawned and set about making breakfast.

From his swag he took his pieces of iron ore and quartz and went to the stamped-out campfire site of the night before. Squatting on his heels, he gathered his dry-rot tinder into a pile beside the small stack of kindling, then proceeded to strike the quartz and iron ore together to make a spark. He blew the spark into the tinder with little effort, the tinder flamed, and he fed it the small kindling until he had a

small fire.

He dined on dried kangaroo meat and sarsaparilla tea. From the sarsaparilla bush he had gathered leaves, and dried them. In his bark cup he placed the hot pebbles until the water was steaming, then sprinkled sarsaparilla leaves on top. Delicious. The early settlers of the colony had made sarsaparilla tea, and only English tea and rum rivaled it as a favorite drink.

Looping the strap of his swag over his shoulder and using his spear as a walking staff, Aaron rose and kicked dirt into the campfire, grinding out every live ember. For an ember could cause a bush fire, and a bush fire was a dreadful thing. A bush fire was a sweeping inferno and could outrun, surround, and engulf a man in minutes. And this had been a long drought. Grass, trees, and underbrush were crisp, a tinder box ready for the spark that would ignite it.

He had come upon this creek the evening before. The billabong was only a trickle, and Aaron estimated that by tomorrow it would not even exist. Therefore, he must move on.

He paused at a rustle in the dry grass on the bank of the creek and smiled as a brush-tailed rat kangaroo no bigger than a kitten hopped from the grass, its tail looped around a bundle of grass that it would carry to its home and there build a nest, using its tail again, this time for shaping the nest. It hopped away unconcerned about the two-legged animal peering at him.

Aaron looked about him. He was surrounded by forest, but across the creek a tall hill rose, taller than any he had encountered yet. He decided to climb it and see the country, see where he had been, where he was going.

Big country, he thought as he climbed the hill,

using his spear as a staff. He estimated that he had roamed the country for three months, and he had not yet come upon either his horse, a campsite, a man, or any other sign of civilization. He was surprised about that, thinking that he should at least have seen a native. He climbed, picking his way among granite and sandstone rocks, perspiring beneath his hair shirt. Grunting, he came to the top of the hill and paused to catch his breath. When he raised his head, his breath caught in his throat.

A plain stretched before him awash in varying shades of blue; an azure plain of almost treeless hills, blue-green with nutritious grasses, ribbons of trees here and patches of forest there, and the low indigo-shadowed hills on the horizon undulating to—he frowned. To the sea?

To what sea? Was that far, far sapphire horizon the sea?

His heart began thudding and he quickly took note of the position of the sun.

"I'm facing south," he said. "I've been traveling mostly east in an effort to find our trail, but—but I've never been this high and seen this far. Did I wander south the four or five days I had the fever? Did I run south after the snake bit me? Have I been near the ocean on the south?"

He gazed over the plain. There might be a river there. There had to be. Could he find water? His mind toyed with the idea of going south. But south is farther from civilization, his reason told him. And who knew how long his good fortune at finding meat and water would last? He remembered his days of starvation just weeks ago. The times he would have wept for water had he been able to produce the moisture for tears.

He laughed bitterly now, a sob catching in his

throat. Beyond him was the far horizon he sought. This was what he had wanted all his life, to explore new land.

But he had learned that dreams were only distant relatives of reality. Adventurous, wild fancies had turned to clawing for survival. His study of flora and fauna was not for writing in a book, but to stave off gnawing, wrenching starvation. And until now, each far horizon had yielded only another hill like the last he had climbed, and each rare running creek had proved a dismal failure that might be only a memory tomorrow.

But every venture must yield experience. And this . . . this . . . Aaron stretched out his hands toward the plain below. This was what Cranston and hundreds of other graziers in New South Wales were wanting to know about, to own. A promised land. He dropped his arms. But like Moses, he could not enter.

Because death stalked him like some loathsome, sleepless creature, death clothed in the hide of starvation, dehydration, a native spear, a poisonous insect or reptile. Aaron shuddered and looked at his arm where the snake had bitten him. It was normal now, though still a bit paler than the other arm. He attributed its final healing to the wombat.

The wombat was a dark furry animal about the size of a small dog. Aaron had watched a wounded wombat stuff damp, moldy leaves into the wound in its side. There had to be a reason for that. And after three months in the bush alone, observing nature, he had decided that for every disease, every wound, there was a cure in nature. Man had only to find it. So he had packed his open and running wound with the moldy leaves. His arm had begun healing within hours. He must mention that to his father when he returned. If he returned.

He looked up at the sun. The sky was bleaching out as the sun climbed high in the east. Ungodly heat would bear down soon. Aaron removed his shirt and tied it like a cape over his shoulders. Sweat and air would cool his bronzed chest and the shirt would shade it. And he must be going. Always north and a bit east. He had survived thus far. A man who had purpose usually did. His purpose was Penelope. He must tell her all that he had seen. He must hold her again in his arms, touch her, make her his. Make the thing he had done to her right in the sight of God and man. He had to return. And he knew she would be waiting.

There were other purposes for returning too. Mum. Sweet Mum, working at her ledgers. And Grandmum in her rocker chair, dreaming an old saint's dreams. And his father. And Mark. Deen. And the uncles, Aunt Fran. His friends. The farm. The Hawkesbury. Sydney. New South Wales. Faces. He missed faces.

He took one last look at the plain. He would mark his route now, ink it in on the map in his brain. Report it to the governor. There would be men to follow him. Men who would go all the way to the sea. Perhaps he would be among them.

But for now, death rustled in the dead grass at his feet, and Aaron turned away, made his way down the hill. He glanced at the white, fluffy cloud overhead, the first he had seen in three months, saw in its shape and configuration a lamb.

Penelope kept her hand under the ewe's muzzle, holding the animal's head up, keeping the muzzle pointed slightly upward, for in such a position a sheep would not offer to run away, would remain

compliant and patient.

"It was a most generous wedding gift, Reverend Marsden," she said, smiling up at the corpulent minister as he stood mopping his ruddy face with a handkerchief. "A fresh ewe. Who would have thought of it but you, sir?"

The reverend finished mopping his round face and said, "John Macarthur, perhaps?"

She let go of the ewe and captured the lamb in her arms and stood up with him. "No. The Macarthurs did not give us a ewe, they gave us a stud ram instead." She laughed. "Surely you saw that robust fellow in the paddock."

"I did not. But I shall look at him when I pass by again. Merino?"

"Yes. With the most fabulous curling horns."

The reverend almost smiled, a rarity for him. "I'm not sure I want Macarthur's ram to freshen my ewe."

Penelope knew the reverend was attempting a jest, but she knew there was a grain of truth in what he said, too. For there was rivalry between the reverend and John Macarthur.

Marsden stuffed the handkerchief into his coat pocket and said, "Rest assured, my dear Mrs. Aylesbury, that John Macarthur may go down in history as establishing the sheep industry in New South Wales, but it was I who took the fleece from my sheep to England, and it was my wool with which King George made him a suit." He shook his head, making his jowls quiver. "I am a friend of John's, but—" He paused. "I'm glad the lamb is well. He was born out of season, but he is a true Merino."

Penelope nodded. "Yes, he is. Our first lamb. Thank you for your priceless gift."

"You are so welcome." The reverend gazed around him at the clean, parklike pasturelands. "Excellent

pasture, even though we are in drought. I see why John Macarthur selected this area for his second farm. Yes. Botany Bay is just east of here, swampland. And west all the wooded foothills of the mountains. Excellent place for you and your . . . ambitious husband.''

Penelope's smile remained, but she squinted her eyes speculatively and Marsden saw it.

"Oh, I don't mean ambition is unsavory, my dear. I am an ambitious man myself. I meant that he is hardworking, very . . ." He smiled. "Trying hard to do well, to make something of himself." Marsden frowned at his own words and shook his head. "None of this is coming out right. He . . . will be an excellent solicitor, already is. And so popular with his constituents. Most of them."

Penelope finally smiled and said, "Yes," and dropped her gaze to the lamb's white wooly head. "Mark is a good man."

"Yes. No doubt." Marsden whipped out his handkerchief again and mopped his perspiring face. Then, looking up at the sun he said, "It must rain soon. We must have rain. This drought is miserable. And the heat—well, I just wanted to visit my parishioners to the south, and I especially wanted to see how the lambing of your ewe went. And I am so glad Mark decided to join our faith."

Penelope set the lamb down on the grass and watched as the little jumbuck loped playfully to his grazing mother and with a flutter of its tail nudged her side and sought its dinner. Penelope squinted at the reverend and smiled. "I'm so glad you came." Her eyes went past him to the tall form of Mark coming across the pasture on foot toward them, home from Sydney for the day. The reverend turned after a bow to Penelope and strode to meet him. Penelope

followed slowly and watched as the two men greeted each other and shook hands.

"Excellent lamb," Marsden said. "Your good wife is a fine shepherdess."

Mark's crystal eyes went to Penelope briefly. "She—we are planning on purchasing a few ewes from John Macarthur and hope to speak with you later about buying some of your mixed breeds."

"Your wife told me. She is already very astute at determining a good Merino when she sees it."

Mark's eyes flashed. "So am I."

The reverend seemed to rear back a little. "Well. Yes. Of course."

"Yes," Mark said.

Marsden mopped his face as Mark gave a wry smile and asked, "Will you come in for tea? Or better, for a glass of port?"

The reverend replied, "Mrs. Aylesbury has already indulged me, thank you. And I must be getting back to Sydney before dark."

"So soon? I'm sorry you didn't come at a time when you could visit with me . . . as well as with my wife." Mark smiled quickly. "However, I understand. Perhaps another time."

"Oh yes. Absolutely." The portly reverend turned to Penelope. "Good day then, missus." He nodded again to Mark. "Good day, sir."

"Good day, reverend," Mark replied and stood beside his wife and watched as the graying minister lumbered across the pasture toward his carriage waiting in the back dooryard. Then he turned to Penelope, his blue eyes clear and sparkling as they searched her face. "What did he want?"

Penelope took her husband's arm and began to walk back toward the house. "Only to visit his parishioners and to see about the ewe." She smiled at

317

him. "How did the trial go?"

"I won." Mark grinned. "I won easily. I convinced the judge that no worker should be made to wait for his wages longer than a month. If the employer did not have the ready currency, he should not have employed the worker."

Fitzhugh had gotten more settlers and emancipist clients since Mark had won the Crawford-versus-Cranston case than their firm could handle. This last case was a test case where a wealthy pure merino had hired an ex-convict brick layer to build his house, then had delayed paying him on the grounds that he had no ready cash. The ex-convict had come to Fitzhugh, and Mark had represented him in civil court. Not only that, but again Rodney Livingston had represented the accused. It was a case almost as popular as the Crawford-versus-Cranston case.

"I'm so glad you won. Congratulations."

Mark nodded, took her hand, folded it over the crook of his arm. "You should have seen Rodney Livingston's face when the judge ruled in my client's favor."

Penelope shuddered. "Be careful of Rod."

Mark laughed. "No problem there, dearest. I can handle Rod." He smiled down at her, "But I much cherish your concern."

Penelope said nothing. One should be concerned for her husband, shouldn't one?

"The lads are clamoring for a party to celebrate. But I told them it must wait. You already have a housewarming to give, and with your condition . . ."

"There's nothing wrong with my condition. If they must celebrate your success, then let's give a housewarming ball and do it then. I've been thinking how Mother would do it. We'll have it, and soon. Perhaps we should discuss it together with Mrs.

318

McWilliams and Arthur tonight.''

"I don't know anything about preparing for balls. And I thought ladies kept to themselves pretty much when they were . . . When they were . . .''

"Large with child? If that's so, ladies are foolish. I'll have the ball. I may not dance, though.''

"I want you to play the harp for us.''

"Oh, but Mark—''

"I want you to show these poor, uncultured, uneducated lads what a superb hostess you are, how beautiful and how talented. You must play the harp. Please, Penelope. Every emancipist and currency lad and lass in the colony will be there. Young and old. And I want to show them what a prize I have in you as a wife.''

Penelope lifted her skirts and stepped over a tree stump. "You make me sound like a—a commodity.''

He thought about that, then nodded. "In a way you are. An excellent hostess, beautiful, talented and—'' He glanced at her. "Fertile.'' When she only looked at him, he smiled. "All the things men long for in a woman, except . . . passion.''

Penelope's mouth tightened and Mark looked up at the sky. "But that will come in time. You'll see.''

She wanted to say, Will it? But she didn't.

After a few moments he asked, "What did Marsden have to say?''

"Reverend Marsden and I talked about sheep, mostly.''

"Did he . . . say anything about me?'' Mark gave some effort to behaving nonchalantly, but his curiosity showed when he glanced at her out of the corner of his eye.

"Yes. He said you were an ambitious, hard-working man. A good man.''

"Ambitious? What did he mean by that?''

319

"It was only a compliment."

Mark was silent. Then he said, "The ol' bludger. There's a story going around Sydney now that he married a poor Hawkesbury farmer and a girl from the Parramatta factory last month and recently he went around to see how the new wife was working out. The farmer told him that she was cantankerous and refused to cook meals or work in the fields. So Marsden took his horse whip to her. Later, he saw the farmer in Parramatta and asked how the wife was doing. The farmer told him that ever since the reverend had whipped her, the wife was docile and working hard."

Penelope's mouth was open in horror. "I don't believe that. Where did you hear that?"

"The tavern. It's gossip. If she had been a pure merino woman, Marsden wouldn't have whipped her. But since she was an emancipist—"

Penelope interrupted, "Please, Mark, let's not get into that."

"No, let's not. I'm in too good a humor." He sliced a sideways glance at her. "One more bit of gossip, though."

"I hate the kind of gossip you hear in the tavern."

"You have to hear this."

"Oh?"

"Guess who has as large a belly as yours."

Penelope fixed her eyes on her husband's and curiosity overwhelmed her reticence. "Who?"

"Annabelle Moffett."

Penelope's mouth flew open again as Mark nodded. "Oh, but. Annabelle isn't—"

"No, she's not married."

"But—"

"An emancipist's daughter will have to face the gossips. Whereas—"

"Whereas *I* was saved from gossip by you?"

"Well—"

Penelope took her arm from his and gathered her skirts in her hands. "Poor Annabelle. I'm so sorry. Who do you suppose is—"

Mark glanced at her again, his wide mouth upturned slightly at the corners. "There's a lot of speculation about who the father is. And since no man has stepped forward to claim the dishonor, and it's public knowledge who Annabelle is smitten of, the gossips could come to only one conclusion."

The cold, clammy hands of dread seized Penelope, and she felt the babe leap in her womb. Some unseen vice gripped her heart, and it seemed that she had grown suddenly stiff with age.

"Aaron," Mark said.

The ground tilted once. The house, looming rectangular and white before them now, swayed.

Mark placed his arm about her shoulders as her trembling hand went to her face. "I'm sorry," he said. "It wasn't my intention to upset you. It's only gossip, after all. Mere speculation. The father could be anybody. But they *were* seen together at Owen's Landing. Let me take your arm."

She let him guide her into the shade of the veranda. Penelope, who asked no aid or solace from anyone, let him guide her into the house, even as he watched her closely. Finally he asked, "Are you all right?"

"I'm fine," she replied, keeping her voice steady. He was watching her as she stood in the hallway pretending to smooth her skirts. "I need to freshen up before tea, though, if you'll excuse me."

"Can you manage the stairs? You look pale."

"Quite well, thank you. Will you tell Mrs. McWilliams for me that we would prefer tea at half-past five tonight?"

321

"Certainly." Mark bowed politely to his wife, and Penelope made her way carefully up the stairs. She kept her back straight and her face composed. She managed the steps and came to the gallery corridor, went into her room, and shut the door behind her softly.

Her first inclination was to throw herself onto her bed and weep, weep and beat her fist against the wall. Anger and pain fought with each other for control of her emotions. Her breath stayed deep in her lungs, and she could neither breathe it out nor take much in.

Reason stepped in cool and sweet and told her that the possibility of Aaron's being the father of Annabelle Moffett's child was only gossip and speculation. But jealousy rushed in to smother reason with its hot dragon's breath and argued that Annabelle loved Aaron. Everybody knew that. And Annabelle's father had always viewed Aaron as his future son-in-law. And certainly, with Aaron back from England, Annabelle would not have been seeing anyone else.

But Aaron loves *you*, reason told her, with its faint, dying breath. He told you he loved you. You saw his eyes when you made love, and you *know* he loves you.

Loved, whispered the voice of doom. Loved. With every passing day that Aaron is lost in the bush his chances of survival grow less. He's probably already dead.

Penelope held on to one of the four posts of her tester bed, trembling and listening to the voices of her emotions.

You must remember, Aaron is your half-brother, shame said from a dark corner of her mind. What right have you to listen to jealousy? You and Aaron are guilty of incest. And Mark is your husband. You

are not being true to Mark, who rescued you from scandal. Rescued you and your family from scandal, and yet you continue to dream of Aaron, your half-brother, and that is adultery. You are guilty of incest and adultery.

Penelope gritted her teeth and held to the bedpost, her body shaking so violently that the bed clattered, while the demons in her tormented her.

Then love touched her tenderly and smoothed her brow with its soft hand. What Aaron and I have together is love, she thought. I refuse to acknowledge shame, guilt, doom. Aaron and I are above all that. Even if Aaron is the father of Annabelle's child because of passion, he is the father of *my* child because of love.

Penelope's lungs expanded, and she drew in a deep breath. Reason told her that Annabelle was the one to be pitied. Annabelle would have to face her pregnancy alone. There was no one to help her, to shield her from it.

Compassion swept through her on butterfly's wings. Yes. It's true.

"Poor Annabelle," Penelope said from deep inside her soul, and her grip relaxed on the bedpost and she turned her pale face to the window where the dying light of day was streaming in. "Brave Annabelle." Penelope turned again and saw her image in the tall mirror on the wall, a mirror Mark had bought from a sailor of misfortune. "It is Annabelle who deserves Aaron," she said aloud. "Because she is facing her shame with courage, and she refuses to name the man." Penelope's smiling eyes filled with tears. "She is more worthy of Aaron than I am."

Chapter XVII

Annabelle wiped her hands on her apron as she watched her father ride into the dooryard. Then she hurried out of the house onto the veranda shading her eyes. From here, she could see that his expression was not cheerful. Her heart sank.

Glenn swung off the horse and let Moley, his convict groom, take the horse. Glancing up at Annabelle and back at his feet, he approached the house. He wiped his nose on his sleeve and stepped up onto the veranda.

"Pa?" she asked anxiously.

Glenn sighed through his teeth, dipped the dipper into the water bucket sitting on the water bench, and took a long drink. He hung the dipper back on its nail, squinted at Annabelle, and shook his head. "It was Henderson from Bathurst, all right. And aye, lass, he went by the Aylesburys'. News is that Buck Crawford has ridden into Bathurst for the fourth time for supplies, and still no sign of Aaron."

Annabelle's eyes misted.

Sally Moffett appeared in the doorway, concern etched on her ruddy face. "What of poor Deen?" she said, glancing at Annabelle.

Glenn propped his boot on a stool. "Deen's been out there over a month now, and every native in the district 'as been alerted, but Aaron could run into a 'ostile tribe that ain't acquainted with Buck and Deen and—" He glanced at Annabelle.

"Pa, how does it look for Aaron?" she asked needlessly. She already knew how it looked, because she had already asked the same question dozens of times.

"Bad." Glenn watched her face, seemed about ready to cry himself. "The longer a man's out there by 'imself, the less likely 'ee is to be found, little girl." He turned abruptly away from his women to face the yard. "Young and with not much experience in the bush—"

Annabelle wiped tears from her eyes with her apron and could hear her warm-hearted mother sniffling behind her.

"It's my fault," Glenn said. "I shouldn't 'ave talked Buck into letting us divide up and go out on our own. Even for a short while."

Sally Moffett took her husband's arm. "Come in for a cuppa tea, Glenn. An' there ain't no one blamin' ya but yourself. And Jack Summers says it was everybody's idea to split up, Aaron's most of all."

Glenn shook off his wife's hand. "Aaron was an adventuresome lad. It should 'ave been us older ones that forbid 'im goin' off on 'is own like 'ee done." Glenn stepped off the veranda and strode over to stand beneath the big gum tree that shaded the back dooryard.

With a sudden sharp intake of breath, Annabelle peeled out of her apron, wadded it into a ball, threw it into a corner of the veranda, and began to hurry across the dooryard toward the stables.

"Annabelle? Annabelle!" her mother called from

the veranda. "Don't you go off ridin' that 'orse, love. It ain't safe fer ya!"

Annabelle didn't care. What did it matter? If Aaron was dead, she didn't want to live anyway. Aaron dead? Oh, dear God. With a sob she ran into the stable, glad to see none of the servants were inside. I'll ride the mare down to the river where Aaron and I used to play, she thought. If he's dead I'll know it there.

She took Ginger out of her stall, and by the time she had blanketed and saddled the mare, someone was darkening the doorway. With tears streaming down her face, she glanced up to see her father standing inside the door looking at her.

"No, you don't, Annabelle. I ain't goin' ta let ya ride out on that mare. Like yer mum said, it ain't safe fer ya."

"What do I care? And why do you care?" Annabelle said, jerking the cinch under the mare's belly. "You wanted a boy and you got me. Then you wanted Aaron for me so you could have a son. Now he's probably dead and—"

"Shut yer mouth, girl. That ain't true about me not wanting my little girl. Your mum and me never felt that way. And I don't like that kind of talk. Why's it only when you're upset with Aaron you talk like that? Yer a merry lass otherwise. But when it comes to Aaron you talk crazy."

"I'm not your little girl anymore. I am the millstone around your neck. I am going to have a native child. I have disgraced you and Mum, and with Aaron probably dead why should I want to—" She put her boot in the stirrup, but a firm hand caught her arm, spun her around.

"Look here, girl," Glenn roared, "that native child you're going to 'ave is Deen's. An' there ain't no man

326

more honorable than Deen Crawford, and I'd be proud to be 'is grandpa, if it weren't for a whole colony of men who would 'ang Deen. And the child, too, in time.''

Annabelle leaned her sweaty forehead against the mare's flank and fought terrible tears.

Glenn's face smoothed out and he laid his hand on her shoulder. "Annabelle. Girl. Don't you care for Deen even a little?"

Annabelle let the tears slide down her cheeks now and tasted their salty wetness. "Only as a friend, Pa."

"Then let 'is little child live."

Annabelle heard the soft footsteps of her mother as she approached and put her arm around her shoulders.

"'Sides, Annabelle," her mother said softly, "that's our grandchild inside you, love."

Annabelle bit back the sobs that threatened to well up inside her and shook her head.

Sally released her and sat down on a milking stool while Glenn leaned against a post that supported the roof of the barn. "'Twas spring," Sally began softly. "The Crawford family was new in the colony, and Mr. Crawford had died. Aaron's mother, Milicent Crawford, had taken over the runnin' of the Crawford farm. Glenn and me decided to go 'unting kangaroos and we invited Buck Crawford, just a lad of sixteen then, to go along. 'Ee and Milicent went and we 'ad a fine time. Glenn and me saw then what a man Buck was. Took to the 'unt like a born bushman, 'ee did. And from then on your father and me watched 'im go bush little by little. Then we 'eard that Buck came home one day and caught Matthew Aylesbury out in the yard, started a fight with 'em. For 'ee thought Matt had somethin' to do with a party of white men who rode into a native village and

massacred some natives. One of the ones killed was Buck's native woman. And 'is little son, Deen, was missin'. 'Course, Buck found out Matthew had nothin' to do with the massacre, and 'ee shoulda known 'ee wouldn't, considerin' Dr. Aylesbury is such a fine man, but Buck wasn't thinkin' straight. Musta loved the woman and the little boy. Well, in a few months Buck found Deen with a native family who had escaped the massacre."

Annabelle raised her head to look at her mother.

"Buck was always a good bushman, love. And 'ee 'as the respect of several tribes of natives out there. So has Deen," Glenn said. "They'll find Aaron."

Annabelle looked at her father.

"Deen'll keep lookin' because Aaron's 'is cousin. And 'ee'd keep lookin' even if Aaron wasn't 'is cousin, 'cause 'ee knows you care for 'im, though I imagine that breaks 'is heart."

Annabelle looked away from her father's searching look when her mother said, "And Buck. 'Ee'll look for 'im because Aaron's 'is nephew and because Buck loves 'is sister Milicent more than anybody on earth, I think, and won't want to bring back bad news to 'er."

Annabelle observed her parents. Two farm people, ex-convicts. Sally Baines Moffett had been convicted for being in possession of stolen goods back in England in 1795 and sentenced to transportation to New South Wales. Once in the colony Sally had been assigned by the Superintendent of Convicts to one of the officers of the New South Wales Corp, the Rum Corps, people called them. The assignment of women convicts to single men was, of course, leaving the women no choice but to prostitute themselves to their masters, and Sally had suffered three years under the dominance of the drunken officer until he had died and she had been given an unconditional

pardon by Governor Hunter.

Glenn Moffett had been convicted of setting fire to a jail and sentenced to transportation. He had served on a chain gang for seven months, after which he was given a pardon. He had met and married Sally just two years before the Crawfords came to New South Wales and, the Moffetts had settled on the land just west of the Crawfords' property. They had proved to be efficient farmers and had gained the respect of all the settlers along the Hawkesbury. After Macquarie's arrival in the colony, her parents, like most other Hawkesbury settlers, had begun to realize a profit for all their hard work. Now the Moffetts were considered "well off," though not extremely wealthy, and had a title free and clear to seven hundred acres of rich bottom land, were at present assigned twenty-two convict laborers, and had two emancipist house servants.

Now, Annabelle told herself, I have shamed them. But as she searched their open, honest faces, she could detect no shame in them, just a quiet, simple pride that had turned a little sad. As convicts, they had known insufferable shame many times. Perhaps a person's cup of shame can hold only so much in a lifetime and the Moffetts' cups had filled up long before they had married and left no room for any more of it. Looking at them now, Annabelle saw only love, a gentle love for their daughter who should have been a boy. Love for a girl who should have received a beating. Her hands went to her abdomen and her eyes went to the door of the stable where the blinding sun burned the outside with its relentless rays.

Out there somewhere was Deen looking for the man she loved. Out there was Aaron somewhere. She must keep this child safe for Deen, her friend. As

for Aaron—

Suddenly, Annabelle knew that Aaron would return. Knew it. And something else surfaced in her mind like a whale rising to the top of the sea. Aaron would find out that she was carrying Deen's child. He would know, as everyone knew, that she could not marry Deen. He would find out that Penelope was married and carrying Mark's child. What then? What then? Perhaps Deen's child would be the cause of her winning Aaron. It was not the way she would have wanted to win him, but it was a way. A smile trembled on her lips as she looked at her mother, and when Sally opened her arms, Annabelle rushed into them and wept as she had done as a child.

But this time, she was weeping with a secret joy.

Deen squinted across the rolling plains below. It was an uncharted plain, with groves of trees following dry creekbeds and undulating hills and meadows gray and bristling with long, dry grass. Heat waves shimmered in the low places. The parching, merciless sun beat down upon the plain burning up grass and trees, even the air one tried to breathe.

Deen's keen eyes moved slowly over the treeless hills. Some long-buried sense stirred. Something was out there. He removed his wide-brimmed hat and ran his sleeve across his mouth, replaced his hat. Somewhere behind him his father, Buck, and thirty natives were combing the forests. Deen had ridden ahead to search. They would never rest, never stop until Aaron was found. Alive or dead, Buck intended to bring home what was left of his sister's son so that she could either stop worrying or stop hoping. And he, Deen, must find the man Annabelle loved.

There. On the side of a hill. Something was not part of the landscape. He could not distinguish a shape or a movement. From this distance it was only a shadow that was not a part of the wild bush. His neck hair bristled with apprehension as he hesitated. Finally, he leaned the reins on the neck of the horse and the faithful animal began to descend the hill, picking its own way among the dried wattle and sunbleached boulders.

When he gained the flat, Deen did not hurry the horse. In this dry heat a horse or a man could use up too much energy, too much of his body fluids in only seconds. A man, or an animal, must go slowly.

Prolonging the trek to the object on the side of the hill, dreading what he might find, Deen noticed the clouds overhead, white clouds scattered across the sun-bleached sky, the first clouds he had seen in months. Over the hills to the west clouds with blue-gray bottoms hung. Rain clouds—if they did not dry up before they gathered.

But was the thing on the side of the hill Aaron? Had Aaron remembered about the frogs?

As Deen guided his slow-plodding horse toward the hill he was remembering the native myths about water, how when the earth was young, old Tiddalick, the giant frog, drank up all the rivers of the earth, the billabongs, the lakes. How the other animals and men were thirsty, and how Goorgougagae, the kookaburra, decided they must make the frog laugh so that he would release the water. So Kangaroo danced, Wombat twirled, but ol' Tiddalick would not laugh. Finally Noyang, the eel, began to spin on his tail, and old Tiddalick began to laugh, and out of his mouth came water, filling all the creeks, rivers, and lakes.

Deen looked up. Frog? Were you too late for

Aaron? Did Aaron remember to dig frogs and drink their water?

Almost fearfully, his eyes focused on the hill again. Bones.

Deen swallowed. They were bones. Bones picked clean. But too large for a man's. His horse shied and snorted at the heap of bones as he drew near, and Deen reined him and got down. The heap was familiar, bones of a horse picked clean by crows, a hide shriveled. The carcass was so clean, not even the flies swarmed it anymore.

Deen bent down and kicked the bones aside, knowing already that this was Aaron's horse, and that it had died of thirst. He bent down and lifted what was left of a swag that had been chewed on but left intact. Damned dingoes.

Aaron without a horse in the bush—

He untied the rope and rummaged in the swag. The journal confirmed that the horse was Aaron's. Deen noticed the notes to Penelope, folded them without reading them, and stuffed them back into the swag. No map. No musket in the scabbard. He scratched his chin and thought about that.

Then he lashed the swag onto his own horse and remounted. Fearfully, he began a slow search for Aaron again. If his horse was here, surely Aaron couldn't be far away.

His hair had stood straight on end all day in a strange static charge of the atmosphere. The air was still and hot, but something caused Aaron to be restless, uneasy. If he removed his hat, his dry hair would rise as if some high, motionless wind were lifting it. His beard bristled and every movement caused sparks to dance over his hair shirt. He looked

up at the sky where the clouds had been gathering for days, at the high, white fluffy clouds with dark bottoms.

He prayed for rain. It had been two days since he had seen water, and the water in his skin bag was getting low. Four or five swallows was all that was left. Those menacing clouds gave him hope.

Aaron trudged on, going north and a little east, keeping close to trees and low places where he might chance to find water, using his spear as a staff.

He had seen himself in a rock bowl of water a week ago and had not recognized himself. His beard and hair were long and matted. He wore a hair shirt, a kangaroo skin hat, and boots he had made. His trousers had worn out and he had fashioned some out of wallaby skins, and he had coated every inch of exposed skin with mud to protect it from the sun and from insects. He was Elijah in the wilderness. He ate insects and roots and any animals he could find.

Elijah had been searching for God, too.

Aaron felt a rumbling beneath his feet and looked up at the sky. His sun-scorched eyes searched the clouds, now boiling slowly, moving together, merging. Another rumble. A slow grin stretched across his mouth. Rain. By God, it was going to rain. The drought would end—for him and for the farmers and graziers at Bathurst and the Hawkesbury and Parramatta and Windsor, Castleraugh, and Sydney. He dropped his spear.

"Please, God, let it rain," he cried. "Please, let it rain!"

As if in answer, a zigzag flash of lightning shot from the clouds to earth, striking a hill a mile away. Thunder boomed and shook the earth.

Aaron jerked off his hat, and laughing, threw back his head and spread his arms. "Rain, rain, rain," he

laughed. "I'm saved. I'm saved."

A bolt of lightning cracked the air, three fingers jabbed the soft sides of the clouds overhead, and thunder took the earth and shook it awake.

Clouds moved together and mingled and rolled over one another blotting out the sun, and the heavens boiled. Bolt after bolt of lightning stabbed the air and shattered the stillness into trembling fragments, followed by thunder that beat its fists against Aaron's chest and rumbled under his feet while he danced.

The elements grew more menacing, the flashes of lightning and rumbling thunder were continuous now. Aaron capered, the heavens grew dark, but there was no rain. The dry atmosphere seemed charged with expectation. The earth held its breath and waited, while the heavens threatened violence and promised life.

Then Aaron's delight stilled as he stood hat in hand and watched the spectacular display in the heavens. Crooked white fingers danced through the clouds stabbing into their soft substance, drum thunder rolled and boomed, crashed and shattered the air. A ball of white light danced across the tips of the trees on the hill before him and paused atop the highest, dimmed, brightened, then disappeared. His beard and hair bristled and popped, but it was not until the bolt shot down and exploded a gum tree that Aaron realized the danger.

The tree flamed but did not catch on fire. A rush of white death cracked the air, and Aaron found himself sprawled on the ground as the thunder trod across his body, and he felt the earth shudder beneath his breast. He lay blinking and staring, watching the electrical display, seeing black rolling clouds rearing their heads to the west.

Then he smelled smoke.

He sat up, sniffed the air, his eyes going west, west where the lightning danced across the sky. Smoke. "Oh, my God," he whispered. The clouds on the western horizon had a sickening gray-yellow hue. Smoke. The dry trees, the dry grass must have caught in a rush of flame, sending sparks snapping into the charged air, catching other trees and grass and sending the flames racing east before the wind, racing toward Aaron.

Bush fire! "Bush fire!" he cried. And even as his feet began to act before his brain did, he saw the first kangaroos coming toward him. A bush fire that he could not yet see, driving them before it. He was running now, running for his life—but to where? For the thousandth time he cursed the endless bush, that continuous, tree-covered bush that went on for countless miles, dry trees, dry grass. There was no sanctuary.

Gray kangaroos, a dozen at first, sprang toward him and past him, then thirty more on either side of him and on ahead. Small, large, heedless of the gasping, running man they had not yet learned to fear. He ran, going east, his only hope to keep ahead of the fire until the rain came—if it came. Now dingoes ran like starved dogs among the roos, and two emus ran past, wings lifted, necks stretched out, and the air overhead was filled with birds fleeing before the rush of smoke. Aaron paused, looked back. Gum trees ignited, exploded, living torches that set their neighbors afire, and now the flames were a reality, and the sickening smoke filled the sky.

He ran, stumbling over flat plain, and the fire's roar filled the air, fed by long, dry grass that should have nourished cattle and sheep instead, and by dead brush that had given up the struggle for survival too

soon. The wattle, the vines, other brush that had grown companionably with the trees now became their enemies, aiding the fire. Another glance back showed Aaron that the fire was moving north and south as well as east, attempting to surround him. Yes, he thought, this is the way of a bush fire, rapid, terrible, awesome—deadly.

His lungs ached, but he ran, his legs pumping up and down, carrying his body east, and the roar increased, and now he could feel the heat on his back. Roos bounded, scattering on either side, wallabies, and animals he could not distinguish hopped and ran past, while flocks of black crows and white cockatoos and wild pigeons flew shrieking overhead. He jerked back his head, looked up at the sky. No rain, not a drop. A red spark fell on the grass just in front of him, and the grass sighed and gave itself up to it in a rush of brilliant yellow.

Aaron avoided the fire and ran on now, stumbling. His mind shut out the sight of kangaroos on fire bouncing past, emitting shrieks, shut out the feel of the heat on his back, shut out the roar behind him, the white flashes overhead, the rain of red fire that fell all around him now. For his only thought was to run, to keep running until his heart burst, or the fire caught him. In some sickened, remote corner of his brain he realized this was the second time he had run for his life. But this time there was no escape.

Run, Aaron, run.

To survive four months in the bush, surviving hunger and thirst only to meet death like this—

The moan he heard came from deep inside himself, because he knew any moment his shirt would catch fire. He stopped, shedding it, and that was when he felt the wetness. He looked up, and rain beat down on his face. He turned about. The fire was nearly upon

336

him, but the rains were coming. Suddenly the lightning shattered the air, split open the heavens. The frog laughed and water gushed from its mouth. Rain. It poured down, blotting out the sight of the fire, and Aaron stood unbelieving as a great cloud of smoke and steam rose from the fire like a hand from hell and smothered him.

He coughed as he became engulfed in smoke. Gasping for breath, he tried to find a pocket of air. He clawed at his throat, which closed against the smoke, and he fell to the earth. But even then, the dying fire blew its smoky breath over him and he could not breathe. To survive a bush fire only to die from its smoke—

He reached up once and pulled at the smoke before he arched his back and gave himself up to blackness.

"Ah, 'tis a sign of good fortune to have two early lambin's on the same property," Mrs. McWilliams said, wrapping her hands in her apron. "But you shouldn't be out, missus. A lamb's not as important as a baby. It'll be angry he'll be if Mr. Mark finds out, and lookin' like a storm, it is."

Penelope was rolling up the sleeves of her thin dress. "I've no choice. And anyway, pray that it *does* storm, Mrs. Mac."

"But missus—"

She had seen the ewe go into labor earlier in the day and had brought her into the newly built shed with its pungent gum wood walls and grated batten floor. It was only a small, square shed now, but Penelope had plans for adding sweating and catching pens, and bins to it someday. But, for now, just this square room would do. She would have to add to it later, after Mark got over being upset about her having had

337

this small square shed built. Though Mark swore they had no money for such goings on as buying sheep and building sheds and hiring more convict laborers, it wasn't the money at all that worried him. It was her interest in something besides her husband.

Putting those treasonous thoughts aside, Penelope shook her head at the ewe's appearance as it stood on a straw mat she had made for its bed. The ewe had not yet delivered. Penelope had sent for help from the Macarthurs, but no one had come yet to help her.

Well, the sheep was hers and this was one of her good Saxony Merinos, and she must do what needed doing. Young ewes that had never delivered a lamb before often had difficult labors; she knew that, and she also knew there was a way to help.

"Please fetch me a bucket of water and some linens," she told the apple-cheeked Mrs. McWilliams. The plump woman left the shed shaking her head, and Penelope got on her knees beside the wooly Merino ewe.

The ewe's eyes were dull, and moisture had collected around its muzzle. It strained down, and a soft wheeze came from its throat, but otherwise it did not complain. Penelope ran her hand over the docile head and stroked its back. Then she peered at the bulging vulva and sat back on her heels. Judging by the ewe's appearance, she couldn't last much longer, and the longer the birth trauma lasted, the less likely it was that the new lamb would survive.

Penelope glanced about for the rope she had placed on the floor, found it, and laid the ewe on her side in the straw, crooning to it as she looped the rope around its neck.

Getting down on her knees was getting difficult because of her own growing abdomen, but she had to do it. As she had told Mrs. McWilliams, she had no

choice. Tentatively, Penelope slid her fingers into the ewe's vulva, and shutting her eyes, slid her hand into the warm, damp birth canal, probing, feeling, until by touch she located what felt like a hoof. "Oh, dear Lord," she whispered. "Where's the other hoof?"

"Interesting."

Penelope only glanced at Mark, who stood in the doorway of the shed now. "The ewe can't deliver," she said as her fingers searched for the other hoof. But in the tight warmth beside the hoof she could feel, not the other hoof, but the spongy softness of a little muzzle.

"And you shall play midwife?"

She saw him take the pail of water from Mrs. McWilliams, who hated the sight of blood and fled from the barn. Feeling a flash of irritation at his intrusion, Penelope did not answer him. Her hand on the ewe's rump was trembling with fear for her prize ewe and its firstborn.

"The merino, Penelope Cranston Aylesbury, on her knees in a sheep shed. Delivering a lamb."

Penelope waited until the ewe strained down again. Then she began to pull on the lamb's leg. Slowly, the leg inched toward the outside, but retracted slightly when the ewe ceased straining down. Penelope glanced at Mark. "You could help."

"Me? A mere currency lad helping two merinos?" he teased, and smiling, he squatted on one knee. "What can I do?"

"Hold the ewe still. She's kicking me."

Mark caught the ewe's neck and leg and held her. His eyes met hers and he smiled. "We won the Stinson-versus-Goodill case."

"I'm glad," she said, pulling the lamb's leg as the ewe strained down again, and when the hoof

339

appeared at the vaginal opening, she sighed and waited for the next uterine contraction.

"No, you're not glad for me," Mark said softly, while his mildly accusing eyes searched her face. "Not really. You are a grazier first, my dear, and Mark Aylesbury's wife second." He gave an exasperated sigh and looked briefly about the shed. "Doing things like building this shed without my consent."

"It was with my birthday money from Father, Mark."

"Your money is yours. My money is ours. Isn't that fortunate for you?"

Penelope shut her eyes very tight.

"It doesn't matter to you that because of me Fitzhugh is the most popular solicitor's firm in New South Wales."

She was thinking that Mark's complaints were neither angry nor bitter, just statements of fact that always made a point. "It does matter," she said, yet she knew that her disinterest showed. He was her husband, and yet somehow she could feel no pride for him, no pleasure in him. His return home every evening after a day in Sydney brought her only discomfort.

Knowing she could be crippling the lamb, but determined to save the ewe, she pulled with all her might at the next contraction. At the sight of a muzzle now, she smiled. "Oh, dear God," she whispered and ignored her husband's probing eyes upon her. He said no more, but held the ewe until the lamb emerged beneath her hands. It stirred and thrashed on the floor of the shed, and she smiled to see all four of its legs moving. She knew that one must immediately put the lamb at the mother's muzzle, else the mother would not accept it. Crooning, she

pushed the lamb to its mother, who sniffed and began licking it.

"Penelope Cranston Aylesbury, midwife. You did a bonzer job, as Stuart would say," Mark said, still watching her. "Stu won't believe it when I tell him."

She smiled, ignoring her damp hand, and watched the ewe and her lamb, listening with a wondrous rapture at the beginning bleats of the damp little thing slowly uncurling with each lick and nudge of the ewe's tongue and muzzle. The ewe was one of her purchases from Elizabeth Macarthur, along with sixty other ewes and two prize-winning rams. Her flock numbered near one hundred.

Mark's soft chuckle interrupted her musings. "I met Rodney Livingston on the street today, face-to-face. We met in front of the hospital, on the board walk. There wasn't enough room for two men to pass each other, so either Rodney must step aside or me."

Penelope waited and when Mark did not go on she asked, "Well, who stepped aside?"

"Both." He smiled quickly when he saw her surprise. "Who should come striding down the walk but old Robert Campbell, my father's partner in trade. He showed no sign of stepping aside, so we stepped off the walk. Campbell tipped his hat to both of us. But Livingston told me, 'Aylesbury, there will come a day when it shall pleasure me to bash your impertinent face permanently.'" Mark's eyes flashed with both anger and amusement.

Penelope sighed disgustedly, despising his enjoyment of the fray.

"And I replied, 'Really? Well, it will please me even more to obliterate yours.'"

Penelope changed the subject. "Mother was able to engage the band for the ball, Mark. I knew if anyone could get them to give their time, she could. She even

341

offered to help me with the preparations, but I refused. I did accept her offer of six of her servants to help the night of the ball."

"Good. The band has a week to learn the new waltz you wanted. And by the way, I was able to speak with the Superintendent of Convicts and am being assigned two servants. A female cook and a shed hand to help you with the sheep."

Penelope's smile was genuine this time. "Wonderful. Thank you."

"It was what you wanted, wasn't it?" he asked, watching her expression closely. "Don't I always get you what you want if it's within my power?"

"If it's within your power."

"The only thing I don't like is the more people we hire, the less privacy we have. And I enjoy my privacy with you, my love." He stepped closer to her, causing her to turn away, feeling the stiffness in her back and arms as she washed her hands in the basin of water he had set on the stool. Drying her hands, she turned back to face him only to find him close, towering over her. Recognizing the look, she was dismayed, dreading what might follow. The ways of a man. She turned away again, but he caught her, brought her against him gently.

"I need you, Penelope. When the judge ruled in my client's favor again today, the first thing I thought of was you, of wanting you."

She saw his hunger, her body felt his urgency, and she hated herself because she could not, would not respond to him. "No, Mark. I—I feel poorly today," she lied, and he knew that she lied.

His breath was hot on her ear as he lowered his face to hers. "That bed of straw. In all my life I've never made love in a bed of straw." He sensed her shock and took a quick breath. "I need you now, Penelope."

342

She shut her eyes, shook her head, and felt his kiss upon her neck, his hand as it moved to her breast before she placed her hands on his chest to push away.

He raised his head and looked at her, his breathing rapid and loud in the small shed as each beat of his heart shook his body. His requests for her body were always pleas, and she almost wished they were demands, for the pleas were harder to turn down. He read the rejection in her eyes and shrank from it, shutting his eyes and saying between clenched teeth, "Why? Why can't you love me? Why can't you want me as I want you?"

Why? Because I have incestuous inclinations? Because I love another man, one I have no business loving? One who is probably—probably—

"Aaron is dead, damn it."

A great, invisible fist knocked the breath out of her. She stared at him, searching his expression for some new truth.

Mark's intense, angry eyes dropped from the pain he saw in her face. "At least, I heard in Sydney that Buck came back to Bathurst recently. There has been no sign of Aaron. Four months in the bush—" He stared solemnly at her as she turned away and began to untie the rope from the ewe's neck.

They both heard the thunder, a great rumbling, and their eyes met. It meant rain. Desperately needed rain, an ending of the drought, a replenishing of the creeks and rivers, a renewal of the grass in the pastures. Mark took her to him again, held her to him. "Sorry I frightened you. I didn't intend to. Truly." He kissed her gently and she endured it, trying hard to find something pleasant in his kiss and embrace as his hands roamed over her body, cupping her buttocks, pulling her to him, fitting his erection

343

against her abdomen. With one hand he reached down and began to pull her skirt up.

"No," she whispered desperately. "Mark, not here!"

"Why not?" he asked against her mouth.

"In the shed? Mrs. Mac—"

"Is preparing tea. Yes, yes. Now. Here."

"My God, no!"

"You are my wife," he whispered, his hand going under the skirt, even as she struggled against him. He cupped her between her thighs roughly. "You promised to obey."

"No." She pushed at his hand.

"I haven't demanded much."

Desperately, she pushed his face away from hers and clawed at his probing hand. "Mark, please."

"Have I?" he hissed between his teeth.

"Not—not here. Not in the shed."

His hand was still gripping her thigh painfully, while the other had clamped on her jaw, holding her face still, upturned toward his. She saw the anger and the desperation in his eyes and pitied him. Pitied him, but did not love him. His grip released suddenly. "Very well," he said, releasing her. "Inside then? Now?"

He would undress her, kiss her body, delight in her, run his hands over her, caress her, and she would endure it, distressed at his desperate need, suffering his lips upon hers. She did not hate him, but neither did she love him. She nodded.

Smiling, he indicated the door with his outstretched palm. "After you, Mrs. Aylesbury."

Smoothing her skirts, Penelope took one last look at the new lamb suckling its mother, smiled faintly, and walked toward the door of the shed.

Outside, the first warm drops of rain were minting

dark brown coins in the powdered dust of the yard, and white flashes of lightning whitewashed the darkening day.

Over at the Cranstons', her father would be giving orders for the servants to drive the sheep closer to the house and latch the barn door. Her mother would be shouting for the servants to close the shutters and save the windowpanes from the hail. In Parramatta, Reverend Marsden would be giving thanks for the rain, and in Sydney the merchants would be speculating on how the rain would affect their investments.

The drought was broken. But as Penelope stepped upon the veranda of Mark's house to go in and up to the room to allow what she must, she was wondering if Aaron knew. If Aaron knew the drought was broken.

A face.

A familiar face. Curly hair.

Another familiar face floating above him with a flat-crowned hat on its head and an emu feather in its band.

He blinked back the smoke, but saw light above, dappling through the leaves of trees. The smoke was in his brain, then, not surrounding him. He took a deep, trembling breath of air. Fresh air, cool air, damp air. He came to himself then, as if his conscious spirit had just reentered his unconscious body. He took a moment to remember who he was.

He was Aaron Aylesbury. And he had survived.

Chapter XVIII

Mark was immensely pleased. She had played like a professional. She had given it her best effort. His applause was the most enthusiastic in the crowd. Emancipists and currency lads and lassies had politely paused in their conversation to watch Penelope Aylesbury as she took her place on the platform, sat down on the chair, and tilted the harp toward her. They had clearly expected to enjoy the music of a harp, because most of them had never heard a harp played before. But when the soft sounds sifted through the ballroom like gold dust in the sun, jaws dropped, and a respectful silence had filled the room. They had had no idea Mark's wife could play like that. He had seen awe on their faces. And they had asked for three encores. He was pleased and walked from amidst the loud applause to take her hand.

She appeared weary, but that would pass, and besides, her face was flushed with pleasure.

"Beautiful," he said. "You did beautifully, Penelope. Listen to them. You have won many admirers tonight."

"Thank you," she said, still blushing.

"Listen. The band is ready to begin. And I'm told it's customary that the host and hostess begin the first dance of the evening."

Ladies noticeably with child did not dance. But, as in all things, Mark was defying society's standards and mores in requesting the first waltz. Penelope could refuse. After all, she had not once obeyed a request of his out of fear or even duty. But she did not refuse him. Because for three hours now, Mark had withheld the details of Aaron's return from her. She knew he was enjoying her suffering, her wondering. His eyes had barely left her this whole evening, watching for a sign that she might be overtly excited, delighted, or even upset. And she *must* know, must find out about Aaron. All she knew was what Mark had told her when he returned early that afternoon from Sydney. He had stood, face dark with quiet fury, eyes bright with an unspoken fear, mouth smiling sardonically, mocking the shock on her face.

"Yes, Owen Crawford put into the cove and came to my—our office with word from Father that Aaron was brought home last evening."

"Was *brought* home?" Penelope's poise had failed her.

It was all he had volunteered as he handed his hat to Arthur and asked for a glass of port to be brought to the library.

Penelope had followed him into the library. "But what else, Mark?"

Deftly he had parried her every question about Aaron with a question of his own about the preparations for the housewarming. Causing her to suffer, knowing she was suffering and enjoying it. She saw his enjoyment of it even now.

She blushed now to think that she had almost begged him for more information about Aaron and

347

he had kept on replying, "Later, later, my love."

Later I shall be gone, gone to see for myself, she had vowed. But she had dressed shakily in her full-skirted azure gown trimmed in sapphire satin, with the handmade lace, the perfect foil for her light complexion and shining hair. Diamond tucks in the bodice at her back afforded her more ease of movement, and the scoop neck revealed, perhaps, too much full bosom. Fran Aylesbury had added to the dress a train of cotton lawn, fitted under the neckline and trimmed with French lace, to float like gossamer behind her as she walked. Penelope had let Mrs. Mac help her put up her hair, weaving a string of pearls, which her mother had given her, into her tresses. And she had greeted the arriving guests, smiling nervously as she stood beside her handsome husband.

But was Aaron well? she had wondered as she greeted her guests.

The guests had arrived in carriages and on horseback, friends of Mark's with their sweethearts and wives, mostly young men, but there were a few prominent older men, solicitors, a judge, merchants, ship owners, graziers, farmers, officers. All emancipists or small settlers or the Crawfords' friends from the Hawkesbury district. The invitation had been open to all, as most housewarmings were. But the exclusionist crowd was noticeably absent, ignoring Mark and Penelope Aylesbury's housewarming, a social slap in the face that was not only expected, but accepted. The Cranstons had not come, Penelope's mother pleading illness. And the Aylesburys had declined because of Aaron's return, according to Mark.

The large ballroom, with its row of seven windows overlooking the veranda, was festooned with the banners and braid of the military, and flowers from

the Cranston gardens. Not to be outdone, the Aylesburys had sent over linen damask cloths for the refreshment tables. The house candles and candelabra and lanterns had been lit just before Penelope performed her pieces on the harp. The ballroom was bright with lights and laughter and gaily dressed women in pastel-colored ballgowns, and gentlemen in blacks, blues, and browns, and sprinkled with the scarlet and royal blue coats of the military.

Penelope's mind had not been on hostessing, but she had gone about greeting guests and giving orders to the various servants automatically, a fixed smile on her face, while her heart fluttered periodically in her chest. She had heard whispers, too.

"One can't tell for sure, but if you'll look very closely you'll see that her stomach is not flat."

"You must admit, the wedding was rather sudden."

"Hush. Mark Aylesbury is an honorable man."

"More honorable than his brother in similar circumstances. If indeed she's . . . you catch my meaning."

Only the friendliness of most of the ladies present, the beautiful band manned by members of the military band, and the sheer numbers of the guests had kept thoughts of Aaron just barely on the edge of her panic.

Penelope overheard other talk, too—that Penelope Aylesbury was a perfect hostess. Being the daughter of pure merinos, Oliver and Elaina Cranston, she had been brought up a lady. Trained by her mother and pampered by her father, Mark's wife was the envy of every currency lass present, because of her birth even more than her beauty. Penelope felt envious eyes following her as she greeted her guests, laughed,

made small talk, saw that each guest met others and that each guest was introduced to the refreshment table where six young convict girls blushed and served the punch and cake. She had thanked the guests for their gifts of food, vegetables, and fruit, live young sapling trees and shrubs, rose cuttings for the yard, candlesticks and figurines for the house. And when Stuart Mays, with a blushing young currency belle on his arm, presented her with a fluffy yellow kitten, Penelope had laughed and said, "Mercy!"

Stuart's black eyes had flashed. "Ah, so Mercy she is! Mercy is one of the first cats in the colony. She was born aboard the *Egret,* which just put into Port Jackson today. A right proper English cat born aboard ship and freshly weaned."

Penelope, smiling, pressed her cheek against Mercy's soft fur, while Stu whispered to Mark at her elbow, "I think there's something brewing amongst the Livingston crowd tonight."

"Ah," Mark had said smiling, while his eyes grew hard. "Let them brew."

They had been interrupted by Jory McWilliams and a young man Penelope had not met. They roared with Mark and jested, and Penelope had turned smiling to greet Dr. and Mrs. Redfern as they came through the door.

The children were few, and those who had arrived were quiet and proper. New South Wales loved their children, but they trained them to respect authority and to obey. One word of caution or instruction was all it took to subdue them. Mothers watched their daughters and the gentlemen their sons.

Penelope had handed the amber-eyed mewling kitten to Mrs. McWilliams and continued to greet her guests, until at last it seemed every guest had arrived, had someone to talk to, and something to drink. It

was then she had done what Mark wanted: gone to the platform the new convict laborers had built on the south end of the ballroom and played her harp. But as she played her thoughts were of Aaron. *Always of Aaron.*

Now Mark led her out onto the polished floor, properly, as an English gentleman should. She knew that, like Aaron, Mark had learned the ways of a gentleman during his stay in England. That included learning how to dance. The waltz was in its infancy. There seemed to be no proper way to do the thing. The gentleman took the lady's right hand and either held it at shoulder height or out straight, while his right hand rested on her dainty waist, and the lady's left hand rested on his shoulder. There was no real pattern to the dance as there was the minuet, only a rhythm, a definite rhythm, as Penelope had taught James.

She gathered her train up and placed her hand on Mark's shoulder, and Mark took her hand, then fell into the rhythm of the waltz with surprising grace. His eyes laughed at her, slightly mocking, as his smile stayed fixed, as did hers. The other dancers began, and her embarrassment was relieved somewhat as the floor filled with other couples caught up in their own inspired interpretation of the dance.

"The party is a success already, thanks to my lovely hostess," Mark said.

She nodded without speaking.

"Yes, I've heard many compliments, Penelope. What a perfect wife for me you are." His eyes swept the milling guests. "I've counted over a hundred."

"One hundred twelve."

He smiled. "Ah. One of the largest dances ever, except for a governor's ball."

"I notice Governor Brisbane disdained to attend."

351

"I will remember that."

Penelope's smile stayed fixed. "What have you heard of Aaron? Mark, you must tell me now." Her eyes revealed her anger and determination, for she would not be denied news of Aaron any longer.

Mark's blue eyes darkened and glinted as he looked down at her and whirled her around. "I told you. Aaron is home."

Penelope's anger flared, and she no longer pretended to smile. "That's not enough, Mark."

"It's all I know."

"If that's all you know, you should be ashamed."

Mark's chin set. His smile was a grimace, and he would not reply.

"Very well. If you don't find out, I shall. I'll go to your parents' tomorrow morning early."

"You wouldn't. Not without me, Penelope. I won't allow it."

"You can't stop me."

His face flushed with anger and his blue eyes snapped. He opened his mouth, shut it, opened it again. "Deen and Buck Crawford brought him home yesterday. They found him five days ago on the edge of a smoldering bush fire in the rain. He was overcome by the smoke."

The small sound that escaped her was an expression of both horror and relief, but it distressed him, caused his mouth to thin and his hand to tighten painfully on her waist. "Yes, go on," she prompted.

"Rumor is that he looked like an animal and even the natives were afraid of him."

Penelope shut her eyes. But he was alive. And home. And nothing else mattered. "Is he well now?"

"I'm not sure."

"Then you should find out immediately. He is your brother."

"And *your* lover?"

She stopped and he stared down at her, his cold eyes gone hard, his nostrils flaring. She wanted to slap him, not because of his insolence, but because it was true. "I would like to sit down, please."

Mark gripped her arm, wanting to hurt her, wanting to take her shoulders in his hands and shake the thoughts of Aaron out of her head. In his crazy, wild scheme to win her, he had harbored hopes of her learning to love him; he had even been confident of it for a while, until it became apparent that she was not going to return his love. It had gradually dawned on him that she had given her heart as well as her body to Aaron, and that the heart was gone. It showed in her unresponsiveness when he made love to her. In her lack of enthusiasm at his little successes. It maddened him. Made him beat his head against the stone wall of his social position, drove him to scheme and work in order to insure success. No, not success. Prominence, wealth, power. Oh, to have *power*.

Angrily, he led her through the crowd of dancers, these brightly gowned guests who were oblivious to his pain, oblivious to the fact that his wife did not love or respect him. He had won her, but Penelope Cranston was just a shell. His brother had her heart, soul, and mind. Blindly he delivered her to the group of ladies seated in the chairs against the wall near the refreshment table.

"You're needed in the library."

Mark dragged his gaze from his wife as she sat down fanning her flushed face, and stared at Stuart, the muscles of his jaw tight. He did not reply.

Stuart saw that Mark had not comprehended what he had said. "I say, mate, you're needed in the library."

Mark uncurled his fists and did not look at his wife

again as he followed Stuart through the throng of talking and laughing men and women. The sweet strains of the band irritated him now, and the faces he had sought so eagerly before he now hated. What he wanted more than this damned party was to take his wife to her bedchamber and hurt her, strike her, make her promise to leave Aaron alone, not to see him, ever.

Stu opened the door of the library, held it open, and Mark went through it only to stop abruptly just inside the door.

In the room twelve men sat and stood, a frieze of the current fashion in men's wear in their finery, their trousers and swallowtail coats, waistcoats and ruffled shirts, their polished boots and their canes. Most were young, young currency lads near his own age, but four were older men, three of them emancipists.

The library was well furnished now. Penelope had bought two Morris chairs, which she said blended with the Crawford desk and chairs. His father had purchased a globe on a stand for him, and between Penelope and his father the built-in bookshelves had slowly begun to fill with fine books. Books were rarer in the colony than musical instruments. Penelope had draped the wide window in deep royal velvet, and the carpet that covered most of the floor was a royal purple and gold thing of much beauty, from Persia.

"Shut the door, Stuart." The man who spoke was an emancipist named Ephriam Barlow. Mark knew him only because he was one of the colony's rags-to-riches merchants. As Mark's eyes moved around the crowd, he realized that the men in this room represented the liberal faction in the colony, some of the most prominent men in New South Wales.

Barlow hooked one thumb in the pocket of his

waistcoat and said, "There's no need to delay the issue we've been discussing here tonight, Mark." Barlow glanced around the room. "I'll come straight to the point. As you know, the Bigges report has done this colony almost irreparable harm, and the time is ripe now to repair that harm."

Bigges had been sent to the colony by the English government during Macquarie's governorship because the government had been receiving numerous complaints of Macquarie's mismanagement. Of course, every one in the colony knew who had complained. The same men who had complained and caused trouble with every governor the colony had ever had. Macarthur was the ringleader of the colony's exclusionists who wrote complaining to the home government because Macquarie had attempted to reinstate emancipists to full social and political positions. Macquarie had believed that once a man received a full pardon, he should receive all the rights that any other free man had.

Although emancipists greatly outnumbered the wealthy free settler exclusionists, Bigges had been courted and won over by the exclusionists, and it was his report that the British government used as their bible in dealing with its colony in New South Wales. Now, emancipists were no longer appointed to the magistracy, they were not called for jury service, and no emancipist, no matter how prominent and wealthy he had become in the colony, could be appointed to the legislative council. The emancipist had no say in the laws by which he was governed.

"You know what we need, Mark. Trial by jury, the right to serve on a jury, the right to be a part of our own legislature, and so on?"

Mark nodded, his eyes darting from one face to another, his mind frozen in what might be a

shocking possibility. Could it be—

"I have just returned from America," Barlow said. "The Americans wanted essentially the same freedoms that we do, but they gained theirs by going to war with the mother country." Barlow shook his head. "We don't want that. Not war. We don't want Australia to become another America."

"Nor another England, either," Jory McWilliams put in.

The currency lads nodded. It was the older men who had come from England who did indeed want Australia to become another England. Which didn't make sense to the second-generation Australians.

Mark's gaze came away from the faces before him and fixed on Barlow. "I know this. Why are you telling me these things?"

"We need a leader."

Still Mark's mind refused to grasp what Barlow might be saying.

"We have William Wentworth, but he's still in England in law school. We need a man who's here now. We need a young man, a popular man. We need, in short, a currency lad, but one whose parents are well respected in the colony. We need that lad to be well versed in the law, in politics—someone who has been abroad, who has a little—shall we say— English polish, but not too much. A man who can win the loyalty of every currency lad, the respect of emancipists, who is not afraid of the exclusionists, and one who has the dash and verve it would take to gain the attention of the governor."

Mark looked at Stu, who had leaned against the wall, crossed his arms over his chest, and was eyeing him with that scheming sparkle in his black eyes.

"And we need a man who can win audience with King George."

356

Mark's eyes darted from Stu to Jory, then to Barlow again. "So?"

"For days we've been taking a poll, amongst ourselves, without your knowledge, because you were one of the prospects. And we've concluded there's only one man in the colony who fits the bill, Mark. You."

Mark frowned, glanced at Stuart, felt all the blood in his body going to his face and sending shock waves to his brain. He voiced his only doubts aloud, "But I'm too young, too new—"

"Too young? Too new on the colony's social scene?" Barlow smiled and strolled over to Mark's desk, where Mark had earlier piled all the papers he was working on, plus a couple of law books, so it would look as though he had been extremely busy. Barlow nodded. "Yes, it's true. But you've—pardon the pun—made your mark in the colony already."

The others laughed and it was Stuart who said, "But don't get the big head yet, Mark. Here's the most important reason we picked you. Your father was a personal friend of Governor Macquarie's."

That irritated Mark, and it showed. "Macquarie is in disfavor with London because of the Bigges report."

Barlow spoke up. "What governor wasn't? Yet, they all had their say sooner or later. They published their memoirs, their rebuttals against the political slander, they gained the ear of king and commoner alike, and had at least a little influence in Parliament. So shall Macquarie. And that is *your* link to Parliament, Mark."

No one spoke. The room was quiet, only the faint, sweet strains of the band could be heard through the closed library door, and a low, even hum of guests' voices. Mark was astonished that these men, these

357

influential, prominent men, had chosen *him* as their leader. But he was wondering. In the course of history, did men usually embrace a cause and carry that cause forward to be followed by others? Or did the others with a cause choose a man among them to lead?

Confusedly, he spread his hands in front of him. "Why must we have a leader?"

"Men who actively propound an ideal are an unruly mob without one. A faction with an ideal must have a spokesman. A thousand voices talking at once only results in confusion. One voice can be heard and understood."

Dr. Redfern, a wealthy emancipist physician who was a good friend of his father's, spoke up now. "We'll be behind you, of course, offering support and advice. You see, Mark, a spokesman's voice is never his own alone, but the voices of hundreds, sometimes thousands."

"Still," put in Barlow, "men are like sheep. They must have a leader to look to, to believe in." He put his hand on Mark's shoulder. "Come, Mark. This isn't anything new to you. You've spoken out on the issues before."

"In Foster's tavern," Stu said, smiling.

The currency lads who knew him best guffawed.

Barlow turned to Stuart with a smile. "Ah, but many a political battle has been fought and won in taverns."

"True," Stuart admitted, still smiling.

Mark smiled too, and when Barlow turned back to him, he asked, "What must I do?"

The older man shrugged. "Do whatever has to be done, Mark. You were born to be a politician. You'll know what needs to be done when the time comes."

Mark laughed softly as the men agreed and began

talking among themselves. His emotions were in turmoil as he accepted a few jibes from his friends. Elation consumed him, along with incredulous pride. What would Penelope say? What would his father say? He would indeed leave tomorrow for the farm to check on Aaron, to tell his father about this. He would—

His mind seemed to burn, and he was barely able to speak with the others on the issues of trial by jury, of emancipists needing a voice in the government.

"You see?" Stuart said, coming to stand by him. "I told you you were a born leader if you could only believe it yourself. You have admitted to being the leader of our small group within the faction."

Stuart talked on, but as Mark tried to listen to what the other men were saying among themselves, he became aware of another sound, a shouting, calling. He put his hand on Stuart's arm. "Listen."

Stuart paused. The band had changed its tune and was now playing an Australian folk song called "The Man is Home From the Bush." The men in the room hushed talking and listened as Mark strode to the door, opened it. Something was happening. He strode across the hall to the ballroom, noticing that the crowd of guests was looking toward him as he entered. They surged toward him, causing him to wonder if the whole world knew that New South Wales had chosen him to carry the banner of freedom for the emancipists and was coming to congratulate him.

But then he saw that the eyes of his guests were not upon him at all, but on a tall, lean man whose back was toward him, and as Mark watched, his guests converged on the man, patting his back, gripping his arm, jostling him, congratulating him, and only when the man turned his head to smile at Mr. Macrae

did Mark recognize the profile.

Mark's countenance fell in direct proportion to his spirits. For the man he had not recognized at first was his own brother.

Penelope watched open-mouthed from her place near the refreshment table as the guests surged toward him, greeting him, shouting welcome home, and plying him with questions. He was thin, almost gaunt, slightly haggard. His response to the barrage of questions was meager. A word here, another word there, and all the while his eyes were sweeping the room, picking out a face and moving on. Aaron.

Suddenly, as if her feet had a will of their own, she found herself threading her way through the throng of guests toward him, her lips, her heart, her whole being uttering one word: Aaron. Her heart thudded, her ears were deaf, her eyes blind, but her mind cried out: Aaron.

It took her an eternity to reach him, and even then she could not approach him. The guests did not move away. Then his eyes met hers, held hers. She saw his anger, his unbearable anger, before he looked away.

She frowned. She must explain.

"How did you manage to survive?" a man asked her beloved.

His lips moved briefly in answer. His eyes came back to hers, darted away.

Of course, he was angry. She would explain. And as she waited, she noticed that he was thinner, taller, that his shoulders had gotten wider and the muscles of his neck more solid. The boyish grin was gone, and the old, soft curiosity in his eyes was replaced by hard-won knowledge. His hair was crisp from the

sun, his skin tanned as deeply as a native's. Her pulses thudded in her ears and her impatience to get rid of her guests caused her to push and shove until she stood before him.

"Aaron. Oh, Aaron. Welcome home," she said.

His brown eyes rested briefly on her face. He bowed formally and said, "Penelope."

She reached toward him, but he said, "Congratulations . . . sister-in-law." His coldness shocked her into speechlessness, but his eyes made a brief, pain-filled journey from her astonished face to her belly and up again. Hell was in his eyes at that moment, and then he turned his back on her.

Frantic, she touched his arm as the guests jostled her, but he ignored her. She maneuvered to face him again. "We want to welcome you home," she cried.

"Home?" His eyes roved around the room, for, of course, this was Mark's home. And hers.

"Aaron, please! You must listen," she cried, but her voice could not be heard above the others', and the band had begun a waltz again.

Frustrated, Penelope glanced at the band leader and saw why. Mark had given instructions for him to begin the waltz. Oh, so like you, Mark, to divert attention from your brother. But at the same time, she knew that Aaron was not enjoying the attention at all, was barely even sociable.

Sociable? He had been in the bush for four months, how could he be sociable? You must listen, Aaron, she cried, but her words were drowned in the noise. Listen to what? she questioned herself. For suddenly it occurred to her that she could not explain, could not reveal to Aaron that he was her half-brother.

In an agony of humiliation at his rejection of her attention, she watched Mark coming toward Aaron smiling, and the guests stepped back. Brother was

going to greet brother after one of them had experienced a terrible ordeal, and they did not want to hinder that.

"Aaron," Mark said when he stopped before him. He put his weight on one foot. "I heard that you had come home."

Aaron stood tall and easy and his steady gaze met Mark's. "Did you?" he said without smiling.

"Penelope and I had planned to go to the farm tomorrow to see if you were all right."

Aaron said, "Now you won't need to, will you."

"I understand Deen found you."

Aaron did not reply, and Mark shifted to his other foot, a little embarrassed because others were listening. "Things have changed since you left."

Aaron's eyes never left Mark's face. "So I've heard."

"Welcome to Penmark," Mark said, gesturing toward the ballroom floor where the dancers had begun again.

"Thank you."

Penelope opened her mouth to say something when Stuart Mays touched Mark's arm. "Sorry to interrupt, Mark, but we've trouble out front."

Mark and Aaron kept eyeing each other soberly, messages passing between them that each understood, but which no one else did. Finally Mark excused himself and turned away, glancing only briefly at Penelope, and the confrontation over, the guests turned away also, leaving Penelope still standing before Aaron.

Casually, he folded his arms over his chest and looked at her. There was not a flicker of interest or anger in his expression now.

Words failed her at first, but finally she said, "There is a reason for everything. You must believe that."

362

"Undoubtedly." His eyes flashed with anger now. They were changing eyes, the eyes of a man experiencing a wide range of emotions and keeping them all carefully concealed. Gone were the laughing eyes of the young man, the troubled eyes of the young physician. His quick smile was gone, too, and the gentleness. He was empty of words and full of experience now, experience that had hardened him. His face seemed carved out of granite, and when she touched his arm, it felt like stone. "I waited for you until—"

"Until my brother came along."

"Until there was no time left." She had sworn not to tell Aaron the child was his, because the bad blood that was now between Aaron and Mark would boil over and stain them all, including the child. Perhaps someday when the anger and hurt had subsided she would tell him. But now it would only mean trouble. And she could never tell him that her father was also his.

A slow, angry smile stretched his mouth. "Your namesake, Penelope, the lady who waited for Ulysses for years, would be proud of you. How long did you wait, Penelope, one month? Two?"

"Aaron—"

He started to turn away, but she grabbed his arm. When she did, he paused, looked down at her hand, and it was then she caught a glimpse of his pain. But when his eyes met hers again, the pain was gone and only anger remained.

"You're so thin," she said, not willing to give him up. "You've suffered."

His eyes swept down to her belly, up again to her face. "You're fat. You haven't."

Anger flared in her, anger because he did not know of her suffering, of her love for him, did not trust her

love enough to know instinctively that there was a reason why she had not waited for him. "Why?" she asked, her jade-green eyes searching his face. "Why did you bother to come here tonight?"

"I was in Sydney visiting the governor. I heard of the housewarming." He looked past her, his eyes searching the guests. "And I wanted to see for myself. You in my brother's house."

All her agony surfaced then and she said softly, "And now that you have?"

"Now I can get on with my life," he said and turned away. "Without thinking of you again."

She stood and watched him walk away. Someone was rushing past saying, "C'mon. There's trouble outside." And the guests surged out of the ballroom into the corridor, Penelope among them. When at last she found herself on the veranda, she saw that the lights from the lanterns in the gum trees gave the scene in the front dooryard a sinister quality. And that it was Mark, with twelve of his closest friends, facing Rodney Livingston and his mob of young merinos.

It was obvious to Mark that Livingston and his crowd had been drinking. Over in Foster's Tavern, likely. He was angry as hell at this. They were here to make trouble, and he had trouble enough of his own, with Penelope and Aaron together in the house. But he stood face-to-face with his foe, hooked his thumbs in his waistcoat, and said sarcastically, "Welcome to Penmark."

Livingston sneered and glanced at his smirking friends. "Did you hear that, mates? Penmark." He looked at Mark again. "Now isn't that clever? One would almost believe you were born to such pomposity, Aylesbury."

Mark kept smiling. "To what do we owe the

pleasure of your company, Livingston?"

"The mates and I decided we wanted to give you a gift, Mark, a *small* token of our regard for you." Livingston gestured to the two young men near the cart parked beside the veranda, and while Mark watched, they tipped the cart and guests scattered as a load of manure slid with an odorous rush onto the veranda.

Fury leapt in Mark's eyes as he met Livingston's laughing ones. "If that is your regard for me, what have you done for my wife?"

"We have a special gift for her, not so onerous, for we believe that she is a victim of circumstances. Her token is in your own paddock." Livingston's eyes went suddenly to the veranda where Aaron now stood alone, the guests having vacated to escape the stench and soil. "We were even thoughtful enough to bring you a welcome home gift, Aaron."

Suddenly Joe Greer brought a cradle and set it in the yard. The guests gasped in horror. There was no need for words. The cradle board was engraved with the insignia of Moffett Farms, a bounding kangaroo. Mark's eyes darted to Aaron. Had he heard of Annabelle Moffett's condition?

Aaron allowed a small smile to stretch his lips. So the merinos suspected that he was the father of Annabelle's child. Good. That meant that they did not suspect Deen. The past five days passed quickly through his mind as he stood with the manure at his feet, the lantern lights causing the shadows of the antagonists to dance in the bare, grassless yard. Mark and his friends were watching him for a reaction to Livingston's insult.

The smoke of the bush fire had shut out the air from his lungs, and in those last seconds before unconsciousness overtook him, Aaron had been

certain he was dying. A part of him had died, that old Aaron, but when he woke to see Deen and Buck's faces, he knew he had been given a new chance. God was no more real to him now than ever, and the reason, the purpose of his existence was no clearer to him than before. But now he did not need a reason to live, to be. Just the living, the being was now enough. And if God had a reason for allowing suffering, then it was His business, and Aaron no longer cared what it was. For in his own hands and brain he had the means, the skill to ease that suffering, and he could use the skill now without demanding answers.

Deen and Buck had carried him on horseback to a native camp and plied him with water. He had wakened in a native village.

"Now if you aren't the damnedest awful sight," Deen had said when Aaron tried to sit up. "Even the natives are afraid of you."

It had taken Aaron a day of eating and drinking and resting before they could set out over the mountains for home. Meantime, Deen had raced ahead to tell Mum and Father that he had been found. A bath, a shave, clothes, and Aaron returned home, thinner, browner, maybe wiser. In the next few hours, as his mother had sat beside him with his father staring at him puffing on his pipe, Aaron had caught up on the news. Mum had told him gently about Mark and Penelope's wedding. Aaron had flown into a rage, swearing in his mind he would thrash Mark. That was before reason took over and told him, Why not? Mark had always loved her, and he, Aaron, had never spoken to her clearly about marriage. And if she had thought him dead, as it seemed everyone else had— But then the loss of her caused him to spring up from his chair and run to the yard, where he vomited up his last meal as if the

vomiting of it could purge his soul of the agony, the pain of losing her.

The news of Annabelle's pregnancy came to him late the same afternoon. Glenn Moffett had been the harbinger of those glad tidings.

Glenn had come over to welcome Aaron home, and when the preliminary greetings were over and Mum and Father had left them alone on the veranda, Glenn had pulled a bottle of rum out of his saddle bag and popped the cork with glee.

"Wanted to drink to your return, Aaron," he had said, handing the rum over to Aaron.

The rum had settled in Aaron's stomach like a hot stone, which melted and slid through his veins like molten tar.

Glenn leaned toward him. "Man, I have got me a problem."

Aaron had lowered the bottle from his lips. "Don't tell me. Annabelle."

"Aye. But it's your problem too, Aaron. Me and your father talked about it and 'ee decided I should be tellin ya. Annabelle's . . . well . . . Annabelle's . . . ah . . . fresh."

Aaron frowned, handed the bottle back to him. "Fresh?"

"You know." Glenn made a motion with his hand to indicate Annabelle's large belly.

Feeling the effects of the rum, the news did not shock him. Nothing could have shocked him, he thought. "No," he said doubtfully.

Glenn nodded. "Aye." He took a deep drought of the rum and passed the bottle back to Aaron.

"I hope to God the guilty man has stepped forward to claim her hand." Aaron said and tipped the bottle up briefly.

"He did, only there's a problem with that."

367

Aaron caught Glenn's watery blue eyes intent on his face and lowered the bottle slowly.

"The man is Deen."

If Glenn had hit him in the face, Aaron couldn't have been more astonished. "Deen!"

"Of course, you know there's no society nowhere that would condone any such marriage."

Aaron had looked doubtfully at Glenn out of the corner of his eye. "This trick won't work, Glenn."

"What trick?"

"This new ploy of yours to marry off Annabelle," Aaron said, shaking his head. "It won't work. I don't believe you."

"Bulsht, Aaron. It ain't no ploy. 'Tis the truth. Ask your parents. Ask Deen. Ask Annabelle 'erself."

Aaron stared at him and realized he was telling the truth. "Damn," he whispered. And he began to realize slowly where his duty lay, duty to the family, duty to his friend, Annabelle. A family member had wronged a girl. And he—he was the only one available who could make it right. He passed his hand over his face and said damn again, but made Glenn no promises.

The next morning early, this very morning, he had taken the *Milicent* to Sydney. During the voyage, he had approached Deen. "I heard about Annabelle," was all he said.

Pain, sorrow, humiliation passed like phantoms in Deen's eyes and then were gone before he replied, "Do I burn at the stake?"

"If you do, we all do."

"I want to marry her, Aaron. I love her."

"I know. But you know you can't."

Deen had nodded. "She was not at fault. I forced her."

Honorable men did not discuss such things, so Aaron only gave Deen a doubtful look and sauntered

away to another part of the boat. It was never mentioned again. He had stood on the deck of the sloop remembering that once Cranston had wanted someone to start a cattle station for James near Bathurst. Aaron had been toying with the idea himself. Brisbane had just promised to send the surveyor-general out to the area he and the others had charted. Aaron didn't have his map, but he had his carefully kept journal and his memory. And the idea of marrying Annabelle was not noxious to him. He had always liked Annabelle, but he did not love her. Never would.

Now he looked at the cradle in the yard with every young merino in New South Wales and every friend of his and Mark's waiting for his reaction. He had to make a quick decision, quicker than he had wanted to.

Aaron smiled sardonically and stepped off the veranda. Slowly he approached Livingston and came to stand before him, eyeing him steadily, giving him time to become wary. "If you are besmirching the honor of a lady, I'm ready to defend it, Livingston," he said.

Livingston's dark eyes flashed in the lantern lights and he smiled. "Which one?"

Anger leapt in Aaron's eyes, and it was the first time the possibility of Penelope's having become pregnant before her marriage occurred to him. "Both," he replied steadily.

Those were the words the young men wanted to hear, and they eagerly began shedding their coats and rolling up their sleeves as Livingston and Aaron stood like two roosters, eye-to-eye. The older men in the crowd rushed about forbidding any show of violence and the ladies exclaimed and scurried inside.

"Stop this. I won't have it," Penelope cried,

coming to Livingston. "You, Rodney, take your drunken friends away at once!"

Livingston ignored her, so Penelope turned to Mark. "You must stop this. I'll have no fighting on our property."

Mark ignored her as he continued to roll up the sleeves of his shirt.

She turned to Aaron. "I demand you stop this at once. You've no right."

Only a sideways glance, and Aaron said, "Haven't I?"

His head exploded then. Rodney Livingston couldn't contain his anger any longer. He suspected that Aaron was not only the father of Annabelle's child but of Penelope's, too. His hate had to be assuaged, his hurt avenged.

Peace shattered like a dropped china dinner plate. Fists made contact with jaws and skulls cracked, while women screamed. All around Aaron men struggled and sprawled in the dust. Every blow to his face and abdomen sent a thrill through him. The pain was better than sexual release, and each blow he delivered in turn was a purging of his angry soul. In the fury and confusion of the moment, Aaron made a vow to bash every damn merino present at least once. Side-by-side he and Mark fought, struggled. Once Aaron saved Mark from getting hit from behind with a gumwood plank. And Mark caught Fredrich Shearer just before he swung a picket off the fence at Aaron's head. The brothers had fought like this side-by-side before, often over the same girls.

Currency lads grinned through bloody teeth and aimed fists at bruised merino faces and received blows in return. The currency lads had saved up all the frustrations of being second-class citizens for just such moments as this. And though the emancipist

370

women and currency lassies screamed and squealed their horror, they wouldn't have missed watching the fray for the world.

Like a dust storm crawling with creatures, the free-for-all drifted from the front yard through Penelope's newly planted orchard at the side of the house, to the back dooryard where only the moonlight lit the faces of antagonists and spectators alike. Aaron was aware that Penelope had sent the men servants to halt the fight, but the servants were getting bashed along with the rest.

Finally Aaron found himself gasping for breath and standing over a young merino he didn't even know. The fight was halting because the men were exhausted. Hair in his face, Aaron looked about for the man who had started it all and saw Livingston staggering up from the ground, holding his sleeve under his bleeding nose. One by one the other merinos began to hunt their horses. Aaron looked around for Mark.

Mark's new blue trousers were torn beyond repair and one eye was swelled shut, but he dusted off his behind slowly, catching his breath, and when he looked about, saw four men sprawled unconscious in the yard. Others were hobbling about. Then he saw Aaron. What did Aaron mean by replying to Livingston that perhaps he was fighting for both women?

Mark clenched his teeth and stumbled once as he made his way to Aaron. Aaron was bent over examining his own torn trousers, and sensing Mark's presence, straightened to look him in the eye.

"You," Mark gasped, his chest heaving from his recent exertions as he stabbed his finger into his brother's chest. "If my wife's honor needs defending, I'll do it myself."

371

Aaron didn't give any thought at all to the blow he delivered his brother. He and Mark had fought each other more often than they had fought others together, and he was aware that Mark was picking a fight now. His blow made a crisp cracking sound on Mark's cheekbone.

Mark staggered back, but caught himself before he fell. His cut lips peeled back from his teeth and only the whites of his eyes showed as he waded in and delivered a blow of his own. This pain from Mark was far more exquisite to Aaron than that delivered by any merino, and the pleasure of the contact of his own knuckles greater when the target was Mark's face.

The brothers fought desperately, grunting, moaning, sprawling in the dust, rolling over and over. Mark was taking out all his frustrations on Aaron, Aaron whom his wife loved, whom his father loved best. Aaron, who was legitimate-born and who was first in the hearts of his family. He wanted desperately to see his brother's handsome face marred, scarred. He wanted frantically to beat that face again and again.

And Aaron beat Mark for loving Penelope, for marrying Penelope, for impregnating Penelope, for taking what was his, the woman who had been his for years.

"Stop! Stop!" screamed Penelope as she ran into the yard after the men. She caught Aaron's arm, but he shook her off, so she caught a handful of Mark's shirt and pulled, but he shrugged free of her and went at his familiar adversary.

But something had snapped in her mind. She did not want either of them hurt, and she waded into the fray unmindful of the flaying fists, pulling their shirts, grabbing their arms and screaming the same

372

thing. "Stop!" The smell of sweat and dust from their bodies assailed her senses as she pulled arms and shirts, and finally Mark stood holding his arms away from himself because she had his shirt in both of her hands pulling with all her might. "Stop! Stop!"

"Good God, Penelope. We've stopped," Mark shouted, gasping.

She moaned and tears mixed with the dust on her face as she peered at him through the locks of hair that had come loose and hung down in her face. "Oo-oo-oo," she said and spun in his hands toward Aaron, who stood gasping for breath, bloody, his eye black and menacing. "Oh you, Aaron. I'd be ashamed. To come here and fight like this." She turned then to Mark. "How terrible, Mark. We'll be the laughing stocks of Sydney. And at your own party. Shame on you. Shame on you for fighting your own brother." Her hair slung as she turned from one to the other. "Don't you dare lay another hand on Mark in his own yard, Aaron Aylesbury! Fighting like small boys. Behaving like savages. Have you no self-control? There's no reason on earth to come to blows with anyone when things can be settled by words. Must you behave like street brawlers?"

Jory McWilliams had come limping up to Penelope and was saying, "Mrs. Aylesbury? Uh, Penelope? Oh, Penelope?"

Finally she focused furious eyes on him.

"Your new lamb?"

Her face paled even in the moonlight.

"Them pure merinos have dyed it black."

Penelope's mouth popped open and her eyes slid to Rodney Livingston who stood grinning at her with one boot in the stirrup as he prepared to mount his horse. Then, lips pressed tightly together, Penelope went to Rodney and took a wide swing.

The pop the palm of her hand made on his cheek echoed in the shocked stillness that followed the brawl, knocking his hat off. "You beast. You miserable cur. Get off my property at once. You and all your miserable hordes. And don't you ever set foot here again or I shall call the army."

Grinning, Livingston picked up his hat and jammed it onto his head, mounted his horse and motioned for the others to do the same.

Hands on her hips—something Elaina Cranston had taught her daughter never to do—Penelope watched the merino men kick their horses and ride out of the yard and out into the dark track. She turned to the milling guests. One look from her signaled them that it was time to depart.

Emancipists and their children had been born to struggle and strife. Many of the parents had been born in the streets of London, and many of the currency children had been born in the streets of Sydney. They had been more delighted by this fight tonight than offended. Indeed, the fight had been more entertaining than the dance. So they did not take offense when they saw that Penelope Aylesbury wished them to leave. Besides, seeing her crack Rodney Livingston in the face herself had raised her several notches in their esteem.

Penelope allowed the guests to bid her, Mark, Aaron, and each other farewell. She watched them mount their horses, fill their carriages. Then as the dust of the departing guests wafted across the yard, she saw Crutchfield bring Aaron his rented horse. Aaron was just putting his foot in the stirrup when Penelope demanded, "Where are you going?"

Aaron swung into the saddle. There was no expression on his battered face now. "To Sydney."

"But why? You can stay the night here."

374

"No, I can't."

Penelope turned to Mark. "Tell him. Make him stay."

Mark was beating the dust out of his coat. "A man has to do what he has to do," he said.

"Oh, but Aaron," she pleaded. "If you go now it may be a long time before we see you again."

Aaron shifted the reins of his restless steed to his left hand and his eyes flashed in the light coming from the lanterns. "And neither you nor I really give a damn, do we?" With that he reined his horse about and set off across the yard at a gallop.

Sick with new grief, Penelope watched him go. Her father had spoken to her about wanting Aaron to start a cattle station in the Bathurst district for James. And there was Annabelle heavy with child, Annabelle who could never hold her head up in Parramatta or Sydney again. Penelope knew what it was that Aaron must do. Anger and pain and jealousy warred for first place in her heart as she covered her mouth to keep from screaming out into the night, *Aaron, I love you.*

"The night is cool. Come inside," Mark said coldly.

Penelope walked with her husband to the house. But on the veranda she paused until she heard the last of the hoofbeats of Aaron's horse.

Part II

1825-1829

Chapter XIX

The plains. It was the tireless bush of the outback pausing from the business of growing trees, taking a deep breath, letting the gum trees and wattle give way to tall, lush grass. It was country tailor-made for raising cattle. In the low pasture and on the sides of the hills, cattle grazed, brown, black and white, solid black.

Aaron reined his horse atop a rise and viewed the country—undulating land with few breaks, laced with sometime creeks, which were followed faithfully by stands of gum trees and wattle and pea vines, just to remind the careless stockman that on either side of this vast, rich plain was bush country, thick, wild, dangerous. No one was more aware of how dangerous the bush was than Aaron. Yet, his memories of being lost in it just a little over two years ago were good. They were thrilling memories, with just enough recollection of hunger and thirst and blazing sun to cause him to respect them, as one respects the concept of a just and vengeful God. The bush *was* God in a way, a God Aaron could accept in spite of its mercilessness to the weak. It had made him understand better the vagaries of human nature,

sickness, suffering, the joy of being alive and well.

He passed his hand under his nose. He was aware that his experience in the bush had been invaluable to him as a stockman. In helping him locate water holes, mainly, besides toughening something deep inside him that made the hardships of raising cattle not easier, but more understandable.

He was the boss stockman, but that did not exempt him from the work on Cranston's cattle station, and this time of year mustering cattle in mobs of fifty or sixty was a daily task. Cattle in this back country were like people, tending to separate into mobs of fifty or more, each mob branching off from the others to find their own territory. And like today, the ringers, mostly jackaroos, young men new to cattle mustering, had to muster the cattle and draft them for branding.

Aaron had spent all morning drafting stray cattle, driving them into the mob, like the mickey, a young bull, he had just driven into the mob below. Some of the breakaways had been driven from the mob by older bulls and were in no mood to be dallied with. But that young bull had learned the sting of the rope and was more afraid of it than the jealous bull, and went snorting and loping into the mob.

Aaron surveyed his world. Below, his best ringer was in the process of drafting a calf, a cleanskin without a brand, chasing it, swinging the rope over his head. The catch rope was attached to the end of a pole, and on the rope's other end was the loop that the ringer would toss over the cow's horns or head. Then the ringer would take a turn or two of the rope around a tree. Other ringers would run to secure the animal's feet. Through the gray dust Aaron could hardly see the ringers branding a cow below.

This drafting and branding were only part of the

work. There was the bangtail muster when they counted the cattle at each water hole, cutting the hair on the tails of the ones that had been counted. And there was the job of riding the boundary to keep cattle from straying or being stolen by a cattle duffer. They made musket balls for their muskets, they drove cattle from one water hole to another, and they broke brumbies for riding.

It had been a hard two years, but Aaron had thrived on it. Clad in his usual blue shirt, moleskin trousers, riding boots, and cabbage tree hat, he knew every inch of Cranston's land and much of his own. He had developed many of the cow-manager and cattle-catching skills himself, had learned a lot about cattle, but had a lot yet to learn.

One thing else he knew well. Mrs. Mark Aylesbury could keep her sheep, with their infernal stupidity, their bleating, the cleaning and the dipping and the shearing involved. He would take the cattle any day. And he was not unconscious of the fact that a stockman was a hell of a lot more dashing than a shepherd. Maybe someday on his own place, after he had established his own cattle station, he might raise a few sheep. The future of the country's greatest industry might be in sheep, but the future of the country itself was in cattle. And someday, there would be a way to process meat for exportation that would broaden the market for beef.

Meantime, he was learning his second trade as stockman, and perfecting his first as a doctor, and practicing both.

"She's done, Aaron," Sig, his best ringer called.

He meant the branding. Castrating was done on the mob of cattle below.

Aaron raised his hand to show he had heard. Someday they would have yards built for mustering

381

the cattle, and he'd be able to yard the cattle instead of catching and branding them in the open country. The mustering would be a hell of a lot easier then.

Tucker-time. Aaron could go for a bit of tea. Stringy-bark Joe and Damper Dan had been assigned to drive the cattle to the north boundary, where there was good watering. So, for all practical purposes, today's muster was finished. Time to head back to the big house.

He wished to hell he hadn't thought of Mrs. Mark Aylesbury and her sheep, though. Now Penelope's face haunted him. Sometimes he thought of her often, sometimes seldom. But whether or not he was thinking of her in the front of his mind, he could not help but think of her when he saw a sunset or a dawn or a new spring flower he'd never seen before. But a man shouldn't think about another man's wife, even though he knew she should have belonged to him, did belong to him in a suspended plane of some strange netherworld.

The plains spread out again as he let the little horse pick his own way down the hill. Out there to the south he had wandered lost, but since then, while he was struggling with the cattle station for Oliver Cranston, a man named Evans had discovered a plain to the south and west of the Bathurst district. Cunningham had discovered a pass through the mountains to the Liverpool plains up north. Now, because of Aaron's report to Governor Brisbane and because of talk concerning his belief that he had once been near the sea to the south, an Australian named Hume and his British partner Hovell sought official support for an expedition south—and had received it from the governor. They had left in October. It was November now and no one had heard from them. Aaron had burned to go with them, but he had

382

Annabelle to think of and his duties at the cattle station and his duties as the only physician west of the Blue Mountains. Acres of new land were being opened up now, and Aaron was jealous, jealous that he had not been the man to discover those districts.

But now you've a responsibility you never had before, his father had told him when Aaron had announced that he was going to marry Annabelle.

Dr. Matthew Aylesbury had been furious at first that Aaron was not going to take a position in either Sydney or Parramatta.

"I'm going out behind the mountains to start a cattle station. For Oliver Cranston. I'll take Annabelle with me," he had told his father on that memorable occasion.

Matthew had been silent with smoldering rage. "For Oliver Cranston, eh? You defy me at every turn."

"No, I'm not defying you, Father. Cranston has made me an offer, and it's something I want to do. I need to take Annabelle away from here. And I intend to practice medicine outback. There are no doctors at all in that new district."

Aaron had to admit that his father's anger had both hurt him and given him pleasure. Matthew had fumed and stewed and thought about it and finally said, "Well, at least you'll be using your knowledge and skills as a doctor." But he added with a glare that would have killed a snake, "That is, if you can find time to heal after your infernal duties as a stockman."

Aaron had wanted to say what the American Benjamin Franklin had said: God heals but the doctor takes the fee; but he didn't. Mainly because Matthew Aylesbury had never exacted a fee from a patient in his life.

Now Aaron smiled up at the azure sky where a

383

flock of white cockatoos flew overhead, and he watched them settle like a flurry of snow in the pasture to his right. He spurred his horse and the animal bobbed his head going down the slope toward the station below.

It did seem he was defying his father at every turn. And there were seldom any pleasant words between them. There were times though, when he visited home briefly, when their mutual interest in medicine drew them together.

"I saw a wombat stuff moldy leaves into its wound one day when I was in the bush, and I did the same to the snakebite wound. The wound began healing within hours," he had told his father.

It was over a cup of tea at the tea table in the living room. Matthew had mused, and Aaron had observed his handsome face smoothing out as he smiled. "Mark's mother was a dairy maid in England once, and she told me how the dairy maids, when separating cream, would set aside a small jar of the cream in a warm place for about ten to twelve days until it formed mold on the top. They would then heat the cream until the mold settled to the bottom of the container, and then they would dip out the cream on top that wasn't moldy and seal it in jars. She claimed the cream was excellent for healing sores and wounds."

Aaron and his father had looked at each other musing about that.

"Could it be," Matthew had wondered aloud, "that it was the mold they *weren't* able to get out of the cream that did the healing?"

The two physicians had pondered it together. Strange that Aaron should treasure that moment when he and his father saw eye-to-eye as men, as physicians, as friends.

Aaron had crossed the north run now into the yard. He could see little Jessica playing in the yard and wondered what kind of mood Annabelle was in today.

"It's all tacked down, missus, but like that the breeze can't get in much," Toady Chun said, rubbing big calloused hands down the sides of his trousers.

"And neither can the centipedes, Mr. Chun," Annabelle snapped. Then, shuddering involuntarily, she folded her arms across her breasts.

Toady Chun ducked his head, shook it, and said, "If that be all, missus, I'll be goin' back to the paddock."

Annabelle was biting her lip, looking closely at the bare beams, running her eyes slowly across each one, and, satisfied there were no centipedes on the beams, ran her gaze slowly over the tops of the door jambs and the window jambs.

"I say, missus, if that be all I'll be goin' out to the cattle yard, if it please the missus."

Annabelle looked at him quickly. "Yes, yes, go, Mr. Chun. But please stay within calling distance."

"Yes mum," the handyman said and walked out the door.

Centipedes a foot long. Spiders that spun tunnel webs, and snakes. There were scorpions farther west, but Mrs. Webb had said she had seen scorpions around the Bathurst district before.

Once when Jessie was a year old Annabelle had dreamt that Aaron's grandmother came to her and told her something was wrong with Jessica, and Annabelle had wakened and gone in to see about the child only to find a centipede seven inches long crawling on the head of her cradle. Ever since,

Annabelle had had an unreasonable fear of the horrible things. She had been afraid of them before, but here, back of the mountains near the Bathurst district, they were much longer than near the Hawkesbury, so large their skins were shells.

There had been centipedes on the bare beams, and sometimes one could hear them scratching on the plaster between the inside and outside walls of the house. At such times Annabelle would cry and shudder; she, Annabelle, who had grown up in the wilds along the Hawkesbury and used to play with toads and harmless insects with Aaron, Mark, and Deen.

When she had married Aaron and moved with him to the Bathurst district, she had felt a great surge of triumph, for she had won him at last. No matter how, she had won him. It was enough that he had asked her to marry him shortly after returning from being lost in the bush and finding out that she was pregnant. *And that Penelope was married,* her conscience reminded her often.

Annabelle had not been afraid then. She and Aaron had stayed at the Thompson sheep station while Aaron had the plains west of Bathurst surveyed and laid claim to the land for Oliver Cranston. She had helped build this sturdy, practical house. So strong in body then and unafraid, so unafraid.

But something happened to a woman here. Annabelle had servants, but she had to fight the dust storms, the droughts. And when the droughts broke the deluges came, and people waded ankle-deep in the mud for days, and that was when the snakes were everywhere. Ants swarmed everything you set out on the table, mosquitoes at times were so thick around a person's face that one couldn't see beyond them. Flies were constantly everywhere. A strong woman, after a

386

while, got used to it, or learned to live with it. Annabelle had. But it was the centipedes that did it. And since she had become afraid of the centipedes, she seemed to be afraid of everything.

It will pass, Aaron had told her again and again. This abnormal fear will pass.

Annabelle looked around her. This was not a small house. It was larger than the one she had grown up in back home, and Aaron had slowly accumulated some furniture for it. Each time he went home, he carted back some pieces over the mountains. Annabelle had Mrs. Chun to help with the cleaning, and Aaron had seven ringers, not including James himself, barely fifteen.

Annabelle missed seeing her parents, missed home, but she would not go back. No, not for a hundred—

A shriek in the yard startled her from her musings and she hurried to the door, that tight, cold fear gripping her, fear that something awful was going to happen.

But all she saw was Jessica running on short, pudgy legs across the dusty yard, her skirts catching in her legs as she ran crying, "Unca Dames! Unca Dames!"

Annabelle squinted against the ungodly glare of the sun and saw a lone rider coming down the track from the east. Yes, it was James. She had never quite forgiven Aaron for allowing James to live on the station. Allowing him? The station would be James's when he turned twenty-one, she reminded herself.

She put her hands on her hips and watched James scoop the little girl up onto the horse and set her in the saddle in front of him. She must tell James not to do that. What if Jessica fell? Or the horse shied and stepped on her?

Another motion caught her eye and she turned her head to look north. Aaron. A ghost of a smile touched her lips and she felt the tightness of her scalp loosen and her dim vision clear, and suddenly she was no longer afraid. Not even of centipedes.

Gathering her skirts in her hands, she stepped off the veranda and out into the yard shading her eyes, watching him. James and Jessica were forgotten as she watched her tall, suntanned husband, with his short crowned hat, approaching on his horse.

Aaron raised a hand in greeting, reined the animal at the nearest paddock, dismounted, and handed his reins to O'Reardon, the horse tailer.

She smiled, watching him come to her with his long, even stride. People were confused about Aaron Aylesbury. Some called him doctor, some called him Aaron. The sign on the veranda post read: Dr. Aaron Aylesbury, physician. But he was more a stockman than a doctor, a self-taught ringer who with or without Mr. Cranston's money would have been a success.

Aaron had taken a wild untamed land and built a cattle station, one of the first west of the Blue Mountains. James had said that he had built it with Cranston money but with Aylesbury sweat, and it was true. Aaron ran six hundred head of cattle on the station, and they had thrived.

"G'day," he said smiling and coming to give her a cursory peck on the forehead.

Annabelle pretended mild annoyance at his peck. Mustn't let her love or her delight show at all. A man could take a woman for granted if he knew she depended on his every whim for her very existence.

"I see James is back," he said.

"Just back," she replied. He was watching James riding toward them, so Annabelle looked at him out

of the corner of her eye. In her mind she caressed his broad, deep chest, slender midriff and waist, his tan, handsome face, his eyes, which were the color of the soil around Bathurst.

"Papa, I wide wif Unca Dames," Jessica shrieked in her curious, high-pitched voice.

"I see. I see," Aaron said, and laughing held up his hands to help the child down.

Jessica at nearly two years old still had her baby fat, but when she turned her face to Aaron, Annabelle was reminded again of her uncanny beauty. Her strange eyes were blue, a violet blue, something that puzzled everyone until they remembered that both Sally and Glenn Moffett had blue eyes. They were trimmed with feathery black lashes the same satin black as her hair. There was no sign of native blood in her features. Her nose was slender and upturned on the end, her lips only slightly full. Her coloring was darker than Annabelle's, but then most people's coloring was. She was Deen's child, but no one would ever guess. The only hint of native in her was the loose ringlets of curls that covered her head.

Jessica hugged Aaron and he hugged her briefly. He loved her, but men in New South Wales did not show affection much for offspring or wife in public.

Aaron greeted James. "Everything in order back home now?"

"Aye," he said, glancing at Annabelle.

Aaron put his hand on James's shoulder. "You don't have to talk about it now."

James had not yet gotten his full growth, but one could see he was going to be a tall man like his father, with the same dark good looks. "I want to, though. Yes, everything went well."

"I would have gone back with you, you know."

"No need. Your family was well represented."

389

"That's good."

That's good, thought Annabelle, knowing that the Cranstons and the Aylesburys had always been at odds. But funerals always brought people together, even enemies.

"Where's Dan? Did he decide life out here was too difficult for him?"

"He stopped off in Bathurst. He'll be here later this afternoon." James smiled at Annabelle. "Has Missus Chun any tea?"

"Mrs. Chun always has tea ready and you know it."

Aaron turned to his wife. Annabelle had kept her thin, raw-boned good looks even after Jessica was born, but she was not the laughing, giggly girl she had once been. Now she had a certain abruptness of manner, a hesitancy to smile, a reticence in accepting friendships. She had few friends anyway, because there were almost no women in the district, but she had not complained.

Aaron carrying Jessica, the two men followed Annabelle inside.

The house was a typical vertical split slab house with the slabs laid horizontally. The fireplace was made of handmade clay brick and dominated the one large room that served as kitchen, dining room, and living room. His and Annabelle's bedroom was beyond the big room, and Aaron had plans of building on to the east side when Jessica was a little older. The slab floor was Annabelle's pride, and she had polished it until it gleamed. This main room was large, since it served many purposes, and it still retained a pungent gumwood fragrance.

When the three of them had sat down at the table with their tankard of tea, James, studying his tankard said, "She was lovely in her coffin."

390

Aaron and Annabelle's eyes met, but Annabelle dropped her gaze.

"My father was calm and there were no tears. Reverend Marsden spoke beautifully. Your parents stood back behind most of the others there at the graveside, though it is no secret to those of us in the family that Mum . . . loved your father, Aaron." James looked up at Aaron. "I believe in speaking the truth when it can't hurt anyone anymore. Incidentally, Mum died in your father's arms. Penelope was there and called him at the last moment, though Dr. Redfern was already there."

Aaron pressed his lips together and nodded. As Penelope used to say, the Cranstons always looked at the Aylesburys, but the Aylesburys only looked at each other.

"Oh, Mark sends his regards to you both."

Aaron nodded and dared not look at Annabelle, for she would undoubtedly guess what he was thinking. *And what did Penelope say?* One of Cranston's servants had come for James when it became apparent that Mrs. Cranston was dying at last—at last, after years of trying to. Aaron had sent one of the ringers with James for safety's sake.

James took a deep breath. "Father spoke to me about the pasture to the south, Aaron. He wants you to have it surveyed, wants to see a plot of it as soon as possible."

Aaron let his boot drop to the floor as he leaned back against the chair. "I've got to go into Sydney soon, anyway. I'll stop by Cranhurst."

"Oh Aaron, must you go?" Annabelle said so quickly that Aaron glanced at her. He knew she had spoken before she had thought.

"I've supplies to buy, Anna," was all he replied, and it should have been enough. He knew why she

was afraid for him to go. She was afraid he would see Penelope. They had lived in the Bathurst district a little over two years and he had made perhaps six trips over the mountains for supplies. Once he had purchased and driven a mob of cattle from Cranhurst to the station here. Each time he had gone over the mountains he had gone to Cranston's house and to Sydney, but not once had he seen Penelope.

Annabelle should know that the thing between Penelope and himself had died long ago, apparently for Penelope when he had left on the exploring expedition, and for him the moment he heard she had married Mark. Still, Aaron felt Annabelle's eyes on him every damned time James mentioned Penelope or Mark's name. Women. A fickle, suspicious lot.

But, Annabelle was his wife, and he ought not be so quick to get irritated at her. "Why don't you pack some clothes for you and Jessie and come along," he said, to make up for his abrupt words. "Spend some time with your parents." He watched the little flickers of emotion play over her face: doubt, fear, shame. Not once had she gone back over the mountains since he had brought her here.

Annabelle's first impulse was to say no. People would stare at her, maybe even at Jessica. But she did not want to be away from Aaron and— She looked about the room, remembered the centipedes. She nodded brusquely. "Yes. I think I'll go."

"Good," Aaron said. "James, I'll be leaving you in charge of things here, as usual."

James grinned. "Thanks, boss."

Aaron smiled, too. For a lad, James had taken to cattle droving quickly, and no man, jackeroo or seasoned ringer, ever mistook him for a jackeroo. He was almost fifteen and didn't have his full height, but

392

he was going to be tall and slender like Cranston. His eyes were dark, as was his hair. He was handsome in an easy-going sort of way, and one of these days, there'd be dozens of broken-hearted belles west of the Blue Mountains, simply because there was only one James Cranston. "We'll leave the day after tomorrow, then," Aaron said.

Annabelle was thinking that if this trip wasn't too dreadful, perhaps she would go every time Aaron did from now on. Jessica was old enough to travel well, and she did want to see her parents more often. She wanted to get better acquainted with Aaron's parents, too. And perhaps she might do some shopping in Sydney. She rose and gathered the tankards and took them to the washing table in the kitchen part of the room.

And besides, she thought as she set them on the worktable top, this way I will know where Aaron is at night.

Later, as Aaron was undressing for bed, he happened to glance at his wife, lying with her back turned toward him, her blond hair spread out on her pillow, spilling over onto his in neat folds. Arranged carefully. It was his signal. She wasn't aware that he knew that when she arranged her hair that way she was deliberately trying to seduce him without seeming to.

When he needed a woman, Aaron always turned to his wife, as a man should. Annabelle was always compliant and submissive. When he touched her, she had that it's-my-duty look on her face, but he knew her. Knew her well. Annabelle needed a man often. Some women did, and there was no harm in that as long as it was their own husbands whom they

wanted. And he knew for certain that Annabelle had never looked at another man since their marriage.

Aaron did not love her as a lover; he loved her as a companion, a help-meet, and as a body. She stirred no deep passions in him, but she was there when he needed her, and he gave her what she needed in return.

He crawled into the bed and reached over, touched her shoulder, made the request he knew she wanted, "Anna?"

"Mmm?"

He bent and kissed her neck. She sighed and turned toward him with the its-my-duty look on her face. He had to smile, but hid it by kissing her cheek, then her lips briefly.

Her body remained slightly rigid as he turned her over onto her back. She looked up at him, and in the lantern light he could see that her eyes were dark, as they usually were when she needed him. With a physician's aloofness he had once concluded that the phenomenon of Annabelle's darkened eyes was because the pupils had dilated, dilated with desire. And her breathing gave her away, too. It was already too rapid.

He bent and kissed her mouth lingeringly as his hands moved over her body. He did not intend to trouble her about taking off her gown. The same thing could be accomplished with the gown on. His hand massaged her body, caressed her breasts through the gown, and as his own desire began to grow, he could feel Annabelle unfolding like a flower beneath his hands.

Aaron could drift away like this, his eyes shut, caressing a woman's body, with the lust in him growing so that he could meet her demands.

Annabelle's assumed reticence never lasted long.

394

Already her breathing was quick, her legs moving restlessly as he kissed her, caressed her body.

Suddenly she pushed him away. With a gasp, she said, "Let me take off my gown, so it won't get soiled."

Aaron smiled to himself and drew back, watching her yank the thing up over her head and toss it with abandon onto the floor. He knew that she wanted to be naked, as he was. And that was all right. It made the lovemaking better.

She lay back down, naked, eyes dark, waiting, rigidly waiting. He bent again to have his own desires quenched and hers, too. He ran both hands over her body, caressing firmly, and soon her narrow hips were undulating. He saw her grit her teeth. Her hands went to her own breasts and pulled them up, his signal to caress and love them, which he did. He suckled each one methodically until he was throbbing with the need for release. But he waited. He kissed her mouth again and massaged her thighs, teasing, until at last she reached down and forced his hand between her legs. He caressed her there until she was arching against him, and she took her lips from his and whispered fiercely, "Aaron, please . . ."

He complied with relish, thrusting into her, then sliding rhythmically in and out until she wrapped her legs around his waist and jammed herself against him.

He thrust rapidly, hard, gritting his teeth and willing himself to last until she had obtained her relief. When he heard her groaning deep down in her throat he knew he had accomplished what she needed, but not until she fell back against the pillow and her legs released him did he allow his own release. It came in quick, painful spurts over and over, until at last he was spent and rolled off her onto

his side.

Their breathing mingled in the quiet room. Annabelle still moaned with the dying waves of her relief.

Finally he said, "Shall I get your gown?"

"Please."

He handed her the gown, which she took and examined carefully for insects and spiders before slipping it over her head and arranging it carefully over her legs. Without looking at him, she placed the linen cloth between her legs to catch his fluid, then rolled over on her side with her back to him as if she had done her duty and could now get on with the business of sleeping.

But Aaron knew if he touched her again she would respond. He knew that if he coaxed her, she could be wild with unbridled passion. He also knew that her sexual release was real, love fulfilled. While his was artificial, only a purging of lust, a release from a gnawing reality, like the release one received from a stiff drought of rum. And, like the artificial relief one received from spirits, he always woke with the need still there. Always there.

How long, he wondered as he drifted into sleep, could a man go before he had to experience the right thing?

Penelope watched as Owen Crawford tied another "sold" tag onto the lovely living room table. She loved the things he made, or rather the things he designed. His workmen did the physical work on his things now. His furniture had its own smooth lines, very little fancy work. "Provincial," they would call it in Europe. But Owen's furniture lacked the unnecessary carvings and frills, was completely

functional, and each piece was stained a much lighter color than European furniture. His pieces graced every emancipist's home and each married currency lad's in the colony. Crawford pieces were seldom found in exclusionists' homes, though she knew a few of the young merinos who had gotten married had purchased some pieces for their homes. It was a standing jest that when a merino was questioned about why he preferred Crawford furniture, he would reply, "The Crawfords are pure merinos themselves. Why not?"

And indeed they were. Crawfords had come over from England as free settlers, just as the Cranstons had, and none had ever been convicted of any crime. But they had been poor, and no one considered them in the same social strata as people like the Livingstons, the Macarthurs, and the Cranstons.

She smiled at Owen Crawford now and said, "Thank you for personally showing me the pieces."

"Quite welcome," Owen said, smiling.

"I know you are a busy man."

"Not too busy to accommodate my own family, Penelope."

The man was so agreeable Penelope thought it a shame he had never married. "Mark will settle the account with you when you deliver. When will that be?"

"I've a boat going down the coast the day after tomorrow. We can take it then."

"Wonderful. I hope to be home by then. I'm staying with Father until tomorrow."

"How is he doing?"

"Well. I'm glad he isn't grieving too much. But then, they say the grief is worse when all the family and friends have gone back home. Still, I think he will do fine."

"And you?"

"I'm fine, too. I have Mark to think about and Eric—" It suddenly occurred to her that Eric wasn't at her side. Turning, she scanned the warehouse for his dark, tousled head. Her eyes slid over tawny-colored oak chairs and sleek polished teakwood tables, farm implements along the wall, a wagon wheel.

"Excuse me. I seem to have lost my son," she said breathlessly.

Owen grinned again. "I saw him riding that wagon tongue over there not two minutes ago."

Penelope's eyes widened. "Oh, dear!" Turning from Owen, she called, "Eric? Eric! Oh, dear." Gathering her skirts, she hurried about looking under the furniture and finally decided he must have gone out the door. Her scalp prickled with apprehension, for the river was terribly close. In a panic, she hurried out into the glaring sun.

In the dusty yard, men milled about, some carrying wooden planks, others driving bullock carts full of metal and tools. The forge was close and she could hear the clang, clang of a hammer on anvil, and the pounding of hammers down by the river where the boats were being built. "Eric! Eri-ic?" she called, shading her eyes and looking east. But there was no sign of her two-year-old anywhere.

"Is this yours, madam?"

Penelope turned around and received a blow she would never recover from. Aaron stood holding Eric in one arm and a small girl in the other. Her vision dimmed momentarily as all the blood drained from her face. It was like a dream. Or a nightmare—Eric in the arms of his own father. She was so stunned that for several seconds she could not make her limbs or her lips move. As she stared speechlessly, she

398

realized that the little girl in his other arm was Jessica, Deen's child.

Aaron's face was expressionless, but his eyes glinted with some emotion she could not identify, and she did not miss seeing his frame jerk as if he, too, had received a physical blow. They stared at each other and neither spoke for a moment.

"Yes. That's my son," said Penelope after a moment.

"Then I'll deliver him to you."

Penelope took Eric from him, the brush of Aaron's hand against hers sending shocks through her. She set Eric on his feet immediately, suddenly too weak to hold him. "Thank you," she said breathlessly.

Aaron was still looking at her with that same unyielding look in his eyes he had had when he told her and Mark farewell in their dooryard the night of the housewarming ball. "I would advise you to keep him better in tow in this place," he said finally. "There's too much that can hurt him."

A sudden defiance came over her and up went her chin. "Or there is much that *he* can hurt in this place. He's a very curious child." *Just like you were. Oh Aaron, just look at him and see that he's your son. He has your hair, your eyes, your face, your build.*

But Aaron would not look at the boy.

"And this is Jessica?" Penelope continued quickly.

A ghost of a smile touched his lips as he said to the little girl, "Show Aunt Penelope what a big girl you are. What's your name?"

The little girl was beautiful, with dark hair and blue eyes. She dimpled as she smiled, and in a high-pitched voice replied, "My name Dessie."

Penelope laughed and Aaron mumbled solemnly that she couldn't pronounce her J's yet.

There was an awkward silence. He seemed to be

lingering. At last, he said, "Excuse me. I've a message to give Owen."

Penelope inclined her head as he brushed past. She shut her eyes tight. He was handsomer than ever. Not as gaunt as when she had seen him last, still broad shouldered, deep chested, hard muscled, and to her he was beautiful. But her practical self told her that her heart shouldn't be racing or her pulses pounding like this. That this was her brother, and even if he hadn't been, she was a married woman and he a married man and— She turned slowly to watch him through dimmed eyes, his easy stroll as he carried the child into the warehouse without looking back.

Penelope picked Eric up and hugged him before hurrying across the dusty yard to her father's carriage where Cricket sat pretending he hadn't seen a thing.

Rodney Livingston had been going over the Cranston estate for two hours. It seemed Elaina Wyndham Cranston's English property would go to Oliver Cranston now. No living relatives except Cranston, James, and Penelope. Anger suffused through Rodney. If it weren't for James, Penelope would inherit the estate after Cranston's death. Penelope and that bucket of crap, Mark Aylesbury. Damn. Anger flared now as he thought about it. Penelope should have been *his* bride. He could never understand what she saw in the Aylesbury brothers.

"Rod, you need to go to the courthouse and make sure Oliver Cranston has registered Penelope and James's births," Rod's senior solicitor, Jude Holt, said now and tossed another stack of legal documents on his desk. "If he hasn't he'll need to in case of his own demise. Just to make everything legal. As if it

mattered in this godforsaken hell hole."

Rodney smiled and stood, grabbing his hat. Holt had never liked New South Wales, so why didn't he return to England? Because of some secret something in his past?

At the courthouse Rodney found that the birth of both Penelope and James were indeed registered. He smiled bitterly as he fingered the crisp page where Penelope's birth was registered. She was born only a couple of months after himself.

Something occurred to him. He wondered, just curiously, if Mark's name was registered at all. Glancing furtively to the side to see if the court clerk was watching him, Rod took down the canvas-covered book labeled "A" from the shelf, plopped it on the clerk's desk, and began to leaf through it. His finger came down on Mark's birth date. Registered legally. Mark Troop. Troop had been his mother's name, his bastard's name. But he had been legally adopted by Matthew Aylesbury, according to the next document in the book.

The Aylesbury files were thick and interesting. Here was the document registering the marriage of the Crawford woman, Milicent, to Dr. Aylesbury, all legal and proper. And next was a document registering Aaron's birth. Whoa. Wait a minute.

Rod's scalp prickled as he flipped back and forth between the two documents. Aaron's birth date was four months before the Aylesburys' wedding. *Before* the wedding. Ah ha! Oh ho! Rod's mouth was open almost as wide as his eyes. "Well, I'll be damned. Aaron's a bastard, too," he said aloud. Chuckling, Rod leafed through some more of the documents. Here was a record of the court trial that had sentenced Matthew Aylesbury to five hundred lashes and thirty years on Norfolk Island. The good doctor had been a

convict at the time he was assigned to the hospital in Parramatta, and he had been convicted of selling opium. But another document showed that the accusation had been false; he had been released, and given a full pardon.

But what was rich was, that he, Rodney, had discovered something nobody else knew. That Aaron Aylesbury was a bastard. But whose? Another quick scan of the indictment against Matthew showed that he had previously been given a ticket of leave to attend to the broken leg of Owen Crawford. And the dates were right. A competent solicitor who was used to investigative research could easily deduce what had happened. Matthew had been given a ticket of leave, had visited the Crawfords to set a broken leg, and while there, had impregnated Milicent Crawford. Then he got sentenced to Norfolk, and while he was there Aaron had been born. When Matthew was released and given a pardon, he came back, married Milicent, and made everything legal.

Rodney pondered that. There was something about that whole Aylesbury-Crawford-Cranston bunch that was abnormal. Namely, they kept having children out of wedlock. Somebody had used the term "oversexed," once and he decided that must be the case with these people.

Rod closed the dusty book and nodded to the suspicious clerk that he was finished, and left the building. He chuckled all the way down the street, wondering just how he could use this juicy bit of knowledge to make the Aylesbury brothers suffer.

Chapter XX

Her father had said that Aaron would be coming that evening to discuss the purchase of some new acreage in the Bathurst district, which explained why Aaron had been at Owens Landing yesterday. So she must leave, she and Eric. She must get out of the house and away before he arrived. It wouldn't do to see him again.

But first, Penelope wanted to visit her mother's grave, to place some spring flowers on it, and so she had left Eric with old Greta, who was doing some marketing in Parramatta.

Now, as she was picking her way among the gravestones in St. John's churchyard, she removed her bonnet to let the soft breeze stir her hair as she lifted her face to the sun. It had been a pleasant summer. There had been rain, and the lambing season had been a good one. She smiled as she thought of her lambs and how strange it was that when the colony was new, cattle had multiplied twice as fast as sheep, but now such an odd occurrence was in the past, and sheep, who were prone to multiple births, were multiplying all over the colony three times as fast as cattle. It irked her

father, who still maintained a healthy prejudice against jumbucks.

She paused for a moment, slightly dismayed, for she saw a man standing in the graveyard ahead of her. But she went on, and as she drew closer she could see that he was standing at her mother's grave. Hat in hand, he turned as she approached, and his dark eyes narrowed when she paused again, hesitating to approach.

For he was a shabby, tall man with an old patched coat and baggy black trousers washed so many times they were smoky gray. His hair and beard, which must have been blue-black not many years ago, was now shot through with gray. The black irises of his eyes were surrounded by bloodshot whites, and Penelope was puzzled that they were misted over with tears. He said nothing, just stood and stared at her, while an old dog at his heels lazily scratched a flea behind his yellow ear.

There was something about him that was familiar, and despite his shabby appearance, she was not afraid of him. "Hello," she said.

He seemed frozen to the spot, staring, his lips came open once. Then he smiled slightly and bowed.

"I'm Penelope Aylesbury," she said. "And this is my mother's grave. Who are you?"

The man stared. "Penelope. Aye. It would be you." When she only raised her brows, he went on. "I had heard you married Mark. I was surprised. I thought 'twould be Aaron."

Penelope frowned. "Who *are* you?"

The man looked her up and down without any reservation whatever and replied, "You have only to look in the mirror to know who I am. Except for the eyes, and they are hers."

Penelope shook her head in bewilderment at his words.

"Sorry," he said. "I'm Rolph Danbury. Your father-in-law's cousin."

Penelope remembered Rolph, the man who had been sentenced with Matthew Aylesbury in England because he and Matthew had been accused of burning her father's corn cribs. Rolph had been assigned to the Crawfords as a convict laborer after his arrival in New South Wales and had been pardoned at the same time as Matthew. Aaron had loved Rolph, but Rolph had a mistress—rum—and had gone off with it plodding the tracks as a swagman, a tramp, going from farm to farm seeking work and not staying long enough to form any attachments. But why was he here?

Rolph saw her glance at the new mound and half turned toward it, indicating it with his hat. "Did she suffer?"

"Not much. No one really knows what she died of. True, she had consumption, but it was in its early stages. It seemed that she had willed her death for years."

A soft moan came from Rolph as he stared at the mound. "Should have been me instead."

Penelope was beginning to see something, to see that Rolph had an attachment for her mother.

"Wasn't she happy?" he asked.

Penelope knelt beside the new white stone with the deep carvings on it and laid the multicolored flowers on it, then rose. "Mother was seldom happy. When she would become very melancholy she would plan a party and invite all our friends. The band would play and someone would give a reading of a poet, and we would all dance, and for a while she would be happy,

405

or nearly so." Penelope glanced at Rolph and saw his complete absorption in what she was saying, so she went on. "It always disturbed her that New South Wales is over thirty years old and yet we have no real poets or artists or musicians. She used to become distressed and say, 'Oh, Australia will be hundreds of years old before we have a world-reknowned artist of any sort.'"

Rolph smiled a little. "She should never have left England. She was jolly back there—or almost so. Though she had a dreadful temper."

Penelope studied him. So Rolph had known her back in England. "Yes, she always had a terrible temper."

Rolph's eyes went beyond her to some distant memory. "I remember once when Matt and I—" he paused, looked at her. "I'm sorry. Just an old man's memories."

Penelope smiled. "You aren't old. You can't be more than forty."

"When a man has nothing in his brain anymore to measure time by except memories, then he is old."

Penelope frowned again. "Are you going to see Dr. Aylesbury?"

"Aye. I'll stop by Parramatta hospital and perhaps stay a night at the farm this time." He cocked his head. "I hear that Aaron is a stockman out back of the mountains."

"Yes."

"Maybe someday I'll go there."

"He would love it, Mr. Danbury. I'm sure he misses you."

He smiled at her. "Your eyes are your mother's, only you see out of them differently. Are *you* happy, Penelope?"

She glanced down at the toes of her slippers and away to the distant hills. "Why do you ask?"

406

"Is there a child?"

"Yes. Eric, my son. Two years old."

Black eyes searched hers carefully. "Is he a healthy lad?"

She smiled. "Too healthy."

The black eyes grew moist. "Ah. Perhaps someday—"

"You would be welcome at our house. Mark and I live south of Sydney. Ask anyone directions to our place. But will you excuse me now? I've a trip to make." Penelope hesitated, wanting to ask Rolph some questions, but not knowing what the questions were she wanted to ask. "Good day to you, Mr. Danbury."

"And to you, Penelope."

She turned and made her way again between the headstones, feeling his eyes on her as she went. Why did he stare? His words kept stirring up some old, forgotten emotions, emotions perhaps that did not belong to her at all. When she climbed into the gig and gathered the reins in her hands, her brow was knit with bewilderment.

She should never have left England . . . Did she suffer? . . . She was jolly back there . . . Terrible temper . . . You have only to look in the mirror to know who I am. . . .

St. John's church slid past the gig as it rattled onto the road toward the marketplace.

You have only to look in the mirror to know who I am . . . Did she suffer? . . .

Penelope's brow smoothed out. Why, Rolph loved her. Rolph Danbury had been in love with her mother. Her lips parted in wonder. And I never knew.

You have only to look in the mirror to know who I am.

A cold hand slid down her spine.

You have only to look in the mirror. . . .

No. It wasn't true what he implied. He was, after all, just a drunken swagman. But he had known Elaina Cranston back in England. He had been a hired farm hand on the Crawford farm just over the ridge from the Cranstons' farm along the Hawkesbury.

You have only to look . . .

No. Penelope shut her eyes. No. I won't believe it. For if I am not Oliver Cranston's daughter, then Aaron is *not* my half-brother, and if he's not my half-brother, I have made a horrible mistake!

I can't think about that. Not now. Penelope gripped the reins until her knuckles were white. I cannot think about that now. It would complicate things too much, and things are complicated enough as it is. With Aaron's child and Deen's . . . Oh, dear God.

Goat cheese. He loved it. He didn't know why New South Wales had more goats than any other animal. Everybody hated goats, everybody had always hated goats. Even the great men of the Bible used the goat to symbolize the devil and his flock. He hated goats, but loved goat milk and especially goat cheese.

Deen chewed his midday meal, goat cheese and yeast bread. He didn't have time to have tea; he'd have some later on the sloop. As soon as Crosby arrived with Penelope and Mark's furniture and got it loaded on the *Elvira*, he'd have to be off and running for Sydney.

Deen's nose itched and he ran his hand under it. Damned gnats everywhere. Soon the mosquitoes would be thick and— Suddenly he had the feeling he was being stared at, and his hand froze halfway to his

mouth. Slowly he cut his eyes to the side and his head followed.

She was a thing of beauty. A tiny thing with chubby arms and legs, blue eyes and a head of curly black hair. She was standing alone, staring at him. Ants crawled under Deen's skin, for he knew beyond any doubt that this was Jessica.

He stared. This was the result of his love? Then how in God's name could that love be wrong?

This is my daughter?

She is blood of my blood, flesh of my flesh.

She is as much mine as Annabelle's.

Annabelle. Deen dragged his rapt gaze from the little lass and looked about him. Instead of being disappointed that Annabelle was nowhere to be seen, he was angry. Damn it. Did she let this baby roam around alone?

He looked back at Jessica. She was so beautiful that he began to have doubts that she was his. "Hello," he said.

Jessica smiled.

"What's your name?"

"Dessie."

A quick smile conquered Deen's mouth. "Dessie who?"

"Dessie . . ." She paused and fixed her mouth just so. ". . . Awsbewy."

Deen rose slowly to his feet, so entranced the rest of the world ceased to exist. "Where's your mum?"

Jessica turned and pointed and Annabelle, frowning, skirts gathered in her hands, came hurrying through the trees on the path to the river. When she saw Deen she stopped, took in the scene, dropped her skirts, and came to stand beside Jessica.

Deen marveled at her beauty, her tanned skin, the freckles across her nose and cheeks that were more

prominent now, her hair more golden. Today her eyes were amber. A great wave of agony began in the pit of his stomach and he was surprised when she spoke.

"I see you have met her."

Deen did not trust his voice for a moment. "Aye. She's beautiful."

Annabelle almost smiled, and it was then that Deen perceived that smiles were rare with Annabelle these days. "How have you been?"

"The same," Deen replied, which was a lie. No man was ever the same once he had lain with the woman he loved.

"I want to thank you, two years late. They said you found Aaron."

Deen smiled quickly. "He would eventually have found his way back. Buck and I only hurried up what would have happened anyway. Your husband is a survivor."

"Perhaps he might have found his way, perhaps not."

They stood looking at each other in awkward silence. What *did* two people say when one had loved and lost and the other had loved and won? "Are you happy, Annabelle?"

Her eyes flickered away from him, came back, fixed on his. "What's happy? I have Aaron."

"Your life outback . . . is it hard?"

"Not really. I don't have much work to do because we have servants. Some of the women out there work hard and get old early. Most are poor."

"But there's something . . ."

"It's—it's the climate, so many insects, the—the lack of social ties." Annabelle's eyes hardened and her expression became taut, but she smiled suddenly. "But someday things will change. There'll be more

410

people. They'll push the bush back and—"

Deen had only one split second more to confirm his belief that all was not right with Annabelle before he heard the cart coming. "And Aaron? He loves you?"

Her eyes went dark gold. "No."

The cart rattled into view with its burden of furniture. Deen grinned quickly and picked Jessica up in his arms, did a little jig with her, and listened to her throaty giggle. Then he handed her to her mother and bowed low. Playing the clown. Because others were coming into view. Always playing the clown. And as Annabelle took Jessica in her arms she said where he could barely hear, "But he's good to me. Very good to me."

Deen nodded, relieved, did a jig for Jessica, capered for the eyes of the others. As Annabelle walked up the path toward the trees, Jessica waved to him over her mother's shoulder. "Bye, bye," her lips said.

"Bye, bye," Deen said waving. And he mustn't show undue regard for the child. Eyes were on him. He turned away. Deen turned away with a grin that was a lie.

"It'll be our own newspaper."

Mark's mind wasn't on newspapers. It was on Penelope. Ever since she had come back after her mother's funeral she had seemed different somehow, more distant. Not that she was ever more than polite to him, anyway.

"Mark, it will be W. C.'s newspaper!"

Mark looked up from the letter that Stuart had plopped in front of him on the desk. Stuart was perched on the railing beside the door. Mark was sitting at the desk. Fitz was out. It was noon and

411

Stuart was here, as usual, doing his duty, keeping the cock robin of Sydney up on the current issues. Not that he needed to be kept up, for once he had assumed the role of leader of this little faction for government representation, Mark had done it well. In theory, the citizens, including emancipists, now had a legislative council, a nominee body with the power to advise the governor. And the right to trial by jury had been extended to the citizens. But it was all limited. Limited power irked Mark, for limited power was no power at all. He compared the citizens' limited power to his influence over his own family. He had earned his father's approval, but that was limited. He had won the right to bed Penelope, but that was limited by her coolness toward him.

Mark's fist came down on his desk with a bang and he glared at Stuart. "Who the hell is W. C.?"

"Sorry. It's William C. Wentworth. He's been admitted to the bar, you know—"

"He's the first Australian to be admitted to the bar."

"Aye." Stuart stood up. "But there's a rumor he'll take over for us, start a newspaper that will give us the voice we need. And—" Stuart punched Mark's shoulder. "You and he can join forces. His father and yours are good friends."

Mark looked out the window through the dusty panes. "Aye. D'Arcy and Father work together at the hospital."

Stuart's black, fanatic eyes danced. "We've arrived. Wentworth's mad at the Macarthur family because Macarthur's daughter refused his marriage proposal. There's no rancor hotter than a lover scorned."

"If you're trying to quote Shakespeare, you missed." Mark glared at Stuart, not certain whether he was glad Wentworth was returning with such

412

aspirations or not. He, Mark, had led the men to gain representation, though limited, and he wondered if Wentworth could do better.

"Cheer up, mate," Stu said. "Your future is brighter than ever. And the prime minister's seat is closer than you think."

Mark looked at Stu. "What? Prime minister!"

Stuart bounded his thin frame to the door and placed his hand on the door latch. "There's talk. Once we are a separate nation, we'll need a prime minister, won't we? It's several more years into the future yet, but— So who is more qualified than you?"

Mark stared.

But Stuart grinned and slammed out the door. Mark watched him through the window striding down Macquarie Street, greeting all he met vigorously as Stuart did everything, vigorously. Prime minister?

A slow smile stole across his mouth. He had dreamt of being head of a legislative council, of being appointed judge advocate, but never had it occurred to him—prime minister?

Mark stood up. My God, what a thing to look forward to, to work toward. He went to the hat rack and took down his hat. "Smith," he called into the clerk's office to the little man they had hired to keep the ledgers since their practice had grown so much. "I'm going for a walk."

"Aye, sir, Mr. Mark."

Sydney. Mark strode down the street avoiding the potholes. Have to complain about the slow fixing of potholes in the streets, he thought. He nodded to a lady passing him, a lady who looked a little like Betty Scoggins. He smiled to himself.

He was oh, so discreet. He went to Betty only at night. She wasn't near as beautiful as Penelope, but

413

she would do the things he needed, give him what Penelope never would, a good screaming tussle in bed. His loins ached even now. He ought to stop by on his way home, but—not unless it was dark.

Mark didn't consider himself untrue to Penelope. Seeing a whore wasn't being untrue to a wife, and every man did it. Especially the young ones. He smiled. Hell, even his own father had, else he, Mark, wouldn't have been born. Only Matthew Aylesbury had visited Mark's mother before his marriage to Milicent. Had he been true since? He wondered.

He was still wondering when he saw Rodney Livingston coming down the walk toward him. Uh oh. Another confrontation, and he'd be damned before he'd get out of the way so Livingston could pass. Mark felt the muscles tighten all over his body, his teeth set, as he came face-to-face with his worst foe.

But Livingston smiled. "G'day, Aylesbury. Fine afternoon."

Mark's lips curled into a sneer. "It was until now."

"Ah, but you never know how good a day is going to be until it's done. So many things can happen. You are a fool, Aylesbury, but you don't know it. Going around all the time thinking you're inferior to your brother."

Mark shook his head bewildered.

"You're not, you know. Did you ever look into the Aylesbury records? You know, registration of births and such things?"

Mark eyed Livingston keenly, wondering what he was getting at.

"I did a few days ago," Rodney said. "Did you know that Aaron's date of birth was registered before your father's marriage to Milicent Crawford?" Livingston watched the shock registering on Mark's

414

face, enjoying his vulnerability. He was planting a seed that might grow to cause no telling how much trouble for the Aylesbury brothers.

It was a long moment before Mark could find his voice. "You liar."

Livingston's eyes snapped. "See for yourself. It's all down in black and white."

While Mark glared, Livingston eased past without either of them stepping off the board walk. Mark stared after him, a kind of panic seeping into his bones, a horror, a revulsion so great he was frozen to the spot for several moments. Then he came to life, looked about. It couldn't be. Not after all these years. Would his father have let him believe that he was the only bastard? No. It wasn't true.

But Mark rushed to the courthouse and told the clerk there a lie about his having to check family records. Trembling, he opened the canvas-backed book and leafed through the crisp old papers.

Twenty minutes later he was out on the street again, almost stumbling as he went, blindly headed toward the Rocks, toward Foster's tavern. Had to see Stu . . . no, he needed to be alone . . . had to clear his mind . . . had to sit in a dark corner and think. . . .

One long drought of stringy bark, the currency lads' name for beer, cleared his jumbled mind somewhat. Mark's heart was still thudding hard, his pulses pounding in his temples. The shirt under his fine coat was soaked with perspiration, his hand trembling on the handle of the tankard. Aaron was a bastard, too.

Mark wept. He bent his head down and wept. No one noticed. The tavern had only two customers and they had spoken to him and left him alone. Mark wept for the years he had envied Aaron, wept for the times he had faced the kids who called him bastard,

415

wept for the way he had given in to Aaron the great, Aaron the son-of-a-bitch.

Mark brooded over the fact that his father had let him believe Aaron was born legitimately. Although he had never mentioned Mark's illegitimate birth, Mark had always imagined his father regarded him as illegitimate every time he looked at him. And Milicent Crawford, that strong, beautiful woman whom every man and woman in the Hawkesbury district admired. A free settler who had the guts to marry an emancipist. The bitch. She was nothing more than a whore. Aaron had been conceived during that pass his father had received to go to Crawfords' farm to set Owen's leg. Aaron born out of wedlock.

Mark wanted to rage, to throw the tankard of beer at the wall, to scream and rage and cry out, "Aaron Aylesbury's a ba-aa-stard!" to the world.

Oh, he would tell Penelope. First thing when he got home. He wanted to see the look on her face. Wanted to see her horror, her disbelief. Oh yes, Penelope, my love, you shall be the next to know. You—

"Mind if I join you?"

Mark's nostrils flared as he looked up into the face of a bearded swagman. "Leave me the hell alone."

"You're Mark?"

Mark glared teary eyed, angry at the man as he took the chair across the table from him. No stringy bark for this man. He held a bottle of rum in his hand. "Who the hell are you? I said leave me be."

"I'm Rolph. Don't you remember?"

Mark's head jerked back. "Rolph!" At first he didn't believe it. Then, as he looked closer at the man, he recognized his eyes, his hair. He'd heard that Rolph had come back to see his father a few times

416

while he was in England, but this was the first time Mark had seen him since he was about nine years old, when Rolph had first struck out on his own.

Rolph grinned through his tangled beard. "Here's to old times," he said. As Mark stared open-mouthed, Rolph tipped the bottle up, opened his throat, and poured the rum down as if it were only spring water. When he lowered the bottle from his lips a third of the quart of rum was gone, and he didn't even flinch. Rolph smiled, though. "Nectar," he said. "Nectar for the soul."

Mark stared with his mouth open a little longer, then said, "How can you drink like that?"

Rolph's eyes were bloodshot now and he smiled. "How? I'll tell you how. Practice. Lots of practice." He grinned, took another swallow, then leaned across the table toward Mark. "Wanna know why? I'll tell you why. It's to forget, to kill the pain, the guilt."

"What pain? What guilt?" Mark had his own pain, but he had a feeling that if he pried a little he might discover something of interest to him.

"Guilt. You know it was because of me that Matthew got sentenced to this godforsaken place. It was me that was involved in the plot to burn Oliver Cranston's corn cribs in England, not Matthew."

Mark had heard the story, but not from Rolph's point of view.

"Matt came to Cranston's farm to get me to go home before I got into trouble with the rest of the rioters. I threw him a torch and he caught it, and then Cranston appeared with his friends and there we were." Pain passed over Rolph's face. He tilted the bottle up again. When he had taken a long pull he went on, "So Matt and me got sentenced to transportation. The voyage in the prison ship was

417

hell. Matt suffered awfully. His medical practice was done for, he had to leave his mum and sister behind, his father had just died . . . awful." Rolph shook his head and drank the last drop of rum. "And the pain. Know what? I was in love with Elaina Cranston."

Mark stared at him with a little amusement. This drunken tramp in love with Penelope's mother?

"Matter of fact," Rolph said, swaying a little as he peered at him from red, watery eyes, "you are my son-in-law."

Mark laughed and leaned back in his chair. "You wish."

"No," Rolph said frowning. 'You are. I am Penelope's father, not Cranston."

Mark smiled and hoped nobody had overheard this fool. "You lie, Rolph. You're drunk and you're dreaming."

"Elaina told me herself."

Mark frowned because he realized that sometimes a drunk fool could reveal more things than a sober scribe. "How can that be?" he said scornfully.

"Elaina came to Parramatta one day to see Matt. He sent her away. I came along on the Parramatta Windsor road. It was a muddy, rutty road then, no houses much. A big storm came up. We rode on her horse. I made the horse leave the track. We got washed away by an overflowing creek. I rescued Elaina. That's when I took her. I forced her against her will in the mud." Rolph peered at Mark, his body swaying back and forth.

Mark's heart had stopped, his breath ceased, and through his teeth he hissed, "You're a friggin' liar."

Rolph shook his head. "I'm not a liar, and unfortunately, I'm not friggin', either. I'm impotent."

Mark felt his face drawing up like a prune as he

418

stared at the fool in front of him.

Rolph went on, "I took a lady I admired to a cottage. There we were a-all alone. Her naked, me hurting for her." Rolph shook his head. "Couldn't do a damned thing. Nothing happened. Matt says it's my state of mind. Would take so-ome lady to fix it. Some lady." Rolph nodded, the lids of his eyes half shut. "But the story 'bout 'Laina and me? Zz-true."

"Fiend," Mark hissed.

"Beast. Tha's what she called me. But she never tol' Oliver. She tol' me that Penelope is mine."

Disbelief rocked the order of his world. Mark tried to speak and no words would come. He wanted to call Rolph what he was again, a drunken fool liar, but when he spoke it was to say, "How could Elaina Cranston have known Penelope was your child?"

Rolph shook the empty bottle of rum and belched rumblingly. With difficulty he held his eyes open and attempted to sit straight. "You oughta know," he slurred. "Cranston an' 'Laina didn't sleep much together." He nodded. "She knew."

Mark stood up abruptly, regarding Rolph as he would regard a revolting snake. "Don't you tell this. Don't you ever tell that lie to anybody." And all the while Mark knew it wasn't a lie. Penelope had never resembled Oliver; she looked like— God. She looked like Rolph!

Rolph sighed. "I haven't tol' anybody but Franny."

Mark backed away, still staring at Rolph. "Don't you tell another soul. It would . . . would hurt Penelope."

Rolph, even in his drunken state, shook his head and said, "It isn't Penelope you're worried about, Mark. It's you. Your reputation. You son-in-law. You son-of-a-bitch."

Mark backed into a table, then spun on his heel and strode across the room. The patrons in the tavern stared as he plunged out the door. Outside he leapt on his horse and jerked the reins. Blindly he ran down the street. Heedless of carriages and bullock carts and pedestrians, Mark rode furiously out of town, and it was not until he was galloping down the track toward home that the full impact of what he had just learned hit him. Penelope, his beloved, ladylike pure merino Penelope, was a bastard.

Would he tell her? Did she know? No, she didn't, and he wouldn't tell her, not until the right moment.

The laughter began deep, deep inside him, deep where the little boy, Mark Troop, still dwelled, deep where all the humiliation and hurt was harbored carefully. Penelope and Aaron bastards. Even Eric was a bastard.

Mark threw back his head and laughed at the sky. The whole friggin' world was a bastard.

Chapter XXI

The truth was, there was no such thing as a pure Merino. The Merino was a mixture of breeds, rams from Bengal bred with ewes from the Cape of Good Hope. Many of the Cape's sheep, hairy creatures brought to the colony by Governor Philip on the first fleet, were bred and raised for meat, not wool. But men like John Macarthur and Reverend Marsden had crossbred the Bengal, with Spanish sheep, or Saxony sheep, from which most of Penelope's flock had come. Reverend Marsden and Macarthur, among others, believed that the primary industry of Australia would eventually be wool, and Marsden had advised Penelope as a serious grazier to breed for fine wool.

Slowly, without incurring Mark's displeasure, Penelope had fenced the sheep runs on their land, and had built the sweating and catching pens and the bins onto the original square sheep shed, until the shearing shed was complete. She had used part of the money she had inherited from her mother's trust fund. But she had to do it slowly, else Mark would brood and go off for a day or so in a fit of blind jealousy.

Being a successful female grazier wasn't easy. But then, she hadn't expected it to be. Men, including their convict laborers, did not recognize women in authority, hesitated in taking orders, grumbled, ran away, and procrastinated, until she solved that by pretending she was merely carrying out her husband's orders, because he was such a prominent young man in the colony that he was too busy to see to mundane daily chores about the station. Penelope had learned to say, "Mr. Blackmon, Mr. Aylesbury says he wants the Saxony ram to go into the north paddock with the crossbred ewes." Or, as she had said two days ago, "Mr. Blackmon, Mr. Aylesbury says it's time to muster the sheep into the west paddock and run them through the wash."

Shearers this time of year were hard to find because every grazier was shearing, so Penelope had to post notice in Sydney and Parramatta for shearers and give a date on which she expected shearing to be done. Shearers came wandering in, swagmen mostly, but there were a few who were of a new breed themselves in the colony, a breed of men given to shearing in the season and to other tasks when the shearing season was over. These men were experts at it. November was late for shearing, but Penelope had to wait her turn. Today, the shearing had begun.

Convict laborers had mustered the sheep in from their different paddocks and drafted them into the yard outside the shed, and several were penned inside in catching pens. Penelope watched, being careful not to give orders, but when she saw that a shed hand or a shearer was slow, she would tell her station boss, "Mr. Blackmon, I would hate for Mr. Aylesbury to see that shearer there, for don't you think he's a bit slow?"

If Blackmon ever caught on to her tactics, he never

acknowledged it, probably not even to himself, but she knew it galled him to have shortcomings pointed out to him by a woman and that was what drove him to demand speed and perfection from the men under him. Better to drive, threaten, and bribe to keep men on their toes than to have Mrs. Aylesbury point out something he had overlooked.

There was one force even greater than a station boss in getting the shearing done and that was the spirit of competition among the shearers. A shearer was a daisy if he couldn't shear more than two hundred sheep a day, and the big cheese of the day was the man who had sheared the most. Men became famous among their cohorts by shearing more sheep than they. "Fine country this is," her father's friend, Mr. Bateman, a cattle grazier from Bathurst said one day, "when manhood is measured by how many fleeces he can cut off the hide of some go'damned wooly."

At the moment Penelope stood with arms folded watching a young native boy catch a bleating sheep out of a catching pen and shove it through a drop gate into a sweating pen. The sweating pens were where the sheep were sheared. Clip, clip, clip, clip went the shears in each of the four sweating pens as shearers bent over the docile sheep. A good shearer could do two hundred fifty to three hundred sheep in seven or eight hours. Penelope had barely a thousand adult sheep, so if the men were driven, they could probably finish today. They had started at sunup.

One shearer was a native, short, long-armed, fast. He was a typical shearer, able to cut the fleece off all in one piece, the fleece clinging together as if on a hide. The classer, Mr. Baker, took the fleece, flipped it onto the classing table with a deft flick of his wrists, and it spread on the

423

table like a carpet. He would class it, keeping the inferior belly wool apart from the coarse back and side wool. The convict shed assistants went over each fleece with fingers working too rapidly to see, picking out burrs and stains. Then the coarser parts were removed and the rest of the fleece rolled, breech to neck.

Slam! The fleece was into the bin with other fleeces of the same grade and baled, then the bales went to the wool press.

The wool press. Penelope shut her eyes. That purchase had sent Mark into a rage to begin with, then a sulk, and he had not come home for two days. It wasn't that he objected to her spending her own money. It was the fact that she *had* her own money. But a good wool press was important to the whole setup of a shearing shed. She did not regret her purchase.

After the wool was pressed, it was weighed. Her scales were new, too, purchased from Owen Crawford.

If the shearer and their classers and assistants objected to a woman's being present in the shed, they didn't show it. The physical demands on their bodies during shearing discouraged any prurient thoughts about their grazier boss, other than the fact that she was present.

At two A.M., Hambone, the old emancipist cook Penelope had borrowed from Cranhurst, and Mrs. McWilliams sounded the gong on the back veranda and called the workmen to tucker. They served wallaby stew from huge camp ovens and gave each man a damper and a tankard of strong tea. Penelope watched as the shearers, shed assistants, and grader sat down under the gum trees in the yard and ate their stew from tin plates. The men were allowed thirty

424

minutes, a smoke, and back to work they went for another four hours.

At five-thirty-six exactly the last sheep was branded, sheared, doctored, and turned out into the yard, and the convict drivers herded them into their paddocks just as Mark came home.

He reined his horse, dismounted, and handed the reins to Dugan. He strode over to Penelope with that strange gleam in his eye, dusting off his trousers with his glove.

"G'day, Mrs. Aylesbury," he said.

"Good evening."

"Are they done?" he asked, glancing at the shearers gathered in the yard.

"Just done. In time for you to pay them."

"Ah. And I shall pay them now," he said loudly for all the men to hear. Then as they turned to go into the house, her hand in the crook of his arm, he asked softly, "Uh . . . how do we pay them?"

She told him.

Mark doled out the shearers' pay, received vigorous thank yous, and then Hambone and Mrs. McWilliams fed them again. Then each shearer and classer headed up the track for Sydney, and Hambone packed his pots and pans in the Cranston carriage and set off for home.

Penelope and Mark dined on beef pie served with a tomato sauce and fresh vegetables from the garden. Mark had lately acquired a direct, strange stare at her, as if he could see into her thoughts and was amused at what he saw.

"I spoke with Father today," he said. "Deen has decided to join Josh Abram's whaling enterprises and give whaling and sealing a go."

"Oh?" she looked up from her plate, saw that amused gleam. "I think Deen will do well at whaling

425

and sealing. And I'm sure it pays more than running the river. The men receive a percentage of the take, don't they?''

Mark's fork clattered against his plate and he stared at her, the gleam turning to a flicker of something else. "Pay. That has become an obsession with you, Penelope.''

She did not reply, only kept looking at him.

"Did you know that more than half your conversation is about money?''

She sighed inwardly. It was going to be one of those evenings when he would brood about something, would keep stabbing the finger of his frustrations into the pit of her stomach. Well, she was weary from the long day and was not going to put up with it. "I'm sorry,'' she said. "What would you have me talk about then, Mark?''

He kept staring at her. "You didn't ask why I spoke with Father.''

"I'm sorry. Why did you speak with your father?''

"I wanted him to . . . clarify something.''

His look was so intense that Penelope felt the blood leaving her face. "Did he?''

"No. It made him mad.'' Mark sat looking at her and remembering how he had gone to the Parramatta hospital and asked to see his father. When they were standing outside under the gum trees he had asked his father about Aaron's birth registration and the marriage registration. His father had gotten red faced and told him that such things were none of his damned affair, and had actually turned his back and gone back into the hospital.

Embarrassed first, humiliated second, and angry third, Mark had mounted his horse and ridden to the farm. Luckily, Milicent was out in the fields and Mark was able to locate the family Bible without anyone's being there to question him. And there, in

her carefully penned hand, was Aaron's birth date, just as the court records showed. And so was the later marriage date, just as the records showed.

Seeing his father, going to the farm, and heading back all the way to Sydney had taken from early morning to early evening, and that was riding hard, pushing his horse all the way.

So Mark was morose and weary and had no patience with anyone, least of all Penelope. And he might, just might tell her what he had discovered. "Yes, I found something out about Aaron that is very interesting."

A cold hand gripped her throat, choking her. Penelope coughed into her handkerchief, kept coughing until she sipped her tea. When she looked at him again, his old amused gleam was back and he smiled. "Did I say something to upset you?"

She shook her head. She was afraid of what he had found out. Something about Milicent Crawford's birth perhaps, or Dr. Aylesbury's, or . . . Aaron's? "It was the pie," she said.

"Of course." A flame leapt in his eye and then he went back to eating, leaving her to wonder why he had brought it up if he wasn't going to tell her what he had found. "Was the yield good?" he asked without looking up.

"Yield?"

He looked at her, raised his brows. "The sheep, Penelope. The wool."

"Yes, Mark. It was. Of course, I haven't got the wool sold yet, but according to the present market value, we'll see a very healthy margin of profit. I'll show you in the ledgers, if you care to see how we managed it."

"Ah. Money again, Penelope. You can't open your mouth without talking about money."

She looked at him wearily, realizing finally that for

the past two weeks his self-doubts had turned to gentle proddings, slight, barely concealed insults.

"You know, my love," he said speaking softly, "you should have been a prostitute." He enjoyed her look of shock and added, "It would be much more profitable for a woman of your beauty than grazing sheep."

Penelope stood up so quickly her chair fell backward. "Mark," she said furiously, "I don't know what is bothering you, but whatever it is I don't think insulting me will help you at all."

"Help? I don't need help," he laughed. "Ah, Penelope, sit. Please sit." He was on his feet to right the chair, and in her ear said, "Sit, my love. You haven't finished your tea."

Penelope sat, hoping his mood had passed, but another took its place as his hand brushed her cheek. He sighed softly and went back to his place at the head of the table and sat down. "Besides," he said, "I need to talk to you about a small dinner party. I'm going to have the legislators here for tea next Monday and I need you to help me."

Penelope frowned. "I had hoped to visit Father for a week, now that the shearing is done, but I can help you plan it and see that the food is prepared before I leave. Mrs. Mac is more than capable of serving, and Arthur is wonderful to help."

Mark's eyes hardened. "I want you here."

Penelope had planned and served as hostess for parties, balls, dinner parties, and meetings for two years for Mark's friends, clients, and political protegés. And during the first month or so there had been a meeting at the house at least twice a week. She had never missed a one, but now that her father was alone, she wanted to visit him more. Besides, she did nothing at his meetings and dinner parties but appear briefly and then go to her room. "Why do you

want me here?"

"You are my wife! And you lend . . . credence to me."

"Credence!"

"You remind men of what I did that no one else could."

"And what is that?"

"I married—" he smirked, "a pure merino."

Determined now to carry out her plan to go to Cranhurst, Penelope stood. "I'm sorry, Mark, but next Monday falls on Father and Mother's wedding anniversary. He may be melancholy. That's why I've sent Eric on ahead."

Steadily, softly, Mark rose and asked, "Are you defying me, Penelope?"

"Defying? No, I'm merely discussing why I need to go to Father's."

Mark's eyes shouted hate at her, then slowly he turned and went to the door of the kitchen, opened it, and called, "Mrs. McWilliams? We won't need your services anymore tonight. And tell Arthur he's dismissed for the evening, please."

"But Mr. Mark. I've to wash up—" came Mrs. McWilliams's voice.

"Do it tomorrow."

"Very well, Mr. Mark."

Penelope stood aghast as she heard the back door shut softly. Mark turned toward her, came to his chair again, and rested his hands on its back. "I don't care to have our private discussions overheard. Has that old hag, Greta, gone with Eric to your father's?"

Penelope nodded.

"Good. Now. I have stated a fact, Penelope. I want you here when the legislators meet."

Whatever was coming, Penelope had as soon get it over with, so she took a deep breath. "I'm sorry. I'll plan the tea for you, but I have sent Eric to Father and

429

I intend to follow Monday."

"No, you shall not."

Penelope's chin came up. "Yes, I shall."

Anger suffused him, his face reddened. "You are defying me," he breathed. "Why? Because you feel I am beneath you? Even though I'm your husband, I am beneath you?"

"Not at all. It's simply that I have a duty to my father as well as to you."

Mark smiled through his anger. "To your father? To your father?" he said and leaned on the table toward her. "Your father, Penelope, is a stinking, shabby, drunken *swagman.*"

If he had slapped her, she could not have been more stunned. Flushing, she stared at him, her lips forming words she could not utter.

Mark pressed his advantage and came around the table to stand before her, thrust his face at her. She stood frozen as he told her Rolph's tale, and ended by saying, "So you, Penelope my love, are the child of a rape, a rape by a swagman."

Her hand shot out and popped him on the cheek, the sound echoing in the sparsely furnished room. She only saw his lips press together before she felt his blow, and it was not until she slammed into the wall that she realized he had struck her. Now he was towering over her, his breath tainted faintly with the wine he had been drinking with his pie.

"You *are* a bastard," she whispered.

"And so are you. Or do they call female bastards bitches?"

She could endure no more and started to rush away from him, but he caught her and said, "Why do you go to Cranston?"

She only looked at him, almost blind with fury.

"He's not your father. He's just a man."

"To me, he is Father."

"Or is it because you see Aaron there?"

She tried to pull away from his grip on her arm. "I have not seen Aaron in—"

"You began to change, to grow more distant from me since you saw him at Owen's Landing three months ago."

She opened her mouth to deny it.

"Don't deny it. Eric told me about 'Unca Awon.' Was that meeting by design? Or was it fate?"

In a rage she attempted to leave, but his hand had gripped her face. "By the way, Aaron himself is a bastard." Mark watched her shut her eyes. "Yes, it's plain in the family records and in the family Bible. Aaron was born before his parents were married. Seems my father received a pass from Parramatta hospital where he was serving as a convict surgeon's assistant and he went to the Crawford farm to set Owen's broken leg. While there, he seems to have tumbled my saintly stepmother and impregnated her. Aaron was born months before my father's marriage to Milicent. So you see, Penelope, Aaron's a bastard too." Mark released her. And while she was assimilating the facts he had just presented and agonizing over them, she was surprised to see the pain on his face. "I—" he began softly. "All these years, I've carefully stayed behind him. I've deferred to him. And I allowed him to play with you. I was ten, eleven, twelve, fourteen—I watched the two of you playing. Saw him kiss you once. When all that time I ached for your smile, for you to just once say, 'Mark, hello!' the way you did Aaron. I ached to touch you even before I understood the meaning. I wanted to kiss you. I dreamed and I wept, but I held back. Because Aaron was the legitimate son of my father and I the bastard." Tears came in his eyes then, the grimace of a silent cry upon his mouth, and in times past she would have gone to him to comfort

him. But not now.

"Ah, how things might have been different had I known that Aaron was a bastard, too. No more legitimate than I."

All her pity for him was used up and she replied, "Except for the fact that your father married Aaron's mother and not yours."

Mark flinched, stepped back, recovered. The quiet in the room was oppressive. "You . . . will . . . stay here Monday," he choked.

"No. I shall not." Penelope gathered her skirt in her hand and brushed past him and up the stairs with Mark's gaze following her.

In her room, she got her trunk out from under the bed, unfastened the lock, threw open the lid, and went to the armoire that Owen had built. From it she took her traveling dress, four afternoon gowns, and a nightgown. Her thoughts were scattered and not one was connected to the other, but she was feeling hurt, guilt, anger. Foremost in her mind was the fact that she had made a terrible, lasting, irretrievable mistake. She berated herself for misunderstanding the few words she had heard her mother speak to Dr. Aylesbury that day and believing that Aaron was her father's son. She knew now, and it was perfectly clear, that her mother had been telling Dr. Aylesbury that she, Penelope, was Rolph's child.

Oh, the terrible mistake! She grieved, but there was fury mixed up in it, too, and pity and hate as she folded her dresses on the bed and placed them in her trunk.

She was placing the nightgown in the trunk when Mark said behind her, "I won't say I'm sorry."

She stiffened, then continued folding her undergarments. "I didn't ask you to. People say things in anger," she paused, "that they don't really mean."

"I'm apologizing for hitting you," he said, "but I

432

meant every word I said."

She resumed packing.

"I would hit you again if you ever strike me again."

She did not pause.

"I've worshipped you, treated you like a queen because I thought I had a real treasure in you and because I thought I had married out of my class. I should have known. Any girl who allows a man to have her before marriage—"

She whirled to face him, her eyes blazing.

But Mark finished, "—is a whore."

She wanted to fly into him, to claw, to hit. Up until now she had submitted to his demands because she pitied him. But no more. Still, she must contain her fury in order to get out of the house.

"In the past I have asked for your favors when I wanted them. Now I intend to take what I want, with or without your permission." He watched her as she placed her hat inside and closed the lid. "Tomorrow you can take it all out again and hang it in that armoire," he said, nodding. "But not now."

She felt his hands on her arms as he pulled her back against him and whispered in her ear, "Now, I need you."

She exhaled a weary breath. "You don't need me. You have yourself."

"Take off the shirt," he said, gently kissing her ear, "it's too much like a man's."

"Mark, I'm going to Father's."

His hands slid down her arms and his breath was hot on her neck. "Though I admit the front is not like a man's." His hands cupped her breasts and his fingers curled into the shirt front. "Take it off, Penelope."

"No," she said. "I don't want your hands on me after what you called me."

It was as if he was not hearing her. His fingers opened her shirt. Two buttons fell to the floor and she could hear them rolling. When she tried to pull away, he held her against him. "Now the chemise."

"Mark, let me go. I will be back home in a week after I visit Father."

His hands went up under her chemise and cupped her bare breasts, gripping hard, then lifted the chemise over her head.

She turned toward him, made a grab for her chemise, but he threw it aside, laughing softly. "Penelope," he whispered, his eyes going to her breasts. And then his hands were on her skirt. "Take it off. You might as well."

"I'll call Mrs. McWilliams," she warned.

"Really? And what will you say, 'Please save me, my husband is taking his pleasure'?"

Horror engulfed her. She couldn't endure his lovemaking like this. She could endure it when he was polite, when he was seeking relief, but not this wanton, insulting way. She struggled against him as he pulled her skirt loose, letting it drop to her feet until she stood naked except for her pantaloons.

"You might as well, Penelope. Penelope Cranston." He tasted her name, enjoying the sound as he looked on her nakedness. She knew what he was doing, savoring the fact that he had married Penelope Cranston, pure merino, a lass above his class—he had thought.

She shook her head. "No, Mark. I'll fight you."

"Do then," he said, as he let his trousers drop to the floor. "Scratch and bite. Leave scratches on my face and I'll tell my friends I had a great tussle in bed with an exquisite whore."

"Your friends. Your friends," she hissed. "It's all you really care about. Your friends, what others think of you. How great you are." On the very edge

434

of panic, she said, "Mark, you don't love me. You can't. You have too much love tied up in yourself to love anyone."

He grabbed her and shook her.

Knowing he would have his way and dreading it, and hating him for it for the first time, her green eyes blazed as she cried, "You can never be a great man, Mark—never!"

It was his fist this time, and Penelope landed on the bed face up. He was on her in a split second, pulling at her pantaloons, yanking them off until her legs stung and he was on top of her straddling her, naked from the waist down. He began yanking his coat off, his shirt, even as he straddled her, threw them as hard as he could across the room.

She stared, not believing what he was doing to her.

When he was completely naked, he smiled down at her. His mouth came down hard on hers and she brought her knee up, catching him on the thigh though she had aimed for the groin. Revolted and filled with horror, she watched the frenzied pain on his face, but what she felt most was shame.

"Penelope. Penelope Cranston," he said, and bruised her breasts with his hands, kneading them roughly, straddling her still. "Fight, then. Fight if you must. Let me give you a reason to fight. Here, take it in your mouth."

Another wave of revulsion, and Penelope managed to turn on her side, then her abdomen, and to crawl toward the head of the bed. "Mark! You don't know what you're doing!"

"But I do. Very well," he said. "Behave like a bitch, you'll be treated like a bitch." His strong hands gripped her thighs and pulled them up to meet his engorged manhood.

Penelope's screams went into her pillow, her hands clawed and pulled the linen, but his thrusts

went into her at an angle that brought her horrible pain because she was closed to him and he was not gentle. He thrust, opening her up. On his knees, he went into her again and again until at last she felt his hands dig into her thighs. And he gasped, gasped again, gasped until at last the pain eased and there was only a wetness where the pain had been.

He collapsed on her, his breathing hot and ragged on the back of her neck, and while she wept silently, angrily into her pillow, he ran gentle hands over her arms and neck, whispering, "It didn't hurt much. I wouldn't commit sodomy with you, gentle Penelope."

And why not? she wondered. You've done everything else.

"You aren't hurt?" he asked softly.

She did not reply.

"I wouldn't hurt you."

You already have, in a dozen different ways.

She felt his body slide off her, but he did not go away. His hands slid over her buttocks as he said, "I wouldn't, though there's no harm in it."

When his damp finger entered her gently, she rolled away from him. "You've had your pleasure," she gasped. "Now please leave me alone."

"Mmm," he moaned with his eyes shut. "In time. In time." He pulled her back to him and again his hands were on her buttocks. "In . . . time," he whispered. He held her hips with both hands, then again his finger went into her in the place that was not natural. "Penelope. Some women take pleasure in lovemaking. You never have. Let me . . . let me try this way. Perhaps you might—"

She could contain her horror no longer. Penelope screamed. She drew in a deep breath and screamed and screamed as loud and as desperately as she could.

Mark scrambled from the bed, crying, "Stop! Stop

436

it! I'm going!"

When she turned on her side, he was standing beside the bed looking down at her, and she couldn't help but smile through her tears because he was no longer erect but limp and flaccid.

"My God! You'll bring everybody in the yard." He hurried to the window and looked out. "See? You made all the servants come out of their huts. They're standing out there listening, with Arthur and Mrs. McWilliams, too." He turned to her angrily. "Damn you, Penelope." He picked up his trousers and stepped into them. "Now I'll have to tell them you saw a spider or something."

Penelope lay now with her eyes shut. She would go to her father. And stay. She would leave and not come back. Because if this happened once, it would happen again. And she couldn't bear this degrading kind of thing he had said and done to her. "Go then," she said hoarsely.

But Mark buttoned his trousers, pulled on his boots, pulled on his shirt and his coat, setting his clothes to right, then came to stand over her. "I—" he began softly. "I—" He paused. Then, "Whatever else I feel for you, Penelope, I do love you," he said. Then he turned and left the room softly.

"Must you go so soon?" Annabelle asked. "Isn't there someone he can send who can purchase the cattle you need?"

Aaron was pulling on his boots and looked up at his wife. Annabelle's face always glowed when she was expecting a child. As a doctor he had seen many pregnant women, and none were graceful. But some carried their fetuses with a kind of pride-stance. They walked with their bellies thrust out like a rooster thrusting out his craw when he struts. But not

Annabelle. She carried her burden like a bucket of slop to the hogs without pregnant dignity or mother pride. And she did not just waddle, she heaved. She was only five months gone and already she looked like she was going to deliver a calf, not an infant. He teased her unmercifully about it, and she loved every minute of being pregnant. He hoped she would carry this one to term. Since Jessica was born, she had miscarried twice.

He finished lacing his boots and stood up. "Anna, no. Cranston and I are going to Sydney together. The shipment of cattle is already in the yards in Sydney and I have to hurry. Besides, that shipment of smallpox vaccine is in and I need it for that tribe of natives over on the Evans Plains."

"Then let me go with you."

He smiled and took her chin between finger and thumb. "No. You're too far gone this time."

Annabelle smiled a little. "You're just angry because I was two months gone when we went last time and I didn't tell you. You're punishing me."

"If you made that five-day trip over the mountains, you'd have the baby prematurely, and I don't want a scrawny son," he teased. He got his hat and took the valise Mrs. Chun handed him.

He had just gotten word that morning that Cranston wanted him immediately. A new breed of cattle had been brought on a ship from France, and Cranston wanted Aaron's opinion before he purchased any. Aaron had Annabelle pack his clothes, and Jack O'Reardon, the horse tailer, packed his gear for a quick trip over the mountains. He was going alone, but Cranston would send some of his drivers back with him if he brought cattle.

Aaron kissed Annabelle farewell, mounted his horse, touched the brim of his hat, reined the mount around, and set the horse at a canter down the track

toward Bathurst.

Explorers, Hume and Hovell, had returned from their trip south. Oxley, the man who had first explored the Macquarie river, had been wrong in saying the land to the south was desolate and good for nothing. The land to the south all the way to the sea was some of the best grazing yet discovered. Though the two explorers had fought and argued, they had opened up vast tracts of land for grazing and blazed a trail from Sydney going south, over the mountains, and on south to Port Philip just across the Bass straits from Van Dieman's Land. Reports from the settlers on Van Dieman's Land, the large triangular island across the strait from Port Philip, declared that there was good grazing there also.

Aaron wanted a start of cattle on his own land soon. He figured that in six years when James took over the station, he himself would have a good start on his own acreage, that which the governor had allotted him for his part in opening up the plains to the south.

He also yearned to do some exploring west and north. The wild unexplored country still beckoned him. But for the moment, he must get over the mountains to Cranhurst.

On the fourth day after he left the Bathurst district, Aaron rode into the yard and Oliver Cranston greeted him.

"You must have flown," Oliver said.

Aaron dismounted and handed his reins to Cricket, saying, "I swear, mate, you get shorter every bloody time I see you." He had traded friendly insults now for two years with Cricket, his father's old prison-mate.

Cricket clicked his teeth, of which there were few these days, and grinned, "T-t-t-taint me growin' shorter, ye bloody friggin' bludger, it's you gettin'

439

taller. Never s-s-saw a man your age that didn't know when to s-s-stop growin'. 'Fore long a man'll g-g-get a crick in 'ees neck lookin' up t' ye.''

"Cricket, I've always wondered what you did to get transported," Aaron said, tucking his handkerchief in his back pocket. "You're too little to have done anything very serious."

Cricket squinted at him from beneath grizzly gray brows. "I got s-s-sentenced for b-b-beatin' the bloody 'ell out of a smart arse young doctor, that's what." But Cricket couldn't pretend annoyance any longer and grinned, slapped Aaron on the back, and took the horse away.

Aaron turned to Cranston. "No, I didn't fly. The road's improving. They're carving one lower down in places now. Pretty soon a carriage will be able to go over it without men having to tie a rope on it to keep it from plunging down the grades. You should visit your own station, Oliver. It's growing, spreading out, cattle everywhere."

"I will when I get a station boss here I can trust." Cranston leaned on the paddock fence. "Ought to hire my own daughter. She manages her own sheep like a man."

Aaron noticed that Cranston's eyes narrowed and the muscle in his jaw was working in and out. He was not in a good humor. Aaron reached down and picked up his hat, which he'd just dropped.

"Or maybe I should hire your mother. She's the same kind of woman as Penelope. Strong and—" He glanced at Aaron and changed the subject. "I bought the whole yard of cattle."

Aaron frowned. "Already?"

"I decided to do it before some bugger beat me to it. Had them driven overland from Sydney and thought you could pick and choose those you want to take

440

back with you. What you don't take I can keep here, and experiment with some crossbreeding."

Aaron sensed someone watching him, sensed it and felt his body break out in perspiration. His heart started doing funny things, too, and he had to take deep breaths, but he did not look toward the house. "Do they look good?"

"Excellent. Good stamina. I think the best of the lot will do well outback of the mountains on coarse grass."

"Good beef cattle?"

"Yes. But before I take you out to see them, let's have tea. Hambone has sconces made and I'll have him put a shot of gin in the tea."

"You've bribed me," Aaron said, grinning.

Aaron and his father's old foe strode toward the veranda. The afternoon sun was blazing bright, beating down on their backs, but that was why men wore broad-brimmed hats and why houses such as Cranston's had deep, shady verandas.

Aaron stepped up on the veranda and finally allowed himself to look over at the figure who sat there, realizing that this was the real reason he had hurried so to get to Cranhurst, the real source of his eagerness to return. He had not even allowed himself to realize it until now—and he must never let her know.

She was sitting in the rocker chair Cranston had bought for Elaina Cranston from Owen Crawford years ago. Dressed in white cotton lawn, she was fanning her face slowly and waving away the annoying flies. She was more beautiful than ever and she drew his eyes to her, held them, made his heart race, his hand tremble as he removed his hat. She was the reason for his existence. Penelope.

Chapter XXII

She poured their tea with trembling hand and was glad he did not look at her. After his first cursory, "G'day, Penelope," when he had come up on the veranda, he had scarcely noticed her. And perhaps that was good, for he might have seen her confusion, her flushed face, heard the pounding of her pulses.

"Thank you, my dear," Oliver said. She poured her own tea, set the silver pot on its tray, and nodded to Hambone, who set the cabbage tree basket of sconces onto the table.

"Tell me how things are going with you," Oliver said. "How's Annabelle and little Jessica?"

Aaron sat tall and handsome and very tanned, as brown as he had been when he returned from the bush over two years ago. His shirt was the same brown as his trousers, with two breast pockets for carrying things. He had run a hand through his hair so that it was almost neat now. His shoulders were broad, and when he took a scone from the basket, the muscles of his forearms stood out. She wanted to touch him.

Aaron swallowed his bite of scone. "Annabelle is due to have our child in March."

It was a stab of pain, but Penelope endured it.

"But she's well. She helps me sometimes with my work. Is a good physician's assistant whenever I need help. She can stand more unpleasantries than I can, but she's deathly afraid of—of all things, centipedes—"

Oliver smiled coolly. "And so would I be. March, eh?"

"Aye. If my calculations are correct. And Jessica is growing tall."

"Is James well?" Penelope asked, keeping her voice steady.

"James is a fine stockman," Aaron replied, without looking at her. "Knows his cattle, knows his work. Catches cows faster and easier than any man I know."

Her heart was skipping beats and she sought desperately for something to say. What finally emerged from her confusion was the urge to argue with Aaron. "Such a waste of time, catching cattle. Isn't it a pity the beasts are so incorrigible one must throw ropes over their heads and tie them up before much can be done with them?"

With easy grace, and not a flicker of rancor, Aaron set his cup of tea down. "That's the difference between cattle and sheep," he said, without looking at her. "Cattle, unlike sheep, don't need much done with them."

"There's branding."

"Done once a year, and only on the cattle that haven't been branded before."

"So is shearing."

"On every sheep every year. The more sheep you obtain the more you have to shear. Brand a cow, let 'em go. Shear a sheep and you have to mess with all that wool." Aaron cast one glance at her. "Then set a

443

shepherd looking out over the mob because sheep are too stupid to fight off dingoes. You can let the cattle go and they take care of themselves."

"Then why is it costing Father so much each month for salaries for all those stockmen?"

Aaron opened his mouth for a quick rebuttal, but Oliver broke in because he had seen that both their faces were getting red. "How *are* the new ringers fairing outback?"

Aaron replied. While Penelope burned and grieved and hurt and chastised herself for it, the men talked of cattle runs, the price of beef, types of grasses, mustering, droving, branding. At any other time, Penelope would have drunk in all the information about the station in spite of her prejudice, but she could not concentrate on their conversation now. She was feeling a heat emanating from Aaron, her old friend, her old lover, something so powerful she was drowning in it. And they ignored her, talking on about men's business, and, after all, wasn't that what Aaron had come to do?

At last tea was done and the men went out together to the south run where Oliver had driven the cattle, and Penelope went up to her old room. There she took off her afternoon dress and put on her riding dress, a soft, sensible brown muslin trimmed in brown cotton braid. She secured her hair close to her head with combs, then went out to have Cricket saddle Brindle, a brindled gelding who had taken a liking to her earlier in the week. And then she rode toward the ridge.

She told herself that she was going there to enjoy the view, see what changes had taken place. She told herself that she was a sensible married woman and that now that her argument with Mark had had time to cool, she knew she would go back. His mild

display of brutality had been because she had been stubborn, after all. A man had a right to ask his wife to be in attendance at important functions. A man had a right to make love to his wife. She knew his problems and sympathized with him. He had been in awe of the Cranstons from the beginning, had thought he loved her from the beginning. Now it seemed that none of them were born greater than the others, and Mark resented those years he had felt inferior.

He was truly a bright man, popular, good at his profession and respected. She should be proud of him, she should do as he said. Learn to get her way by methods other than defiance, just as she had found a way to manage Mr. Blackmon and the hired men.

On the ridge, she saw that the trees were a little larger than when she had been there last, but curiously, the path up the ridge was not grown over on the Cranston side. That other traveler had used it as often as she had.

The ridge was the same. Cranston trees stopped on the Cranston property line, right down the middle of the ridge. And to the north Aylesbury property sloped down to a patchwork flood plain of the Hawkesbury.

Penelope dismounted and let the horse's reins drag, took in a breath of air. She sat and thought of her sheep. It was breeding time, and here she had run away like some defiant adolescent. And Mark had let her go, had said no more to her about it, behaved with gentlemanly grace. Had seen to the carriage for her and to her trip from Sydney to Parramatta. She felt at once triumphant and ashamed.

Oh, the country here was beautiful, still wild to the north. To the west, a way had been found through the Blue Mountains, but they were still wild and

untamed, violet today. Tomorrow they might be azure or indigo or sapphire. She wanted to see them up close, to cross them, to see the other side where the air was dryer and men and women tanned quicker and the bush stopped and went around to the creeks. And what was beyond that? No white man knew, but the settlers called it Nullabor—no trees. Was there a desert, then?

She propped her elbow on her knee, her chin in her hand, and looked down at the Aylesbury farm. She told herself that she had come here because she might see Eric playing in the dooryard below. She told herself that she wanted to see if the ridge was the same, if the country had changed, to see the winging flight of the pink-breasted galah. It had nothing to do with the fact that Aaron must pass this way going home to his parents' farm.

She heard the horse's hooves plodding on solid earth, heard the clatter of gear, the creak of leather, but she did not turn her head. The hoofbeats paused. The horse snorted. Penelope turned her head slowly.

"Sorry if I disturbed your musings."

She straightened. He was still astride his horse, tall, handsome. He pushed his hat back away from his forehead with his thumb, a smooth gesture that told her he had done it a thousand times before.

"I was hoping to see Eric," she replied.

His expression did not change. His horse stamped one hoof. "Eric?"

"My son is spending the next two days with his grandparents," she said, nodding toward the Ayles-bury farm.

His expression still did not change, and he did not look away. "Strange. It never occurred to me that Eric was my parents' grandson."

Penelope smiled gently. "I know."

446

His eyes narrowed at her, and he dismounted and slowly came to stand beside her. She saw his leg stiffen as he put all his weight on one foot. "Does my brother strike you, Penelope?"

Of course, she knew he could not have helped seeing the bruise on her left cheek, put there three days ago by Mark's fist. Her father had seen it too, had asked about it, and she had given him the same reply she would give Aaron.

"No." Her hand went to the bruise. "I bumped it on the shearing shed door on shearing day."

He kept looking at her. "You're lying."

Penelope rose and faced him. "I'm not lying. Your brother does not strike me."

She saw his desire to believe her warring with his knowledge of bruises, and it was a long time before he said, "Because if he does, I'll kill him."

"What right have you to say such a thing?"

"He is my brother and has no right to strike any woman."

She turned her back on him and heard him move.

"I'll be going now," he said.

"Yes."

"I'll tell your son that his mother misses him."

Penelope shut her eyes tightly. "Yes, tell my son that." *Talk to my son, Aaron. Look at him. See who he is. Please. Please.*

"You'll . . . be coming back to Cranhurst?" she asked, turning back.

He already had one foot in the stirrup. "Tomorrow, for breakfast. I have to go to Sydney and pick up some smallpox vaccine." He mounted and looked down at her. "Perhaps I'll go visit Mark at his office."

"Yes. Do that."

"Or will I need a pass of some kind, since he is so important these days?"

"I resent your attitude."

Aaron nodded. "Yes. You are a dutiful wife. You would."

She saw the pain in his face then. "Aaron, there was a reason for what I did, not waiting for you."

"If there was, it can't be discussed now, can it? It's too late, Mrs. Mark Aylesbury." He kicked his horse and she watched him as he rode down the slope toward his parents' farm.

Angrily she grabbed up the reins of the brindle gelding, mounted and rode down the side of the hill. What a fool she had been, trying to explain, trying to make him understand, trying to make him—*make him what, Penelope?*

Oh, fool. She would never hope, never think of him again.

The next morning at breakfast she took a portion of the eggs and a biscuit and handed the bowl to Aaron, who did not look at her, had not spoken to her, except for the cursory good morning.

Aaron and her father began talking about cattle again, and today the conversation unnerved her. "Cattle, cattle, cattle," she finally chirped, interrupting them. With a glance at Aaron, she said, "You really ought to run a few sheep on your station outback, Father. You're missing out on a growing market. You'll be sorry someday that you let people talk you out of it. Everybody else runs cattle and sheep together."

"Uh uh," Aaron said, leaning back in his chair with only a glance at her. "I'm not going to be responsible for sheep. I don't like sheep. I don't know anything about sheep."

Cranston frowned in thought as he stirred his tea. "In time perhaps I should buy sheep, try to run them with the cattle."

"Then you'll have to hire a shepherd," Aaron said, rattling his spoon on his plate. "And shed hands. And you'll have to build a shed and pens. Bring over a wool press."

"And scales," Penelope said, smiling to herself as she sipped her tea.

"And build cottages for all the new men because we're full at the outback station."

"Speaking of cottages, Father, is that old cottage still on the old Breedlove property?"

Cranston was reaching for a biscuit and his hand paused for a slight moment, then went on to pick up his biscuit. "How did you know about that?" he asked, looking at her closely.

"I found it once on a ride. Of course, it was all boarded up, but in good condition." She didn't mention that she had seen it only the day before yesterday, made a point of seeing it. It had been repaired, and she had taken it into her head suddenly to sweep it out, dust it, wash the wine glasses, shake out the fresh linen and replace it on the bed.

"Ah. Yes. The cottage is still there," Oliver replied.

She pretended innocence by asking, "What was it built for?"

"Why . . ." he hesitated. "Once, years ago, I had thought of sending a man out to live there to operate a still I had." He smiled quickly. "Yes, when rum was outlawed, most every farmer had a still."

"But you never ran one?"

"Briefly. Things changed fast in the colony even then. A brewery was started in Parramatta."

"And the darling cottage was never lived in?"

"No," he cleared his throat and pasted butter on his biscuit.

She smiled at him. "That cottage was not built for

449

a man."

Oliver looked up at her quickly, saw her direct smile. His handsome dark countenance colored. "What are you suggesting? That I had planned on carrying out some clandestine affair?"

She shrugged. "What a shame no one ever occupied the cottage. It must be in terrible disrepair."

Oliver let out his breath. "I—as a matter of fact, I recently fixed it up. Repaired it. It needs a little cleaning up, though."

"Why?"

"What are you getting at, Penelope?"

Again she shrugged. "Nothing. Just curious."

Cranston salted his pork generously and said, "I thought I would go there to read. To think."

"To dream?"

Oliver stared at his daughter again. "Yes. Perhaps."

Penelope was aware that Aaron was eating his breakfast voraciously and did not seem to be listening at all. Sometime while he was lost in the bush, he had forgotten how to let his expressions show. His face was as inscrutable as his plate.

Yet she felt it, that something coming from him, had felt it at tea yesterday, on the ridge, felt it now, a carefully controlled passion, a seething, smoldering desire, a love of such intensity she was certain no one had ever felt such a love before.

But the men turned the tide of conversation to cattle again, and sheep and the newly explored country to the south. Her hand brushed his when she passed the pitcher of milk to him. She saw a ripple under his white shirt, a flash in his eye. Was it her imagination?

I love you, Aaron.

The world had stopped turning. They were

manikins talking, Aaron and her father and she, puppets in a puppet show. None of it was real anymore.

He spoke of going to Sydney. He rose. They talked about the vaccine. They went outside. Aaron touched his hat. Bid them farewell. Said he would return in two days, after which he would take the cattle west. And then he was gone, riding down the track going east to Sydney.

She gave him thirty minutes before she mounted the brindle and set off down the path skirting the ridge, going west. Penelope believed that women were born with a power, a quiet power few men would acknowledge. There were prostitutes and willing women everywhere, but for each man there was only one woman who had the power. The power to communicate without saying or writing a word. The words were in her body, in the way she moved, the lids of her eyes, the smoothness of her speech. And she had the power to know he would come to her.

Wouldn't he?

The track was long. She did not remember its being this long. She kicked her mount into a trot, then a canter. A flock of parrots rushed up from the grass along the side of the track, squawking, setting the kookaburras to laughing in the trees to the right. Overhead a wedge-tailed hawk circled, casting its shadow over the track and the grass and the trees. Something scuttled into the grass at the side of the track, and a single green and yellow parakeet peered at her with one bright eye from the branch of a low-growing wattle and chuckled deep in its yellow throat.

But would he be there? Doubts assailed her, drowning all her confidence in the woman power.

He had been hurt because of her marriage to Mark.

He was still angry. He was married. His wife was pregnant. He was an honorable man. He would not think to come to her. And even if he thought of it, he wouldn't do it. And he would not have understood that she would come to the cottage. Oh Aaron, what am I thinking about? I'm married, too. And I am an honest woman as you are an honorable man. He had business in Sydney. Hadn't she seen him going down the track to the east, not the direction in which she was going?

I will turn around, go back. Go home to Mark.

But the trees parted suddenly. The little cottage with its two multipaned windows stood covered in blossoming pea vines. And he was there.

He had removed his hat and coat and tie, and his shirt was open at the neck. He was leaning against a tree near where his horse was tethered, watching her. She rode slowly to the cottage, not taking her eyes from him. She dismounted and tethered the brindle and looked up at him. He had not moved; neither had his expression changed. But he unfolded his arms and opened them to her.

She went to him, and it was as if time had not passed since she was in his arms. His warm mouth met hers halfway, sending shock waves of pleasure clear down to her toes. His mouth moved on hers, with hers, eager, desperate, almost painfully. Desperately he held her to him, pressing her to him, and with each beat of his heart against her breast she grew weaker. When he took his lips from hers she whispered rapidly. "Aaron, Aaron, I love you, have always loved you, didn't you know?"

He gripped her shoulders and his desperate eyes devoured her face. "My God, Penelope, I've needed you."

"And I have needed you."

With a low moan, he pulled her inside the cottage door, and kicked the door shut, took her mouth again, held her so close to his thudding heart she could not breathe. She dug her fingers into the hard muscles of his back and wanted to climb inside him, to melt there, to be him. They clung desperately to each other for a long moment. And finally his trembling hand moved to cup her buttocks and pull her against his hardness. She felt him shuddering as great surges of passion enveloped them both. His hand was tugging at her bodice, and Penelope pulled away and began to undress. She undressed, hurriedly, wildly flinging the clothing to the side. He stood back, and she saw the wild need in his glazed eyes, so enthralled with what he saw before him that his hand paused, forgetting to unbutton the rest of his shirt. Then the shirt was off. Boots flew against the wall and trousers got kicked aside as he pulled her to the bed. All of it happening so quickly and wildly, neither took time to look at the other. There were only impressions.

The soft mattress beneath her, his hard, lean body half on top of her, his warm mouth searching her, his tongue finally exploring, his hand kneading her breasts, until she felt her own wetness between her thighs, a swelling and an aching there. His ragged breath on her face caused her to shiver; his soft, low moans, his desperation was the love song she needed.

And Penelope was losing herself, grasping him, pulling him to her as she arched her body against him, trying to absorb him, and her own hands pulled at him. Wildly she realized that she had never felt this way before. It was as though if she didn't have him she would die, and all her emotions cried out for him, cried, I love you. And all her insides were knotted in her abdomen.

He gasped, and as she parted her thighs for him slid inside her unhesitatingly, with one long, deep, gentle thrust. Her lips parted and for a moment there was no breath in her, and then she lost control. She raised her legs and grasped his buttocks and pulled him in tighter against her, and her hips moved rhythmically.

He let his breath out. "Oh, my God," she heard him say between clenched teeth. Then he started moving inside her, moving slowly, sensuously.

"No, faster. Hard. Please," she gasped.

Aaron gritted his teeth and thrust inside her, unable to endure the pressure building inside his entire body. She was beautiful, so achingly, painfully beautiful, her body, her face, her breath, her taste, her smell, the feel of her. Unconsciousness threatened him as all of the heat and passion rushed to where they were joined so intimately. He stiffened and let it burst out, burst to fill her, to fill her velvet depths with his love.

She cried out from deep down in her throat and he knew she was experiencing the same release as he. He kept filling her, emptying into her, until her damp body began to relax, and when he was empty of all the urgency, he lay down on her and kissed her damp eyelids, cheeks, lips, neck.

For a time she lay as if dead, her lips parted, arms and legs askew, and he lay against her side, his face buried in her neck, his hand resting on her abdomen. Outside the breezes whispered in the gum trees, and parakeets chirped.

Penelope's eyes fluttered open, observed the round beams that supported the roof of the cottage, the sunlight filtering through minute cracks in the wooden shingles. Then she became aware of the shuttered window beside the bed and turned her head

to look across the room at the fireplace, the shelves with their gleaming wine glasses, the small round table and chairs. And she smiled and kissed his damp forehead.

"Ah," he said. "She lives." When Aaron raised up to look at her, he was the boy she knew, the young man who had made love to her two years ago near this cottage, close to the old still.

"Do I live? Or am I in paradise?" she murmured.

"I think we're both in paradise," he said. "My Penelope." She raised up on her elbow and his eyes took in her breasts, her neck. "Aye, paradise."

Smiling, she ran a finger over his lips and he grabbed her hand and pressed a kiss in the palm. Her eyes grew sad and she said, "There was a reason why I did not wait for you—"

He sat up quickly. "Let's not talk about that."

"But I want you to know that I misunderstood something my mother said and I thought you were—"

"Penelope." He ran his fingers through his hair. "That—that world outside this cottage does not exist. Not while we're inside this cottage. If we allow ourselves to think beyond these walls, there'll be guilt, and unpleasant memories."

She sighed. "I should feel guilty, I suppose, but I don't."

His eyes ran slowly over his beloved's face, neck, collarbone, and registered pain.

"And so should you," Penelope said softly. "There's Mark and there's Annabelle, and I think this is called adultery."

"Hush!" he said firmly, taking her chin in his hand. "Nothing and no one exists outside this cottage, my love."

Quickly, her brief period of guilt passed, and

455

another moment later she was once again smiling, running her hand over his wide, bare shoulders, enjoying the perspiration she had caused on his skin, enjoying the texture of the dark curling hair on his chest. "Oh, I do love you."

His eyes played over her features again and he smiled slowly. "And I love you. Do you know when I first knew that?"

She shook her head and ran light fingers over his jaw, loving its strong, solid lines.

"The day I first saw you in Campbell's warehouse. You were with your father. And I was with my mother and my little sister Jessica. I think we were five years old."

"And I thought you were the most beautiful boy I had ever seen."

He smiled. "And now?"

"More so."

Smiling, he played with a curl at her temple and ran the back of his fingers down her neck, drinking in her beauty, her perfection, bathing in his love for her, his unblemished love.

"Did you see Eric last night?" she asked, taking his hand and kissing it.

He nodded, still smiling, and placing his hand on the side of her face. He wanted to remember the shape of her soft lips, the tilt of her perfect nose, the shape of her emerald eyes, each dark curling lash. Remember it always. "I had to spank the daylights out of him."

Suddenly Penelope's eyes widened and she scrambled up and stared at him in horror. "You *what?*"

He sat up. "I spanked him."

Penelope gasped. *"Spanked* him!"

"Aye. That I did."

"But—but why?"

456

"He ran away. Had every servant on the farm looking for him. Mum was searching the ridge, but I found him."

Penelope's eyes were shooting hot darts at him; her gentle sweetness had turned to explosive anger. "Where was he?" she shrieked.

"Would you believe that he was on the track headed west? Told me he was 'going bush'!"

Penelope looked away from Aaron's amused face. "How can you spank him. I've *never* spanked him."

"That's obvious. He's a brat, Penelope, and you're going to have trouble with him if you and Mark don't take a firm hand."

"Mark doesn't—doesn't pay him any attention at all."

"A pity. All the more you should."

She looked at him quickly, angrily, her mouth tight. "I do. I am with him constantly."

"And mothering him and letting him get away with hell," Aaron said, propping his head in his hand. "What a boy needs most is a father."

"Well, is that so? Listen to you. You—you—you're with him one time and you spanked him!" Suddenly tears sprang to her eyes.

"Not true. I found him at Owen's Landing that day. He was running away then, too."

Tears rolled down her cheeks. "It's a wonder you didn't spank him then."

"If I'd known he was my nephew the moment I found him, I would have. It's a serious thing to let a boy get by with, running away."

Penelope started crying, sobbing, letting the tears gush out. Didn't he see? Didn't he know?

He gathered her warm, naked body into his arms, his hand massaging her hip bone. "My precious love," he murmured in her ear, "I didn't spank

457

him hard."

"He'll hate you," she cried against his hairy chest.

"He doesn't. He spent the rest of the evening following me around."

Now the tears really came and she sobbed against his neck.

"I never saw you cry. Don't. Don't," he said, stroking her hair, cupping her head in his big hand and pressing it to his face.

When Penelope got control of her grief, she murmured against his neck, "What did your mum say when you spanked him?"

"She bit her lips to keep from giving me a piece of her mind. She spoils him unmercifully, too."

Penelope sniffed. "And your father?"

"When we told Father, he thought it was funny, Eric running away like that saying he was going bush. I've threatened to do that since I was five years old, and he certainly didn't laugh at *me*."

Penelope smiled. "I like your parents."

"Good. They like you, too, but they wish you'd visit them more often."

"I will. I've made up my mind. From now on, I'll visit often. But—Father; you know."

"I know. He wouldn't take it too kindly."

Penelope sighed and shut her eyes. This was her man. This was Aaron, the father of her child, even if he didn't know it.

As his hands began a slow journey up her side to her breast he said, "The neighbors are all laughing about Mark's son who wanted to 'go bush.' I think Eric started a new saying in New South Wales."

She sighed again and her mind followed the route of his hand as it grasped her breast and moved down again to massage her abdomen. She could hear his heart speeding up, feel his breath quicken on the top

of her head, and once again he was carrying her away with him. She turned over on her back and stretched out, took his beloved head in her hands and brought it down so that his mouth locked with hers.

He explored her, every inch, every crevice, lovingly drinking in her smoothness with his hands, her beauty with his eyes. He went slowly this time, allowing all the paralyzing sensations to diffuse through him as he massaged her breasts, tasted the nipples, felt their soft, achingly tender texture on his tongue. He suckled them one by one, stuck one in his ear because it felt good, ran his hand to the triangular patch of curling hairs at her thighs, tugged them gently, ran exploring fingers over her, into her where their love had mingled, then cupped her buttocks in his hands, squeezed them, kissed her between her thighs until her hips began their restless movement, and her breath came in ragged gasps.

"Oh, Aaron. Oh, please. I can't stand it."

He smiled, thinking he couldn't either, for his manhood burned, throbbed for release. Eyes shut, he turned her over to love her back. He must love all of her, have all of her, because this was the last time, the only time. He groaned with that knowledge and straddled her, caressing her back and waist with both hands, then moved his hand to her buttocks, heard her gasp.

"I won't hurt you," he promised. And after he had caressed her thighs and buttocks, she moaned at last and spread her thighs, uttering a soft sound. He gritted his teeth and slid into her vagina slowly, gently, and when he felt her buttocks tighten, he paused, waited. She moved then, pushed her hips up toward him, and he moved in farther until she had taken all of him.

She gasped with the exquisite pleasure of it. Aaron

almost exploded in her then, but he waited and then began a slow moving in and out, in and out until she matched his rhythm with her hips. A sweet gurgle came from her and he thrust into her faster, gently, until he felt her stiffen. This time she cried out with a loud, ecstatic wail that sent him into a frenzy. He spurted in her again and again, until the perspiration ran down his hips, his face, and mingled with hers.

Then he collapsed on top of her with a moan.

Never, never had he felt like this. Never had it been so explosive, so exquisitely painful. So complete.

They drifted off into a kind of twilight doze together, bodies and limbs entwined, tangled. Perspiration mixing, breath mingling.

When she woke, he was dressing, looking at her with a dreamy half-smile on his face. "Good afternoon."

She smiled. "It was, wasn't it?" Her smile faded. "You're going—"

"I must. Sydney is a long way."

She shut her eyes. "Oh Aaron," she groaned at the thought of their parting.

"Hush. We had this moment. And as long as we are in this cottage today, we still have it."

"I'll never leave, then."

"There's that other life outside, my Penelope." His eyes caressed her face. "Ah. We did have this moment."

"Do you think—"

"No. This can't be again. You know that."

She knew. But his saying it wrenched her heart out. "Yes," she whispered. "I know."

He finished dressing and stood looking at her. "But I can live on this. I can remember this day. I can treasure this. But my love, please avoid me. Please,

Penelope, make it easy for me. For us both. There's Eric, Mark, Annabelle, and my child yet to be born. Too many lives to get involved. Too many to hurt."

She knew, of course. Two married people living miles apart. Nodding, she closed her eyes and said, "I will stay away from Father's if I hear you are coming. If I'm there and you arrive, I will leave. I won't do anything but speak to you if we meet on the streets of Windsor or Parramatta or Sydney. And I will never talk of you." She opened her eyes. "But please don't ask me to stop loving you."

She saw a world of agony in his face as he opened the door. "Would I ask something of you that I can't ask of myself?" he said softly.

And then he was gone.

Penelope heard him ride away, but she still felt him inside her, inside where all her dreams and hopes and love were kept.

Now he had gone to that world outside, and so must she. For as he said, there were Eric and Mark and Annabelle, and others. Others who must not know. Must never know. Their love had to be a private treasure. And they must be puppets on a stage acting out before others their roles as sister-in-law and brother-in-law, and never, never let their love show.

Chapter XXIII

"Two years ago, August eighteen twenty-six, our legislative council deliberated and recommended that all crimes and misdemeanors be tried by a jury of six officials or magistrates and six citizens, just as it is in England. In England anyone once convicted of a crime but receiving a full pardon is eligible for jury service. But the emancipists of New South Wales? Ah, that is different matter."

The crowd in the warehouse meeting hall roared, "Hear, hear!" The applause sounded like a springtime hailstorm, as young men called out to the speaker on the podium. They begged for more and Mark Aylesbury gave it to them. His blue eyes had a fanatic gleam as he spoke, and leaning over the speaker's stand, he cried, "Justices are chosen from amongst our citizens. But who are the citizens chosen? The more respectable citizens, of course, and we know who in this colony are considered respectable."

"Hear, hear!" the crowd roared.

"We also know," Mark cried and had to repeat his words when the hall quieted, "we also know who chooses the justices."

When the roar of the crowd subsided again and the din ebbed to a low mumble, he went on. "Oh, citizens of New South Wales have trial by jury, all right, but who chooses the juries? Not the emancipist, friends. No. Never. The emancipist is home tending his turnips while the exclusionist sits in judgment of his turnip patch."

The guests at the party went wild. Actually, Mark wasn't saying anything the crowd of emancipists and currency lads and lassies didn't already know, hadn't already read about in Wentworth's paper, *The Australian,* and discussed and fought over in the taverns. But through Mark and his friend W. C. Wentworth, the emancipists and currency lads vented their anger at the home government in England, at the conservative exclusionists in the colony, and even at times at the governor himself. New South Wales had begun as a penal colony, was still run as a penal colony, even though it had been a crown colony of England now for four years. The full rights of free citizens were still not given to emancipists, those former convicts who had served their time and had received full pardons, even though they were in the majority in the colony. And prejudiced sheriffs and magistrates almost never chose a currency lad to sit on a jury.

Mark had simplified the matters in his speech. The emancipist tended to the business of living—tended his turnips—while the exclusionist ran the colony, trying the emancipists' friends and sons, sitting on the juries, making the laws, enforcing the laws.

Finally the crowd silenced and Mark went on. "Our trial by jury is in the developmental stages. We *have* gained ground, though inch by inch only. And we have the home government thinking, ladies and gentlemen. For our Governor *Darling—*" He

463

grinned after emphasizing the new governor's name, while the crowd roared with appreciative laughter. "Our Governor Darling is going to have to reply to Lord Bathurst, our home secretary in England, about how he is trying to control our newspaper. Know what that means, ladies and gentlemen? That means that *The Australian*, our voice, is getting through to somebody. For, and this is important, this is the greatest mark of a governor's disdain—he has drawn up a bill proposing a stamp act on—" Mark paused and grinned and held up his finger. "Not tea, ladies and gentlemen, but on newspapers."

The men laughed.

"Now our home government sees that our governors are being placed in a precarious position, of being unable to carry out their duties as strictly military governors, because we, gentlemen, have a voice. We are being heard. And so. Today we have received word that a Constitution Act is being drawn up by Parliament that any legislation that is proposed in this colony must be certified by an entire body of justices, not just the governor alone. Gentlemen, this colony's governor's position is weakened at last."

The floor vibrated under Aaron's feet as he watched his brother on the podium. The noise subsided.

"You see what this means? We've got to get a few emancipists and liberals on that bloody judicial body!"

The crowd roared again.

"So that we emancipists, we native-born, we small settlers, we currency lads, we liberals, we, the backbone of this colony, we, the majority, will be able to tend to *our . . . own . . . turnip patch!*"

His last words were almost drowned out by the roar

of the crowd. The roar went on and on.

Near the veranda door of the warehouse, which was used often as a meeting hall, Aaron stood, arms crossed, leaning against the wall. James stood with him, James the son of an exclusionist, but who sympathized with the liberals.

"I wish he had said something about the squatters," James said.

"He will, in time. If it's popular to do so," Aaron said. "Right now on that issue he's at his wait-and-see stage."

James nodded. "Meanwhile men are pouring over the mountains, squatting on land that doesn't belong to them, and which they are unable to buy. Why doesn't Mark and his crowd do something about getting the government to allot free land so that the squatters, who are full citizens of this country, wouldn't be committing a crime just to obtain a little land?"

Aaron just shook his head. The British government had auctioned land and given free land grants, all right, only to men with capital, usually Englishmen, and as favors to special people. As usual, that left out the Australian-born and the emancipist free settler. So the poor settlers were taking matters into their own hands and crossing the Great Divide anyway, moving across the land with their cattle and sheep, and when they found unoccupied land, they were squatting on it. They were trespassers in the sight of the law, but most station owners had decided that if the squatters respected the station owners' rights, they would respect the squatters' rights. And the squatters would graze their cattle and sheep until the water ran out or some exclusionist acquired the land legally; then the squatter would move on.

Aaron watched as Mark came down off the podium

465

amidst cheers, laughter, and much back-slapping. He smiled. How does it feel to have a future prime minister of Australia as a brother, the men kept asking Aaron. How did it feel? Like nothing. It wasn't Mark's popularity or his political position Aaron envied. It was Mark's wife.

His eyes went to her now. Penelope Aylesbury, graceful, beautiful. Aaron and Penelope had seen each other at a distance, at one governor's ball and two king's birthday balls, three times over the past four years, since their time together in the little cottage near the still. But they had kept away from each other. Carefully kept away. And yet, it seemed only yesterday he had made love to her in the cottage. A memory that kept—

Aaron shook the thoughts from his head. He shouldn't have come here tonight, but since he was in the area he couldn't very well ignore the invitation to attend the Constitution party, especially since Mark was to make the speech. Ah, but it wasn't Mark, was it? The reason you came, Aaron Aylesbury?

Women. They did complicate things. Here he was away at mustering time because of Annabelle. During the past two years she had been pregnant twice and had miscarried late in each of her pregnancies. Aaron had been wild with frustration, berating himself. What kind of physician am I that I cannot deliver, from my own wife, a viable fetus?

So he had brought her to her parents' house for two months before she was due to deliver, to be near his father, his father who had years of experience at this sort of thing, who was considered the best doctor in the colony. Aaron had left her to stay there and had gone back to the cattle station at Bathurst.

But now that her time was close, he had come back over the mountains and planned to remain here until

she delivered.

"Aaron! I'm glad you came!"

Aaron turned from studying the form of his beloved moving among the crowd, smiling, looking like a living flower, dressed in a rose-colored gown, to face his own brother.

Mark held out his hand and Aaron took it. "Nice speech."

Mark was grinning—Mark grinned a lot these days—and said, "W. C. read the outline of my speech and is going to print it in *The Australian* tomorrow. He calls it my turnip-patch speech. Can you imagine it in the history books someday? That ought to open some school lad's eyes. Remember how ol' Baldwin used to label famous speeches like that when he taught us history?" Mark hit Aaron gently on the biceps with his fist. "Made you remember the speech, didn't it?"

"Occasionally."

Mark turned smiling to James. "James," he said, offering his hand.

James took it with the sardonic amusement of a typical skeptical nineteen-year-old. "Perhaps the history books will call you Ol' Turnip someday, Mark."

Mark roared with laughter.

"Parful speech. Parful," said a white-headed old gentleman as he stumbled against Mark. He was holding a tankard of rum that threatened to spill as he righted himself. "Parful speech."

Mark thanked him, calling him by name, then turned back to Aaron and James and took both their arms. "I need to talk to you both after the party. Think we can go to Foster's Tavern for a while? This punch is like rainwater, and all they have on the refreshment table is little cakes. I'll be famished."

Aaron's brown eyes cut over at James. "Well, I need to get back to Annabelle. Wanted to leave for the farm tonight."

"Oh!" Mark exclaimed. "How is Annabelle?"

"Close to her time."

"Again?" laughed Mark.

Aaron eyed him without expression. "Aye. Again."

"Well! I wish her well. Brought her to Father this time, did you?"

The lids of Aaron's eyes were shut halfway. "Aye. I brought her to Father this time."

"Well, I won't keep you long. For old time's sake, Aaron. I haven't talked to you in years for any length of time. I want to pick your brain, mate, about the squatters outback. You too, James."

James said, "You go, Aaron. I'll find Jessica and take her to her Aunt Milly."

Mark looked at Aaron. "Jessica?"

"Our daughter. We're staying at the hotel with Mum and Father."

Mark's countenance fell. "Oh yes. Lovely little lass. Wonder why Father didn't stay after my speech. I wish he had stayed and at least congratulated me."

"Father wanted to get back to the farm, too. Leaving tonight. Because of Annabelle."

Mark nodded thoughtfully, looking at the floor. "That explains it, then. The reason he didn't stay. I hope he liked my speech. Do you think he did?"

"I'm sure he did," Aaron said, without enthusiasm.

"Well, what do you say about meeting me at Foster's for a bite to eat?"

Aaron nodded. "Very well. For just a little while."

"Good." Mark said, slapping Aaron on the back, his former exhilarated mood returning. "I'll tell

Penelope to go on in the carriage without me. I'll stay the night in Sydney. Wait right here, Aaron. I'll say my farewell to the boys and tell Penelope to go on home without me. I'll be right back."

Aaron's hand closed over Mark's arm. "You are sending Penelope home at night alone?"

Mark's smile wilted a little. "No. There's the driver."

"No road is safe at night for a woman."

"Listen, Aaron. Penelope is no ordinary woman. She can take care of herself."

Aaron didn't like it at all, but he perceived that Mark was going to send her on anyway, whether or not he went with him to the tavern. But it wasn't any of his business. Not any at all.

Mark's blue eyes flashed—a spark of anger and resentment—but his smile remained. "I'll be back."

Aaron watched his brother making his way into the crowd of loudly talking guests, then turned to James. "Sorry, friend."

"I don't mind. And Jessie needs to get to bed."

Aaron nodded. Lately the people in the colony were bringing their children to gatherings and leaving them mostly to their own devices. The children added to the excitement of these political affairs, for some reason. Aaron wondered what little Jessica had found to do.

"Watching a chooky lay an egg."

Eric frowned. "You can't watch chickens lay eggs."

"You can so. I've done it before," Jessica said. She was tiptoeing and peering into the chicken's nest. A plump brown hen was setting on it, jerking her head and watching Jessica warily. The barn where the

469

chickens had their roosts and their nests was next to the meeting hall and belonged to one of the men who liked to hear her Uncle Mark talk and was at the party. The children were running at will in and around the hall, but only Jessica had ventured into the barn to see what there was to see, and Eric had followed her.

Eric had only seen her twice in his whole life. Once when she was very little and which he didn't remember, and then tonight. He had been playing with other lads, and had seen her go into the barn by herself. He had been watching her out of the corner of his eye. You didn't look at girls straight out, because you had to pretend you didn't care whether they were around or not, but you looked at them out of the corner of your eye so you'd know what they were doing and they wouldn't know.

He had been watching Jessica out of the corner of his eye because she was his cousin, whatever that meant. He had decided that a cousin was like an aunt or an uncle only littler.

"What happens?" he asked skeptically.

She pressed her lips together. "Well, the chicken grunts and the egg comes out."

Eric was still skeptical. "Where?"

"Under her tail."

"It doesn't. It comes out her belly like baby people."

Jessica rolled her beautiful blue eyes and sighed disgustedly. "My father would call you a stone head. Don't you know that babies come out where the mother wee wees?"

Eric blushed painfully and his hands went to cover his face, but only for a minute. "Oh-oo. You said something bad."

Jessica sighed again. "Don't you know anything? My father is a doctor and he says there's nothing bad

about the human body or what it does."

The conversation was so embarrassing that Eric couldn't stand it any longer, so he squatted down and poked at an ant with a piece of straw. But he looked at her out of the corner of his eye. She was pretty. The prettiest girl he had ever seen. She had blue eyes and whiter teeth than anybody he had ever seen. And because she was looking at him now, he stood up and cocked his head, covering his embarrassment by saying, "I can beat up any boy I see in Sydney."

Jessica shrugged. "So can I."

Eric wasn't making much of an impression so he kicked a piece of cow dung hard and said, "You'd better watch out for me."

"Why?"

"Sometimes when I'm really feeling mean, I kiss girls." He glanced at her.

Her blue eyes danced. "That doesn't scare me either, Eric Aylesbury."

"Well, it makes some girls cry."

"I wouldn't cry. Crying's for babies. But you'd better not let my father ever see you kiss me; he might spank you again. He did once when you were little and ran away from my grandparents' farm."

Eric had heard that story a million times and hated it. He didn't remember Uncle Aaron's spanking him, but he knew his uncle would. Uncle Aaron was a stockman. That meant he raised cattle. Eric thought he was the most powerful man in the world and he bet he could beat up every man in Sydney. The whole colony even. Maybe even the whole world.

Her eyes were watching him, which made him itch all over, so he looked up for something to do and jumped up, catching the beam that went across the top of the chicken part of the barn. "My father is going to be a pry inister someday."

"My father says your father is a wowser."

471

Eric stopped swinging and dropped back down. "What's a wowser?"

Jessica frowned. "I don't know."

Eric put his hands on his hips. "Well, it doesn't matter. My father hates me, anyway."

"I don't believe you," said Jessica, shocked. "Your father can't hate you—he's your *father*. Maybe he's only mad at you."

Eric shrugged. "Maybe." And maybe he hated his father and wished his father was somebody like Uncle Aaron or Uncle James. Somebody not so busy. "I wish *I* lived on a cattle station."

"Perhaps you shall when you get big."

Eric shook his head. "When I get big I'm going to run away. And I'll never come back. Except to see my mother once in a while."

Jessica was staring at him, looking so sad that Eric felt terrible. He felt so bad he wanted to make her smile. So he stared at her for a moment, then he stepped close to her and smacked her a kiss on the cheek. She looked so surprised and her cheek was so smooth, that he turned and ran in embarrassment and fear. He ran until he ran smack into somebody.

Mouth open wide in horror, Eric looked up at the tall form of his Uncle James.

"Eric, lad," James laughed, tousling his hair. "Why the rush? What's going on? Why are you in such a hurry?"

Horror overwhelmed him, and Eric cried, "It's Jessica! She—she—she's watching a chooky lay an egg!" Then he sped off across the yard in the gathering dusk. He fell once, but got up furious at his pain and ran toward the meeting hall where he would find his mother and hide behind her. As he ran, he had great visions of Uncle James furious with him, and Uncle Aaron coming after him to spank him. All because he had kissed Jessica when she

472

hadn't asked him to.

In the barn Jessica's mouth was open and she bawled aloud, tears gushing down her cheeks. Eric had kissed her and her face was burning with embarrassment. But she wasn't crying because Eric had kissed her, she was crying because when he had, she had inexplicably let loose and wet her very best pantaloons.

"So you think they'll give it a go? I mean get behind me if I try to get legislation through that will let a man have title to land after he's squatted on it for a few years?"

"Mark, I don't know. I think so, though you've got to realize these men are in the remote outback, beyond the mountains, and won't read a newspaper or hear much news for months." Aaron toyed with his glass of wine and marveled at the amount of beef steak and kidney pie his brother had eaten, and the amount of wine he had drunk. Mark had gained a little weight since he'd seen him last, but on Mark it looked good, gave him a look of solidity he hadn't had before.

Mark forked in the bits of meat quickly. "Mmm, Mmm. But soon," he said, holding up a piece of beef on his fork, "we'll have a settlement at Port Philip. And one up the coast at Moreton Bay. Towns along the coast. With newspapers."

Aaron nodded. "I heard."

Mark chewed quickly. "Especially Port Philip on the southern coast. There's men coming across the Bass Strait from Van Dieman's Land with cattle and sheep, men going up the coast, spreading out over the land driving the cattle and sheep. The overstraiters and the overlanders will fill up the southern coast. At least as far as Hume and Hovell

explored. The more towns, the more contact the squatters will have with Sydney."

"Aye," said Aaron, leaning back in his chair. "The country I roamed over six years ago when I was bushed is filling up, being settled. But still the population is incredibly sparse for the colony to be over thirty years old."

"That's one thing doctors are good for. I hope you're spreading the word. You go all over out there around Bathurst, don't you? Talk to a lot of men? Tell them we're fighting for their rights back here in Sydney."

"I do that." Aaron watched him drink his wine. The man could quaff a pint of it in a hurry. And he wondered if he made love to Penelope the same way. Aaron winced. Dammit. Shouldn't think like that. Shouldn't let himself think about that at all.

"'Smatter? Bad wine? I'll call ol' Foster over and give him hell."

"Never mind."

"He owes me a favor. Not this cheap pee water."

"Never mind, Mark." Aaron glanced at an old clock on the shelf over the tavern fireplace. "I have to go. Have to get up early and go upriver to the Moffetts'."

"To Annabelle?" Mark stopped chewing and studied Aaron's face. "Rather domesticated, aren't you? To let a Sheila take you away from male company? Even your wife?"

Rage flew into Aaron's face, but he didn't reply. Mark had been "picking" his brain for over an hour now, asking questions about the squatters, what they did when water ran out, how they lived, what direction they were moving, what they talked about, what hopes, what dreams. They hoped what all men hoped for, better graze farther on, a place to put down roots and raise a family, enough food to eat, children.

And dreams of a good life in the remote future, of sitting in an easy chair on a deep veranda smoking a pipe, with a tankard of rum in hand, watching the convict laborers chop the wood and hoe the fields, and, as one old squatter put it, watching the jumbucks fornicate them into a fortune.

"Things are changing," Mark said, pouring wine into Aaron's glass. "Like Macquarie said. When he came here this was a jail, but he left it a colony. Only now it's a country. A new country. And the goal," Mark said, lifting his tankard, "is to become a commonwealth."

"I'll drink to that."

They did.

"And not like Father wants and Cranston wants. They want another England," Mark went on. "But it will never happen. We will be a new nation."

Aaron observed his brother closely. Mark did have a vision. He had a purpose, a vital purpose. Men like Mark had built nations before.

"Not like America," Mark was saying as he ate. "Cranston and Macarthur and all that crowd want a plantation system here like in the southern states in America. Big landowners like themselves, with the land in the hands of a few and worked by cheap convict laborers, like the Negro slaves in America. But where would that leave blokes like you and me, Aaron? Will you be a station boss forever? Or will you own your own land? No, we'll not have a slave system here, not a plantation system either. It will be land for the taking for any man, rich or poor. Or I'll die trying."

Yes, Mark had a vision.

Suddenly, a man entered the tavern and stood looking about. He spotted Aaron and came to him. It was the overseer on Glenn Moffett's place. "Dr. Aaron?"

475

Aaron said, "Aye?" and rose expectantly.

"It's Mr. Moffett, 'ee sent me here."

"What is it?"

"It's the baby, sir. It's decided to expedite matters, sir."

Aaron looked at Mark. "My God, it's probably here by now. It's early again."

"Go. The farm's four hours away. Good luck, mate."

Aaron hesitated, then turned, grabbed his hat off the hook by the door and went out.

Mark stared after him. "The bloody bastard forgot to pay his docket," he said. Then he shrugged and commenced scraping his plate clean.

Aaron knew the sound. Annabelle pushing. His mother had gone on to the Aylesbury farm with Jessica. But Aaron and his father had come straight to the Moffetts'. They had gone from Sydney to Parramatta for Matt's medical bag and from there over the toll road to Moffetts' farm.

"Hear that, Father?" Aaron said as the two men dismounted from the two horses they had rented in Parramatta.

"She sounds like she's been at it a while," Matthew said.

Sally Moffett met them on the veranda. "Oh, thank God, Aaron. 'Ello, Matt. She's been at it for eight hours." When Sally saw the horror on Aaron's face, she said, "Oh, not that hard, son. It started easy, early this morning, and built up slow, but the pushin's doin' no good."

"Bulsht," Glenn said from his chair deep in the shadows of the veranda. "She's been at the pushin' six hours."

Aaron caught his father's worried look, and both

went inside the house.

Sally led them through the big room that served as kitchen and dining room, the room people called the living room, and across a narrow hall into the front bedroom. This had been Annabelle's room as a child. It consisted of one bed, a small dressing table, an armoire, a mirror, and a washstand that doubled as a bedside table. The room had one window, which was shuttered. As a result, the room was dark and musty.

The first thing Matthew did was tell Sally to open the shutters and let in the light. When she did, sunlight flooded in and lay in multipanes across the linen sheet under which Annabelle lay. The room smelled of her efforts, perspiration, stale breath, urine.

"Get the window up, Sally. Let's have air," Matt said, rolling up his sleeves. Aaron stood back. His father was the senior physician here, the authority. He recognized it and respected it.

"Annabelle," Matt said, taking her hand.

Annabelle's lids fluttered open, her eyes rested on Matt. Then they moved to Aaron. A ghost of a smile appeared on her mouth.

"It's not too awfully early this time, Anna," Aaron said, smoothing the hair away from her damp face. His throat closed up with emotion. His wife was a plain woman, but not ugly. Her features were spare, her nose small and straight, her lips thin, and there was a faint sprinkling of freckles across her nose. Today her cheeks were flushed with her efforts, her eyes unusually bright and deep gold. Aaron loved her, as one person loves another when they have lived together and shared the ups and downs of life. Six years she had been his wife and worked beside him. She was his companion, but even now he was aware that a companion was all she was to him. Still, he loved her as he loved his mother, his father, his

477

uncles, his friends.

Matthew, with the expertise that came with experience, said, "Annabelle. I'm going to examine you to see what's taking my grandchild so long to get here. It will hurt a little, but I'll be as easy as I can."

Annabelle nodded and grasped Aaron's hand.

Matthew Aylesbury drew the sheet down from her body and sat down on the edge of the bed. Aaron knew what he would do. So did Annabelle. Matt inserted two fingers into the birth canal to feel for the baby's head. With the other hand he palpated her abdomen, trying to determine the baby's position.

At that moment a contraction began, and Annabelle's whimper grew to a shrill, high-pitched shriek. Aaron watched Matthew's brow. A man could tell a lot by watching another man's brow. He watched it knowing, knowing what his father was thinking.

Annabelle swam. She swam from one isle to the other and when she reached an island hoping for rest, she had to let go and go on to the next one. Because somewhere in this turbulent sea was a paradise where the air was cool and birds were colorful and everything was quiet. She knew that the stormy sea was pain, the islands brief respites from the pain, and that if she could swim long enough without drowning, she would reach the paradise where there was no pain. The only thing was, her heart kept missing beats.

". . . breech," came her father-in-law's voice. "But I'm not sure. Feels strange. Aaron, see what you think."

"But Father. You know more—"

"I know I can't feel the head."

She released her husband's hands and swam the stormy sea, panting, reaching, kicking until she came to another island, but this one had a rocky shoreline and did not give her much rest. The waves

pounded her body, threatened to wash her away.

". . . frank breech, Father," came Aaron's voice.

Aaron and Matthew looked at each other. With a low groan, Annabelle pushed off for the next island.

"Anna, we're going to use the forceps . . . cold . . ." came Matthew's voice.

She nodded, understanding. She had assisted Aaron once. She knew. She caught one glimpse of father and son working down there between her legs, heads almost touching. Aaron was pressing her abdomen because her pushing wasn't strong enough, his father was using forceps. Their voices came and went over the roar of the waves.

"There's meconium, a bad sign for the fetus," Matt said.

Aaron's voice sounded frantic over the roar of the waves, "Father, I don't like her pulse."

"Damn. I can't turn the fetus. It has to turn, and fast, Aaron."

"Help us, Anna. Push. Hold on, Anna."

"Aaron, I can't turn it. Try."

"But if you can't, I can't."

"You have to try, son."

". . . can't get a handle on this."

"Push, Annabelle. Push for Aaron."

Annabelle tried very hard, pushed with her feet, pulled with her arms, but the island was so far away, and she was so tired. Aaron couldn't rescue her, nor his father. Deen? Could Deen? He had once.

"Father? That's the umbilical cord. . . ."

". . . cut off fetal circulation. . . ."

"It's stopped pulsating."

"Damn! See if you can dislodge it from the vaginal wall, Aaron. Otherwise the baby's circulation will be cut off. . . ."

Annabelle opened her mouth for air, cried out, but even crying out took too much energy and it made the

island seem farther away. So she concentrated on one hand at a time, one arm over the other.

But don't you remember, Annabelle? You can't swim.

"I can't find her pulse, Aaron."

"We've got to—"

Teeth bared, Aaron pulled. With forceps and with hands, he pulled the fetus through the birth canal with each uterine contraction. But now the contractions were weak and his father was pushing on the uterus, giving it help. Both men perspired, both knowing time was important, both knowing it was probably too late for the baby. The umbilical cord had prolapsed, was looped out of the birth canal, and the baby's buttocks, which were presenting first, was compressing the cord against the vaginal wall, cutting off the fetal circulation. Aaron pulled, and tears poured out of his eyes as he pulled this male child with all his might. Then the buttocks of the fetus pivoted as it came down, and finally Aaron delivered the body, the child's legs lying alongside its abdomen. "I've got to deliver the head," Aaron said desperately.

"Yes." Matthew's voice was quiet.

Then it was there, the infant blue-gray with the cheesy vernix coating its wrinkled body. It did not breathe. Aaron cleared its mouth of phlegm and water and still it did not breathe. He cursed and slapped the tiny bottom, but the infant unfolded with its head down and did not breathe. He slapped it again, his tragic eyes going to his father. But Matthew's face was stern. "Aaron? Aaron?"

Aaron stared at him and his eyes went to Annabelle.

Annabelle made one more breast stroke to reach the island, but it was too late. She was too tired. So tired. And giving in to the cool sea was easier.

"Anna! Anna!" She heard Aaron calling her from some faraway place. She made one more attempt to reach the island, but her arm wouldn't come up any longer, and she was so tired she let the sea wash over her, wash her under. Because there she wouldn't have to struggle anymore.

"Anna, Anna!" Aaron shook her furiously. Kept shaking her, but there was no breath, no pulse. Wildly he turned to his father. But Matthew was working with the infant now, placing his mouth over its mouth and nose and giving it breaths of air. The little blue chest rose when he blew, but there was no movement in its limbs. None.

In a fever, Aaron held Annabelle to his chest, and from his mouth came a moan, "What happened? What happened?"

Matthew worked for another ten minutes on the infant, and when he felt no heartbeat, no pulse, he finally lay the infant down and looked at Aaron. There was a world of suffering in his face. Aaron laid Annabelle down at last on her pillows and sat with his hands covering his face. When he looked up, his father was cleaning up the bloody newspapers and linens beneath Annabelle's legs, his shoulders drooping, his movements slow.

Aaron stared at him, at the dead infant on the bed beside Annabelle, at Annabelle white and still as death. He snorted bitterly. "Father and son. We made a fine team. We lost them both. Not one. Both! I'm through. I'm not going to touch another patient. I can't even deliver my own wife."

Matthew turned to him slowly, anger etching his handsome face with deep grief lines around his mouth, down the middle of his forehead. "Haven't you ever lost a patient before?"

Aaron answered impatiently, "Yes, yes, yes."

"A woman in child labor?"

"Yes."

"An infant?"

"Yes, but what does that—"

"What makes you think that Annabelle and this infant had any better chance of living than anybody else just because she was your wife? You should know, Aaron, that there are circumstances beyond our control in which *people die*. You, of all people, should know that no matter how hard we try and how much skill we apply we can't *make* people live. This infant was too large for her and it was turned wrong. And there was something, something wrong with her heart."

Aaron shook his head.

"We're doctors, Aaron, not gods. As for us as a team, I'm proud of how coordinated we were, how skilled. You did the best goddamn forceps delivery I ever saw in all my years as a doctor. And to be very frank with you, Aaron, I'm so damned proud of you and your skill that I'm having a bloody hard time feeling sorry for you."

Aaron stared at his father through the misty wall of grief. And then he had the war of tears. You didn't let tears come, though, you fought them. You held your grief in, and kept your sense of loss mostly to yourself. The pressure in his chest increased as he kissed his wife's pale hand. And as he grieved silently, he wished he could have loved her more. Wished he could have loved her half as much as she had loved him.

He grieved for the child too, the infant boy that never breathed. But then, he had grieved only a little less for those four other premature infants Annabelle had delivered over the years.

Aaron wandered out of the room in a daze of grief. Matthew was in the living room telling Sally. Sally

482

cried out, wailed. Glenn moaned.

Dust under Aaron's feet. The sun on his back. He was walking, but he didn't know where. Perhaps if he had loved her more . . . perhaps she did not have the will to live. Perhaps her heart was broken and couldn't hold together under the stress.

And why had Jessica lived and his infants did not? Did his seed poison Annabelle, that she couldn't deliver a child of his own?

Aaron walked a long time, and when he became aware of where he was, he was surprised to see that he was on the veranda of the Aylesburys' house. His mother was standing before him. He looked up. He was a little boy again. "Mum, we lost her. Lost them both."

Milicent Aylesbury's face grew old before his eyes, but she opened her arms and held him, and for one brief moment he let himself be a little boy again and he let tears dampen the shoulder of his mother's dress.

A shadow passed across the sky, and Deen, at the helm of the whaling vessel, looked up, saw nothing but a blue and cloudless sky. The sea was rough, spindrift showering the air with foam. But some deep instinct intruded upon his peace of mind, disturbed him. His hair bristled, his skin crawled, and cold perspiration broke out over his body. He looked across the ocean toward the north, and the image seemed clear. Annabelle's arm sunk beneath the murky water of the sea.

Deen's mouth stretched into a grimace, and his ship's mates stared in astonishment when he threw back his head and cried to the sky, "Annabe-e-elle!"

Chapter XXIV

It always happened that way. No matter how hard he tried, no matter how he proved himself, no matter how well he did, Aaron always received the praise.

Mark was sitting on the Cranstons' back veranda looking out across the yard. He could barely see the paddock, the stable, or the sheds for the mist and the rain. He couldn't see the mountains at all. They were veiled in mists almost as black as his wife's veil. Damn him. Damn her.

Mark gnawed on the knuckles of his right hand and went over and over the funeral ceremony held in the church in Windsor. The sun had been shining then, filtering in through the windows onto her coffin, a coffin built and carved so beautifully by Owen Crawford. All the old friends were there, all the uncles. But did any of them say much to him about his appointment? No. They were all caught up in Annabelle's death. Why? Because she was *Aaron's* wife, not his.

It was unfortunate, Annabelle's death. A shame, of course. He was the first to admit that. But people were morbid. They'd rather talk about death than life. At the Moffetts' after the funeral, the friends and

neighbors had gathered to pay their respects again to the family, and there was a banquet of food spread out on planks under the gum trees in the yard. The talk had been of Annabelle:

Isn't it a shame, she was so young.

And poor Aaron had to see both die.

They did everything they could for the poor woman.

It's the good who die young.

And she was the Moffetts' only child.

Mark hadn't moved an inch in two hours, sitting here on the veranda in this chair. Oliver had gone to check on his precious new bull in this ghastly rain. And God only knew what Penelope was doing. They'd just made it home from the Moffetts' before the rain started. Damned weather.

No one said much about his appointment. He was the first man ever to be appointed by the legislative council of New South Wales to carry a proposal to Parliament in England about the squatters, and very little was said about it. Not even by his father.

"Congratulations, Mark, on your appointment," his father had said, but Mark could tell his mind was far away, and he hadn't said another damned word about it. There had been no "I'm proud of you," no questions about it, no inquiries as to when he'd go, what he'd do or say. But Aaron? Oh ho! How many times today had his father gotten that disgusting look on his face and said to somebody, "Aaron was incredible. I couldn't manage to turn the infant. If it had been up to me, it would still be unborn. But Aaron did it. He managed the delivery." Personal stuff a man ought not talk about. Birthing details didn't interest anyone but women. His father had made a fool of himself.

Mark gnawed, one hand folded over the other. He

didn't expect much from Aaron; he had been in a daze. The night after Aaron had left Foster's Tavern to go to Annabelle, Jory and Stu had come in and announced that the council had met secretly and chosen him, Mark, to go to England. That was two days ago. Had Penelope said much? No. Just, "I'm sure you'll do an excellent job, Mark." No "I'm proud of you," from her, either.

No questions today from the friends, either. Not even Stu. Maybe Stuart and Jory and the others thought they'd ask him all about his plans later this week, but he had news for them. He was leaving tomorrow and he wasn't going to tell them. Rot for brains. The entire colony. Give 'em the choice of talking about the future of their country or a funeral and they'd choose the bloody funeral every time.

"Father?"

Aaron surrounded by Jory and Stu. His father's eyes going to his favorite son every other minute with a look of concern.

"Father?"

Mark barely moved his head to look at Eric who was standing beside his chair, intruding on his thoughts.

"Mum says you'll get me a drink of water, sir. The dipper's too high and I can't reach it."

Mark glared at the boy. "You don't need a drink of water."

Eric frowned. "I do. I ate ham at the Moffetts' and it made me—"

"I *said* you don't need a drink of water. It can wait."

"Mum said for me to ask you—"

"Go tell your mum if she wants you to have a drink of water she can get off her duff and get it herself."

Eric stared at him with those big brown eyes so

much like Aaron's and Mark was filled with fury.

"But Mum's lying down and I—"

Mark lunged at the boy, intending to whale him, but Eric was too fast and jumped back with a cry and ran into the house.

"Brat," Mark muttered as he settled back in his chair.

No, and he hadn't forgotten that at least ninety people had carried food to Aaron that day in the Moffetts' yard and Aaron had merely shaken his head. But when Penelope took Aaron a plate of food? He took it, of course. And Mark hadn't missed the look that passed between them at that magical moment. No, he had seen it. That look wasn't a sister-in-law, brother-in-law look. What a fool he had been. There must have been something going on between them all these years. Yes, Penelope coming to see her so-called father, and who else? Aaron?

Their secret was clear to him at last. She would hear that Aaron was going to be in the area, so she would go to her father's. And probably Aaron sent her a message. Or perhaps he just showed up here at the house. In fact, perhaps Oliver Cranston knew the whole thing was going on and condoned it. It was clear to him that Oliver liked Aaron better than his own son-in-law. Mark knew why, too. Aaron was the son of the woman Oliver Cranston had always wanted, had probably tumbled a time or two too, who knows? Hadn't he, Mark, found out that Milicent had had sex with his father before their marriage?

"Mark, may I ask why you threatened Eric?"

Mark didn't move his head. Instead, he cut his eyes up at Penelope standing beside his chair, still in the black dress she'd worn to the funeral. "Because he doesn't understand the word no."

487

"Exactly why did you tell him no?"

Mark unfolded his hands, sighed and stood up, her angry gaze following him as he stood. "Because if he wants a drink of water every five minutes he should get it himself."

"The dipper—"

"Then let him bloody well climb something to get it, like everybody else." Mark didn't like the puzzled look she gave him. "I wish he'd be a little more self-reliant—"

"Self-reliant!"

"Instead of being wet-nursed at the age of five."

"What on earth is wrong with you today? You've been this way since—"

"Since I saw you making eyes at Aaron."

Penelope's mouth popped open. "What?"

"I saw him looking at you like you were something he'd like to eat."

"Mark. I'll not listen to this. I simply—"

"You giving him the cow's eyes."

"Oh!" Penelope breathed, her face flushing with fury. "I gave him a plate of food, he took it, and not a word passed between us."

"Do lovers need words?"

Penelope stared, her green eyes snapping. "You would say this about your brother on the day of his wife's funeral? How could you?"

Mark hooked his thumb in the waistband of his trousers and glared at her. "It was easy. Because it's true."

Penelope whirled to walk away, but his hand shot out and caught her arm and jerked her back. Eric was standing in the doorway staring, horrified, and it only fueled the anger inside him. "Don't ever walk away from me when I'm talking, Penelope."

488

"You're not talking, Mark, you're babbling nonsense."

He held her arm, hating her, loving her, wanting to hurt her. "Look at me, Penelope, and tell me that you have not been in Aaron's arms since you and I married." He saw a flicker in her eyes. Somewhere in their angry depths he saw a flicker of guilt. "Yes. Tell me."

"You incorrigible beast," she hissed.

His hand caught her on the mouth, and her shock was so great, she just stared. "We're going home. Now. Get your shawl and the rest of our stuff. We're going. Now!"

"No. We will not."

Mark grabbed her and started shaking her. "Damn you, Penelope. Why must you always defy me!" he cried, so angry he was blind.

Eric made a lunge at him and started beating his leg with his fist, a furious, shrill shriek of rage coming from him, and all Mark heard in his own fury was, ". . . my mother. My mother . . . alone!"

With one sweep of his hand he sent the boy slamming into the veranda post, and then he pushed Penelope away from him. There was a flutter of black as she ran to Eric and gathered him into her arms.

Mark was both ashamed of himself and angry as he stood shaking with rage. "I said, get ready. We're going home."

"I knew it."

He whirled around to stare at Oliver Cranston standing in the rain, one foot on the veranda.

"I knew you were striking her." Cranston's black eyes narrowed as he stepped up on the veranda. "And by God you'll not do it again."

Still angry, Mark snarled. "I don't strike her, and if

489

I do, it's none of your damned business."

Cranston shook with fury as he came slowly toward Mark. "It's my business as her father and as a gentleman."

Mark couldn't help but smile. "As a gentleman perhaps, but as a father?" he laughed, but his head exploded with pain and he slammed into the house. When his vision cleared, he heard Penelope order Cranston to stop, saw her clutch his arm. Mark shook his head to clear it. Seething, he said, "You aren't her father, Cranston. Her father is a drunken—"

Penelope shrieked, "Stop. Hush, Mark!"

A great surge of pleasure shot through Mark, a surge of power, the power to hurt a pure merino. "Rolph Danbury is Penelope's father."

Cranston's face went quickly from red to white. "You scum," he hissed and threw off Penelope's restraining hand.

"It's true. Ask Rolph. Ask Fran Aylesbury, ask my father. Ask Penelope herself."

Penelope saw the white horror on her father's face, and all she wanted now was to comfort him, to erase the hurt, the horror she saw there. "Father, it doesn't matter. Let it be. He's just upset."

Oliver kept staring at Mark, staring with such speechless fury that Mark looked away, looked at Penelope.

She gave him the look she'd been saving up for years, a look that left nothing hidden anymore. The look told him that she not only pitied him because of his old, tangled resentments, but that she feared for him, and that he had become loathsome to her, as loathsome as some slimy creature that might crawl up from the marshes of Botany Bay.

Mark read the look and took an involuntary step backward, as if someone had just thrust him through

490

with a two-edged sword. His hand went to his abdomen. "We're going home. Now. Get ready."

"No. You'll go home alone, Mark."

He made a weak attempt to smile. "I leave for England tomorrow, remember?"

"Yes, thank God."

His lips went white as he stared at her. Then he went blind with rage and wrenched her hand from Cranston's arm, and with all his might he propelled her out into the yard in the rain. "Get to the carriage. Now!"

Her feet slipped in the mud as she crouched, holding her arms out for balance. "No! I'll never go back to you, Mark. Never," she screamed above the roar of the rain.

He went to her, caught her arm, but something caught him, spun him around. Cranston's fist aimed for his face, but Mark ducked, and with all his strength gave Cranston a blow to the abdomen.

Oliver crumpled like an old stick and fell into the mud. Eric's screams maddened Mark as he grabbed Penelope's arm. He dug his fingers in, twisted, aware of the servants piling out of their huts staring. Let them. It was a domestic matter, and they would not dare interfere. He saw Cricket hefting a plank, coming at him, and Boston stumbling toward him. Mark got ready to push the little freak in the mud, take the plank away from him, and use it on Boston, as he continued to jerk Penelope toward the stable where the carriage stood. But in the thundering rain, he did not hear the hoofbeats.

Suddenly, he was caught in a whirlwind. His face exploded and blood blinded him. Aaron's angry face and flashing teeth were before him. Something raised him up off the ground, gave him another blow and another and another before he even had time to raise

491

his fists. He lay in the mud and rain tasting blood, swallowing blood, and he could not see out of one eye. His head thundered with every beat of his pulse.

"Get in that carriage, you son-of-a-bitch," said Aaron's face.

Mark's body rose of its own accord, his feet hardly touching the ground as Aaron half carried him to the waiting carriage. Cricket's face appeared in his peripheral vision. Suddenly Mark was sitting in the carriage holding the reins in his hands even as unconsciousness threatened, and Aaron was holding the horse's bit, rain plastering his hair to his head and soaking his black suit.

"I came to tell you farewell," Aaron shouted through his teeth. "Now I'm telling you good riddance."

Suddenly the horse lunged forward and Mark fought the reins to gain control of it.

As the carriage moved away, Aaron delivered Penelope without a word to the veranda, leaving her with Cranston.

He said nothing. There was too much pain inside him. Too much that would take a long time to heal before he could speak again.

He turned, took the reins of his horse from Cricket, mounted, and rode off, going north toward the ridge.

Penelope watched as the carriage rolled past, Mark driving, hatless, only glancing at her and her father and Eric on the veranda. She felt no regrets. Her life for the past four years had been given solely to Mark. As his hostess she had worked and planned to entertain his friends. She had totally served him. As his wife, she had submitted to his erratic moods, heights of joy, deeps of depression, with their accompanying sexual results. And she had listened to his problems and his boastings, as a wife should. But

492

he had been increasingly unfaithful to their marriage. Gossip had come to her in the form of whispers from her friends. He was seen going into a particular house south of Sydney, a house that belonged to a prostitute. He had flirted with women in her presence at parties. This from a man whom she had never loved.

The carriage wheels left deep tracks behind in the soft mud and the carriage itself soon vanished through the rain.

No. She did not hate him. But neither would she mourn his departure.

"Is it true?"

Penelope turned to Oliver Cranston, searched his tragic face with her eyes. Then she smiled. "Who can truly say? Rolph claims that Mother told him that I am his child. But you know how Mother liked to imagine little intrigues. Besides, you are my father. Always shall be."

Oliver looked at her sadly. "Yes. You will always be my little girl," he said.

"You are a hard taskmistress, Mrs. Aylesbury," Mr. T.J. Crume said as he pulled on his gloves. "If your wool had not been of such excellent grade and quality, I would not have paid you such an atrocious price for it. For I can offer any price to the wool growers in this colony and they'll take it." Crume ran speculative gray eyes over Penelope's form, clad in an immaculate riding dress of deep green muslin.

Penelope had seen the appraising gaze several times as she had watched the speculator from England examine the bales of wool her shed hands had so carefully classed, baled, pressed, weighed, branded, and hauled to the wool warehouse near

Sydney cove.

"You say your husband is in England?"

"Yes, Mr. Crume. He left over five months ago."

"Mmm. He should have taken you with him. Voyages to England are a boring six to eight weeks."

Penelope turned and began strolling out of the warehouse. "My husband shall not be bored, Mr. Crume." He has himself, she thought. She came out into the spring sun, followed by the wool buyer.

"I say, have you any objections to taking tea with me at the tavern where I'm staying, Mrs. Aylesbury? I need someone to keep my last evening in Sydney from being boring."

"I have no objections at all, Mr. Crume," Penelope replied. "But I can't. I must return to the farm at once. Work keeps me from being bored." She observed his smile vanish. "Good day, sir."

Mr. Crume muttered a begrudging good day, and Penelope made her way to the bank. After she had deposited her receipt for the season's wool, she went to the street in front of the warehouse where she had left her carriage. As she approached she was at first surprised, then strangely apprehensive when she saw Stuart and Jory McWilliams standing beside it.

"Hello, Stu. Jory," she said cheerfully. "My goodness. Surely you both aren't finished working for the day. It's barely past noon."

Stu looked at Jory, whose face paled. Both men were staring at her strangely, their hats in their hands. It was their expressions that told her that something was wrong, and at that instant she became aware of crowds of people near the wharf. But that wasn't unusual; there were often crowds at the wharf when a ship had just put into port. But Penelope knew. She knew as surely as if they had already told her. "What is it? Stu?" she demanded softly.

494

"Penelope . . . a ship that just came from the Cape of Good Hope just put into port."

Penelope waited. Mark was dead. He no longer existed. She grasped the side of the carriage for support for what she knew was coming. "Please go on," she whispered.

"The captain on the *Bartlet* just gave a report to Campbell. There was a storm at sea. Near the Cape. Two ships foundered, but the *Blundell* went down and all the passengers were drowned." Stuart's face was twisted with agony, his face very pale. He kept shaking his head and searching for words, Stu who was never without words. "I . . ." he shook his head again. "Penelope, there were no survivors."

"The *Blundell* was Mark's ship?"

He nodded. "Aye."

She felt all the blood draining out of her face. "Is it official, Stu?"

He nodded.

She looked at Jory, whose eyes were damp, and he was biting his bottom lip. She felt faint. She felt overwhelming sorrow. Mark was her husband. She experienced regret that she couldn't have loved him, been a better wife. She shook her head. Her vision cleared. She could not suffer for Mark, not anymore. A cool breeze came to stir the lock of curls in front of her ears in the shade of her bonnet. She felt the color rush back into her face, flushing it. "Dear God," she breathed.

Stuart took her arm. "I'm sorry, Penelope."

She leaned on him, aware of a small crowd of people gathering close. They knew Mark's carriage, Mark's wife. They had heard of the tragedy. "How many men . . . ?"

"Over five hundred. They're not sure yet," Jory said softly.

"Oh, dear God. All those families . . ." Penelope looked up at Stuart.

"Most of the men on board were sailors from England. We think there were about nine men and two women on board from New South Wales," Stuart said.

Penelope pulled away from him slowly and held on to the carriage. "Thank you, Stu. Jory."

"What are you going to do?" Jory asked.

"I'll take the rig on home first. Then I must go to the Aylesburys'."

"Word has already been sent to Parramatta hospital to Mark's father," a man said from nearby.

Penelope nodded, and Jory helped her up into the carriage.

"We'll go with you, Penelope."

"That won't be necessary."

"Will you be all right? May we drive you home?"

"No. Thank you. I—I'll be all right."

Stuart stood looking up at her. "For whatever else he became, Penelope, he did much for this colony."

"Yes," she said, letting tears come. "He did that." She nodded and clucked to the horse. The carriage lurched forward and she turned it about to head down the street.

Stuart and Jory stood there. They knew about her and Mark's relationship. They would understand and respect the fact that she was not prostrate with grief. They knew of Mark's moods and tempers, and they knew about his visiting prostitutes, and his hatred of Eric. They knew, above all others, of his complete absorption in himself, and they knew she had not lost her love, but her greatest source of agony instead.

*   *   *

496

The memorial service for the passengers of the *Blundell* was held two weeks after the news came to Sydney of the ship's loss. Penelope sat in St. John's church with Milicent Aylesbury on one side of her and Eric on the other. Beside Eric sat Oliver Cranston. Beside Dr. Aylesbury sat Aaron, who had been sent for. No one questioned her lack of tears. What tears she had shed for Mark had been shed in private, and the tears she had shed were familiar, tears of pity.

Aaron had seen her briefly outside the church and had said only, "New South Wales will miss its favorite son."

Yes, and that sentiment was echoed a hundred times that day, because it was true.

When the service was done, Aaron left for Bathurst, the Aylesburys returned home, and Penelope went to her own farm. A year of mourning had to be gotten through somehow.

One year from the day of the memorial service for the passengers of the *Blundell*, Penelope went to Parramatta to see Frances Aylesbury in the same small brick house she had lived in since she had arrived in the colony.

"You're closing Penmark?" Frances said, pouring the tea into a dainty china cup. "But Penelope, that's such a waste."

No one had seen much of Penelope over the past year. She had stayed quietly at Penmark, raising her sheep, running the house, visiting her father and the Aylesburys often.

"That's one reason I'm here," Penelope said. "You're opening a manufactury in Sydney and mentioned once you wanted to move there. Well,

would you consider staying at Penmark? I won't exact any rent. I'll just want you to see that it's kept up, for I don't want to sell it. There won't be any sheep there anymore, and you can do with the runs what you wish."

Fran poured cream into their tea. She said nothing as she watched Penelope sip her tea. Then, "I'd want to pay the rent."

"I won't accept any rent payments."

"Then I'll make improvements as I see fit, with your approval, of course." She did not know where Penelope was going and she didn't ask. "And of course, when you return to Sydney, you will stay at Penmark."

"You will, then?" Penelope was grateful to Fran. And so relieved. She would hate to have to dismiss the servants and board up the house.

Fran nodded, smiling.

"Thank you," Penelope said, reaching out to touch her hand. "Your living in the house and keeping it up will help me a great deal."

Frances smiled at her again. "Well, so, my lass. You mentioned that you came for two reasons. What's the other?"

Penelope set her cup down with a clatter and looked at Fran silently. It was a long moment before she replied. "Is Rolph Danbury my real father?"

Fran had long ago learned to hide her emotions and their accompanying facial expressions, and there was not a flicker of surprise on her face as she said, "Why do you ask?"

Penelope told her about seeing Rolph at the graveyard that day, about Rolph's seeing Mark in the tavern and what he had revealed. She finished by saying, "And don't deny it, Fran. You've been carrying a torch for Rolph Danbury, your cousin, for

years, haven't you?"

Fran stared at her. "Whatever gave you that idea? Why, I'm in my forties, Penelope, and a spinster. And Rolph's been away for years."

"And it's a family secret you were in love with him."

Frances Aylesbury did not blush.

"So, tell me. Is he my father?"

Fran sighed. "Yes."

Penelope nodded. "I thought so. And there's another family secret. Was Aaron really born before Milicent and Matthew were married? Is he truly Matthew's son?"

Frances smiled. "Milicent Crawford never knew any other man existed besides Matthew. Yes. I can stake my life on it. Aaron is Matthew's son."

"That makes Aaron my second cousin?"

"Or your cousin twice removed." Fran shook her head. "I don't know. I never did understand the second- and third-cousin thing, and cousins twice removed. Just say, Aaron is your distant cousin."

Penelope smiled gently for the first time since she had arrived at Fran's door. "I want to help Rolph, Fran. I want him to have anything he wants, money, clothing, food, and I want Penmark to be available and open to him when he needs a place to stay. That's why I persisted in finding out how you felt about him."

Frances cleared her throat and glanced at her. "With him and me both in the house with only the servants present, that should certainly make the gossips' tongues flap."

Penelope smiled. "When you see him, tell him . . . tell him I want to get to know him."

"Tell me yourself."

Penelope's eyes widened, and she turned in the

direction of the voice behind her.

In the doorway that led to Fran's kitchen stood a man, a tall man with dark hair shot with gray. His eyes were black. He was handsome without his beard and without the red in his eyes. He grinned at Penelope and bowed, and had he not been her own father, she might have blushed at his handsome courtliness. But what was he doing here? Penelope turned her quizzical gaze upon Fran.

Fran's face was absolutely unreadable. "Rolph has been fixing things about the house," she explained rationally.

Penelope turned to Rolph.

Rolph grinned. "Lots of things."

Penelope looked at Fran.

"Windows that won't close. Door hinges, chinks out of brick . . ."

"Ax handles," Rolph offered.

"Yes. Ax handles," Frances said, avoiding Penelope's gaze.

"In fact, Franny's learning how to fix a few things herself," Rolph said, his eyes shining roguishly.

Penelope looked at Fran again. Not a flicker of expression showed on Fran's face, but two spots of high color had appeared on her cheeks.

Penelope bit her lip to keep from either laughing or weeping. "You heard my offer then, Ro—Fath—whoever you are?"

He nodded. "And who knows? I'll probably accept the offer, from time to time."

When Penelope looked at Fran again, Fran said, "He doesn't stay in the same place long."

Penelope nodded. Swagmen seldom did. On the other hand— Penelope rose. "I have other business to attend to, so I'll be going." She offered her hand and Fran took it. "Mrs. McWilliams will get in touch

500

with you to make arrangements for your move to the house."

Fran nodded and kissed her on the cheek. "Have a safe journey."

Penelope gave her hand to Rolph. "And I was feeling so sorry for you, not having a home."

Rolph shrugged and Penelope kissed his cheek. Then she left the house.

Penelope surprised several people in New South Wales that day. Uncle Tad Crawford was surprised when she bought twelve horses and four mules. Uncle Owen was surprised when she bought two ox carts and two drays. Uncle Ben was surprised when she bought the two yokes of oxen Owen said he had for sale. And the entire population of Sydney was surprised when she hired eight drovers, complete with dogs.

She said good-bye to the Aylesburys and to her father on a hot summer day six days later. Then she said good-bye to Penmark. No one gave much thought to her going, for it was customary for a widow to make a journey after her year of mourning was over. It helped to put some of her grief behind her, and to lend her more perspective about her future.

But there was little suffering in Penelope as she turned her face away from Penmark.

The endurance of the bush horse was uncanny. Out here behind the mountains Tad Crawford's horses had thrived. They weren't grain fed, but lived on the grass. They were a light horse with good feet and good temperament. They could work all day in sweltering heat, sometimes at over one hundred degrees, be turned out at night, and hobbled to fend

501

for themselves.

Aaron had made a great discovery about the horses he had bought from Tad for stock horses in the Bathurst district. They thrived in the comparatively dry climate. They were healthier and had more stamina and were not bedeviled by as many insects as most horses.

Without a good stock horse raising cattle would have been impossible. And Aaron was fortunate; he had a good horse tailer in O'Reardon, who managed his horses with dexterity and delight. Aaron leaned on the fence now watching James ride the buck-jumper in the cattle yard, hanging on to him with his knees only, stirring up more dust than a mustering might have. This was only one of James's skills. Even if he hadn't been Cranston's son, James would have been in the highest position as a stockman by the sheer weight of his talent in horse tailering, mustering, droving, and branding. His judgment was good, too.

The horse in the paddock gave one last kick with his back legs and began trotting around the yard snorting. James would ride him, show him the tricks of the reins, and in time that young horse would be one of the best stock horses on the station.

"Boss?"

Aaron turned to face Damper Dan, one of his best ringers, but already he was hearing the bells.

"Boss, it's an overlander comin' down the track," Dan said, squinting east. "And by God, it looks like a big-time squatter."

"Maybe 'ee's already got property around bought an' paid fer," Stringy Bark Joe said, picking his teeth with a gum tree swig.

"He'll want graze and water, boss," Dan said. "And them's jumbucks he's got. Them sheep can

502

sure stomp up good pasture."

"Don't see no cattle," Sig said, coming to stand with the others.

Aaron stood up straight and watched the stream of sheep pouring down the side of the hill to the east, like clouds in the eye of a storm. Must be two hundred of them, he thought. A man could hear all that infernal bleating clear to Hades. "Sig, the overlander can have the run to the west bordering my property where the creek is, but see that he understands he must move on at dawn tomorrow morning."

"Aye, boss."

"And have Tom and Chad keep an eye on them. That's a big outfit, and I don't want any of my cattle duffed."

"'Ees bound to be 'urtin' fer beef, all right," Joe said. "For I'll wager 'ees been eatin' mutton all the way from the 'awkesbury River."

The men watched as the sheep kept pouring down the hill, attracting the other men in the yard. Jessica was suddenly beside Aaron and stuffed her hand in his.

"What is it, Papa?" she asked in her high-pitched sing-song voice.

"An overlander, love."

"Are them sheep?"

"Aye, lass."

"Will there be any baby shee-eep?"

"Lambs, Jessica. I'll wager there'll be a few."

Now came a team of bullocks over the hill pulling a dray, and as the ringers stood staring, another came over the hill.

"Look at it. 'Ee's movin' 'is 'ole bloody station," Joe exclaimed.

Among the sheep rode drovers on horses whistling to their sheep dogs, low, short whistles, or long

503

questioning ones. The dogs were dashing in and out among the sheep, keeping them coming straight for the station.

"What do you make of it, Aaron?"

Aaron glanced worriedly at James, who had come to stand beside him, squinting at the procession pouring over the hill. Now came two bullock carts loaded with what looked like furniture.

"That's a wool press," one of the ringers said.

"Some overlander moving his entire sheep station," Aaron told James with a frown. "I wouldn't be surprised if he's not bringing his damned sheep shed with him."

The sheep kept coming, closer and closer, not veering away from the station, and Aaron was getting angrier and angrier. Not even a squatter would be so brash as to run his mobs right into a man's homestead. Aaron looked for Mrs. Chun, who was standing on the veranda. "Mrs. Chun, keep Jessie inside." To Toady Chun, standing bowlegged and belly-over-belt beside him, he said, "Get my breech loader." To James, he said, "This is no ordinary overlander. I don't know what's on his mind, but whatever it is, let's be ready for him."

Men sprinted for their muskets, and by the time they came to stand in the yard behind Aaron, the sheep were approaching the yard. They flowed in and over it, bleating, leaping over each other as sheep will do. The dogs ignored the men and darted at the sheep, nipping at their heels, barking, narrowing the mob, keeping it in line as it flowed around the stockmen still standing agape and helpless in the yard. It was a sea of sheep, over five hundred heading west now, and Aaron was mad as hell. The gall of this overlander!

The sheep drovers riding amongst the mobs

nodded with such friendly aplomb to the stockmen that the ringers forgot they had muskets in their hands and waved back.

The sheep flowed past, but the bullocks, carts, and drays halted at the eastern edge of the dooryard, and that was when Aaron saw the overlander. An overlander with a child riding on a horse behind him.

Stringy Bark Joe nudged Aaron. "Bloody gee, boss. That overlander, 'ee's a woman!"

Aaron squinted, took a good look. The overlander wore a dress. And then he thought he recognized her. No, surely not.

But it was. *Penelope*.

Aaron looked at James. James lowered his musket and a slow smile stole across his mouth. He glanced at Aaron, and then motioned to the other men with one hand, dismissing them. The ringers lowered their muskets, began to saunter away, looking back over their shoulders. And smiling, James went away to find something else to do.

Penelope approached on horseback, dressed in a dark gray skirt and a cabbage tree hat that shaded her face. As Aaron stared, she reined the horse before him, looked down at him, and for a moment she said nothing. Then, "It's time you ran sheep with Father's cattle, Aaron, so I brought a few with me."

He kept looking up at her speechlessly, his emotions a turmoil, unbelieving, and yet his heart thudding in his chest told him it was true. This was not some crazy, exotic dream.

She removed her man's hat and tossed her head to loosen the folds of her hair and then smiled gently down at him. "I've also brought you your son."

Son!

Aaron's muddled brain did not comprehend. Son?

505

His eyes moved to Eric sitting solemnly astride a brindle gelding, holding a yellow cat in his arms.

Son? *My* son?

Perspiration suddenly broke out all over him. Penelope had been pregnant when he had returned from the bush. Gossips had said she had had too large a baby too soon for everything to be proper.

Eric. My God. Eric. Yes. How could he have been so blind? So this was the reason. She was pregnant, he was off in the bush. . . . His soul overflowed and tears threatened, and any time that happened a man had to move. He held his hands up to his son.

He lowered Eric to the ground, ran his hands briefly over his face. Yes, the eyes, the hair . . . oh, my God. He gripped him by the shoulders and swallowed the lump in his throat. Then he released him.

Love overwhelmed him as he raised his hands up to Penelope.

When she slid into his hands and then into his arms, the world narrowed to her body, the feel of her and all her curves against him, her lips, hair, eyes. He kissed her and she opened her lips to him. With shaking breath he kissed her harder, bruising her, wanting her, feeling her soft, sensual response. They clung desperately to each other, not hearing, not seeing, only feeling, only feeling everything, especially each other.

Then Aaron felt eyes on him. Slowly he took his lips from hers and looked out across the yard. The men were busy doing other things, not looking, purposefully not looking, so he cut his eyes down and to the side. Eric and Jessica stood side-by-side, looking up at them soberly.

Slightly embarrassed, Aaron said, "Uh, Eric, lad, why don't you and Jessica go see the new calves in the paddock?"

Eric nodded. "Aye," he said, and took off toward

the cattle yard followed by Jessica and the yellow cat.

Then Aaron looked at Mrs. Chun, who glanced down at her shoes when he saw her on the veranda. "Mrs. Chun, will you see to the children for an hour or so? Mrs. Aylesbury and I have some . . . serious business to discuss."

"Oh aye, Mr. Aaron," she said, blushing and nodding a greeting to Penelope. And then she hurried away after Eric.

Aaron looked at Penelope and smiled slowly. Then he raised his hand to indicate the door of the house. "Mrs. Aylesbury?"

Together, they went inside.

Mrs. Chun paused and looked back, just as the door shut. Her brows shot up, and when she heard the bolt slide home, her mouth popped open. But when two brown arms reached out and pulled the bedroom shutters to she said, "Oh dear!" not certain she approved at all. Indeed! However . . . blushing painfully, she went toward the children again.

Eric climbed onto the fence and looked down at Jessica who was leaning on it observing twin calves in the yard. "Don't you want to ask how long I'm going to stay?"

Jessica, pretending disinterest, said, "No."

Eric said, "Well, I'll tell you anyway. We're going to stay forever."

Jessica smiled in spite of herself. "I'm glad. Now I'll have somebody to play with."

"Aren't there any other kids around here?"

"Not on this station. All the men are bachelors."

"What's a bachelor?"

Jessica sighed and rolled her eyes. "Don't you know anything? Bachelors are men who don't have any children."

Six-year-old Eric philosophized, "Maybe that's because they aren't married. Men don't have children

if they aren't married."

Jessica thought about that and nodded agreement.

For a moment neither spoke, but Jessica sighed and Eric kicked the fence with the heel of his boots. Finally Eric said, "Animals have babies and they aren't married."

Jessica sighed. "That's different."

"Why?"

"People aren't supposed to talk about such things."

"But you said your father said it was all right because it was about the human body."

"We're talking about animals, Eric Aylesbury."

They both blushed. He had seen the sheep copulating and she had seen the cattle. And it was awful. They were painfully blushing, so to ease the embarrassment Jessica said, "Do you want to see the baby frogs?"

"Aw, I see frogs every day."

"But these are tiny, tiny. No bigger than my thumb."

"Well, all right." Eric slid off the fence.

Together they ran toward the grove of gum trees that followed the creek below the paddocks.

"Children! Children, don't go far," Mrs. Chun called, reaching toward them.

Overhead the pink-breasted galah flew in noisome flocks going west. From the distance came the sound of tinkling bells and bleating sheep. A crow called his universal caw, caw in the trees near the creek, and in answer an awakened kookaburra laughed frantically.

From the shed came the sound of hammer on anvil, from the north a cow bellowed softly. In the paddock the new horse whinnied. But from the big house with its wide, deep veranda, there came no sound at all.

If you enjoyed this book we have a special offer for you. Become a charter member of the ZEBRA HISTORICAL ROMANCE HOME SUBSCRIPTION SERVICE and...

Get a
FREE
Zebra Historical Romance
(A $3.95 value) No Obligation

Now that you have read a Zebra Historical Romance we're sure you'll want more of the passion and sensuality, the desire and dreams and fascinating historical settings that make these novels the favorites of so many women. So we have made arrangements for you to receive a *FREE* book ($3.95 value) and preview 4 brand new Zebra Historical Romances each month.

Join the Zebra
Home Subscription Service—
Free Home Delivery

By joining our Home Subscription Service you'll never have to worry about missing a title. You'll automatically get the romance, the allure, the attraction, that make Zebra Historical Romances so special.

Each month you'll receive 4 brand new Zebra Historical Romance novels as soon as they are published. Look them over *Free* for 10 days. If you're not delighted simply return them and owe nothing. But if you enjoy them as much as we think you will, you'll pay *only* $3.50 each and save 45¢ over the cover price. (You save a total of $1.80 each month.) *There is no shipping and handling charge or other hidden charges.*

———— *Fill Out the Coupon* ————

Start your subscription now and start saving. Fill out the coupon and mail it *today*. You'll get your FREE book along with your first month's books to preview.

0-8217-1841-X

E'D CLAIM THE
UTBACK—THEN TAME HER
USTRALIAN HEART!

ZEBRA/0-8217-1841-X (CANADA $4.95) US $3.95

Wild Surrender

Gina Delaney